PRAISE
Lisa Wingate

THE SEA KEEPER'S DAUGHTERS

"Readers will delight in this compelling saga that sweeps from past to present, coastline to mountains. Compassion and forgiveness pave the road to redemption in this gem of a book. *The Sea Keeper's Daughter* is a keeper!"

MARY ALICE MONROE, *New York Times* bestselling author of *The Summer's End*

THE STORY KEEPER

"Lisa Wingate's latest novel, *The Story Keeper*, pays homage to all young women who dared to rise above the life into which they were born, to find the life they were destined to live."

CATHERINE HOSMAN, *Killeen Daily Herald*

"Wingate is, quite simply, a master storyteller. Her story-within-a-story, penned with a fine, expressive style, will captivate writers and non-writers alike."

BOOKLIST

"Wingate's latest tale is beautifully crafted and has so many layers to appeal to readers—history, a contemporary love story, a bit of mystery, and details about the book-publishing industry."

ROMANTIC TIMES

"Not since *To Kill a Mockingbird* has a story impacted me like this."

COLLEEN COBLE, *USA Today* bestselling author of *Seagrass Pier*

"For anyone who enjoys master storytellers such as Adriana Trigiani and Karen White. *The Story Keeper* . . . transports readers across time."

JULIE CANTRELL, *New York Times* and *USA Today* bestselling author of *Into the Free*

THE PRAYER BOX

"A careful eye to detail and a beautiful, lyrical style reminiscent of those of Mary Alice Monroe and Patti Callahan Henry."

STARRED *BOOKLIST*

"Journeys begin with one single step . . . in Wingate's masterful exploration of the road to redemption. Relatable characters and vivid portrayals of events both current and historical create an enchanting, memorable pilgrimage into the fullness of faith and love."

PUBLISHERS WEEKLY

"With a gift for crafting a story that digs into how a person's past can shape their view of themselves and of hope itself, Lisa Wingate never disappoints to deliver a first-class novel."

USA TODAY

"*The Prayer Box* is a masterpiece of story and skill."

DEBBIE MACOMBER, *New York Times* bestselling author

"*The Prayer Box* is Lisa Wingate's best work so far! Tandi's story is an enchanting take on family ties, redemption, and allowing oneself to be swept up into a river of grace regardless of one's past."

KAREN WHITE, *New York Times* bestselling author of *The Time In Between*

OTHER NOVELS BY LISA WINGATE

"A rising star in the world of women's fiction."

ROMANTIC TIMES

"Lisa Wingate is a glorious storyteller!"

ADRIANA TRIGIANI, *New York Times* bestselling author

"Gripping . . . compassionate and lyrical . . . reminds us that it is love that changes our world."

PATTI CALLAHAN HENRY, *New York Times* bestselling author

THE SEA KEEPER'S DAUGHTERS

THE SEA KEEPER'S DAUGHTERS

LISA WINGATE

Tyndale House Publishers, Inc.
Carol Stream, Illinois

Visit Tyndale online at www.tyndale.com.

Visit Lisa Wingate's website at www.lisawingate.com.

TYNDALE and Tyndale's quill logo are registered trademarks of Tyndale House Publishers, Inc.

The Sea Keeper's Daughters

Designed by Dean H. Renninger

Edited by Sarah Mason

Published in association with Folio Literary Management, LLC, 630 9th Avenue, Suite 1101, New York, NY 10036.

Library of Congress Cataloging-in-Publication Data

Wingate, Lisa.
The sea keeper's daughters / Lisa Wingate.
pages ; cm
ISBN 978-1-4143-8690-4 (softcover) — ISBN 978-1-4143-8827-4 (hardcover)
1. Restaurateurs—North Carolina—Fiction. 2. Inheritance and succession—Fiction. 3. Hotels—North Carolina—Fiction. I. Title.
PS3573.I53165S43 2015
813'.54—dc23 2015014930

Printed in the United States of America

28 27 26 25 24 23
12 11 10 9 8 7 6

For those who chased stories
where none had gone before,
the Federal Writers.

May history remember you kindly.
But most of all,
may history remember you.

The one story you didn't tell
was your own.
I hope this tale does you justice.

Acknowledgments

Writing fiction is the strangest of professions. Here is a job in which your task each day is to listen to the voices of people who don't exist and describe events that never were. It's the adult version of Let's Pretend.

Yet even games of Let's Pretend are better when friends are involved—real friends, not the type you conjure up in your head. Many kind people contributed to the making of this book, so I'd like to take a moment to offer my undying thanks.

First and foremost, I'm grateful to the Federal Writers, whose work was far-reaching, revolutionary, fascinating, and sometimes dangerous. They probed the corners of a hidden America, knowing that even when we have little else, our stories still have value. I am so very grateful for all the stories they saved from extinction.

As always, I am incredibly thankful for my family. Thank you to my husband and my sweet boys for supporting me through late nights and crazy schedules, and to my mother for being my official assistant and helper, but also my mama. Not everyone is lucky enough to have a helper who will honestly tell you when your hair looks bad . . . or when a manuscript needs work. Thank you to my sweet mother-in-law for helping with address lists and for loving my grown-too-soon boys and to Paw-paw for making sure the next generation knows the family stories. Thanks also to relatives and friends far and near for loving me and helping me and hosting me as I travel. You're the best.

I'm grateful to my favorite digital designer, Teresa Loman, for beautiful graphics work, to Ed Stevens for constant encouragement and help with all things technical, and to my wonderful Aunt Sandy (also known as Sandy of Sandy's Seashell Shop) for help with early readings and for contributing beautiful sea glass jewelry for book giveaways and gifts. Thanks to Duane Davis for book tour help and for incredible proofreading. Thanks to Virginia Rush for lending an eye to the manuscript. Enormous gratitude to talented author friend Julie Cantrell for being an amazing critique partner.

To the people of the Outer Banks, thank you for not only a warm welcome each time we visit, but for your patience in answering questions. A special thanks to Jamie at Duck's Cottage Downtown Books in Manteo for always making our visits there a joy and for help with the research on the history of Roanoke Island. A more charming town than Manteo can't be found anywhere. Everyone should come for a short stay . . . or a long one.

In terms of print and paper, deep gratitude goes out to the talented folks at Tyndale House Publishers. To Karen Watson, Jan Stob, Sarah Mason, Maggie Rowe, and Cheryl Kerwin, thank you for being a fabulous publishing team. To the crew in marketing, publicity, art, and sales, thank you for using your talents so well. You are the ones who help these stories fly to the hands of readers.

Lastly, I am grateful to reader friends everywhere. I love the connection we share across the miles. Thank you for recommending the books to friends, suggesting them to book clubs, and taking time to send little notes of encouragement my way via e-mail, Facebook, and Twitter. I'm indebted to all of you who read these stories and to the booksellers who sell them with such devotion. Thank you for joining in my games of Let's Pretend.

May this journey bring you as much joy as you have given me.

CHAPTER 1

Perhaps denial is the mind's way of protecting the heart from a sucker punch it can't handle. Or maybe it's simpler than that. Maybe denial in the face of overwhelming evidence is a mere byproduct of stubbornness.

Whatever the reason, all I could think standing in the doorway, one hand on the latch and the other trembling on the keys, was, *This can't be happening. This can't be how it ends. It's so . . . quiet.* A dream should make noise when it's dying. It deserves to go out in a tragic blaze of glory. There should be a dramatic death scene, a gasping for breath . . . something.

Denise laid a hand on my shoulder, whispered, "Are you all right?" Her voice faded at the end, cracking into jagged pieces.

"No." A hard, bitter tone sharpened the cutting edge on the word. It wasn't aimed at Denise. She knew that. "Nothing about this is *all right*. Not one single thing."

"Yeah." Resting against the doorframe, she let her neck go slack until her cheek touched the wood. "I'm not sure if it's better or worse to stand here looking at it, though. For the last time, I mean."

"We've put our hearts into this place. . . ." Denial reared its unreasonable head again. I would've called it *hope*, but if it was hope, it was the false and paper-thin kind. The kind that only teases you.

Denise's hair fell like a pale, silky curtain, dividing the two of us. We'd always been at opposite ends of the cousin spectrum—Denise strawberry blonde, pale, and freckled, me dark-haired, blue-eyed, and olive-skinned. Denise a homebody and me a wanderer.

"Whitney, we have to let it go. If we don't, we'll end up losing both places."

"I know. I know you're right." But still a part of me rebelled. *All* of me rebelled. I couldn't stand the thought of being bullied one more time. "I understand that you're being logical. And on top of that, you have Mattie to think about. And your grandmother. We've got to cut the losses while we can still keep the first restaurant going."

"I'm sorry," Denise choked out. With dependents, she couldn't afford any more risk. We'd already gone too far in this skirmish-by-skirmish war against crooked county commissioners, building inspectors taking backroom payoffs, deceptive construction contractors, and a fire marshal who was a notorious good ol' boy. They were all in cahoots with local business owners who didn't want any competition in this backwater town.

Denise and I should've been more careful to check out the environment before we'd fallen in love with the vintage mill building and decided it would be perfect for our second Bella Tazza location and our first really high-end eatery. Positioned along a busy thoroughfare for tourists headed north to ski or to spend summer vacations in the Upper Peninsula, Bella Tazza 2, with its high, lighted granary tower, was a beacon for passersby.

But in eleven months, we'd been closed more than we'd been

open. Every time we thought we'd won the battle to get and keep our occupancy permit, some new and expensive edict came down and we were closed until we could comply. Then the local contractors did their part to slow the process and raise the bills even more.

You're not the one who needs to apologize, I wanted to say to Denise, but I didn't. Instead, I sank onto one of the benches and surveyed the murals Denise and I had painted after spending long days at Bella Tazza 1, in the next county over.

I felt sick all over again.

"The minute we have to give up the lease, they'll move in here." Denise echoed my thoughts the way only a cousin who's more like a big sister can. "Vultures."

"That's the worst part." But it wasn't, really. The worst part was that it was *my* fault we'd gone this far in trying to preserve Tazza 2. Denise would've surrendered to Tagg Harper and his hometown henchmen long ago. Denise would've played it safe if only I'd let her.

Yet even now, after transferring the remaining food inventory to the other restaurant and listing the equipment and fixtures we could sell at auction, I still couldn't accept what was happening. Somehow, someway, Tagg and his cronies had managed to cause another month's postponement of our case with the state code commission. We couldn't hang on that long with Tazza 2 closed but still racking up monthly bills. This was death, at least for Tazza 2, and if we weren't careful, the financial drain would swallow Tazza 1, leaving our remaining employees jobless.

"Let's just go." Denise flipped the light switch, casting our blood, sweat, and tears into shadow. "I can't look at it anymore."

The click of the latch held a finality, but my mind was churning, my heart still groping for a loophole . . . wishing a white knight would ride in at the eleventh hour, brandishing sword and shield.

Instead, there was Tagg Harper's four-wheel-drive truck, sitting in the ditch down by the road. Stalker. He was probably scratching his belly while sipping a brewski and smiling at himself.

"Oh, I hate that man." Denise's teeth clenched over the words. "I'd like to . . ."

I couldn't help myself—I took a step in Tagg's direction.

"Whitney, don't get into it with him. There's no telling what he's capable of."

My despair morphed into a feverish anger. I'd never hated anyone the way I hated Tagg Harper.

Denise's hand snaked out and grabbed my jacket. "Don't give him any more satisfaction. It's bad enough that he'll see our equipment on eBay as soon as we post the listings. Jerk. Honest competition with his restaurant, I can handle, but this . . ."

"I'd just like to . . . walk down there and nail him with a kick to that great big gut of his." The past few months' drama had driven me to think about refresher courses in Tang Soo Do karate, a pastime I'd given up after leaving the high school bullies behind, twenty years ago. I hadn't told Denise, but someone had been prowling around my cabin at night.

As usual, my cousin was focused on the practical, on achieving *containment*. "We need to concentrate on digging out financially and keeping the first store alive."

"I know." The problem was, I'd been adding things up in my head as we'd made our auction list in the mill building. What we'd get for the supplies and equipment wouldn't even take care of the final utility costs here, much less the legal bills we'd amassed. With the flagging economy and the need to absorb as many Tazza 2 employees as possible into the other restaurant, I wasn't even sure we could make payroll. And we *had* to make payroll. Our employees were counting on it. They needed to pay their bills too.

Guilt fell hard and heavy, settling stone by stone as we crossed the parking lot. If I hadn't moved back to Michigan five years ago and convinced Denise to start a restaurant with me, she would've still been in a nice, safe teaching job. But I'd been sailing off a big win after quitting an upper management job, opening my own bistro in Dallas, proving it out, and selling it for a nice chunk of change. With four hundred thousand dollars in my pocket, I'd been so sure I had the perfect formula for success. I'd told myself I was doing a good thing for my cousin, helping her escape the constant struggle to single-handedly finance a household, take care of her aging grandmother, and pay for Mattie's asthma care on a teacher's salary.

Denise, I had a feeling, had been hoping that our starting a business together would somehow defeat the wanderlust that had taken me from culinary school to the far corners of the world, opening top-of-the-line kitchens for a multinational restaurant conglomerate.

"See you in the morning, Whit." A quick shoulder-hug and she disappeared into her vehicle, cranking the engine, then crunching across the leftover ice runoff of a polar-vortex winter. Rather than disappearing down the driveway, she stopped at the curb, near Tagg's truck. Through the cold-smoke, I could feel her watching, waiting to be sure I made it to the road without spiraling into a confrontation.

It was so like Denise to look after me. Since her long-ago days as my after-school babysitter, she'd always been fiercely protective. Like the rest of Mom's family, she'd worried that I was stuffing down the aftereffects of my father's death, and that Mom was making a mistake by exposing me to my grandmother on far-away Roanoke Island. It was no secret that Ziltha Benoit held my mother responsible for the untimely loss of her son.

Denise had silently understood all the things I couldn't tell my mom, or anyone—the painful inadequacy that had haunted my childhood, the sense that I could never be good enough, the ridicule in the exclusive private school across town, where Mom's music teaching job came with free tuition for me. The awkwardness of not fitting in with the silver-spoon kids there, even though my last name was Benoit. Denise had always been my oasis of kindness and sage advice—the big sister I never had.

Passing by her car on the way out, I couldn't even look at her. I just bumped down the winter-rutted drive, turned onto the road, and headed toward home, checking once in the mirror to make sure Denise was out of the parking lot too.

Tagg Harper's taillights came on just after her vehicle pulled onto the road. My anger flared with tidal force, and I was starting a U-turn before I even knew what was happening. By the time I made it back to the restaurant, Tagg was positioning his truck in the middle of the parking lot. *Our* parking lot. The driver's-side door was just swinging open.

I wheeled around and pulled close enough to prevent him from wallowing out. Cold air rushed in my window, a quick, hard, bracing force.

"You even set *one foot* on this parking lot, Tagg Harper, I'll call the police." Not that the county sheriff wasn't in Tagg's pocket too. Tagg's dumpy pizza joint was the spot where all the local boys gathered for coffee breaks . . . if they knew what was good for them.

Lowering his window, he rested a bulky arm on the frame,

drawing the door inward a bit. The hinges groaned. "Public parking lot." An index finger whirled lazily in the air. "Heard a little rattle in my engine just now. Thought I'd stop and check it out."

"I'll bet." Of course he wouldn't admit that he wanted to get his meat hooks on this place. He was probably afraid I'd be recording on my cell phone, trying to secure proof of the threats, the bribes to officials and contractors, the constant harassment.

Which was why he was smiling and blinking at me like a ninny now.

"It's *my* parking lot, until this is all settled. We reserve the right to refuse service to *anyone*. You're not welcome here." *Don't back down. Not this time. Don't let him bully you.* Gripping the steering wheel tighter, I swallowed hard.

"Heard you were moving out early to save on the rent." His breath drew smoke curls in the frosted air. I smelled beer, as usual. "Expensive to keep a building for no reason."

"Well, you heard wrong, because we've got a hearing with the state code commission in six weeks, and with that little bit of extra time to prepare, there's no way in the world we won't win our case."

His chin receded into wind-reddened rolls of neck fat before he relaxed in his seat, self-assured and smiling. He knew a bluff when he heard one. "It'd be a shame to drag yourself any deeper under . . . what with your *other* business to think about and all."

What did *that* mean? Bella Tazza 1 was outside the county. There wasn't anything Tagg could do to affect it, other than posting derogatory food reviews online, which he and his peeps had already done.

But he was thinking of *something* right now. That was clear enough. His tongue snaked out and wet his lips, and then he had the gall to give the mill building a leisurely assessment before turning his attention to me again. "Guess I'll wait until the carcass cools a little more."

Pulling the door closed, he rolled up his window, and then he was gone.

I sat alone in the moon shadow of my dying dream, once again feeling like the little girl who would never be worthy of dreams, the Benoit name, or anything else.

No matter how far I traveled, no matter what I achieved, that girl remained just a few inches beneath the skin.

Right now, she was telling me this was exactly what I deserved.

Rounding icy curves as the headlights glinted against dirty mounds of leftover snow, I had the urge to let go of the wheel, close my eyes, and just stay wherever the car came to rest . . . until the cold or carbon monoxide put an end to all of this. In some logical part of my brain, I knew that was an overreaction, but the idea of going broke and taking my cousin with me was unbearable.

There has to be a way out. There has to be something I can do. . . .

Yet no miraculous possibilities came to mind during the thirty-minute drive home. Finally, the surface of Lake Michigan glinted through the trees, and I looked toward it seeking the comfort it usually provided. This time, all I could see was a vision of myself, floating cold and silent beneath the surface.

Stop. That. The words in my head were a reprimand, strong and determined like my mother's voice. *You are not your father.*

But occasionally over the years, I had wondered—was there, inside me, the same demon that had taken him from us before I was six years old, leaving me to remember him as a feeling, a snatch of sound, a mist of memory?

Could I, without seeing it ahead of time, come to a place where giving up seemed the best option?

How was the thought even possible for me, knowing firsthand the pain a decision like that leaves behind? Knowing what happens in the aftermath when a person you love enters the cold waters and swims out to sea with no intention of returning to shore?

Someone should tell the dead that saving the living isn't as simple as leaving a note to say, *It's no one's fault.* For the living, it's always someone's fault.

Turning onto the cabin road, I cleared my head and felt the tears beginning to come, seeking to cleanse. Tears seemed like the only thing I had left. They swelled and pounded in my throat as I drew closer to the little lake cabin that had been home since I'd moved back to Michigan. Fortunately, Mrs. Doyne, who lived in the house out front, kept her cabin rentals at 1950s prices. She was more interested in having responsible, long-term tenants than in making money off the property.

Dressed in her nightgown and probably ready to turn in, she waved from behind a picture window as I passed by the house. One of her ever-present crossword puzzles dangled in her hand.

I had the random realization that even Mrs. Doyne would be hurt if I lost myself beneath the lake's quiet surface. *Get your act together, Whitney Monroe,* she'd probably say. *Life goes on.* Mrs. Doyne had survived the death of her husband of fifty years, her one true love. She worked in her gardens, volunteered all over the area, and mentored a Girl Scout troop. She had the best attitude of any person I'd ever met and it went all the way through to the core. She was fearless, always up for a new adventure.

There had been a time when I'd thought that if I kept up the facade long enough on the outside, I'd become that on the inside, too. I'd opened world-class kitchens, driven others to maintain the pace, never let myself get rattled when a newbie on a hot line scorched a sauce or a waiter dropped a tray. I'd dealt with corporate higher-ups who weren't much different from Tagg Harper—bloated, self-important personalities bent on showing the world how special they were. I handled things well. I had things under control.

But what I'd never been faced with, what I'd avoided my entire adult life, was the very thing that had been squeezing me dry these past months. I'd never allowed someone else's well-being to depend on my own. Even during a short marriage that had both begun and ended with disaster, I'd maintained my own finances, kept my own life, and so had David. Both of us seemed to prefer it that way. I'd never been faced with the knowledge that my choices, my actions, my *failure* would destroy another person's life.

Turning off the car, I rested my head against the steering wheel as the cold needled through the windows and the engine's chugs settled to dull metallic pings. A sob wrenched the air and I heard it before I felt it.

A breath heaved inward, stung my throat. Another sob pressed out. I lifted my head, let it bump against the steering wheel, thought, *Stop, stop, stop!*

The knock on the window struck me like an electrical pulse, catapulting me upright. Beyond the blurry haze, I made out Mrs. Doyne's silhouette against the security lamps, the fur-lined hood of her coat catching the light and giving her a fluffy halo.

My emotions scattered like rabbits, leaving behind only two that I could identify—horror and embarrassment. I didn't want *anyone* to see me like this, least of all Mrs. Doyne. It would only worry her. She'd been a godsend to me these past few years, and even though I'd tried to keep my financial situation under wraps as Bella Tazza 2 imploded, she'd figured out that things were bad. She'd started bringing me casseroles and offering to wait for the rent if I needed her to.

Like everyone else in town, she wasn't aware of the whole story. All she knew was that we'd had some trouble with the inspections on the new restaurant. I was careful not to reveal more. The truth about Tagg Harper's underhanded dealings would only hurt her. Mrs. Doyne's deceased husband had been one of Tagg's favorite uncles and ice-fishing buddies.

Pretending to reach for my keys in the ignition, I wiped my eyes and then rolled down the window, hoping she wouldn't notice what a mess I was. Apparently it was obvious, even in the dark.

"Oh, honey." She touched my shoulder, and I clenched against another rush of tears. "I guess you heard. I'm so sorry . . ." She seemed to leave the sentence unfinished, its meaning a mystery. What was she *sorry* for? Did she know about the postponement of the code commission hearing? Had she been in it with the rest of the Harpers all along?

Even the question hurt. I'd come to think of Mrs. Doyne almost as a substitute for my mother. They enjoyed all the same things. They both loved music. They both played the violin. They had the same Upper Peninsula accent. Being around Mrs. Doyne was like having my mom back again. Mrs. Doyne was even a cancer survivor. Someone strong enough to defeat the disease that had taken Mom five years ago. It was after her funeral that Denise and I had reconnected and spent a long night talking about life, dreams, and Denise's struggle to pay Mattie's medical bills after her ex-husband refused to keep up the child support. Suddenly, the unexpected offer on my restaurant in Dallas had made sense. All of it seemed meant to be.

"Come on inside." Mrs. Doyne's hand circled my arm as if she meant to forcibly lift me out the window. "You look like you need a spot of hot tea."

I didn't argue. I didn't have the energy. I just went along.

Inside, the house smelled of cats, baseboard heat, and plants in fresh pots. When this year's rebellious spring weather finally warmed up, Mrs. Doyne's garden would be half-grown in the sunroom. How could anyone who lovingly nursed the tender shoots of new life be in on Tagg Harper's dirty dealings? The bullies were getting the best of me again, making me paranoid. I couldn't let someone like Tagg make me lose hope in other people. Good people like Mrs. Doyne.

"Sit," she said, leading me to a sofa space between three curled-up cats. "Let me put the water on."

Sinking down with my cold fingers tucked between my knees, I let my head fall back, closed my eyes, tried to think. A cat crawled into my lap, nestled there, and toyed with the zipper on my coat, its soft purr a lull of comfort.

"I tried to call you earlier when I got the message." Mrs. Doyne's voice seemed far away.

Another month . . . can we hang on another month? There has to be some way to get the money. . . .

Options and options and options cycled through my mind, ending in brick wall after brick wall after brick wall, and then the biggest one of all—the fact that if we went any further with all of this, we risked losing everything.

You can't do that to Denise. You can't do that to Denise and Mattie and Grandma Daisy.

You never should've come back here. You never should've involved them in all of this. It's your fault. It's all your fault.

"I say . . . I tried to call you on your cell phone when the message came."

Mrs. Doyne's words pressed for a response.

"Message?"

The teapot whistled, the high, shrill sound causing the cats to stir.

A spoon clinked, the refrigerator door opened and closed. Cream and sugar. Mrs. Doyne knew. We'd shared more than a few cups of tea these past few years.

"It sounded as if the man had no idea who else to call. He left a message on the recorder while I was at the market. I suppose he found your cell number and reached you directly?"

Her slippers shuffled against the wood floor as she reentered the living room and handed over my tea. The cup was warm, comforting, its chamomile scent sinking in. "I left my phone in the car all afternoon." I didn't tell her I'd done that to avoid the constant flurry of bill collectors.

Mrs. Doyne delivered a perplexed look, settling into her recliner. "I know it isn't the sort of news you need right now, what with your restaurant struggles." Her head inclined sympathetically, her eyes compassionate behind thick glasses. "Are you close?"

"Close?"

"To your stepfather." Frowning, she looked into her teacup, as if she might find the answers there. "I assumed not, given that the neighbor had so much trouble contacting you."

"My *stepfather*?" The words struck like a ricochet baseball, drilling some unsuspecting fan in the head. I hadn't seen my mother's late-in-life husband since her funeral.

It was no accident that my stepfather's neighbor had trouble finding my number among his belongings. The man wanted nothing to do with me.

"Mrs. Doyne, I'm completely lost here. I haven't heard from my stepfather in almost five years. There's no reason he'd be getting in touch, believe me."

"Oh . . ." A hand-to-chest look of surprise. "When I saw you crying in the car, I just assumed the message had gotten through to you. I'm sorry to be the deliverer of such news. The call was from your stepfather's neighbor on the Outer Banks of North Carolina . . . Roanoke Island, I believe he said. He thought you should know of the situation. Apparently your stepfather is in the hospital. He took a fall in the bathroom . . . and he laid there for nearly four days before anyone found him."

CHAPTER 2

"I know it sounds nuts. Just hear me out, Denise." In better days, I might've rethought the idea, especially given Denise's opposition to it, but right now I was elbowing doubts out of the way like a *Titanic* passenger trying to make it to a lifeboat. "Keep in mind that we're talking about an old man who fell in the bathroom and was trapped for four days. Yes, I know that Clyde Franczyk isn't just *any* old man, but I think I'm safe enough going there. Someone needs to, and obviously his sons still don't have anything to do with him, or the neighbor wouldn't be calling me."

"So you're . . . driving to the Outer Banks to save Clyde Franczyk? The man who hoodwinked your mother into leaving *him* what should've belonged to you?" Denise was halfway through prepping the morning bread-basket dough. A cloud of flour poofed from her hands as she flailed them. "Have you forgotten how he acted at the funeral—waving the will in our faces and telling us that we couldn't come get any of your mother's stuff?"

"Of course not." Thanks to Clyde, the graveside service had ended up one step short of an all-out family brawl. "But that building in Manteo is still technically mine. Yes, he has the right to live there as long as he wants, but he can't legally stop me from going in. I might not have been ready before, but it's time to *be* ready. My mom begged me for years to go through my grandmother's things. I just . . . didn't have time to deal with it."

"And now you're going to . . . what? Just march right in there, sort the family heirlooms, sell some stuff, and sink the money into fighting Tagg Harper? Maybe you can talk your stepfather into shuffling off to a nursing home while you're at it, so you can sell the building, too." She coughed on a breath of flour dust. Her eyes were watering when she came up for air—watering and filled with doubt that I could handle the building and all that remained inside it, including Clyde. "Come on, Whit, this is the man who wouldn't even let you see your mother's body until the funeral service. At the very least, he's selfish and possessive and mean. At the worst, he's a con man and a crook. You need to stay away."

"I need to *go*." I didn't want to do this without Denise's blessing. I already felt like I was abandoning her by leaving Bella Tazza.

In reality, I didn't want to go to the Outer Banks at all. Part of me—the old part that had traveled around the world, never staying long enough to form close associations—wanted to turn tail and run away to a whole new life. If it weren't for Denise, Mattie, Grandma Daisy, and the Tazza employees, I could've done it. I wasn't even forty yet. There was plenty of time to reinvent. The restaurant conglomerate I'd worked for would've taken me back in a heartbeat. I could land on my feet someplace far away, let life go on without a thought about Clyde Franczyk and the old waterfront hotel that held almost a hundred years of the difficult, often tragic history of my father's family.

"Believe me, Denise, I've thought this through. In the first place, there's more than one possibility here. At his age, Clyde would be better off if he'd reconcile with his sons and move back to Raleigh. Maybe I can help to make that happen. Not that *they* like me either, but Mom always hoped she could do something to mend those fences. She felt like she was the cause of their issues even though she didn't mean to be."

"So you're doing this for your mom now?"

"It's the best thing for everyone involved. And whether Clyde can be reunited with his family or not, there isn't *just* the building in Manteo to think about; there's all the stuff in storage on the second floor. My dad's family was very well off. Grandmother Ziltha came from money, and she married a Benoit. The Benoits had shipping interests all over the Eastern Seaboard. You can't imagine what was in the penthouse residence when Mom and I worked all those summers at the hotel. There's no telling what might be left."

Denise quirked a brow, her lips forming a narrow, skeptical line. "Whitney, based on what happened at the funeral, you're liable to get shot. And have you even considered that Clyde may have sold anything of value? The man is perfectly happy to live upstairs for free, *and* collect the rent on the retail space downstairs. Who says he'd stop there?"

"I won't know until I see for myself." My spine and my resolve stiffened. "I have to try to do what I can, Denise. It's what my mom would've wanted, and it could make the difference for all of us." I swept a hand toward the empty kitchen, where our hard work was evident in every nook.

Denise portioned dough into glutinous blocks, dropping them on rack sheets as she mulled her answer. "I don't know. Thinking of you going to Manteo gives me a bad feeling.

Maybe some of that's just the history. I was always jealous of you and your mom, taking off to spend summers on an island. It sounded so romantic—ghosts and sea captains and all that stuff. But I'm also being honest here. I'm worried about this and I'm worried about you. I've been worried for a while. Have you thought at all about the fact that you're not just talking about old family heirlooms in that building? Your mom's personal belongings are there. You haven't visited that place since . . . Whit, the Excelsior was the last place you saw her before she died. Are you sure you're . . . in the right frame of mind to be going there now?"

"Now is when Clyde's health issues came up." Given my breakdown last night, I wasn't sure I was in shape to take this step at all . . . but it *was* the right thing to do. "I'm *fine*. And believe me, you have nothing to be jealous of, in terms of the Excelsior building. My grandmother worked us like dogs. Those romantic tales I always told were more fairy tale than reality." I could imagine what my cousins in Michigan must've thought back then. Desperate to defuse the family feud over whether my mother should be taking me to spend time with Grandmother Ziltha at all, I'd concocted wild stories about my gilded summers on the Carolina coast. I'd become so good at invention, I'd halfway convinced myself.

Denise lifted a hand, forming a dough-covered, five-fingered stop sign. "Okay. All right. If this is what you think you need to do, I'm behind you. I'll hold down the fort . . . but I just want you to be careful."

"I will be." But I had no idea what I might be walking into. I'd repeatedly tried the number on the message Mrs. Doyne had given me, and no one had answered. I'd also tried calling the phone number for the third-floor residence—my mother's old number. No response there, either. The hospital in Nags Head wouldn't release any information.

"How long do you think?"

"A week, maybe a little more, depending on what shape Clyde is in and whether I have any luck in getting some dialogue started with his kids . . . and on the condition of the storage in the second floor of the building. It could take me a while to figure out whether there's anything of value left. I don't want you to think I'm abandoning you, but there is an upside. With me gone, we can give my spot to one of the cooks we had to release from Tazza 2. Every little bit helps. If things go well on Roanoke, maybe we can make it until the state code commission hearing, win our case, and hire the whole crew again. I know it seems like a wild scenario, but at least it's . . . hope of some kind."

A long sigh, and then, "Maybe Clyde's kids will come to their senses. I know they were offended when he remarried and sold their mom's land, but family is family."

I went back to measuring ingredients for the morning's run of marinara sauce as Susan, our baker, wandered in the door carrying mascarpone and ladyfingers for tiramisu. She dropped a receipt on the prep table as she passed by. "Had to pick up a few things at the grocery store. Sorry." Her gaze strained toward the receipt. We'd started buying some supplies piecemeal because our credit with most of the food service vendors was shot.

"I'll get a reimbursement to you as soon as I open the safe and stock the cash register."

"I don't have to have the money back today. . . ." Susan deposited the supplies, then snagged an apron off the wall and slipped it over her head. "Just whenever."

I knew better, of course. Susan's husband was semi-unemployed after losing his factory job. They lived paycheck to paycheck, like most of our staff. But also like everyone else, she was devoted to Bella Tazza and to keeping it going. Twice recently, I'd found waitress tips piled beside the cash register. No explanation as to how they'd gotten there, and nobody would claim them. Now Susan was trying to pay for our groceries.

"It's not a problem, Suz. I'll get it as soon as I'm up front."

Denise shot me a frown, and I saw the same sad, nervous feeling that'd been curdling my stomach for a couple months. Were we doing people a favor by trying so hard to hang on? Or was their belief in Bella Tazza cheating them out of the chance to find new jobs before the inevitable happened?

I tucked the receipt in my shirt pocket, right behind the custom-embroidered Bella Tazza logo. There was a time when we hadn't thought twice about ordering fancy embroidered uniforms.

One step at a time, I told myself as I finished the sauce and left it to simmer in the boiling vat. *You can do this. Just take it one step at a time.* As much as I dreaded seeing Clyde, the return to the Outer Banks at least opened up new possibilities. Unfortunately, those new possibilities came wrapped in a layer of old pain.

I tried not to overanalyze as I went up front to stock the cash register. Meanwhile, the hot-line crew was trickling in to do the day's kitchen prep. Soon enough, the front-end crew would straggle through, and the usual organized chaos would ensue, its white noise and immediate needs eclipsing all else. Bella Tazza 1 had been busy since the day we'd remodeled an old café building and introduced our midpriced Italian menu to the community. With ski slopes, a manufacturing plant, and a massive retail distribution center nearby, there were plenty of hungry mouths to feed, and in this county, no political issues barred the way of good business.

Standing at the register, I counted cash to reimburse Susan for the groceries, then dialed the number from Mrs. Doyne again. The more I could learn ahead of time about what I'd be driving into, the better.

When he answered, Joel Coates sounded friendly and laid-back in the way of Outer Banks full-timers. He also seemed really young. Almost like a teenager.

I heard a door chime in the background as I explained who I was and why I was calling.

"Morning. Welcome to the Rip Shack," he said.

"Pardon?"

Joel chuckled. "Sorry. Had a customer come in. So, yeah, the old man doesn't get out a lot. But the dude never skips the Saturday buffet down on the corner. Like, he's there every week. Table by the window. Orders two meals. Eats one. Brings one home in a box. Usually hangs in Creef Park awhile, sits on the bench, scopin' the boats and stuff. Jamie down at the bookstore says that was, like, *their* thing, back before his old lady died."

The flow of conversation stopped suddenly. I felt a sting behind my eyes, realized I was just standing there staring at a handful of dollar bills. I couldn't remember how to count them.

"Awww, man, that was rude. I'm sorry. That was, like, your mom, huh? I remember her a little from before my boss started the shop here. She was real cool. She had lights on the Excelsior building at Christmas and a reindeer sleigh thing on the roof and stuff. At Halloween, she always set up a big ol' table at the curb and gave out candy. Even if you were, like, too old for trick-or-treat, she was super cool with it."

"She loved kids. She was a teacher . . . a music teacher," I choked out, unprepared for the sudden flood of emotion. You never get over losing your mother. The emptiness has ebb and flow like a tide, but it's not controlled by the phases of the moon or anything else you can predict.

Joel filled the void with more information. "Well, listen. I don't got a whole lot else to tell ya. I was workin' here solo Saturday 'cuz it's off-season and it's slow. When the old man missed the buffet down the street, I figured I better just go upstairs and see, so I did. Doors weren't locked, and I thought, *Man, if he went outta town or somethin', he wouldn't leave the doors like that.* So I, like, hollered and I heard somethin', so I went in. Dude was in a heck of a mess. You can kinda guess what somebody looks like after layin' on the bathroom floor four days. He was pretty out of it, but the really whacked thing was, he didn't want an ambulance to come. I called my girlfriend. She works with the hospital, and she was like, 'Get the ambulance *now.*'"

"It sounds like you did the right thing." I tried to imagine the man my mother had reconnected with and married only four years before her death, now frail and old. I couldn't. At the funeral, he'd been in good enough shape to yell at me in front of everyone. His full head of white hair had been neatly combed, his suit crisply pressed, his posture straight, unyielding, testifying to a long military career. He and my mother had dated when she was just in high school, before he went overseas with the Army.

I couldn't picture him in the condition Joel was describing, but I didn't dwell on the image either. As horrible as it was for anyone to be left lying injured and helpless for four days, I still wanted—needed—to keep the walls of resentment in good repair. It wasn't hard. Clyde was the reason I wasn't there when my mother died. It was *his* fault I'd had no idea how serious the return of her cancer was. He'd helped her keep secrets. He'd supported her in refusing further treatment while there were still options available. He'd taken her home to just . . . give up. Which wasn't like her. My mother was a fighter. She loved life.

She loved me.

But she'd been under Clyde's control, somehow. I'd never understood why, after being single since I was five years old, she'd married in a whirlwind, so late in life.

Joel Coates knew none of that, of course. He sounded concerned and sympathetic toward Clyde, as anyone would be, observing the situation from the outside.

"So, Kayla, my girlfriend, does social work counseling. She tried talkin' to him yesterday, but dude wasn't into it. He wouldn't give her anyone to get in touch with for him. That's when I went upstairs and found your number and called. Kayla says that this morning, the old dude, like, ordered himself a cab and busted outta the hospital. I would've gone and picked him up if he needed it. Anyway, that's all I know. Guess he's comin' back here sometime, but he didn't show up yet. No idea how he's gonna make it up those steps, though."

Joel paused to help a customer, while my thoughts and emotions swept in and out rapidly and randomly, like waves rushing ashore, depositing flashes of color and shape only to sweep them away again.

"So . . . you're gonna come see what he needs . . . or get him somebody . . . or somethin', then? Kayla was worried."

"Yes. I'm leaving later today to drive out. I'll be there sometime tomorrow. Joel, would you do something for me? Could you call me if you see Clyde come back?"

A strange pause held the other end of the line, and then, "Well . . . ummm . . . I can write a note for my boss, I guess. I'll be gone taking the surf wagon to a trade show for a couple days. Hope you can talk some sense into the old guy."

"I hope so too." But everything I knew about Clyde told me that he wasn't a man to be talked into anything by anyone. Especially not by me.

CHAPTER 3

A seventeen-hour drive with only a short stopover for sleep gives you plenty of time to think. By the time I wound my way down the last finger of the mainland to Point Harbor and then crossed the Wright Memorial Bridge onto the Outer Banks, I'd cycled through every possible version of the upcoming conversation with Clyde. For some reason, it hadn't occurred to me until I was over the glistening waters of Albemarle Sound that I should've asked Joel Coates not to tell my stepfather I was coming. By now, Clyde might be locked and loaded.

The traffic was surprisingly light on the highway that traversed the Outer Banks end to end. I cut over to the beach road before Nags Head and took the slow way along the narrow two-lane, passing rows of aging saltbox houses that clung doggedly to the dunes.

Maybe in a way I was stalling for time, but it was more than that. Mom had always told me that these particular beaches were special. My father had rented a cottage for the two of them here, years ago. He'd brought her home to meet his mother, but he'd wanted to have her all to himself first. Instead of traveling directly to Roanoke Island, they'd come to Nags Head. Perhaps he was afraid, even at almost forty years old, to deal with his mother's reaction to a hasty four-month courtship and a sudden marriage, particularly considering that his bride was fourteen years his junior. My father had given a benefit violin performance at the University of Michigan and taught a music theory seminar afterward. My mother had been involved in both. He'd noticed the pretty grad student with the thick auburn hair and big brown eyes. The rest was history.

On their first trip to the Outer Banks, they'd shared an idyllic spring day along the shore. An off-season day like this one. The type of afternoon when the water was cold, but the sand was warm and the sky a pristine, clear blue.

Heaven, she'd told me. *I thought I'd stepped right off the map and into heaven. Of course, I was crazy in love too. . . .*

But as evening set in and they traveled to Manteo, the story had taken a darker turn. There, my grandmother quickly ferreted out that her son's surprise guest was not only much younger, but descended of factory workers and farmers and housewives who did their own cooking—men with grease under their fingernails and women with dishpan hands. It became clear that my mother wasn't *the right sort.* She wasn't welcome in the Excelsior or in the family.

I'd always had a feeling, reading between the lines as an adult, that the objections only made my dad more determined to finally stand up to his overbearing mother. Perhaps he shouldn't have. Perhaps, after a lifetime of dealing with my father's intense mood swings, Grandmother Ziltha had a right to fear that my mother's innocent infatuation with him would end in disaster. Mom had never said it, but in so many ways, the two of them were like sun and moon. She was gritty, tough, practical, determined, passionate about having a teaching career. The first in her family to even attend college. He was contemplative, wildly artistic, reckless. A violinist of no small repute. A composer. A dabbler in the art of watercolor. Completely unprepared to live outside the insular world of privileged music schools and concert venues.

Never fool yourself into believing that love conquers all, Grandmother Ziltha had told me when I was thirteen and sweeping sand off hotel balconies in the summer heat while watching local teenagers pass by on their bicycles. *Those without the proper commonalities will only destroy one another. Do not marry out of your sort, should you decide to marry one day.* She'd always made it clear that, as the poor relations, we were to live by different rules.

The insults stung, even though Mom had encouraged me to make allowances for my grandmother. It was no secret that, despite her wealth, Grandmother Ziltha's life had been hard. Her long-ago marriage to Girard Benjamin Benoit Jr. had been short and had ended in tragedy. Benjamin had died at sea the year my father was born. My mother was sure that the losses in Grandmother's life were the reason for her constant frown and unwelcoming personality, and that it was important for me to come to know her as a way of remaining close to my father.

But my grandmother seemed disinterested in forming bonds of any kind. She made polite acquaintance with the hotel guests and the members of her social circle but maintained no intimate ties. She'd raised my father in the finest boarding schools, and the walls in her cavernous library, filled with his certificates, awards, and concert photos, were evidence that she'd made certain her son had the best of everything. His dark hair, blue eyes, and soft features had marked me since birth, but that didn't seem to endear me to Grandmother Ziltha. By all appearances, she tolerated my mother and me because she felt it was her duty to do so. Or because we were all she had left. She'd long ago cut off communication with her own relatives in a dispute over inheritance. She'd managed to alienate herself from the family she'd married into as well.

Thinking of her now brought to mind the hot, vibrant Outer Banks summers, when tourists came searching for a haven in which to leave the world's troubles behind. As a child, I'd always arrived here filled with anticipation and determination. Each year, I'd spun fantasies of finally doing something to make my grandmother like me better. Inevitably, the season ended in disappointment and the ultimate conclusion that I just wasn't good enough to love.

The islands had changed over the years, but in all the ways that mattered most, the Outer Banks was still the same. The spring air flowing in the window grounded me, swept away the sense of being exhausted and out of body. Anticipation sprinkled through the car like salt spray, tickling my senses as I made the turn at Whalebone Junction and crossed the causeway onto Roanoke. Maybe it was just adrenaline, but I felt almost giddy as I pulled into Manteo and passed by the grand old houses there. To my right, Shallowbag Bay peeked between buildings, and a squatty, rebuilt version of the old Roanoke Marshes Lighthouse waited to greet tourists and boats arriving at Manteo's historic waterfront.

Only when I pulled up to the Excelsior building, its elaborate facade and lurking stone gargoyles softened by early evening light, did I recognize my budding anticipation for what it was.

I'd expected, for that brief span of time while passing into Manteo, to find my mother here. I'd imagined her on the Excelsior's third-level balcony, leaning over the scrollwork railings that faced the bay, waving just as she had during my final visit here. That day, she'd tied a bright scarf around her short, cancer-ravaged hair and put on makeup and a colorful sundress. It was all a disguise, an act contrived to hide the truth of how sick she was.

She'd smiled and told me she was excited about the success of the new restaurant in Dallas—the first place I'd ever opened that actually belonged to me, not the corporation. She was delighted to see me settling down at thirty-three and finally giving up the traveling life for something of my own. She understood how hard it was for me to get away to visit, especially now that there was no paid vacation time. I shouldn't worry about it. She was done with the chemo, her hair was even growing back a little. . . .

If only I'd realized, at the end of the visit, that I was sharing a final hug with my mother, I would've held on longer, come back sooner, stopped rehashing our family's concerns about her marriage and Clyde's insistence that they move halfway across the country to live in Manteo.

If you could know—if you could *always* know—when the *lasts* in life are coming, you'd handle them differently. You'd savor. You'd stop. You'd let nothing else invade the moment.

My emotions ricocheted now. The euphoria of seeing the Outer Banks again dissolved into a soft weepiness. Exactly the kind of thing I couldn't afford.

There wasn't time for it.

The salt breeze served as a distraction, a comfort, as I rolled down the window and slowly circled the building, looking things over. Manteo was so startlingly beautiful these days, clean and well manicured—a far cry from the commercial waterfront town my mother had first seen when my father brought her to visit as a new bride. With its old, New England–style homes freshly painted and ready for tourists and the harbor filled with expensive pleasure boats, the place lay blanketed in an old-world charm, a sense of being far from modern life and its concerns.

The appeal had apparently sparked an economic boom in the years since my last visit. Sleek, multistory condos towered where the old drugstores and fish houses of my childhood had once leaned away from the sea. The condos were designed to fit in seamlessly, but neither my mother nor Grandmother Ziltha would've approved. The new buildings undoubtedly blocked part of the harbor view from the Excelsior's roof garden, for one thing.

The uptick in construction probably meant that the aging Excelsior, one of only two turn-of-the-century originals to have survived repeated waterfront fires, was worth far more than it had been five years ago. No wonder the first-floor retail space was full, despite the fact that the place looked tired and ragged, as if it, too, were mourning the loss of my mother, who'd dreamed of restoring its Gilded Age glory. At street level, an upscale ladies' boutique, a jewelry shop dealing in vintage and artisan works, and a small gallery, so narrow that it was little more than a runway with a door on one end, were all closed for the evening. No doubt the store owners were still keeping off-season hours at the first of May.

In another corner of the building, the Rip Shack was also dark. *Surf-n-Sand*, read a blinking neon sign in the window. The shop was the typical kind of seaside place, offering everything from actual surf equipment to paddleboards, beach chairs, flip-flops, swimsuits, T-shirts, and items in between. A handwritten sign wavered in the breeze, clinging to the window by a bit of tape. I let the car roll almost to a stop as I read the message. *Back in one hour-ish.*

No time of departure was listed. The loose way of doing business seemed to fit my image of Joel Coates, the young surfer-voiced neighbor who'd called about Clyde's fall. Since all the other shops were closed for the evening, the Rip Shack probably was too, but no one had bothered to take down the sign.

An SUV and a Volkswagen Beetle sat in the rear alley of the Excelsior. Neither was familiar, but that didn't mean one or the other wasn't Clyde's. I hadn't seen him in five years, after all.

I rolled into an empty spot, climbed out, stretched the kinks from my back, and studied the third-story windows of the Excelsior. No lights, no movement, no signs of life beyond the wavy plate glass. Nothing but the silent reflections of rooftops and sky. The fire escape tempted me briefly. Back in the day, it had been my preferred method of sneaking to and from the building—less chance that I would run into Grandmother Ziltha, assigning me yet another job to do. Escaping her was my greatest pleasure. Unfortunately, catching me was hers. Every summer when we made arrangements to come here, my mother gently reminded my grandmother that *Mom* was the one coming to work. I was here to visit with my grandmother. Every summer after we arrived, it was made clear that my grandmother wasn't interested in a visit; she was doing us a favor by providing an opportunity for extra income, and she expected me to earn my keep, as well.

The hard work didn't hurt me, in truth. It taught me things. Not the least of which was that I wanted to be the boss someday . . . and when I *did* become the boss, I would treat people with respect, not condemnation. Life at the Excelsior had been a good training for life in general.

"Looking for someone?"

I stumbled backward, lost my balance, bumped into a trash can, and made a racket that probably echoed for several city blocks.

There was a guy standing in the back door of the surf shop. Tall, good-looking, wearing a T-shirt. The wetsuit rolled down at his waist was still slick with water.

"Joel?" I asked, but he was older than I'd pictured. Probably a little older than me—fortysomething perhaps. Longish, slicked-back hair outlined his face. Brown, but sun-bleached lighter on the ends. He obviously spent a lot of time by the water.

"Mark. Mark Strahan." He stepped forward and extended a hand, but the gesture wasn't welcoming, exactly. More like curious . . . or suspicious. His chin lifted as he sized me up.

Mark had the kind of rich, caramel-brown eyes a girl shouldn't gaze into very long. A shock of damp hair fell over them after he shook my hand. He swept it out of the way, seeming to wait for me to make the next move. When I didn't, he said, "You the stepdaughter?" It sounded more like an accusation than a question. Something inside me bristled. It also confirmed that he wasn't glad to see me here. "My Saturday clerk said he'd called you about Mr. Franczyk's accident."

"Yes. I appreciate that he did." I squinted toward the windows again, wondering if Clyde was watching us, even now.

"No one's up there." Mark seemed to read my thoughts. "Mr. Franczyk hasn't shown up since he walked out of the hospital. Not unless he came and went in the middle of the night."

"Do you have any idea where he is?" According to Joel's description, my stepfather didn't socialize with anyone or maintain friendships, and he wasn't even supposed to be out of the hospital. Where would he go?

"I don't." Mark studied me in a way that asked a question,

but I couldn't tell what the question was. This guy wanted something. "I've never known him to be gone like this. Not since his wife passed away." Unlike Joel, he didn't apologize for mentioning my mother. Maybe it hadn't occurred to him yet.

"There was no indication of where he was headed? Did he mention any contact with his sons?" Maybe they'd come to get him after all.

"Not according to Joel's girlfriend. He just told them, if they didn't remove the IVs, he'd do it himself. Kayla said he wouldn't give her or the hospital staff next-of-kin information. He told them his family didn't want anything to do with him and vice versa. He left in pretty rough shape. Kayla says it happens, especially when someone's afraid social services might look into it as an adult well-being case."

Something acidic roiled in my stomach and bubbled into my chest. I swallowed hard, trying to quell it. I hadn't anticipated social services involvement or words like *adult well-being case.* "This just doesn't make sense." If one of Clyde's sons *had* finally come to take him back to Raleigh, why wouldn't they have picked him up at the hospital and stopped by here for some of his things?

"Kellie in the jewelry shop might have some ideas. She's been here the longest. But she's closed for a few days and gone across the bridge."

"All right . . . well . . . I guess I'll go look around upstairs and see what I can figure out." I didn't even have the phone numbers for Clyde's sons anymore, but with a last name like Franczyk, they couldn't be too hard to find. I could probably track down their contact information. . . .

"It's your building." The comment was surprisingly sharp-edged.

I turned, blinked at him. "*Clyde* told you that?" Somehow I'd always imagined my stepfather letting everyone believe that the building belonged to him.

Fingers braced on the rolled-down wetsuit, Mark surveyed the nearby ground, his lips pursing in a way that deepened the dimple in his chin. I caught myself wondering what would happen to it if he smiled.

"When we leased the space, he said he only did contracts six months at a time. Said if something happened to him, his stepdaughter would be down here to sell the building quicker than spit off a griddle—his words, not mine."

That analogy sounded like Clyde. No surprise that he would think of me as *spit* or that he would paint an unflattering picture for the townsfolk.

"It's more complicated than that." I wasn't ready for questions about the building. I wasn't ready for any of this. I'd imagined finding Clyde upstairs in the residence, a little battered, but still existing in his usual way. I'd hoped that, based on his health crisis, he might be persuaded to move in with his sons or into an assisted-living facility—someplace where he could get the help he needed. What if he was not only as stubborn as ever, but mentally off now? What if he'd walked out of the hospital into no one's care and was wandering somewhere, addled and bruised? The nights were still cool here. What if he'd fallen again, in an alley or someplace, and couldn't get up? The questions made my head spin, and I couldn't answer any of them. The only thing I could do was go upstairs and wait . . . for what, I wasn't sure.

"Everyone will be wondering about the building." Mark broke into my thoughts. "I know this is a family issue for you, but for us it's our livelihoods. We can't just walk down the street and find another open space to put in a business."

"I understand that." If he knew how *well* I understood, he'd probably be shocked. On the other hand, the decision could come down to their businesses or mine. "I'm not prepared to talk about that right now. Thanks for the information." Without waiting for more questions I couldn't answer, I turned and started toward the side-street entrance to the old hotel stairwell. My mother's key was waiting on my key ring, right where it had always been. Removing it would've been like admitting she was gone forever.

Stepping through the door and starting up the stairs, I reminded myself again that she wouldn't be here. Whatever secrets this building kept, I would have to discover them on my own.

What was waiting here? What had Clyde left behind? Were there clues as to where he might be?

The door to the third-floor alcove was unlocked when I reached it, the cat flap in the bottom hanging slightly askew. At any given time, my mother had been a caretaker of one to a half-dozen wayward felines looking for permanent homes. Wherever she lived, she was involved with the animal rescue organizations. Perhaps Clyde was still sharing space with Oscar and Felix, the duo of tabby kittens I'd found on my first trip here to meet the old flame my mother had suddenly married. Oscar and Felix were an unplanned wedding gift. Being my mother's daughter, I couldn't just leave them in a ditch for the gators.

Maybe Clyde had found them another home after my mother passed away. He didn't really like cats.

When I turned the corner onto the balcony, Grandmother Ziltha's wicker porch furniture was still right where it had always been. In the hotel's glory days, the cushion covers had been regularly washed and the wicker repainted every few years to ward off the salt air. Now the cloth lay faded and threadbare, tiny moats of leaves and cricket parts gathered around the cording. The wrinkles formed dry riverbeds filled with sand. A saggy lawn chair rested forlornly nearby. A matching one had been folded and placed against the front wall.

My mother's chair. Waiting, as if she were expected to return, open it, and sit watching the boats and the tourists come and go.

Beyond the leaded-glass front door, the interior lay shadowy and dim. A gasp trembled into the silence, and it was a moment before I realized that I'd made the sound myself. Everything in the front room was just as it had always been. All of my mother's belongings, still in place. Even a basket of organic knitting yarns and a half-finished angora hat remained neatly tucked beside a needlepointed wing chair in the ornate, bay-windowed parlor that my grandmother had referred to as *the receiving room*.

The screen door slapping shut made me jump, an eerie disquiet settling in its wake. The building creaked and groaned. It always had, but now each sound seemed piercingly loud.

"Hello?" My voice echoed against quiet walls, muted by a myriad of my mother's quilted hangings and fiber arts creations. "Clyde, it's Whitney. Are you here?"

No reply.

I passed silently down the center hallway, checked the kitchen, the living room, the bathroom, the master bedroom, six of the guest bedrooms. No one. I peeked into vacant areas that my mother had closed off when she'd moved in. The library, the drawing room, a ballroom that had been built for grand parties but had never hosted one that I knew of, all looked as if they hadn't seen humankind in a long while.

My courage flagged outside the only guest bedroom I hadn't checked yet—the one my mother had used as a craft room. I stood gripping the doorknob, stiff-armed like a soldier gathering strength for the final full-frontal assault against an overwhelming enemy. Even so, even having steeled myself, I was unprepared. The place where my mother had died was exactly as it had been the last time I'd visited her. The single ship's-wheel bed that had once been my father's waited along one wall, a maple-leaf quilt draped over it. A small dresser sat under the window Mom had always loved because it caught a good breeze off Shallowbag Bay. A stack of books rested on the marble-topped nightstand. Her weaving loom stood by the window, her easel beside it, a watercolor seascape half finished.

One of her scarves lay on the dresser, gray with dust. A paint palette and an artist's brush were gathering dust beside it.

The only thing missing was the hospital bed she'd told me was only there because the hospice service had sent it by mistake. *Oh, Whit, don't fuss about it. It's too much trouble to sort out the paperwork. They'll come get it eventually.* She'd waved a backhand and smiled beneath the water-blue head scarf. *I'm through all the treatments, and I feel okay. Just enjoy yourself while you're here. Tell me more about the restaurant in Dallas. I'm so happy it's doing well. . . .*

Moving into the room, I touched the quilt, ran my hand along it, smelled my mother's favorite bath spray. *Coconut Dream.* She said it reminded her of summer nights on the beach.

Grief rose up, sudden and overwhelming. The next thing I knew, I was grabbing the quilt in handfuls, pulling it off the bed, rolling it and clutching it against me, clinging to it as if it *were* her, then bolting from the room, running into the hallway and through another door, up a flight of stairs to the rooftop garden that had always been my hiding place, my dreaming place, my refuge from the world of others.

The lawn furniture had been left to slowly disintegrate since my mother's death. A fifties-vintage string of patio lights hung weathered and cracked. The remaining plants had grown wild or died. A Lady Banks rose tumbled from a cracked pot, its blooms a feast of yellow. A dead bougainvillea formed a crown of thorns over a leaning trellis. Passionflower vines circled the garden's iron railings, the stems heavy and rebellious. New spring leaves thickened the barricade, creating a living wall.

But even this thicket of my mother's making could not shelter me. Inside this place that she had tended and nurtured back to life, I fell into what remained of a chaise longue, wrapped her patchwork and stitches close, and let the tears come like a storm tide.

CHAPTER 4

The air on the second floor of the building whispered of mildew and decay. It crossed my mind, as I unlocked the door from the stairwell, that my grandmother—who'd always insisted that the cherrywood floors be flawlessly polished and the chair rails along the hallways be dusted to a white-glove shine and the salt haze be washed and washed and washed from the windows—would have been horrified at that smell. She would've found it disgusting that the center of her building was going to rot, decomposing like the meat of a sandwich in a forgotten lunch sack.

Didn't Clyde ever come down here? My mother had stored things like Christmas decorations, gardening equipment, and leftover craft supplies in the empty hotel rooms. Were they as untouched as the one where she'd died? Would I find her treasures waiting here in tiny time capsules?

The long hall, its mahogany wainscoting now clad in pimpled varnish and muted light, stretched wide like a dragon's mouth, toothed with peeling plaster and paint, dust swirls dripping like smoke. Why did Clyde insist on staying in the Excelsior if he wasn't even taking care of it? He couldn't possibly be happy here. He wasn't a wealthy man, but he had his military pension. He could afford something better suited, easier to maintain. Instead, he chose this eerie state of suspended animation.

I'd made the rounds this morning and talked to the people who ran the boutique and the gallery downstairs. The jewelry store owner, who reportedly knew the most about Clyde, wasn't expected back until at least tomorrow. By all accounts, Clyde reluctantly communicated with the tenants about basic repairs and maintenance to the building, but nothing else. He wasn't interested in chitchat or socializing or invitations to wine-and-cheese events in the stores during the holidays. He hadn't endeared himself to the shopkeepers, and they weren't thrilled with the slow disintegration of the Excelsior either.

Unfortunately, they were even less pleased by my arrival. Everyone was worried about my reasons for coming, and I couldn't give them what I didn't have—answers about the building . . . or about Clyde.

After falling asleep on the roof yesterday evening, then waking half frozen under a scattering of stars, I'd gone back downstairs and again found the apartment empty, my stepfather still mysteriously absent. The remainder of the night had me starting at every sound. In the morning, I'd awakened in my mother's chair, wrapped in her quilt and her scents. Even though the building was mine, I felt like a trespasser, a thief about to be caught and punished.

Before anyone could show up and tell me differently, I wanted to get a look at the second floor. No sense arguing with Clyde about the contents if nothing of value remained. If there *was* something, at least I'd know what I was arguing for—what my eventual options might be. If left-behind family heirlooms couldn't buy our way out of the immediate trouble with Bella Tazza 2, my only hope might be the value of the building itself.

A sharp pinch of guilt came with that thought. It was clear enough from the uneasy conversations downstairs that everyone had heard of Patricia's greedy daughter, who wanted nothing more than to turn the family property into profit.

Clyde had apparently salted the ground in front of me. Had he purposely arranged things so that if I ever came here, I'd find the whole town against me from the beginning? Who could say what the man was capable of? He'd manipulated a woman who was on heaven knows what medications, persuaded her to bequeath use of the building and its income to someone she'd only been married to for four years. I had no idea whether the woman who'd changed her will only weeks prior to her death bore any resemblance to the one who'd carefully labeled each of these cardboard containers. *Christmas, Easter, Fourth of July. Exterior twinkle lights. Window candelabras. Wreath and garlands.* My mother had been a lover of all seasons and every holiday. After years of teaching, she owned enough decorations to liven up even a place as large as the Excelsior.

In her e-mails to me, she'd written about how much she adored being one of the full-timers in Manteo. She'd even been in the annual outdoor theater presentation twice before the cancer had come back. Like others on the Outer Banks, she saw assuming a role as one of Sir Walter Raleigh's Lost Colonists not only as a way of preserving history and entertaining tourists, but also as a bit of a lark. Among the citizens here, it was a badge of honor to discuss which characters you'd played over the years. In her younger days, my red-haired mother would've been perfect for the coveted Queen Elizabeth role. As it was, she was happy to play bit parts and help with the musical end of the show.

Standing here by her boxes, I tasted the regret of having been held up by a restaurant disaster the one time I'd planned to come watch her perform in the amphitheater that housed the Lost Colony drama. I should've dropped everything and made the trip, no matter what.

Now here I was, left with only the remnants of her. The crushing nature of the task struck me as I looked down the hall. This place needed so much more than a quick sweep to see if anything remained that could be sold to save Bella Tazza 2. Yes, there were mountains of hotel castoffs and family heirlooms to deal with, but my mother's life—things she cared about—remained here too. I needed time to consider how best to honor her, how to treat these items with reverence, finding the right place for each one, the right person to put to good use what I couldn't bring home. My aunts would want some of her things. Which ones? What should be saved and what should be let go?

Whit's baby clothes, the masking-tape label on a green plastic tub read. She'd probably saved those things in hopes of grandchildren.

At thirty-eight, that was looking less and less likely for me. Yet despite my wanderings, my consuming drive to prove myself in the business world, and my hasty-then-disastrous marriage, my mother had clung to the hope that I would one day settle down in a little white house with someone who really loved me. Someone with whom I would start a family of my own.

The familiar lump swelled in my throat—the one that came with thinking of all the milestones my mother and I would never share. I swallowed hard, sighed out regret. I hoped she knew, even though I'd been stubborn, even though I'd insisted on culinary school and a career far from home, that she wasn't the one I'd been running from. Maybe, in truth, that restless spirit was as much an inheritance as whatever remained in this building, where my father's father had come and gone from the harbor. Perhaps it was the very thing Grandmother Ziltha had disliked in Benjamin Benoit, the adventuring husband with whom she'd once taken over ownership of this grand hotel. They'd shared less than eight years before he'd vanished at sea off Cape Hatteras in 1936. Perhaps I was plagued by the stirrings of my ancestors, who'd heard the siren songs of faraway places, who'd left home again and again to wander.

I felt their whispers, sensed their stories seeping from the walls as I moved down the hall, beyond my mother's stored items, deeper into the past. The first two rooms on either side were filled with hotel equipment—the enamelware rolling carts once used by the maids, shelves stacked with china pitchers and water glasses. Blond bedsteads and dressers hailing from the sixties. Any antiques of value had been sold when the rooms were updated. What remained from the Excelsior's last years of business added up to little more than a removal nightmare, now that the freight elevator used by Old Dutch, the porter, no longer worked. My mother hadn't seen the point in fixing it after the motor died. She'd lacked the funds, anyway. *We need the exercise of walking the stairs,* she'd told me. *Clyde, especially, with his bad circulation.*

Someday when you've got time to sort through what's left from your grandmother Ziltha, you can figure out how to get rid of all the junk. We'll hunt up some big, burly guys to move things. Maybe a little good will come of that and I'll get some grandbabies before I'm too old to enjoy them.

Mom . . ., I'd warned, feeling the familiar tightness and resentment stiffen my spine. Why wasn't a corporate career that allowed me to travel around the world, to live in resorts and upscale hotels, to eventually start my own business, good enough? Why, always, the pressure to consider a road other than the one I'd taken?

Now I wished that instead of scolding her, I'd simply said, *Well, Mom, maybe one of these days, right? If my soul mate happens along. I love you, you know.*

Why had we always been locked in the subtle battles of mother and daughter, each convinced we were right about what was best for the other?

I hope she knows how much I loved her.

Moving on from the first couple rooms, I continued down the hall to the ones near the elevator, where Grandmother Ziltha's possessions had been stored after she passed away. I'd turned eighteen that spring. A scholarship had taken me to Paris for a summer work-study prior to starting culinary school.

The Excelsior had been closed for two years by then, Grandmother Ziltha's declining mental state making it impossible to keep the place going. Mom's e-mails to me had described the sad condition of the third-floor residence, now a disjointed shadow of its former glory. With Lucianne in a nursing home and Old Dutch dead, there was no one to stop a dishonest home health worker from taking my grandmother's fur coats, jewelry, silver services, even antique furniture, as she came and went from the Excelsior. When questioned, she said those things were gifts, given to her out of Ziltha's gratitude. Mom had no way of proving otherwise, nor could she afford the legal battle over it. She simply did the best she could, moving most of the remaining valuables and the smaller antiques down to the second floor, where she could lock them away before leasing out the third floor.

I don't want you to have to bother with that stuff, Mom, I'd told her, the bluntness easier via e-mail. *Just sell it. I can use the money to stay in Paris for school, long-term.*

Her reply had been gentle but determined. *I'll let you go through it when you have the chance. Your father's baby photos are there, and his school records and other family mementos. That's your history on the Benoit side. Just leave it be until you have time for it.*

As often was the case, she'd been right in the long run. Now, the fact that I hadn't squandered the funds from this building on a stint in Paris seemed like a gift. Whatever remained in the packed rooms next to the elevator shaft and the open lounge area could offer salvation for Bella Tazza. Letting go of these things was a small sacrifice compared to preserving the jobs of thirty-five hardworking people.

Around me, boxes and furniture and gray moving pads formed an odd sort of fruit, each ripe with possibility. No telling where I should begin or exactly what I was looking for. I was certainly no antiques expert, nor did there seem to be any sort of organizational system here. The heavy mahogany dressers with ornate mirrors, the tall bedstead leaning against the wall under a dirty canvas drop cloth, the lovely upright piano my grandmother played beautifully, the dining room suite, the hall tree, the massive gilt-framed mirror that had hung in the living room, all were impressive, even covered with dust. They undoubtedly had value, but getting them out of here would be almost impossible without the elevator.

The boxes made the most sense as a starting place. Boxes and dresser drawers and china cabinets. I needed small things I could easily transport, possibly even to the antique store I'd passed on the way into town.

"I guess . . . here we go," I whispered into the quiet air.

Crossing through the maze, I moved to a wardrobe and a

stack of bookshelves that stood together along the salon wall. The bottom drawer of the wardrobe squealed in protest at being dragged open. The space inside was filled with hats and gloves. Despite the summer heat and laid-back atmosphere of the Outer Banks, my grandmother had never gone anywhere without both, her habits left over from an era when meticulous propriety controlled women's lives.

Squatting above the dusty floor, I dug through the contents, temporarily lost in intricate patterns of seed pearls, colorful glass beads, swirling feathers, and the milky shapes of embroidery. A matching pair of gloves lay folded with each hat, the adornments carefully coordinated. No doubt the sets had been created by artisans who were well known in their day. Everything about Ziltha Benoit spoke of the wealth and position with which she had been raised.

The leftovers were interesting to ponder, but not the sort of things I needed. Maybe my mother's theater group could use them as costumes. In an odd way, my grandmother probably would have liked that. She'd always supported the arts.

I stood and opened the wardrobe cabinet next. Dresses hung inside, the type that would have sheathed my grandmother's long, thin frame far before I ever knew her. The finery of a young woman. Beaded and sequined, they must've been pricey, worn to cocktail parties, receptions, and invitation-only dinners among the Outer Banks' most well-known families, or perhaps in Virginia Beach and Norfolk, where the coastal elite supported museums, historical societies, and other philanthropic ventures. In her younger years before the falling-out with her family, she'd involved herself in the business. After the estrangement, she'd withdrawn to the hotel and Roanoke Island, subtly letting her resentment be known by her refusal to keep up appearances.

Standing here among her belongings, I felt as if she were watching me from some darkened corner, pointing that craggy finger and saying, *Do not touch, young lady!*

Her voice was so clear, I paused to listen, to recall the way the languid Old South tones of her Charleston upbringing had given even the harshest commands a musical quality. She'd never called me by my name. I was always *child* or *girl* or *young lady*. The name *Whitney* was too modern and lacked sophistication, she said, so she refused to use it. Her habit of addressing me was, instead, a perpetual scolding. Those years of navigating her tutelage and the staff of the Excelsior had prepared me for the sometimes-brutal process of working my way up from prep cook to executive chef to corporate manager to business owner. It was proof that sometimes the hardest things in life become the building blocks of the greatest achievements.

There'd been a bit of Grandmother Ziltha in that standoff with Tagg Harper in the Bella Tazza 2 parking lot too. She and I did have a few things in common, stubbornness being one and determination to cling to what was ours being another. She wouldn't have liked the idea of my selling off her belongings.

"You'd probably do the same thing, if you were in my shoes. You'd never let someone like Tagg Harper come out on top," I told her as I continued around the room, searching empty dresser drawers, where an occasional yellowed hankie or stocking lay curled in nests of string, wavy gray hair, and dismembered bug bodies. Broken bits of jewelry slid across drawer bottoms and drew trails in the dust. A small, pearlescent box offered up a smattering of spelling bee awards, a Red Cross emblem, a locket, a baby ring, club pins, and a Daughters of the American Revolution Medal of Honor—things Grandmother Ziltha had saved to the last of her life.

Their only value was sentimental now. I left them where they were and moved on to a pile of boxes along the west wall. The dust-draped labels bore my mother's handwriting. *Ziltha's books.* Upstairs, what was now a closed-off room had once been the domain of important men. In years past, its heavy mahogany desk and bulky leather chairs had been privy to the private conversations of the sea captains and shipping magnates who gathered to speak with Benjamin Benoit. During his travels, he'd amassed a world-class library that had stretched from floor to ceiling, the enormous bookshelves woefully overburdened.

No one ever read the books, as far as I could see, and when I came in the summers, I, like the household help, had been forbidden to touch them. They were fragile and of no interest to a girl my age, I was told. Instead, a stack of books from the public library always awaited me in the room I shared with my mother at the end of the hall. I read Grandmother Ziltha's selections occasionally, but *Anne of Green Gables* and *Jane Eyre* felt a bit too close to life during those summers. For the most part, I was too tired to read anyway. If I wasn't too tired, I was sneaking down the fire escape, looking for new friends or cute boys.

What might be among these books I'd always been told not to touch? Perhaps some of them really *were* valuable. It was worth checking, anyway.

I lifted a box from the stack, lugged it to a cracked vinyl chair and looked inside, coughing at the haze of old paper, dried glue, and decaying binding tape. The contents actually seemed to be in pretty good shape, but the box was filled with nothing more than outdated encyclopedias. *Those* hadn't come from the drawing room. The only encyclopedia set in my grandmother's house had belonged to her maid, Lucianne, and had stayed in Lucianne's room upstairs. Grandmother Ziltha had thought it a ridiculous expense for a maid to incur, and she was angry that Lucianne had let a traveling salesman bamboozle her into making the purchase. My grandmother also thought I needed to be reading the classics rather than perusing photos of baboons in Africa and Aborigines in Australia. *Uncivilized,* she had said.

Even reading the encyclopedias had been a tiny act of rebellion, once. I couldn't imagine what it must have been like for my father, growing up under Ziltha Benoit's domineering eye. The ivy-laden boarding schools in Virginia must have seemed like welcome vacations.

Setting the book back in its place, I put the lid on the box and walked back to the pile. Something caught my eye as I tried to wrestle another container free . . . something I . . . recognized? Even with a drop cloth lying over it, the slanted top of an old captain's desk was unmistakable. The desk had always stood in an alcove of the library, a holdover from Benjamin Benoit's seafaring travels, according to family lore. Of all the things in my grandmother's house, this was the one that had most inspired my childhood imagination.

A tug on the dry-rotted covering revealed the beautiful gilded-edged writing surface, the inlay bright and surprisingly free of patina. Leaning across the mountain of cardboard, I caught a glimpse of the ornate cabriole legs and bun feet. "There you are," I whispered, and realized that in some way I'd been hoping for this. Seeing the desk was like reuniting with an old friend.

On evenings when my grandmother was away with her bridge club or gone for other social engagements, I'd sneaked into the library and sat in the wobbly, narrow-legged chair at the small davenport desk. Perched there, I wrote, drew pictures, read books, and dreamed of foreign lands. Distant foghorns and boatswains' whistles had lent the illusion that I was somewhere far away, sailing from one exotic port to another, as my ancestors had.

That comes from long time back in the Benoit family, Lucianne had told me once when she caught me sliding open the writing surface and investigating the tiny drawers behind it. Dried-up inkwells, pens, and blotters still rested within its catacombs.

The captains kept hiding places. You know that? Way back in the day, they sure enough needed someplace to stash their valuables. Someplace nobody'd ever find. She'd checked over her shoulder before showing me the desk's hidden compartments. *Your daddy loved this desk as a little'un too. He'd sit here writing and dreaming and getting that same far-off look to his eye—if your granny didn't have him practicing the violin or the piana, that was. You're so much like that boy. Sometimes it's almost like watchin' a spirit. You be careful of the sea, sweetness. It ain't been good to this family.*

She'd taken on a sad look then, folds of weathered skin hanging heavy around her mouth in the way they usually did when my father was mentioned. Tragedy ran in the Benoit family like eye color. Sad endings lay inseparably tangled with threads of wealth, privilege, duty, and the lure of the sea. Perhaps that was why, the older I grew, the more I'd felt the need to separate myself from the Benoits. And my father.

Perhaps that was also why the sea had always lured me back.

Dragging and pushing boxes, I worked to fully uncover the captain's desk, each move careful and quiet. It was in good shape, considering the long exposure to salt air and the years of being tucked away in a space with little climate control.

It would be small enough to carry down the stairs, if I engaged a little help.

No telling what it's worth. . . .

No telling if there would be anything left inside it by now, either. Perhaps the home health worker had already rifled through it. After the fact, my mother had discovered so many things missing.

Fortunately, the upper compartment was locked, a good sign. The key was still underneath the inkwell slide, where it had always been.

The hand-wrought brass lock turned as if it had been used yesterday.

Old papers lay in the compartment beneath the writing surface—inventory notes, a leather-bound ship's manifest from a journey to Hong Kong, a brass taffrail device. With its metal wings similar to the fins on an arrow's shaft, the taffrail log would've been hung on a ship to calculate the vessel's speed through the water. As a child, I'd secreted this one away many times and dashed to the roof, holding the string and spinning in circles to cause it to turn.

It glinted now, dangling in the window light. The tarnished fins twisted slightly, as if they still remembered the ocean breeze. The pull of an old fascination tugged at me. This desk was my history. Surely there had to be other things that would be easier to part with. Things less precious. If I took the desk and its contents home, I could spend more time with them, find out if they'd belonged to Grandmother Ziltha's mysterious husband and why the desk hadn't been lost at sea when he was.

Stop. Whitney, you can't get romantic about this. Hard decisions would have to be made here. I didn't have room for any furniture in Michigan, nor funds to transport it. If Clyde never came back to the Excelsior, the time to sell the building could be coming sooner than I'd thought.

Keep a business head. Don't go sentimental. Don't.

Setting the taffrail log back in the desk, I hardened myself against the heirlooms and their stories. They were only brass, leather, wood. Of course I would give them up to save Bella Tazza, to ensure that Denise, Mattie, Grandma Daisy, and my employees didn't suffer for my business mistakes. *I* was the one who'd wanted the mill building so badly that I'd rushed into the deal without taking time to wander around town, ask a few questions, get some details about the local climate.

This was my mess to clean up. I would do whatever it took to prevent others from paying the costs.

A clinical determination elbowed aside girlish fantasies as I searched the desk drawers, fingering antique pens and swinging open a compartment made to hold a wax candle and a stamp for sealing letters. The hidden latch that would allow the top of the desk to slide forward was right where I remembered—where Lucianne had shown me years ago. I slipped my hand over it, pulled the pin, and edged the upper compartment forward to expose the three cubbyhole spaces behind the drawers in the base. They'd always been empty, but now items rested in each one. How had those come to be there . . . and when?

In the first compartment lay a brooch, its ornate gold filigree forming a crest that encircled a beautifully faceted red stone. The second space held a tusk-shaped scrimshaw carving of a woman in a billowing dress, standing at the wheel of a ship at sea. Beside it lay a necklace of carved bone or ivory beads, its centerpiece a snuff jar or a locket with a Maltese cross etched into the surface. The third cubbyhole held a book, leather covered and bowed slightly to fit into the little nook.

I removed the items one by one, examined them. The brooch was definitely gold, the large stone probably a ruby, the others possibly diamonds. The head of the crest was emblazoned with a script *B*. Perhaps this had been my grandmother's? Maybe given to her when she married into the Benoit family? No doubt it was old and had value, as did the scrimshaw carving and necklace. Setting down the brooch, I examined the carving, marveling at the intricate image created by etched lines and stained with ink, a masterpiece of scratches. Who was the woman? A captain's wife? A passenger prominent enough to have been permitted to take the wheel? A captain herself? Would a woman have been allowed, even if she were a Benoit?

Was the carved necklace hers? Had she worn the locket close to her skin as she'd set off on the ship, or had it been given to her there—perhaps crafted by a sailor who'd become smitten with her? Or was the woman on the scrimshaw piece only the artist's imagining—a patron saint, a guardian angel? Was she a lover left behind, yearned for during the long voyage from the old world to the new?

I'd never seen any of these things in my grandmother's rooms upstairs, and helping Lucianne remove and dust her endless knickknacks had always been among my summer tasks. Who had selected these treasures and hidden them in the desk? When? Had it happened after my grandmother's death? Long before? Had I even looked in the secret compartments the last summer I'd worked here, the summer I'd turned sixteen?

Probably not. By then I was much more interested in boys.

The book, now permanently bent by the cramped quarters, was a pocket copy of Stephen Crane's "The Open Boat." It could easily have lived its life sandwiched among the Benoit library collection upstairs. I never would've known.

The binding crinkled softly as I lifted the cover. Perhaps it was an autographed copy? An especially valuable edition? The pages fell open, parting almost down the center. A letter, clearly wadded and crumpled once, had been tucked into the spine. Its imprint had yellowed the pages, so that its ghost remained even after I removed it.

"Where did *you* come from?" I didn't realize I'd spoken until my voice echoed into the hanging mist of stillness and forgotten things.

The letter didn't crackle, but unfolded silently, its surface more like fabric than paper. It felt soft beneath my fingers, surprisingly pliable, almost velvety.

The words had been written in 1936. A woman's artful cursive, the carefully practiced penmanship of a bygone day when such things were considered important.

Sister Dear,

It is my hope, as this letter arrives, that you may know how very precious you are to me, as is your dashing husband, Benjamin, though I have only begun to know him in these greatly troubled times since your wedding. Could that have been only seven years ago? How short a while when spoken, yet it was another life, another world when first I met your beau and the four of us strolled in the Charleston garden, nervously warming to your sudden announcement. Mother and the aunts looked on, twittering behind their hands, for you had given them quite the shock, whirling in with your plans to marry. Knowing you, they should not have been surprised at all that you would go your own way. Your Benjamin, with his wild tales of world travels, was so different from any among our family, and from my Richard. I confess, I was a bit jealous of the life into which you would marry.

Yet you always were the bold one, the one to marshal the activities among us children, and I the steady, careful one, happy to follow along with all that you had planned for the lot of us.

How precious were those times! How wonderful the days when all was well.

How necessary, also, that we must release them now. It is fine enough to glance at the past, but one must never focus there overlong. Don't you think?

Perhaps we did not recognize then, in our softness, in the ease of our lives draped in fine lace and pearls, how truly fortunate we were and how fortunes can change. Had I understood it, had I known that one can live with so much less, perhaps my Richard would still be with us today. Perhaps his choices would have been different, that fateful day in '29.

So many quiet nights, I wrap myself in wishing lines that begin with "If only . . ." I know you must yearn for Benjamin when he is gone to sea, particularly now that a baby is finally on the way, but be thankful for the anticipation of his homecomings, and for Benjamin's gainful employment when so many cannot find work.

You have such blessings in the stable fortunes of the Benoits and in your success with the hotel there in Manteo. Your child will never go hungry, nor be marched off to breadlines as so many are today. The world is not what it once was, as we well know from our own family's sad decline. Those years of dress fittings and afternoon socials seem frivolous and far away now. They have become distant memories. My old gowns have gone almost too threadbare to wear to receptions and events about the college, and my work frocks are barely serviceable for minding the reception desk in the dean's office. These will not, however, matter a bit where I am going next.

I know that, upon the news of the closing of the women's college, you had expected that my little Peapod and I would eventually come to the Excelsior for more than just a visit. Please know that what I have to tell you now does not in any way diminish my gratitude over your efforts and the plans you have formed on my behalf. I know you have done this out of love and no small bit of concern over my ability to look after Emmaline and myself. It is also evident that you, Lucianne, and Old Dutch have gone to quite a bit of trouble to make a room homey for us. Will you extend them my thanks for their hard work and kindness? Tell "Old Duck" (as Emmaline still calls him) that she will send more drawings to him soon. She still treasures the toy horse he carved for her during our visit there a year ago. She has since combed the little horsehair tail practically down to the nubbins!

I do wish, Dear Sister, that I had spoken up earlier of another possibility that might come to pass for Emmaline and me. I suppose I had been reluctant to seem ungrateful and, as always, unwilling to go against your leading. I would treasure the opportunity to live by the sea and to whisk away your lonely hours as you await your husband's many returns to home harbors. I adore the very thought of being there for your child's arrival late this summer, but in truth my presence and Emmaline's would only intrude upon time that you and Benjamin should be spending with your wee one when he or she finally makes an appearance. I know that, after so many tries for a baby, these remaining months must be an agony of waiting, but it will happen sooner than you know, and you do not need the burden of a sister and niece to care for in the meanwhile. Similarly, with Daddy's passing and Mama having lost the house in Charleston, we would only be another drain, were we to go there.

Today, I have received the most exciting news, and I hope that you will cheer it as well! Some time ago, in anticipation of the difficulty in finding work after the college's demise, I applied for a position with the Federal Writers' Project, a program in the care of President Roosevelt's Works Progress Administration. The FWP provides a most exciting opportunity for those like myself, displaced from the academic world or from positions in the creative and journalistic arts.

You may or may not, there on the Outer Banks, have heard of this monumental endeavor, but word is that this is a pet project of Eleanor Roosevelt herself! Through the program, our government has created a plan to document and preserve the natural wealth and common history of this nation. Writers, photographers, researchers, and mapmakers journeying along the byways of each state will document all natural wonders and bona fide tourist attractions, in order to encourage travel and promote economic growth. The writers shall also record a sort of history of the people, such as has never before been attempted or even considered worthy of effort. It is Roosevelt's aim that these teams of documentarians in each state may gather the memories, folk legends, and lives of the common man, from farmer to factory worker, from Western cowboy to former slave.

Can you imagine this? Such a magnificent and momentous undertaking! As of today, I have officially been added to the rolls of the Federal Writers' Project. My salary of eighty dollars per month will not, by any means, secure accommodations at the Ritz, but it will provide for our basic needs if we are careful, and the kindness of strangers along the way will surely help as well.

Though most writers on The Project operate in their home areas, I have been tasked to a region in which a field interviewer was recently dismissed for slovenly behavior and underwhelming effort. My job will be to act quickly and judiciously, so as to bring reports from the territory up to speed. To that end, I will soon go to the far western mountains of our beautiful state of North Carolina. I will be traveling in the company of a young cartographer who is charged with mapping and photographing the countryside there for the FWP. I will take along my typewriter and the folding desk that was once Father's, as well as a bare minimum of belongings.

You may be wondering now about Little Pea. Special permissions have been given to allow her to travel along as, at only six, she is considered too young to be away from me for long periods. I suspect that our kindly dean of students here may have had a hand in this arrangement, as in my being admitted to the program at all. Among the writers taking up this task nationwide are many famous names you would doubtless recognize. Even notables such as Anzia Yezierska, Max Bodenheim, and Zora Neale Hurston are rumored to be involved or considering it!

Can you see, Dear Sister, that in this work I will be in fabulous company? Please do not think me ungrateful for your kind plans to take us in. This is simply a better alternative. Emmaline and I will come to visit when we can, though I anticipate that our time in the Blue Ridge could be lengthy. From there, I may move into employment at the FWP state office if a position is available. I will write to you daily and post letters as we come to towns along the way. Forgive me for not traveling to Manteo in person to tell you all of this. I simply cannot, as I am certain you would attempt to talk some sense into me. I know in my very bones that this is an adventure I must undertake and that this journey will change me. I will not allow myself to be turned from it.

Do not worry over me. I look to my upcoming work with great anticipation. I will become a small piece of the vast history of this battered and magnificent country.

Yours always,
Alice

CHAPTER 5

The sound overhead stopped me halfway through another box. I'd been hearing voices from below for several hours as I worked—male voices. I'd concluded that I was over the Rip Shack and that the crew down there was having a good time. There had been numerous spurts of raucous man-laughter and a few high-pitched female giggles. Their day was clearly going much better than mine.

So far, I'd gathered a few antiques and vintage items I thought might have some value, but in reality, I'd mostly come up with old magazines, tax forms, business files from the hotel years, free notepads, outdated phone books, hankies, linens, ashtrays, and assorted sea shells. There seemed to be no rhyme or reason to the items stored here.

Among other things, I'd been hoping for more letters and enough clues to discern exactly who Alice was. My knowledge of my father's family was tissue-thin and filled with holes. I'd always known that Grandmother Ziltha had two brothers she'd broken ties with, and that her mother was an Avondale, a name synonymous with old Charleston high society. But I'd never been told that my grandmother had a sister. Did my father know about Alice? Or was she a secret my grandmother kept from everyone . . . and if so, why?

Maybe I should've left the whole thing alone—I had bigger fish to fry right now—but in some way Alice's letter reached to the deepest shadows in the most hidden parts of me. Had her husband, like my father, *chosen* to leave his family behind, deserting them in the most painful way? Another young mother left alone? Another daughter abandoned, to make of fact and memories what she could? Was the tragic type of loss that had both marked and changed my life a sad form of family heritage? Was Alice's decision to join the Federal Writers' Project an attempt to finally break the cycle of pain that a suicide leaves behind?

I know in my very bones that this is an adventure I must undertake and that this journey will change me.

Had it? I wanted to find out. In some inexplicable way, I saw myself in the words of this woman who'd apparently been stricken from the family record. I needed to know what had become of her.

A sound passed overhead again—something more disturbing than joists offering up ghostly creaks and moans. Those were *footsteps*. Footsteps upstairs, and then three rhythmic thuds. *Boom, boom, boom,* in rapid succession from one end of the building to the other. Too fast for human feet, unless there was an eight-foot basketball player up there.

I let a stack of china rest in a box again, sat back on my heels, and focused upward, taking in the peeling plaster ceiling. The sound came again. *Boom, boom, boom* and then silence. Then *boom, boom, boom, boom, boom,* like the raven rapping at the door in Edgar Allen Poe's poem.

A pulse rushed up my neck, beating staccato accompaniment,

and a tidal sense of dread brought me to my feet. Was Clyde finally home? Could he possibly have made it up the stairs without my hearing him? Maybe he wasn't alone, or maybe it wasn't Clyde at all. Maybe one of his sons had come. Perhaps they were here to move him out, take him someplace where he could get the help and care he needed?

Only one set of footsteps tested the joists. *Squeak, squeak, squeak* . . . and then the pounding, *whap, whap, whap, whap*.

My cell phone rang on the davenport desk, and I jerked upright, lost my balance, and did a backward knee bend over a box. A mound of threadbare velvet curtains broke my fall, and all I could think was, *spiders, crickets, crawly things*. I came up in a hurry, knocked a small pewter pitcher off a box, and watched it fall in slow motion. It hit the floor with a resounding ring and bounced away, the sound filling the empty salon and echoing down the hallway into the hotel rooms.

Below, the hum of first-floor conversation halted.

The pitcher rolled to a stop against the wall. My cell quit ringing. I stood stock still, aware that I'd just made enough racket to wake the dead. Had whoever was upstairs heard it?

The noise came again. *Thump, thump, thump.*

Then nothing.

My cell let out another warbling ring. I grabbed it and answered, breathless, anticipating disaster. The only person who ever called back-to-back when I didn't answer was Denise, and she only did it when there was a problem.

Home and all its issues squeezed through the line and instantly arrived on Roanoke Island. "What's wrong, Denise?"

The question seemed to take her by surprise. "Well . . . nothing really. You didn't call last night. I just wanted to make sure you were all right. Have you talked to your stepfather yet?"

Her hopeful tone begged the comfort of a lie. I had a feeling there was something still unspoken, some new reason she needed me to say, *Yes, it's all settled. I'll be home in a couple days with money in my pocket. Don't worry about a thing.*

"I haven't seen him yet. It's kind of a long story." A glance at my watch tightened my chest even more, the bones aching, so that I felt like Mattie during one of her asthma attacks. "I can't believe you're calling during the lunch rush. Is business slow today?" *Please say no.* We couldn't afford a low take. Not even one.

At least ten different mental scenarios played at lightning speed in the instant it took Denise to answer. I knew why. I was afraid that, in my parking lot standoff with Tagg Harper, I'd poked a sleeping tiger. I should've had the good sense not to lock horns with him again. No doubt that was the family temper coming out. When Grandmother Ziltha went on a rant, linens and improperly washed silverware flew from windows, sooty ashtrays shattered against walls, and hotel staff ran for cover.

"No, it's fine. The lunch has been good, actually. Had the Rotary club take the banquet room at the last minute, and a road crew came in on top of the normal crowd, so it got a little crazy for a while. Dale's home sick from the hot line, and that held up the plate time some, but we were still averaging around nineteen minutes—not too bad. We're slowing down a bit now. I put the blackened tilapia special up for tonight, so I'm sure it'll be busy."

"Good." Glancing at my watch, I stopped pacing, did a double take. I'd been down here longer than I meant to be. The afternoon was already half gone.

"So . . . you haven't even *seen* your stepfather yet?" Denise veered back to the original question, once again pointing to the need for a quick and easy answer.

"Clyde wasn't anywhere to be found when I showed up. I think he might've just come home, though . . . or maybe it's one of his sons. I'm downstairs, but I hear activity on the third floor. Either someone's up there or the place is being robbed."

Denise didn't laugh at the joke. Instead, there was an odd pause, followed by, "Whit, be careful, okay?"

"I was only kidding. I'm sure it's Clyde or someone he sent." I aimed for a casual tone, smoke-screening my mounting dread. The performance wasn't just for Denise's benefit. *Imagining triumph is the first step in reaching it*—a bit of wisdom from a poster we'd hung in the Bella Tazza kitchen to inspire the staff. "Although, considering the state of things upstairs, I'm wondering what kind of mental shape he's in. The place is like a shrine. My mother's slippers are still sitting there beside her chair, even."

Denise stopped to ring up a customer and accept a few compliments on the meal.

"Sounds like they were happy," I said when she came back.

"That was the manager of the highway crew. They'll be in all week. Maybe longer. Good news for us. Those guys can put away some food. They decimated the bread baskets. I think Heather filled them at least ten times. I'm not sure we turned a profit."

"Dough is cheap." I thought that'd get a laugh, for sure. Starting out, we'd had one of our biggest arguments over whether or not to put the "endless bread basket" on every table. "Denise, is something wrong? Other than the obvious, I mean." Even with all we'd been through lately, my cousin was usually in a good mood when she switched into restaurant mode. Our Italian heritage on my mother's side meant that stuffing people brought joy at a DNA level.

Denise's silence was an answer.

"All right, what's going on?"

"Listen . . ." Her tone was weirdly ominous. "Before you have it out with your stepfather, run downstairs and let someone know you're up there."

"Huh? Why?"

A sigh hinted that the real truth was coming. "I just . . . I'm worried about you, Whit. It's a lot to take in, being back there with all your mom's things, and you said yourself, you don't know what sort of mental state your stepfather is in. I need you to . . . be sure you're safe. I can't do this—Bella Tazza—without you."

"Denise . . . *what*?" Where was this coming from?

"It's nothing. I had a dream last night and it kind of freaked me out."

"About me?" This wasn't like Denise at all.

"Yes . . . well . . . sort of. We were out at Gooch Pond—you know where we used to ice-skate? Remember that? And you were just little. Maybe about ten or so. I was babysitting. We were laughing and doing spins and having a good time. Then I was spinning and spinning, and when I stopped, I couldn't see you. I looked down, and you were all grown up, but you were under the ice, staring up at me."

Goose bumps walked over my skin, and I rubbed them away, hugging myself. Had she read my mind? Did she somehow know about my temptation on the shores of Lake Michigan the night before I left town?

The cold traveled to my bones, as if the water were rushing over me now. "Geez, Denise." I lifted the tone of the words, making light of it. But it didn't feel like light. It felt like darkness.

"Just be careful down there, okay? I went by church this morning and said an extra prayer for you."

"Thanks." I couldn't come up with anything else. My mother had raised me in church. I'd left it as soon as I left home. The same kids who'd teased and belittled me in private school had made Sunday school a living torment. I'd never had the heart to tell my mother. She'd always thought she was doing me a favor, driving across town so that I could spend Sundays with my classmates, rather than in the working-class community that still gave us sympathetic looks and whispered about my father's suicide. "I'll be careful; I promise. Don't worry about me, okay?"

Denise paused to engage with another customer, leaving me staring out the window, still strangely chilled.

Outside the hotel, a spring breeze twirled along the alleyway and pressed through the gaps in the window sashes. Atop the captain's desk, the corner of Alice's letter lifted slightly, then rested again. For an instant, I wanted to tell Denise about it, to read the words to her and see what she thought. Then I realized how bizarre that would seem, how impractical given our present situation. I should've been focusing on the search for valuables, not taking time to sift through every scrap of paper, looking for more information about a woman who had to be long gone by now.

Denise was all business when she came back. "Listen, I need to go. The guy from Primero Foods is here with our delivery. Remember what I said, okay? Go downstairs first. Tell somebody you're up there. And keep your phone with you . . . in case things spiral out of control."

"Denise, the man just got out of the hospital. . . ."

"And text me afterward. If I don't answer, it's because I'm in the carpool line, picking up Mattie. They'll write you a ticket in a heartbeat for texting in the school zone."

"Give my godbaby a squeeze for me, 'kay? Tell her I'm sorry I'm missing my day to pick her up at school. Tell her we'll go for ice cream when I get back."

We said good-bye and I hung up, tucking the phone in my pocket and pausing to survey the mess strewn from one end of the salon to the other. I hadn't accomplished much since finding Alice's letter in the davenport desk. Other than sorting out some books I thought might have value, setting aside a few vases, and gathering the vintage hats, shoes, and gloves into a couple old suitcases, I had little to show for my time.

Now, things might be about to get significantly more complicated.

I turned to the sounds upstairs again.

Squeak, squeak, followed by *whack, whack, whack* traveling down the hall.

Leaving the second floor behind, I hurried down to street level, Denise's warning still in my mind. *Tell somebody you're up there.* Who? I hadn't met anyone other than a few of the shopkeepers. I barely knew them, and in general, they saw me as the enemy.

"What's going on upstairs?" Speaking of the enemy, Mark Strahan was standing in the Rip Shack's side entrance. He was dressed in jeans today, along with a gray long-sleeved Body Glove shirt of the sort that surfers wore. The grim look on his face brought back the tension of our original conversation. "Sounded like the roof was about to fall in."

"That was me, actually." I pictured myself doing the Three Stooges move over the boxes upstairs. "I was cleaning out some things."

His eyes narrowed. "Cleaning out?"

"There's a lot of clutter in the old hotel rooms. Just junk, mostly." Why did I feel like such a vulture? I didn't have to explain myself to Mark, or to anyone else.

A quick jerk of his head indicated the building above. "He's back, you know. Mr. Franczyk. I saw him get out of a cab—tried to tell him if he'd hang on a minute, I'd help him up the stairs once the shop was clear of customers. He just waved me off. Guess he made it okay. That can't be an easy climb in the shape he's in."

An inconvenient sympathy came knocking at the doors of my conscience. I kept them securely bolted. "I'm headed up there to talk to him."

A wry, one-sided smirk formed a dimple alongside Mark's mouth, momentarily drawing my eye. He seemed to realize it, and his gaze tried to catch mine. I looked away instead, as he added, "From what little I know of him, I'm guessing that might be an interesting conversation."

"I'm afraid it might."

"You're going to try to talk him into moving out of this building." Mark was astute about my motives—disturbingly so.

"I plan to encourage him to be sensible. He isn't safe here alone. Obviously."

Firmly crossed arms and a stern look made me out for a liar. "You know what's going to happen to this building if you put it up for sale?" He nodded toward the nearby condos. Constructed with period architectural details, gabled roofs, and hand-cut shingles, they weren't an eyesore, but they weren't original Manteo, either. "In this location, with the water view, he'll do everything he can to get around the six-story height restriction."

"He . . . *who*?" Now I really was confused.

Mark gave me a tight-lipped look. "Last year, it was a resort redevelopment over on 64. Three towers, ten stories high each."

He drilled through me with an intensity that quickly bolted me in place.

"I have no idea what you're talking about." That much was the truth. "But no future plans for the building have been made at this point."

A muscle in his cheek twitched, pulling the corner of his mouth again. Downward, this time. "Why do I feel like that's the party line?"

"Are you calling me a liar?"

"More like a mystery. It's pretty clear that you're here for a reason."

"Maybe that *reason* has nothing to do with you *or* your shop." But in all likelihood, Mark Strahan and his shop would become casualties of the situation . . . victims of changing times. There was no way I could take care of the Excelsior long-distance, and even if I could, I didn't want to. Too many memories remained here, and the fact that I'd just spent hours seeking after more information about Alice only underlined the twisted pull this place held. I needed to let it all go and move on.

The owner of the Rip Shack and I stood locked, uncomfortably close, in a test of wills. He wanted me to see his point, and the truth was, I did. I just couldn't allow myself to take on one more problem, especially not one of this magnitude. The building was old, it hadn't been well kept, repeated hurricanes and nor'easters had flooded it, and in general it was a mess.

A quick, sardonic sound disturbed the taut silence. "I *saw* Casey Turner go in your stairway door earlier today." He closed the gap between us even further. "You want to tell me again that you aren't making plans?"

This guy had some nerve, seriously. "I don't even *know* who that *is*. I've been on the second floor working since breakfast, and I haven't seen or heard a soul . . . not until just a few minutes ago."

He backed off a little, fingers drumming on the elastic fabric over a tightly muscled bicep that looked like it came in contact with a weight machine on a regular basis. "You'd be smart to stay away from Casey Turner. The man's a leech."

"Good to know." If Mark Strahan wanted to win the favor of his eventual new landlord, he was going about it in completely the wrong way. Right now, it was all I could do to stay nice on the outside. Inside, frustration and tension were building up steam and looking for a release point. *Let him have it, Whitney. The bigger they are, the harder they fall.*

A delivery van and trailer wheeled to the curb, temporarily breaking the stalemate. The driver bounced out, shaggy blond hair whipping in the ever-present breeze off the bay.

"Hey, boss-dude, wha'zup?" He flashed a quick, dazzling smile that I had a feeling charmed the teenage girls at local hangouts.

"Joel?" I stepped forward, not waiting for introductions. I had a feeling Mark wasn't planning on any. "Whitney Monroe. You called me in Michigan."

"Yeah . . . it, ummm . . . seemed like the right thing to do." A glance flicked toward his boss. Was Mark angry with him for bringing me into the situation? "How's the old man gettin' along?"

"I haven't spoken to him yet. In fact, I was just headed up there. He came home a little while ago, apparently."

Joel's expression changed from relaxed to concerned. "Need me to go with ya? Kayla's been worried about the dude."

Mark gave an almost imperceptible head shake.

Denise's warning about the dream did a spider-crawl up my

back, leaving an unsettled feeling. "I think it's probably better if I go by myself. Thanks, though. After I've had a chance to talk to him, I'll come back down and let you know how he is. I appreciate the phone call the other day. It was a really decent thing to do." I flashed a look Mark's way.

A group of adolescent boys rode by on bicycles and waved, and both Joel and Mark waved back.

"Hey, run by later," Joel yelled. "Got some kickin' freebie videos from the trade show!"

Mark frowned. "Joel, you know the policy. They don't get freebies unless they've been in school all week. *Ask* first. You got Colton in trouble with that stuff for the PS3. His mom said he ditched school and flunked a test." He didn't wait for an answer before disappearing into the shop.

"Yeah, yeah . . . Everyone's a critic." Joel offered an impish grin, then did a half turn in the street, fired a finger pistol at one of the boys, and added, "Little turd."

He wished me luck with Clyde. I thanked him and then made my way up the stairs. A gust of wind wrenched the alcove door from my hand, and I caught it just in time to stop a thunderous slam against the wall. After the fact, I was almost sorry. Maybe it'd be good if Clyde had advance warning. Had my suitcases in the craft room and my coffee cup in the kitchen been noticed?

Or was I arriving completely by surprise?

Dread followed me around the corner onto the balcony, a nervous sweat building under my T-shirt. Across from the wicker sofa, the front door was actually hanging open, the torn screen door squeaking lazily in the breeze—the only sound I could hear as I stood and listened.

Something white fluttered in the shutter—a business card,

tucked between the wood and the brick. Clinging by only one corner, it released its hold with my fingers inches away. I caught it in a full-fisted grab. An instant later, it would've been gone, gliding away toward the water.

On the back of the card, someone had handwritten in an uneven combination of cursive and print, *Call when you have a moment.* Turning it over, I took in the owner's photo—clean-cut guy in a blue polo shirt, medium-blond hair neatly cropped, blue eyes, friendly smile.

The name was familiar, thanks to my conversation downstairs. *Casey Turner. CGI International.*

The man Mark was so sure I was already conspiring with—a real estate developer. So he *had* been here. Mark wasn't making that up. . . .

Three rhythmic thuds echoed out the door, and I stuffed the business card in my pocket like contraband. Moth wings fanned my throat, leaving a dry, dusty, choking feeling as I craned closer, trying to see past the front parlor.

Nothing.

Then suddenly, a thump, another, another, coming toward me this time. A tennis ball bounced from the shadows, crossed the parlor, and landed on the porch. A medium-size yellow dog scrambled after it. Spotting me, it skidded to a stop just inside the tattered screen. Wary eyes narrowed, hair bristled, the dog barked.

I stood there, uncertain and wondering if Clyde had heard. Was he coming to the door? The open air seemed a better place for confrontation. It would be harder inside, where my mother's gentle, creative spirit still lived among her weavings, her collections of shells, lamps fashioned from bits of driftwood, and sea glass artfully woven with wire to create sun catchers.

I couldn't imagine what she'd say if she were here to witness this. Would she be on Clyde's side or mine? Had she really intended for him to keep the building for years on end? Was that her plan, or had he coerced her as she lay close to death, perhaps delirious from the morphine I had no idea she was taking?

Maybe, if she was watching from heaven, she'd been waiting for this confrontation. Maybe she'd yearned for me to set things right.

Did the dead still *want* things? Or was death simply a letting go of all that is held so tightly in life—an understanding of the temporal and shallow nature of the human matters of possession, greed, desire, justice? I wanted to know. I so badly wanted to be certain that my mother was at peace, but it was hard to have much faith in a God who would take someone like her so young.

"Clyde?" I moved closer as the dog relaxed to its haunches, still barring the entrance. It—she—was a motley, flea-bitten thing, part yellow Labrador, part . . . who knew what? Ribs showed through her mud-spattered coat as she sat, legs flopped outward, the feet folding together as if she were adopting a yoga pose.

So . . . Clyde owned a dog? Where had the dog been while he was in the hospital? I hadn't seen any evidence of a pet in the house. No dishes, no toys. My stepfather didn't take very good care of her. A wound on her front leg had healed and crusted with sand.

She growled when I opened the screen and stepped around her into the parlor, but then she huddled low, her eyes rolling upward in a weary way that begged me not to challenge her.

"Clyde?"

Beyond the entry parlor and the front hallway, a recliner snapped upright in a clap of metal and fabric. Like all sounds here, it echoed, traveling easily in a place of so many hard surfaces. Sneaking around had never been easy in Grandmother Ziltha's domain.

"Geddout!" Clyde yelled. A faint shadow shifted the hallway light just past the kitchen. The outline of a head poked in as Clyde leaned from his recliner. "I told you people, I don't need no welfare services. I'm fine. Now git off my porch!" His voice sounded raspy and weak. A series of coughs followed the words, and then, I thought, a groan.

"Clyde, it's Whitney. . . Patricia's daughter?" No answer, so I added, "We need to talk."

"You geddouta here. Said I'm fine!" There was no change in his tone—no increasing level of threat. No hint of recognition. No measure of surprise.

"I'm coming in." I slowed my breathing, squared my shoulders, made myself as large as possible.

The dog's toenails clicked as she belly-crawled in my wake, following through the receiving room, then stopping, then following again as I moved past the kitchen and the double doors to the library, continued toward an evening parlor that my mother and Clyde had used as a living room.

Ahead, Clyde's shadow whisked from the doorway, and both he and the furniture moaned as he rose. Heavy steps crossed the room, moving in the other direction.

He was . . . running away? That wasn't like the man I remembered. He wasn't one to back down from a fight. My few visits here had always been a power play, with Mom in the middle. Now I prepared myself to meet a broken, confused old man, a shell of my former enemy. But when I stepped into the room, white-knuckled fists and a baseball bat waited instead. Thin and stooped, his back bowed, my stepfather looked nonetheless formidable. Despite the fact that he swayed on his feet, I stopped where I was.

The rectangle of light spilling through the parlor door and my own silhouette reflected against his eyeglasses. I saw the dog creeping up behind me, heard her growl nervously, uncertain how to interpret the situation.

I thought of my cousin's dream, her warning to me.

"Clyde, put down the bat. It's Whitney. Patricia's daughter." Maybe he couldn't see who I was. The curtains were closed, making the room unnaturally dark. "I'm just here to talk. Put *down* the bat." I reached for my cell phone. "Clyde, if you don't stop that, I'm calling the police."

I prepared to run. How fast would he be able to move in his present condition? Surely I could make it to the porch and into the stairwell before he could catch me. What about the dog? Was she still behind me?

What would she do if Clyde went on the attack?

I forced myself not to back away, flinch, turn to check the dog's position. The baseball bat slowly tipped, drooping forward, Clyde's thin arm collapsing under its weight. Like a cardboard cutout left standing in the rain, he wilted into my mother's chair, landing first on the armrest, then sliding to the cushion where I'd slept last night among scents and memories.

Sidestepping, I took the edge of the rocking chair by the window, turned, and opened the curtain to let in a spill of murky light. I tucked my hands between knees that felt like they were made of hot wax. The dog, still eyeballing me, slinked past and adopted a defensive position beside Clyde, her nervous panting the only noise in the room. Together, she and my stepfather were a picture of misery. He seemed so much older than I remembered, as if the sea had slowly weathered him these past five years.

"We have some things we need to discuss," I said finally.

He didn't answer, didn't acknowledge that he'd heard me.

"Clyde, I came here for a couple reasons. First, your neighbor called me because he was concerned about you. I'm wondering if you've been in touch at all with James or Jared . . . or anyone in your family, and whether they know about your fall? I thought that might've been where you went when you left the hospital."

Hope crept upward, even though I knew I was grasping at straws. This could all be so simple, if Clyde would only listen to reason. "I think you need to face the fact that it's time some decisions were made. I'm sorry if that sounds harsh, but you've never been one to beat around the bush. The reality is what it is. I'm here to help you in any way I can—out of respect for my mother. I think it's what she would've wanted me to do." It galled me, offering this kindness, even now. I remembered the disruption he'd caused at the funeral, the way he'd announced that none of us had better come anywhere *near* the Excelsior. The shock of my mother's death had held me numb until that moment. Clyde's challenge had brought the pain roaring in.

Yet now, looking at the shrunken remnants slouched and wheezing in my mother's chair, I saw my stepfather as almost a victim too. Old age had come to claim him. Old age or guilt. Or both.

"Don't you bring her into it. You're not here because a her. I know why you showed up here all a sudden. Thought you could sneak in and take it while I was laid up, didn't ya?" He turned my way, his gaze anger-filled, as if somehow this situation between us, this war, were my fault.

Uncertainty niggled. I felt like a shrew, but I willed myself not to back down. I'd been more than generous, never fighting him for the building. But now, I had no choice. "If you're talking about *my* building, yes, I do want it. This isn't a good place for you, Clyde. You could just as easily have been found dead after that fall in the bathroom. You can't stay here by yourself anymore."

He turned his cheek to me, angling toward the opposite wall. Strips of storm-dulled light fell unevenly over his face, shading and highlighting a landscape of lines and folds. Outside, distant thunder rattled the sky. "Woulda been better thataway. Been better if they just didn't find me."

"Clyde, you don't mean that." Something in me softened. I worked quickly to crystallize it again, but it wouldn't take the same shape. "Let me call James or Jared for you, explain what happened and see if—"

"Don't want it. Go home, Whitney. You wait a little longer, maybe next time you come, I'll be outta the way for good. 'Til then, I got a legal right."

I pressed my fingers to my mouth, stopping a torrential spill of venom that would've only made things worse. *Breathe. Be calm.* "I'm not leaving right now. I'll be here for a few days, if not longer. I plan to sort through the mess on the second floor, at the very least. Those were *my* father's family belongings. My mother left them for *me*. I'll be staying here in Mom's craft room. There's no sense in my spending money on a hotel."

Surprisingly, he didn't argue, but only pinned me with a narrow glare and growled, "Don't you touch *a thing* a hers. Don't you even *think* you're gonna take *one thing* outta these rooms up here on the third floor. You'll go through me first."

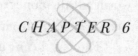

CHAPTER 6

Judging by the look on the antique store owner's face, the verdict on the books wasn't promising. I'd brought in the leather-bound copy of *The Open Boat*, along with several others. The shopkeeper was a friend of Joel Coates's—someone Joel promised I could trust to give me an honest appraisal and possibly an offer.

There were other things I wanted to have evaluated, but the books seemed a safe place to start. In two days of working on the second floor, I'd developed a system that I hoped would make a cleanout of the building and assessment of the contents at least a little more efficient. The first couple of hotel rooms at the end of the hall were my catchall places. In one, I'd collected items that qualified as vintage, but not necessarily antique. In the other, I'd left the old hotel furniture and, box by box, begun to add junk that was only fit for the garbage.

In a corner of the salon, I'd started a collection of bona fide antiques—everything from small parlor tables to a few pieces of jewelry I'd found tucked in odd places, including the brooch and the necklace from the davenport desk.

I'd been hoping to get a feel for things by trying this first transaction. So far, this trip wasn't a confidence builder.

"A few of them are worth a little money as collectibles." The man frowned across the counter, seeming either uninterested or suspicious of my motives. "The rest, I can't use. If you just want to get rid of them, I can give you the number for a guy over in Norfolk who makes shelves and end tables and other folk art pieces from old books. He'll probably take whatever you've got in the building, as long as they're hardbound and the covers have age to them."

"Thanks." I couldn't hide my disappointment. I doubted the man was lying to me, but considering how militant my grandmother had been about not letting me handle the books, the news stung in more ways than one. "Think he'd be interested in old encyclopedias and reference books, too?" It was a nice thought, at least—Lucianne's prized set ending up as art furniture, rather than in a trash bin. She'd like that.

"I imagine he would, if you want to bother hauling them in. I'm sure those wouldn't be worth much. They've gone the way of the dinosaurs, haven't they—encyclopedias?"

"True." We exchanged the look . . . the one you share with people who remember *back when* and sort of miss it.

He turned again to the copy of *The Open Boat*, carefully thumbing the pages. With his grizzly, gray-bearded chin and blue corduroy Nelson cap, he looked like he belonged in the story. "May I tell you something?"

"Sure." I blinked, stood back a little, disturbed by the sudden change in conversational tone.

"Breaking up the collection—whatever remains of Ziltha Benoit's estate—isn't a matter to be taken lightly. I know some things might have been removed from the place during her declining years, but what's left should be cataloged and carefully appraised, so that something of real value doesn't end up in the trash or at Goodwill."

Shock hit first, then indignation, and finally guilt brought up the rear. Guilt and I had become old friends these past few days. I felt its incessant gnawing every time I passed by Clyde, who sat rooted in the recliner next to my mother's, the baseball bat propped nearby as he stubbornly fixated on the blaring television and pretended I wasn't there.

The look on the antique dealer's face was much like Clyde's. It *accused* me of something. Everyone in town, with the exception of Joel Coates and perhaps Casey Turner, whose business-card invitation I still hadn't responded to, had already formed opinions of me. It shouldn't have surprised me that this store owner knew who I was. In this little Mayberry-by-the-sea, the locals were aware of everything. Where I was concerned, the usual friendliness didn't seem to apply. Suspicious looks came my way and whispers followed me in restaurants, the drugstore, the grocery store.

"I'm not sure there's much left," I told him, and a skeptical look came my way.

There was no point trying to explain myself, so I sold him the few books he wanted, then took the number of the buyer in Norfolk. When I had time, I'd call and see if he might make the trip over to pick up the whole library load.

If only the thief had made off with those, rather than jewelry and silver.

Had my mother known how much was missing? Had she even spent any time downstairs, other than to store things there? Had Clyde removed things from the second floor? Maybe sold them?

I wouldn't find out by asking him, since he either didn't respond to my questions or, if necessary, answered with a gruff word or two.

Clyde, I'm going out to grab a hamburger. Do you want me to get something for you?

Mmmmph.

A hamburger, then?

Ummmph.

Do you have food for the dog . . . and a leash? Is there a place you usually walk her?

Mmmrrr-park-rrr-guess.

I'd gathered that the dog was a stray. As nearly as I could piece together, Clyde had taken a cab to a hotel after leaving the hospital. He'd stayed there until he thought he was strong enough to come home and make it up the stairs. Somewhere along the way, he'd found the dog and decided to bring her along. I couldn't fault him for it, even though he wasn't steady enough to take her out for potty breaks. She was a sweet girl, and she needed help. My tenderhearted mother would've rescued her in an instant. Perhaps that was the reason Clyde had done it, even though he and the place weren't equipped for a pet.

Clyde *did* make sure the dog got her exercise, though. Every morning at roughly four thirty, he prepared coffee in the world's loudest percolator, turned CNN on at maximum volume, and threw the tennis ball down the hallway over and over and *over*, so the dog could chase it past my room.

As a result, the dog and I had, in a weird way, bonded. She'd taken to following me downstairs during the day, rather than sitting with Clyde. The second floor was lively with scents and sounds and the occasional scampering mouse. Dog entertainment.

She was waiting for me when I came back from the antique store, still lugging the mostly full book box. My despair must've been showing as I once again added it to the library pile in the hallway. The dog rolled a remorseful look my way and ducked her head.

"It's not your fault."

She lifted an ear, her eyes soulful, worried, weary, and needy. She wasn't asking for much—just a place to be and someone to be near, but there was no way Clyde could keep a dog. She was one more complication in a series of issues that already seemed endless. I'd been watching Clyde these past two days. Family arguments aside, some new plan *had* to be made for him. Sadly, his kids wanted nothing to do with the problem. I'd tried.

Bracing my hands on my hips, I looked past the dog and down the hall, where each dark, varnish-crackled doorway and transom seemed to whisper, *What now? What next?*

Where do you go from here, Whitney Monroe?

Giving up seemed like the most sensible option. This just wasn't a one-woman job, and with the exception of the items from the davenport desk, and possibly the desk itself, I hadn't found much of significant value. Still, I somehow couldn't shake the nagging feeling that I'd missed an important clue—that this place held a secret I should've figured out by now.

"What are you trying to tell me?" I whispered to the building, to its ghosts, to my ancestors.

The dog lifted her head, looked down the long hallway as if she saw something there, then barked, the sound ping-ponging off the walls as she scrambled to her feet.

"What . . . are . . . ?"

A trash pile rustled at the far end of the building. Goose bumps lifted on my skin. What was *that*?

Before I could conjure an answer to my own question, the dog sniffed the air, bayed, and launched herself past me at roughly the speed of a nuclear missile. Her wild flight took her to the end of the hall, where she growled, yapped, and feverishly began digging at the floor under a broken wing chair.

I backed a step toward the salon, tried to see what she was after. Her prey sounded larger than the usual house mouse. No telling what it might be . . . a rat, maybe?

A shudder rocked my shoulders and I backed away another step. Whatever it was, I hoped it escaped, found a hiding spot, and stayed. . . .

The battle broke loose and headed my way. An enormous rat . . . no . . . a *squirrel* was running for its life, zigzagging like a soldier under fire and finally scampering to safety atop the pile of book boxes. The dog hit the stack at maximum force, almost reaching the squirrel's height before gravity, inertia, and rotten cardboard came into play. The tower of boxes sagged, teetered, then tumbled over. Yelping, the dog fell backward in what seemed like slow motion, all four feet running in the air. The squirrel, still moving at normal speed, clawed its way over the dog, up the door trim, and into the frame of the transom, running back and forth and beating on the glass like a prisoner in an isolation cell.

Back on her feet, the dog attempted a full-bodied wall climb, slid back down, howled like a hound with its prey up a tree, then tried again. Globs of plaster fell and dust swirled.

"Stop! Hey . . . no!" I yelled.

Of course, no one was listening. The dog shredded another section of the wall, driving the squirrel up the transom glass, where it slipped, wobbled, then teetered on the ledge, legs flailing.

"I said *stop*!"

Primal instincts took over—mine. I looked around for something, anything, that would either subdue the dog or fend off the squirrel. Squirrels and I had a history.

An umbrella from the trash heap was the only nearby option. Three panels tore in unison when I opened it, but still, it was better than nothing. I had to call off Clyde's dog before something gruesome happened.

I forced myself forward. One step . . . two . . . three . . .

Stretching out my hand, I came within inches of grabbing the dog before the squirrel sailed free, hit my umbrella, fell through, and ran down my back while I screamed like a banshee. The dog bypassed me in hot pursuit, and both ran the length of the building, finally disappearing into the storage room up the hall. Bolting after them, I heard barking, growling and hissing, fabric ripping, objects toppling off shelves, glass breaking.

Nearby, the stairway door burst open beneath an ancient exit sign. I skidded to a stop, and Mark Strahan was standing in the gap, wide-eyed and wielding a golf club as a weapon. We froze, staring at each other, Mark brandishing the nine iron and me splay-legged, clutching my ragged umbrella.

His head tipped almost imperceptibly and his chin dropped. He blinked, blinked again, the serpentine folds over his eyes saying, *Call the men in the white coats, the lady upstairs has gone round the bend.*

"There's a squirrel . . . in here. . . ." The words came in a breathless whisper.

"A . . . squirrel?" The golf club slowly descended until it dangled at his side.

"I don't like squirrels . . . up close." Another heebie-jeebie slid over me, bringing with it childhood nightmares left behind by a petting zoo mugging.

Mark squinted at the threadbare umbrella. "I thought I heard someone screaming."

"It charged at me."

"The squirrel?" The corners of his mouth tugged, and for a moment he reminded me of his younger shop helper. Joel's easy-going personality came with a ready laugh and a constant good mood. He was one of the few people in town who was glad I was here . . . unlike Mark, who typically scowled as I went by or pretended he didn't notice me at all.

Now his stomach convulsed and a puff of air chugged out. "I thought someone was being attacked up here, or . . ."

"It's *not* funny." It was, of course. I glanced up at the fan-shaped hole in the umbrella, pictured a deranged Mary Poppins in sloppy jeans and a paint-spattered *Bella Tazza* sweatshirt with the cuffs cut off. I was out of clean clothes upstairs, and I needed to do the wash, but I'd been avoiding the laundry room. The last load of my mother's things was still there, neatly folded in a basket, seemingly waiting for her to come home. The strange still life of an ordinary day, of future expectations, was too much to bear.

"Trust me. It's funny." Mark's eyes caught the light and warmed. His grin was the kind that could pull you in if you didn't watch yourself. Up close that kind of charisma was dangerous. "What was the umbrella for?"

"They attack from overhead . . . squirrels."

"This happens often where you come from?"

"Petting zoo victim, thank you very much." Folding the umbrella, I considered setting it against the wall, then held on instead. The commotion had temporarily stilled, but if the squirrel came out, I wanted to be able to protect myself.

"Ahhh . . . you're one of *those*," Mark joked.

In the storage room, something heavy slid. Glass shattered. Sweat broke over my skin. "Could you just . . . maybe . . . get the dog out and shut the door? I'll call somebody to come trap it . . . or . . . whatever."

"Leave it alone. It'll probably go back where it came from." He surveyed the walls. "No telling how it got in here. Is there water for it to drink in this part of the building?"

"The water to the second floor was turned off years ago."

"Well then, your little friend must be coming and going. We've had them in our ceilings downstairs several times."

Utter revulsion traveled from my head to my toes and manifested in a full-body shudder. I looked down at the floor, now a known squirrel thoroughfare. "Gross . . ."

"It doesn't happen *all* the time."

"Once is too often."

Mark tapped a finger to his lips, and I could see the wheels turning; I just couldn't imagine where they were headed. "Tell you what. I'll make a deal with you. You let me know . . . say . . . thirty days before you do *anything* about selling or leasing this building . . . and I'll work on your squirrel problem."

The sound of tearing fabric echoed forth, adding emphasis. Both of us looked toward the storage room before turning to each other again.

"That sounds a little like extortion."

His palms slowly turned upward, the gesture annoyingly innocent. "I can leave it. Completely your choice."

He had me and he knew it. He'd probably surmised that I couldn't pay an exterminator. Scratch that. He'd *undoubtedly* already talked to the antique dealer down the block. The details of my book-selling trip were most likely spreading around town like wildfire.

"And you'll get the dog out and close that door first . . . and figure out how to keep the squirrel from getting back in here again?"

"Do we have a deal?"

I bit my bottom lip. Everything in me knee-jerked, rising up and answering, *No. No deal. I'll handle my own problem.*

Everything in me . . . but the part that was squirrel phobic. That part was roughly the consistency of Silly Putty on a hot day. It was whispering, *Just say yes. It'll take you more than thirty days to sort out the future of the Excelsior anyway.*

"Chivalry really is dead, isn't it?"

That actually seemed to hit a sensitive spot. He winced a bit, his mouth hardening around the edges. His hands rested on his hip pockets, his stance firm, a power position. The only thing ruffled about him was the stray shock of brown hair dangling over his forehead. "Do we have a deal, or don't we have a deal?" "Yes, I guess we do."

"All right then." He walked toward me, slowly extending his hand to seal the bargain. What I really wanted to do was poke him in the eye with the umbrella, but I settled for sneering at him as I accepted the handshake. His gaze caught mine and I saw my own reflection against the cool, coffee-and-cream-colored surfaces. He kept me there a moment longer than was necessary.

Despite the bubbling brew of anger and resentment, a weird sort of . . . something else . . . shot through me. I didn't care to analyze it.

"Deal," he said.

"Whatever," I answered.

"Dude, what's goin' on up here, World War III?" Joel was in the stairwell door now, also carrying a golf club. "There was, like, more noise again."

Mark released my hand. "Our friend here has a squirrel problem."

"Oh, man, yeah, that happens." Joel was enthusiastic about the squirrel, but of course Joel was enthusiastic about everything. "One time, I was ringin' up a ticket downstairs. This lady had, like, eighty-seven kids in there, and they were ready to drop some massive change on paddleboard stuff. I mean, like, it was seriously insane. And then there's, like, a squirrel in the ceiling and it must be jumpin' up and down, 'cause the tile over her head is vibratin'." He paused to illustrate and I imagined squirrels falling through the ceiling tiles. "The whole time, there's, like, these little white foam bits coming down like snow, and I'm just pretendin' I don't even see it in the lady's hair, but I'm afraid the whole thing's gonna end up on her head before I get the order done." The story ended with a good-natured chuckle followed by a curious look. "So, where's the squirrel?"

Mark motioned toward the storage room. "In there with the dog."

"Gnarly. Don't let the dog get it."

"Joel, who's watching the shop?"

"Yeah . . . Surf Dude, there wasn't any customers down there."

Mark started toward the door on long, hurried strides, giving orders to Joel as he went. "Get the dog out of there and shut the door. We'll bring the squirrel trap up here after a while."

My mouth dropped open as Mark rushed off. "You didn't tell me you had a squirrel trap!" But he was already headed down the stairs. If I'd known this was something they did regularly, I could've just asked Joel for help. No doubt his price would've been easier to pay.

Joel focused on the tumble of boxes and books behind me. "So, you find anything good today?" He had been more than curious about what was happening on the second floor. If he could catch me as I came and went from the building, he asked about my progress and what I'd discovered. Someone in his family had a flea market over in Georgia. He'd spent his childhood cleaning out old homes and sorting through storage lockers of abandoned belongings. It'd made him a bit of an amateur treasure hunter, even though he didn't seem like the type. He picked things up at estate sales and sold them on eBay to raise surf-travel money and entry fees for competitions.

"Not really. The books were mostly a strikeout at the antique store. Thanks for sending me over there, though. It was worth a try, at least."

"Yeah, sure. No prob."

"He did give me the name of a guy who'd probably take the old books in bulk." Rubbing my forehead, I looked at the results of the dog-and-squirrel melee, scattered down the corridor beyond the salon. "Of course, now I'll have to pick them up first . . . and find some new boxes."

Something clattered in the storage room. The dog bayed, the ear-splitting sound echoing through the building. "Can you just . . . pull her out of there and shut the door before she gets hurt or chases that thing back into the hall? Please?"

"Yeah, hey, no worries. I'm on it." He sauntered to the entrance and shinnied around a stack of mattresses. A bloodcurdling scream erupted a moment later. I was already scrambling to deploy my umbrella before he laughed and shouted, "Just kiddin'!"

"That's *not* funny."

Listening as he tried to locate and coax the dog, I moved a safe distance away, grabbed an empty box, and continued toward what was left of the library pile.

Joel's attempts turned comical. "Hey . . . oh . . . don't . . . Shoot. Wait a minute . . . daggumit!"

The mountain of books looked like it had been the victim of a level-five earthquake. Everything from pocket novels to Lucianne's Reader's Digest Condensed Books and the encyclopedias lay scattered and spewed, open pages torn by scrambling dog toenails, bits of paper everywhere.

"Good thing none of this was valuable." Setting down the box, I scooped up several encyclopedias. Shreds of paper fell out, floating downward like tiny kites losing the wind.

The *A* volume had landed open at *Andalusian*, an entry I'd probably loved in childhood. Like most girls, I'd fantasized about having a horse, even though I knew we'd never be able to afford one. White horses were my favorites. Photos like the ones on that encyclopedia page would've been the stuff of wishes during those lonely little-girl summers here in Manteo.

Something caught my attention as I picked up the book and thumbed through the pictures. There was a stiffness to the back half of the pages, as if something might be . . .

I flicked through, and then, there it was. Hidden right under my nose, all this time. The old postmark showed the envelope's point of origin and the date. *Ruby Ridge, North Carolina, June 7, 1936.* The contents felt stiff and thick, a greeting card of some sort. Even after years of lying between the pages of a book, the envelope showed evidence of having taken abuse in the past.

Yellowed folds crisscrossed it at all angles, and a liquid stain painted an uneven brown watermark over the stamp.

It was addressed to *Mrs. Ziltha Ruby Benoit, Excelsior Hotel, Manteo, NC*. I'd forgotten that my grandmother's middle name was Ruby. I'd seen that name only once, on the announcement for a funeral I wasn't able to attend. I was already in Paris by that time. My grandmother had been buried in the Avondale family plot in Charleston, in accordance with her wishes, but my mom had been the only one in attendance.

The ruby brooch I'd found in the captain's desk made even more sense now—a perfect gift for Ziltha Ruby. I'd seen her wear many beautiful pieces of jewelry during my visits, but never that one. Perhaps it reminded her of the husband she'd lost.

Turning over the card, I investigated the flap, still firmly sealed. Two side-by-side hearts joined with an arrow had been drawn over the closure. Graceful calligraphy above the drawing warned, *Do not open until June 27*.

But this letter had *never* been opened. Whatever it contained hadn't been seen since the sender had tucked it safely inside and dropped it in a mailbox.

What in the world?

I surveyed the scraps of paper littering the floor, recognized disjointed bits of handwriting, saw more pieces here and there among the mound of books.

Letters . . . those were shreds of letters.

Who would've done something like this and for what reason? My grandmother would never have deigned to touch Lucianne's encyclopedias *or* the Reader's Digest books. Had Lucianne rescued the letters after my grandmother had discarded them unread and . . . torn to bits? Was something more sinister at work? Perhaps my grandfather had kept the letters from my grandmother, afraid she would . . . what? Travel to the mountains to join her sister in the Federal Writers' Project, or to bring her sister home? She'd obviously had trouble with pregnancies before. Maybe someone was worried about her putting the baby in jeopardy?

The truth had undoubtedly died with my grandmother, or with Lucianne, or with Benjamin Benoit. No one else would've had access to Ziltha's mail.

Carefully prying one of the envelope's side panels loose, I brought the contents into the light for the first time in almost eight decades. Inside, the colors on the heart-shaped card were still vibrant and beautiful. Above the lithograph of two little girls building castles by a teal-colored sea, the text read:

Will you be my Valentine?
No one else will do.
I try to put my thoughts in print;
I'll settle for a little hint.
I hope you love me, too.

I turned the card over, read the handwritten message on the back:

Happy Birthday, Dear Sister! My apologies for the out-of-season card. It called to mind our many glorious days along the shore, and so I imagined that you would enjoy it and also relive those times in the old summerhouse.

If this envelope should arrive early, I hope you have kept from opening it until our birthday. I cannot resist mailing it to you from the tiny burg of Ruby Ridge. Do you remember when we devoted the whole of the day to constructing a sand castle with a moat and seven towers? You pronounced yourself Queen Ruby. You stood in the gazebo and informed the adults that you would henceforth be addressed as "Ruby" and would no longer answer to "Ziltha."

I so admired your courage. You were always the shining star, the standout, the brave twin. I may never have said as much, but I was envious in my own quiet way. Your nature was to determine your destiny, just as you always have. I do believe I may, at last, find mine on this journey.

Thomas and I have been given a fine, crisp afternoon for travel after having been party to the interesting nature of worship in a small mountain church this morning (most vibrant and boisterous as men, women, and even a child left the pews to engage in all manner of contortions, speaking in tongues, and writhing on the floor before the altar). I have never in my life seen such a thing!

Blessings and love to you, Queen Ruby. Know that Emmaline and I are well. This mountain air may yet cure her of the croup.

I will write more when I am able.

All my love,
Alice

"Alice . . . and . . . Ruby," I whispered, tracing a finger along the bottom of the card before turning it over again to study the image of the girls by the shore. The sister who was never spoken of around the Excelsior was my grandmother's *twin*?

And *Queen Ruby*? The woman I'd grown up visiting was as straight and tightly strung as the laces on a corset. I couldn't picture her playing in the sand, crowning herself queen, or ever having been fun-loving in any way. My image had been of a sullen, lonely, rigid little girl—a younger version of the person I knew, a woman who kept everyone at arm's length. Yet in reality she was one half of a whole, bonded in the womb?

"Queen Ruby . . ."

"Is that your name?" Joel strolled up the hall with the dog in his arms. I realized I'd been staring right through him. I'd forgotten he was even here. "Ruby, huh, girl? That's pretty rad, I guess." He gave the dog a chin snuggle, then set her at my feet. "So, yeah, I shut the door to keep her outta there, but man, it's gnarly in that room now. There's stuffing and pieces of mattresses, like, everywhere. Some cups fell off the shelf and got glass all over the floor. Ruby cut her paws up some, I think. There was a little blood around, but I couldn't see where she assassinated the squirrel or got bit or anything."

I checked the dog's feet. "It does look like she sliced her pads a little. I'll find some antibiotic ointment upstairs."

Joel whisked something from his pocket and held it in the air between us. "Check this out, though."

I stood up to look. A strand of glimmering red beads lay across his palm, the heart-shaped center pendant sparkling in the light.

"Where did *that* come from?" I lifted it and studied it more closely.

"Outta one of the mattresses, I think. Queen Ruby here seriously trashed stuff, but she dug somethin' up while she was at it, I guess."

"This came out of a mattress?" My grandmother had become increasingly eccentric in the years before her dementia was diagnosed. During our last summer of working here, Mom had decided that something needed to be done about it. With Old

Dutch gone and Lucianne planning to move to her daughter's soon, the situation had grown impossible. Grandmother Ziltha railed in front of the hotel guests, went downstairs to the restaurant where the Rip Shack was now and accused them of poisoning her food, tossed a bucket of trash on some kids making noise in the alley. She'd even hit a waiter with an empty luncheon plate.

That final summer with her was an experience both sad and terrifying, even at sixteen.

Maybe in her paranoia after the hotel was closed, my grandmother had begun hiding valuables? Could she have realized the caretaker who was supposed to be looking after her was actually making off with things? Perhaps that was the reason for the treasures tucked in the davenport desk?

What if all the family heirlooms *weren't* gone—what if some remained hidden? But where?

"Those are nice," Joel observed. "Y'know, you find some pretty boss stuff in old houses around here. Guys brought it home off the ships and gave it to their sweethearts or their mamas. That necklace might be worth real bucks. Better look through that room good before you toss out the junk." He cocked his head to get a view of the Valentine's card. "What'cha got?"

I handed it to him and he read it, then turned it over and looked at the front again. "Whoa. That's cool."

"It was inside one of the encyclopedias. I found another one a couple days ago." I grabbed the book, and both Joel and I squinted at it endwise, checking for evidence of anything else between the pages. "The envelope this card was in had never been opened."

"Whoa," he said again. "Like a message from the grave."

A chill passed over me. I didn't really want to think of the letter that way. In truth, these letters weren't just clues to a mystery; they were someone's past. *My* history. My father had an aunt. My grandmother had a sister. "The strange thing is, no one ever mentioned Alice. She and my grandmother were *twins*, for heaven's sake. And it's obvious that they were close. What happened, I wonder?" All my life, I'd wanted a sister, which was why Denise and I were so close. I couldn't help but believe that nothing, but nothing, could cause us to stop speaking to each other.

The dog rolled over and exposed her belly, and Joel scratched it with his flip-flop, his long, tan toes curling over the end. "You got any idea, Ruby-dog?"

"Her name's not really Ruby."

"She looks like a Ruby." The dog closed her eyes, content with the idea, and Joel turned back to me. "You gonna hunt for more stuff up here?"

"Yes, I am."

"You, like, need a hand? I'm a pretty good picker." A curious, slightly hungry look wandered toward the spilled books. "We might even find the letter that's got all the answers in it. Who knows?"

"That'd be nice, but . . . aren't you supposed to be downstairs working?"

Chin popping up, he looked around as if he'd awakened on a whole new planet. He was a nice kid, but I had a feeling this happened a lot. "Oh, crud . . . yeah. Dude. I gotta go."

"Could you grab some of that loose cardboard from the salon and maybe stuff it under the bottom of the storage room door—just in case the squirrel tries to sneak out before you bring the trap back up here?" Could a squirrel limbo under a closed door? I did *not* want to know.

"Yeah, cool, no problem." Joel was already jogging down the hallway, grabbing the waistband of his saggy jeans to keep them from falling off. Without breaking stride, he passed right by the storage room and disappeared into the stairway.

CHAPTER 7

Dearest Ruby,

At times, we unexpectedly awaken from the sleep of our own lives. Today, I have awakened.

If only you and I could share in this grand adventure! By logic of course, I am aware that you are a married woman, expecting a child, and bound to your grand life at the Excelsior, but I yearn for you to travel along with me. If only this could be one of the many far-flung journeys we dreamed of before the terrible misfortune of this Depression.

On occasion, I find myself wishing that we had opted for our girlhood dreams rather than falling to the lure of handsome men and the paths of housewifery. While I would never desire for any person the sad course my life has taken, today it is as if I feel the blood in my veins and the air in my lungs for the first time since Richard took himself away and left me to await Emmaline's birth alone. I realize now how angry I have been with him, how heartbroken, how bitter and how afraid to allow myself to feel. In my years at the college, I was merely existing, merely biding my days. I had condemned myself to death without actually dying. Now

I have climbed from the stillness of the grave, and I see the world in a glorious new light.

Through these letters, I hope to share not only my experiences, but this newfound joy. Joy is not complete until it belongs to more than one. I believe it was the apostle Paul who said as much. Perhaps I should have listened more closely to those long, hot summer sermons at Grandmother's church in Charleston, but we were such rotters, truly! Remember Old Juba shaking her dark, knobby finger at us when we abandoned our beds and swam in the goldfish pond that hot, moonlit night? I do believe, between the four of us, we may have taken years from her life . . . if such was possible.

I fancy that, in this journey of mine, I may in some way honor the child who once danced in the fountain 'neath the moon. I have lost the carefree girl I once was, banished her to some far country and locked her away. The greatest part of me may have gone with her. I have allowed the cutting blades of fear to whittle me down to nubs. I dearly believe it was not fate that brought me here, but God himself. This is the place I will finally find courage and breath and voice. This is where I will find life.

Today, during a most thorough introduction at the state FWP headquarters in Asheville, we recruits were made privy to the inner workings of this monumental endeavor. Rooms there had been filled with the desks of typists and editors. Filing cabinets lined wall upon wall. My mind could scarce take in the magnitude of it all! To imagine that the whole of this space and the people at work in it are devoted to the documentation of our state and its stories, and that similar efforts have been undertaken in every state!

In the end, it is estimated that we North Carolina writers may "fill these halls with well over one million words," so said the leadership of The Project as they gathered us for a pep talk at the facility. Might I also report, Dear Sister, that names such as Manly Wade Wellman were bandied about? I may have sat directly beside or behind some famous writer and not even known it. I was far too afraid to ask.

In the room was such overwhelming excitement as plans were detailed! I'd daresay most of us there forgot we had been forced to sign the dreaded WPA Pauper's Oath in order to qualify for The Project at all. Our mission seemed quite vast and important. We are to create not only a brief guidebook of our state, but a comprehensive encyclopedia to include all natural wonders, the narratives of farmers and former slaves, the stories of soldiers returned from the Great War, the last of those who fought in the War between the States, the folk tales of mountain peoples, transcriptions of famous trials and court proceedings, and all else, our leaders said, "from golf to the Ku Klux Klan." Having the soul of true newspapermen, they desire that no stone be left unturned.

As you can see on the attached page, I've attempted to sketch the scene for you. Mother often said that I had inherited a bit of Father's drawing talent, for it did not come from her. What do you think? Is it true?

I do believe I have rendered the room rather well, and our speaker, too, with his close-fitting round glasses, grim mouth, and intense gaze. Perhaps when I retire from my mission with the FWP, I will take up a position as a courtroom artist. Emmaline and I might become partners in it. She is sending a drawing for Old Dutch, as well. She was a very good girl throughout the day, patiently waiting on a bench with her colors. All were most kind to her, and she became something of a tourist attraction herself. She will be practicing her letters as we travel, and soon enough she will be writing her own notes to you, I'll wager.

I will close for now. I have added to this missive throughout the day as time permitted and now have worked late to finish it. We were given lodgings overnight in a dormitory building maintained by the Civilian Conservation Corps for road crews and other workers. In the morning, we will set out, scattering all directions like leaves in the breeze.

I will write again from wherever the wind blows me.

Lovingly,
Your sister, Alice

P.S. Yes, I am aware that the addition of a postscript is gauche. One should finish thoughts before signing the letter, but I have forgotten a final detail. I have met my traveling companion, the mapmaker. He is younger than I had anticipated, only through his second year in college, and a bit wet behind the ears. At twenty-one, he is barely old enough to qualify for The Project, and is eleven years my junior, but he seems a delightful soul. I do suppose our being selected to travel together is the doing of my dear friend the dean, for my new companion, Thomas Kerth, is a distant relative of his. As I have time, I may attempt a rendering for you in the future. —A

A cardinal landed on the sill and pecked at the window as I slid the torn pieces of the letter's final page into place, revealing Alice's sketches of the North Carolina FWP headquarters. Aside from the scraps that had ended up on the floor during the squirrel hunt, I'd found the remains of letters tucked between encyclopedia pages and scattered in what was left of the packing box. Each letter had been torn to shreds, envelope and all, and as far as I could tell, had never been opened. There was no rhyme, reason, or order to bits that remained, some no larger than my pinky finger. Finding enough of the first letter to rebuild it had turned out to be a complicated project.

From a plywood Santa Claus my mother had always used on our Michigan lawn at Christmas, I'd created a makeshift table, then started gathering the piles in order by the postmark, one scrap at a time. Alice's letter from the FWP headquarters had been written on green ledger paper, which made it easier to ferret out. Like the Valentine's card, it was dotted with stains, the ink partially smeared by seeps of liquid.

It seemed unlikely that this much mail could've been hidden from my grandmother. She must have destroyed the letters herself. The woman I knew would've been the type to respond with fury toward anyone who, like Alice, didn't cooperate with her plans. Typically, when my mother and I came to the Excelsior, Ziltha was embroiled in conflicts with other merchants in town, or with the chamber of commerce, or the credit card companies, or the mechanic who serviced her car, or members of her civic clubs. She'd been the driving force behind more than one hostile takeover of the Ladies' Society, the Arts Council, and the local chapter of the DAR.

She'd lived to stir up a wrangle and then feed off it. Maybe she couldn't forgive her sister for going away, or maybe she'd been jealous of Alice's new opportunity.

Either way, it was sad to read the notes and realize they'd been written as a way of sharing an adventure, but the effort had gone unappreciated. I'd never wondered about my grandmother's past before, but now I wanted to understand how she had changed from Queen Ruby into a woman bitter with people and life. What had caused the reverse metamorphosis, the drawing inward, like butterfly regressing to caterpillar?

The hallway door opened, and I looked up, falling back to the present and hitting hard enough to be off balance for a moment. I grabbed the plywood tabletop to steady myself. It slid in my hands, almost toppling off the base of boxes before I caught it.

"I'm guessing this never made it up here." Mark frowned at me, holding up a small cage that I assumed was the squirrel trap.

I glanced at my watch. Once again, I'd blown a bunch of time on the letters.

"Ummm . . . yeah, I guess not." No doubt I was getting poor Joel in trouble. The look on his boss's face conveyed that this was par for the course.

"I figured." The owner of the Rip Shack looked frustrated and tired this afternoon. "We had a couple day-tour buses come in, and when Joel hit the end of his shift, he was gone like vapor. As usual."

I wanted to defend the kid. Joel was the only friend I had here on Roanoke, and he *had* saved Ruby-the-dog from the squirrel, after all. Aside from that, we shared a common opponent. His grouchy boss. On the flip side, I fully understood Mark's position. It can be hard to get and keep reliable staff, running retail. "Maybe he thought I was coming down to get it."

Mark blinked, eyes rolling upward under thick, dark lashes. "Kids like Joel don't *learn* if you make excuses for them."

"Yes, I know. I own a restaurant back home." I wasn't sure why I wanted him to know that. Perhaps in some way, I needed to convey that I wasn't just a greedy out-of-towner here to pillage and then make a run for it. I had reasons for doing what I was doing. This was a necessary evil.

That didn't explain the hours I'd just spent gathering bits of Alice's letters. There was nothing to be gained from them except the story. But my family history was woven into this place, as was the truth about Grandmother's lost twin sister. I couldn't let go of the building until I had learned what there was to learn.

For the time being, Mark might get his way by default.

He gave the piles of paper scraps and my makeshift table a curious look, like he meant to ask about them. Then, still holding the squirrel trap, he motioned to the storeroom door. "It's this one, right?"

"Yes." I focused on the letters again. "Thanks for bringing that up."

"We made a bargain. I always keep my end of a bargain."

I could feel him watching me. I could also feel myself bristling under the skin. "If you're saying that because you think I *won't*, you don't need to worry. I'm not a liar."

He stood there a moment longer, and I continued to pretend I was oblivious. "Good to know," he said finally. "Is the vicious killer still in here?"

"Very funny." I couldn't resist glancing up as the storage room door creaked open. Mark was looking my way, wearing a smirky, annoying, squirrel-catching smile, as if he relished this opportunity to prove his prowess. Maybe he could charm the thing into his little trap.

"Wish me luck."

"Good luck. Remember, *your* part of the deal, once you catch it, is to make sure it doesn't get in here again."

"No problem. This'll only take a minute." He disappeared through the door, leaving it ajar, so that I felt compelled to monitor the situation and be sure nothing scampered out. "Your dog did a number on this place." His voice echoed against the high ceilings, bouncing past me down the hall.

Ruby, curled at my feet, woke with a start, ducking her head as if she recognized the word *dog*. Maybe it was the only name she knew.

"It's all right." I rib-rubbed her stomach with my tennis shoe. "I won't let the mean man come get you." Ruby was a hard case. Every time I tossed a wad of newspaper or knickknack on the trash pile, she tucked tail and ran for the corner. People had been chasing her away for a while. Why she'd decided to trust Clyde, I couldn't imagine, but she did seem to like him, and so her loyalties were divided at best. Even so, I'd be glad to have her with me when I went into the storeroom to search for further valuables hidden in mattresses or anyplace else.

As soon as Mark removed the squirrel, of course. He'd said it would only take a minute.

He was true to his word, but when he exited, he was empty-handed. My hopes flagged a bit. "You caught it already?" *Because otherwise, you wouldn't be leaving, right?*

A single brow arched upward. His bottom lip hung slack, then flirted with a smile, as if he were waiting for me to laugh and say, *April Fools'!* "You know that the trap has to stay in there until the squirrel gets hungry and decides to go after the bait . . . right?"

"Are you *serious*? I thought you were going to grab the squirrel and . . . well . . . stuff it in the cage or something."

His other eyebrow went up, and he had the nerve to actually snicker. The grin faded as I stood blinking at him, my hands braced on the table.

"Oh . . . you were serious," he said.

"Yes. I was serious."

"Sorry. But that's not how it works. It's not like gator wrestling or snake charming. A squirrel pretty much does what a squirrel wants to do."

"This is *so* not what I had in mind."

"You want me to relay that to the squirrel?"

"*I* could've stuck some food in a box and put it in the storeroom *myself*." Right now, I felt like quite possibly the stupidest human on the planet. Of course Mark wasn't going to walk in there and catch it with his bare hands. With all the junk in that room, he probably couldn't even find it.

He tasted his bottom lip, held it between his teeth a moment. "I can go take the trap back if you want." His expression was so innocent, it qualified as backhandedly snarky.

"No thank you." I bent over the letters again, tucking an annoying fall of dark hair behind my ear. I could imagine what I looked like after a day of digging and sorting and battling the local wildlife. "So, I'm assuming that, for my squirrel-removal dollar, I'm also getting frequent trap rechecks?"

He stuffed my protective cardboard barricade back underneath the door. "I didn't realize there was money in this proposition."

"Good, because there's not. Listen, I don't want to *hurt* the squirrel, but I really do need it out of the way so I can work in there. Soon."

The curtain of hair fell in my eyes again, and I paused to pull the hairband free and finger-comb the sticky mess into a wad, then rebind it. After last night's storm, the air was humid, turning my hair wavy and swelling it to three times its normal size.

I was weirdly conscious of Mark watching me as he

spoke. "Joel said he found some jewelry hidden in one of the mattresses."

I blinked, surprised. It hadn't occurred to me that Joel would give his boss a report. Had Mark *asked* for one? "Yes, he did. My grandmother was eccentric, but always in an obsessively organized sort of way. Toward the end things got bad, though. The caretaker we hired turned out to be a thief. Maybe my grandmother had started hiding things from her, or maybe she was just confused. Joel offered to help me search."

Mark angled away a bit. I'd caught him by surprise. "Just a word of advice. I'd be a little careful about letting Joel know too much of what's going on up here. He's a nice kid, but he's got some issues. He doesn't come from the best family situation and doesn't necessarily hang around with the most savory people. There's no telling who he might mention it to."

I vacillated between being grateful for the warning and once again defending Joel. "The other day, he told me he wanted to start college in the fall, to be a history teacher. He said he was planning to work with the Lost Colony drama this summer to earn extra money for tuition."

"He's trying to get his life together. I hope he sticks with it this time."

That struck a chord. I couldn't count how often in these years since leaving the corporate life, I'd hired good kids with bad pasts and terrible family patterns. It's not easy to change someone's default settings, especially when they have relatives constantly dragging them down, but I'd quickly learned that the by-product of staying in one place was getting involved with people on a deeper level, whether you wanted to or not. As a boss, I couldn't help being attached to those kids, hoping to make a difference. Some of the ones who'd straightened themselves out were like younger brothers and sisters to me now. We'd kept in touch even after they'd moved on to bigger and better things.

A few of the others were among the greatest disappointments of my adult life.

I was struck by a sudden sense of connection to Mark, and just as quickly I felt the need to tamp it down. I didn't want to feel anything toward him.

"Just be careful what you tell Joel." A grim look followed the words. "A lot of kids grow up here on the Outer Banks not knowing much about the wide, wide world. It's a tough transition for them, figuring out what to do with the rest of their lives, other than work at some tourist trap and party like there's no tomorrow."

"I can see where that would be a problem." I thought about Joel—intelligent, good-looking, personable, athletic, interested in history . . . yet seemingly aimless. He was so much like the teenagers I'd known my last few summers here—the ones my mother didn't want me hanging around. They were different from the private-school kids I sat in classes with back home—the kids who were sweating out college prep courses before they left the eighth grade. At the time, the suntanned, freedom-loving island kids had fascinated me. Their lives seemed fun and slightly careless. Their days weren't scheduled like those of the kids in my school. They weren't constantly being shuttled off to music lessons, sports teams, dance classes, and tutorial sessions. The kids here weren't fretting about building a dossier for Harvard or Columbia.

The trade-off for that kind of aimlessness is that, if you're not aiming at something, you never know where you'll end up. I'd learned that on my own, long after leaving the snotty prep-school classmates behind.

"Joel just doesn't need any temptations." Mark's gaze caught mine and held on. "He shouldn't get it in his head that he's got a way of making quick money—legal or otherwise. He needs to *work* this summer, stay focused, build up some savings, and head for college in the fall."

"I understand."

The conversation ebbed, yet we held our places. The air seemed to wait for one of us to disturb it.

"How long has Joel worked for you?" I wasn't sure why I asked, but this being the off-season, Mark could've hired more mature help if he'd wanted to. "When I met the two of you, I sort of assumed that Joel might be your brother, or at least a relative."

The owner of the Rip Shack wandered a couple steps closer, leaned a shoulder against the wall, and crossed his arms over a well-fitted T-shirt that read *Hang Ten*. "Not related. My family is in Norfolk—Mom, Dad, brothers, nieces and nephews. I'd always liked it out here, and about six years ago, it was time for a change, so I sold part of a business inland and came here. I was down the block until a space opened up in this building. Joel was one of the little townies when I first moved to Manteo—like those kids you saw on the bicycles the other day—only with Joel, there wasn't any mama calling around to find him at dark. It was kind of the opposite. She'd kick him out of the trailer while she had guys over, and he'd just have to find a spot to hang out until whenever."

"That's terrible." I had a new appreciation for Joel. He seemed to be doing really well for himself, considering.

Mark nodded. "He got a lot of help from the shopkeepers and other folks around here. Manteo is filled with good people. We try to take care of our own."

"I remember it that way." Despite Grandmother Ziltha's difficult personality, and her penchant for picking fights, the people here had tried to come to her aid. After her death, my mother had cleaned out a freezer full of casseroles. "Well . . . thanks for filling me in."

I turned to the letters again, absently slipping one torn shard under another, piecing together a word. It was time to end this conversation. The newly cordial, conversational Mark was . . . disquieting. I could literally *feel* him still standing nearby.

"There's a charity down on Hatteras devoted to giving teens and young adults here something productive to do—encouraging them to catch a vision for making good out of their lives instead of getting sucked into drugs and the party scene . . . and helping them get into treatment if they do have a problem. They call it Seaside House. One of the churches started it after a couple of drug overdose deaths among their young people. Three different members of the congregation had dreams about the kids going into a house on the shore, all within a week of each other. I would like to get something like that started here. Last year, we lost a girl who grew up with Joel. They were running buddies when they were kids. Townies together. You never saw one on a bicycle that you didn't see two."

Guilt tugged at the hair I had just sloppily refastened in my messy bun. I'd been way too quick to judge Mark Strahan. He didn't like me, but he wasn't a bad guy. *Ever'body got a story,* Old Dutch had told me once when I'd complained about what a shrew my grandmother was. *Ever'body got a reason for what they do. You eat off somebody else's plate, drink a their cup, could be, you'd be that same way.*

"I'm sorry. That must've been hard . . . for Joel and for all of you."

From the corner of my eye, I watched Mark's shadow move closer. He craned to see what was on the table. "I'm hoping we can put together something that'll make a difference. We've got a good group of people, along with several civic organizations and churches, working on what kind of counseling and mentoring, substance abuse help, and activities it might offer. As a matter of fact, I'd like to talk to you about the second floor of this building."

I dropped a scrap of paper and it floated downward. What had passed for idle conversation was really an agenda of sorts, on Mark's part. Not that I could blame him. It was a valid agenda. A really good one. But I couldn't just give away the building, even part of it. "I'm not ready to think—"

Three swift taps overhead stopped me midsentence, and for the first time I was thankful for Clyde's unceremonious method of communicating through the floor. "He does that when he needs something. I'd better go check. I gave him a cane I found down here and asked him to keep it with him when he's moving around. Instead of *using* the cane, he leaves it by the chair, then pounds on the floor with it when he wants to summon me."

The muscles in my neck tightened and twitched, and I felt my heat-ray glare burning a hole through the ceiling. This battle of wills between Clyde and me was exhausting, but he'd win it over my cold, dead body. He may have taken advantage of my mother's sweet, giving nature—*Patricia, where's my this? Patricia, I need that. What's for dessert, Patricia?*—but if he thought I was going to be his slave, he had another think coming.

Scooping up the lost piece of Alice's letter, I set it on the table, scooting the stacks a little closer together, where hopefully nothing would fall off when the hallway door was opened and the air shifted.

"I've got some folding tables downstairs that I use for side-walk sales in the summer. I'll have Joel run them up to you tomorrow." Mark retrieved a shred of paper that had blown his way, then brought it back to me.

"No. That's okay. Don't bother." Favors between us weren't a good idea.

Three more thuds on the ceiling demanded attention.

Mark squinted upward. "Does he do that often?"

"Only when he feels like it. The rest of the time he pretends I don't exist. He's hoping I'll disappear."

"Do you plan to?"

"Not today."

CHAPTER 8

Upstairs, Clyde was in an especially foul mood. Even Ruby recognized it, and after trotting into the dayroom, she quietly retreated to the kitchen. Safer territory.

"Where's supper?" Clyde's voice shredded the peaceful afternoon air with the effectiveness of an invisible cheese grater.

This was why he'd called me up here? I'd left him a ham sandwich before going downstairs. The plate was empty now, piled on the collection of newspapers beside his chair. "It's only five thirty, Clyde. And it looks like you ate your lunch."

"My stomach's growlin'. Where's my pretzels? You're gonna pretend you come here to take care of me, you can at least gimme my food. I'll call that social worker, tell her you make off with whatever you can git your hands on. Eat all my food."

Don't react. Don't give him the satisfaction.

I pulled the cell phone from my pocket. "Well, that's good, because I talked to the boy who works downstairs in the Rip Shack. His girlfriend, Kayla, is the social worker who tried to help you at the hospital. Kayla would *love* to chat with you some more. I think we should call her. Let me get her number real quick. Maybe you can also tell her what happened to the sandwich I left for you and the banana that was in the fruit bowl this morning and the potato chips that were in the bag the dog just grabbed. Did somebody come by and take those, too?"

Clyde's nose scrunched up as if the air had gone foul. "Close the door. All that wind comin' in the screen. Run up the electric bill. Get my service to where I can't pay it. That your plan?"

Breathe, breathe, breathe. Don't go ballistic. That's exactly what he wants. How did my mother put up with this insufferable lout? Why did she? What did she ever see in him? Was she that desperate for someone to take care of after she retired from teaching? "Oh, Clyde . . . I think you've got plenty of income from my mother's rentals downstairs. In fact, I'm a little surprised the building isn't in better repair. There are squirrels getting in. The shopkeepers have been trapping them in self-defense."

"Why'd you think I brung that dog? Thing's part hound. Had a dead snake in her mouth, first time I saw her."

My stomach clenched. Mental image. Gross. "That's disgusting."

A snort. "You quit feedin' her up on dog food, she'll hunt. Rats, squirrels, snakes. Whatever comes in here, she'll root it out."

"Up *here*, you mean? On the third floor?" All I could think was, *Rats, squirrels, snakes. Rats, squirrels, snakes. Rats . . .*

"Stinkin' nutria rats. All over the place. Too big for the stray cats to kill, even. Come right up the sewer. Ten pounds, some of 'em."

My poking around downstairs quickly came to mind. I'd seen mouse droppings, heard a little rustling in the walls. Was something larger lurking in the Excelsior? Surely I would've run across evidence. "Clyde, you *know* that's not true." *Right? Tell me I'm right. Then again, if a squirrel can get in . . .*

"Some tourist jumped in the river, swam out to rescue one,

thinkin' it was a drownin' puppy. Nutria rat. Bit the fella and he had to git rabies shots. Was in the newspaper."

The balance of power in this war of systematic unpleasantness was slowly turning, and Clyde seemed to know it. I couldn't compete with snakes and ten-pound mutant ninja rats.

"*When* was it in the paper?"

"Couple weeks ago. Don't believe me, look it up. Rats so big, the stray cats run away from 'em."

"You know what, Clyde, I haven't got time for this. And I can't come rushing upstairs every time you decide you want something. Stop thumping on the floor. You're wasting your energy, trying to get rid of me." *So there.*

But I did plan to ask the Rip Shack guys about nutria rats the first chance I got.

"Busy stealin' everything you can get your hands on."

We'd been to this very street corner and around the same block before. "You can't *steal* what you already own." No wonder Clyde's sons wanted nothing to do with him. If he was this horrible to them, why would they bother?

"You took her necklace. The gold cross with the pearl in it. Well, you can just put it right back on her dresser, missy. Told you not to touch a thing up here. Not 'til I'm dead."

I blinked, my head snapping back as if he'd slapped me rather than pointing a finger. Did he *know*? Did he remember, or was he only accusing me of this to cause maximum impact?

I couldn't imagine my mother without that tiny gold cross around her neck. One of my earliest memories was of sitting in her lap in church, my head resting on her shoulder, my fingers toying with the cross as I compared it to the one in the stained-glass window. In place of the light radiating from the crown of thorns, my mother's necklace held a small, shimmering pearl.

Every night, she set the little cross by her bed. Every morning, she awoke and fastened it around her neck. One of the first Mother's Day gifts I'd ever bought her was a thin, gold chain to replace the one that was kinked and pinched in a dozen places.

She'd hugged me until I almost couldn't breathe, kissing my hair as she told me I shouldn't have spent my raspberry-picking income on her.

Tears, the hard and unexpected kind, struck me now, a blunt-force blow. "She was buried in that necklace, Clyde. You *know* that." My voice trembled, and I hated the weakness of it. I hated that it had happened in front of the enemy. I hated *him* for bringing me to it.

Ruby slunk past me, whimpering, and rested her nose on the armrest of Clyde's chair, her head pressing so lightly that she didn't even compact the fibers of a furniture protector my mother had woven from fluffy brown yarn.

"Sent it home to her from Vietnam," Clyde muttered, his body sinking into the cushions, almost disappearing as his gaze turned away. Absently, he laid a hand on the dog's head. "Got it at the PX. Didn't cost much."

I felt sick. My mother had been wearing that cross in her wedding photo, the day she'd married my father in a chapel not far from her college campus. Just the two of them and a couple of her girlfriends as witnesses. They hadn't wanted any interference from either side of the family, which, no doubt, would've come. My mother's parents thought a four-month whirlwind relationship wasn't a long-enough trial period, especially considering their fourteen-year age difference. My father's mother, of course, wouldn't have been in favor of my mother's *sort* under any circumstances.

She'd been wearing Clyde's necklace on the day she gave herself to my dad? How could she? Why would she?

My dad was the love of her life. *My dad.* She'd fallen for him at first sight, in the performance hall at his concert. Between musical scores, a theater student had recited a poem from Lord Byron, and my parents' gazes met.

There chiefly I sought thee, there only I found thee;
Her glance was the best of the rays that surround thee;
When it sparkled o'er aught that was bright in my story,
I knew it was love, and I felt it was glory.

After the performance and the seminar that followed, she'd made it a point to linger, and he'd made it a point to shake loose his admirers and meet her. They'd gone to dinner, stayed long after, not parting until she was forced to leave for dorm curfew.

And yet all the while, she'd been wearing *Clyde's necklace*?

Who *was* my mother? Had I never known her at all?

The emotions overwhelmed me, and all I could do was turn and rush up the hall, not stopping until I was out the door and down two flights of stairs, walking the Manteo street and gulping in cool, salt-laden air.

I ended up on a park bench, staring at the sound through a haze of tears, watching the boats come and go from the marina. In the bay, a pod of dolphins rolled and frolicked, and a bird ventured from its hiding place to see if all the people had gone home yet.

Gulls called. Live oaks twittered. A bullfrog sang a lazy bass somewhere nearby. Familiar sounds. The sounds of summer here with my mother, who now seemed like a stranger to me . . . as if, in keeping her secrets, she had negated the life we knew, made it invalid. Had she spent all those years dreaming of Clyde Franczyk? Wishing he would come back? Wishing she'd never met my father, but instead had waited for Clyde to return from Vietnam?

I wanted to wash the thought away. To make it be gone. But no amount of tears could dilute its potency. It burned like acid, the tears of protest blurring my view of the water. Not far offshore, a man in a red kayak paddled close to the dolphins, then stopped to take pictures as they cavorted. *I* wanted to be the one in a boat. I wanted to row and row and row until I was far out at sea, where there was no question about right and wrong, where there were no hidden secrets.

The kayaker made an aft turn, gracefully moving toward shore, gliding along with an expert lack of effort.

I closed my eyes, tried to get my head together, to stuff the pain down and bind it tightly.

A pinprick in my arm made the pain tangible, brought it to the surface again. I slapped, felt the warm spill of blood. The mosquitoes were coming out. I couldn't stay here. Letting my head sink into my hands, I wiped my eyes, tried again to think, to prepare to go . . . someplace. I wasn't even sure where I was headed. I couldn't stand to return to the Excelsior and my stepfather.

Maybe I'd take a page out of Clyde's book and hide out in a hotel in Nags Head for a few days. Run away from everything.

But the truth was, I couldn't afford the price, or the time. Aside from that, Nags Head now seemed tainted too. Who could say if my mother's story about her idyllic lovers' day there with my dad was even true? Maybe it was part of the lie. A figment of the mist my mother had woven like one of her tapestries. Without her here to sort out the threads, I'd never know which were false-dyed and which ran through to the core, which were artificial and which were true colors.

Something buzzed around my ear. I swatted at it, hissing, "Leave me alone!"

"You look like you could use some bug spray." The kayaker had come in for a landing while I wasn't looking. Standing on the dock, he smiled good-naturedly, then reached into his backpack and offered a mini bottle of Off! repellant.

"I'm fine. Really. Thanks." I wasn't in the mood for company, even the friendly kind. I needed time alone to lick my wounds and decide what to do next. I wanted to get in the car and drive back to Michigan, but what would I be going home to? The death of Bella Tazza 2 and the tenuous struggle to rescue the first restaurant from overdue bills? Surrender to Tagg Harper? Watching Denise debate whether she could afford to take Mattie to the hospital for a breathing treatment or should wait this one out and save the money?

I couldn't do it.

"Bad day?" the kayak guy asked. He was still standing there with the bug spray, offering it up, if I wanted to take it.

Swiping away moisture and mascara trails, I sniffled and nodded and hugged my arms tight over the torn-off sweatshirt sleeves, taking a breath and then slowly letting it out. "Not the best."

"Getting a little cool out here now."

I realized that my elbows were welded to my sides, my hands rubbing up and down. "Guess I'd better go in." *Where? Go in where?*

"Hungry at all?"

I turned then, taking him in more carefully, slowly moving upward past a nice-fitting pair of gray Gore-Tex boater pants, a Legend dry top with a color-coordinated hem strip and a bright sunburst that arced over a broad chest. A gold-nugget cross hung there, along with what looked like a pricey long-lens camera and a pair of Oakley sunglasses. The Hobie ball cap had been tipped back far enough that I could see his face in the mix of waning sunlight and overhead security lamps.

Blond and blue-eyed, clean-shaven, with hair close cut over his ears, he belonged on a billboard for upscale outdoor adventure in the Outer Banks. He also looked slightly familiar. Maybe I'd run across him in one of the restaurants here?

Hungry at all? What exactly did he mean by that? Was this a . . . pickup? Between managing the first Bella Tazza and starting Tazza 2 and then battling Tagg Harper, I was out of practice at gauging this kind of thing. I hadn't been anywhere near a random pickup line in forever.

Back in the day, opening corporate eateries in tourist meccas and resort towns, that kind of thing was the norm. Visitors and staff members were frequently looking for love. If you were young and female, you learned to handle it almost out of reflex—reject the creepy ones, maybe date the nice guys a little. Realize that, where business is seasonal, the help is all there for the same reason—because everyone comes and goes and that's the way they want it. That's why you're there too. By silent, mutual agreement, there are no long-term attachments, no painful good-byes. The beginnings come with endings already implied.

An old part of me, the part that had once found satisfaction and some misguided sense of self-actualization in those types of relationships, reawakened, whispered, *Why not? At least somebody wants you.*

I needed comfort right now. A distraction.

"A little." I tested the waters.

A slow smile added to the billboard-photo illusion. It wasn't a false sort of smile. He actually seemed like a nice guy.

The gold cross eased from under his camera strap, as if to offer reassurance that he could be trusted. Unfortunately, it reminded me of my mother's necklace and the argument with Clyde. My stomach compressed into a hard, tight ball. Maybe this wasn't a pickup attempt, but a mercy mission. Maybe he'd paddled ashore here, sensing that an epic meltdown was under way. Perhaps the dinner invitation was an attempt to . . . counsel me? I wasn't up for that. I couldn't deal with well-meaning advice right now.

"Let me go bring the kayak in." Slipping the camera strap over his head, he moved to set it beside me with the bug spray. "Hang on to this for me."

I stood up, finding myself strangely off balance. "You know what, on second thought, I'd better go back home. I . . ." The excuse I'd been about to make, *I left my stepfather without any dinner,* wouldn't even form itself in my mouth. There was food in the refrigerator. Clyde could manage.

But a dinner invitation from someone who'd just . . . paddled up out of nowhere? Probably not such a good idea, especially in my present state of mind. Maybe I'd just go back to the Excelsior and spend all night on the second floor, piecing together Alice's letters and searching for more clues . . . in the dim light of the bulbs that still worked . . . with the shifting shadows and the noises . . . and the squirrels . . . and the nutria rats . . .

"It'll only take a second," my outdoorsman rescuer, my convenient distraction, offered pleasantly. "Think about what you're hungry for. We can walk downtown if you want, or hop in the car and run over to Kitty Hawk. Hit the Black Pelican, maybe. Or whatever else sounds good. No strings. Just dinner, I promise."

Just dinner . . . I needed dinner . . . and someone to talk to. "All right." Downtown, maybe, because there was no way I was getting in his car. I was emotionally wrecked, not stupid.

He started back to the kayak, then paused, turned to me again, and offered a friendly handshake, along with another winning smile. "Sorry. I should've introduced myself. Casey Turner."

The blindside surprise left me temporarily speechless, trying to reel up my chin before he could see my brain tripping over itself. *That* was why he looked familiar—the photo on the business card I'd found tucked in the shutter my first day here.

Don't tell him your name. Give him a fake one. The thought was ridiculous and tempting all at once.

Stay away from Casey Turner. The man's a leech, Mark's warning chimed in.

"Whitney Monroe," I offered, and Casey didn't seem surprised. I had a feeling he'd known all along. Maybe that was why he'd stopped and been so determined to engage me. Maybe this wasn't a pickup attempt *or* a mercy mission . . . but a *business* call?

As he walked away, I caught myself checking to see if anyone was watching. We were right out here in the open. If this got back to the Rip Shack, Mark would be all over it.

Then again, why did I care? It was my prerogative to have dinner with anyone I chose. If I decided to make arrangements to sell my building, I could do that, too. Maybe Casey Turner was interested enough to make some sort of contingency deal and offer cash up front, even knowing that he would have to wait to actually execute the sale and claim possession of the building until after Clyde finally left.

The only thing I had promised Mark was that I would let him know thirty days before I sold to anyone else. Casey and I could work that out too, if he was interested enough in the property. The man was wearing hundreds of dollars of designer outdoors wear for a simple evening of kayaking. He'd just left me with several *thousand* dollars in camera equipment. He could probably afford to do anything he wanted.

I tried to put Joel and Mark and the story about the Seaside House charity out of my mind. *You can't save the world if you can't save yourself, Whit.* That was the truth of it. I had families to worry about at home.

My mind was turning, firming up thoughts, slapping mortar on new barricades as I watched Casey effortlessly hoist the kayak onto his shoulder and carry it to the porch of a nearby building, where he leaned it against the wall like he owned the place. Maybe he did. How would I know? And maybe he wasn't the creep he'd been made out to be. How would I know that either? All I had was Mark Strahan's word, and *he* had an agenda. More than one, actually.

"So, where to?" Casey pulled the car keys from his pocket as he came back across Creef Park. "Your choice." He glanced over his shoulder toward town, as if he thought I'd opt to walk someplace close by.

"The Black Pelican sounds good." The suggestion seemed to surprise him almost as much as it surprised me. "I haven't been there in years."

Whisking off the ball cap, he shook out his hair and stuffed the cap inside his knapsack. I picked up the camera and bug spray.

"Sounds perfect." His words held a sense of anticipation that should've worried me, but for some reason didn't. I was up for almost anything tonight. Anything but returning to the Excelsior, with its mysteries and shadows and its impossible tangle of unanswerable questions.

On the other side of the old boathouse that was now the Maritime Museum, a gold sports car was waiting for us. Convertible. BMW. It matched the shoulder stripes on Casey's dry shirt perfectly.

"So did you get some good pictures of the dolphins?" I made conversation as he opened the passenger door so I could slide in.

He motioned to the camera in my lap. "Take a look. See what you think."

I obliged, scanning the images as we started toward Kitty Hawk and Nags Head.

"Did I get anything?" He turned off the radio, and the quiet seemed more in keeping with the acres of wild salt marsh and lowland maritime forest. In the distance, the sun slowly sank into the water. The dash lights came on in the car, and a plethora of electronic gadgets cast a glow over the camera.

"These photos are awesome." The stop-motion shots captured dolphins breaching, their bodies in sleek, graceful arcs, everything about them radiating pure joy and abandon, sprays of water frozen against the setting sun. "I mean, like, *National Geographic* gorgeous. You're an incredible photographer."

"It's just a hobby." He was surprisingly modest about it. I hadn't imagined him as the modest type, based on the clothes and the car and what Mark had said. "Stress relief. I donate the photos to a group that supports sea turtle preservation. They use them for T-shirts, calendars, sell them as stock photography to raise money. It's a good outlet for something I'd be doing anyway."

Sea turtles. Casey Turner was nothing like I'd pictured. Not the ruthless, bulldozer-wielding, skyscraper-building creep Mark wanted me to believe. In fact, right now Mark seemed the more underhanded one of the two. He *had* blackmailed me over the squirrel trap, after all.

"That's great." I turned off the camera and set it down. "I have a restaurant in Michigan. A few of my employees are really good amateur photographers. I'll have to mention the idea to my business partner. Maybe they could hook up with a conservation group that focuses on the Great Lakes. She loves getting the kids who work for us involved in the community."

He laughed, regarding me with a quirky, sideways look.

"What?" I caught myself smiling back.

"Kids." He laughed again. "That struck me as funny. You're just a kid yourself."

I gave Casey a closer look. At first glance, I'd assumed he was around my age. Maybe he was older than I'd thought, midforties but well preserved. It didn't matter, really. So far, I was enjoying the evening out, and there was the temptation to keep it just that. An evening out, not a business meeting.

Casey seemed content with casual conversation as well. All the way to Kitty Hawk, we chatted about sea turtles, their nesting habits, and what the beach looked like when hundreds of babies hatched and raced toward the sea.

"I've never seen it," I admitted as we pulled into the parking lot of the Black Pelican, an Outer Banks landmark housed in an old Coast Guard lifesaving station. Long ago, my mom had told me the story of how rescuers were dispatched to ships sinking in the treacherous waters off the Outer Banks.

"Never?" Casey exited the car, and I caught myself reaching for my door before I realized he was coming around to open it. He offered a hand to issue me out of my low-lying seat and

I slipped my fingers into his. "I thought you were a longtime regular. I had the impression that you grew up here."

It was the first thing he'd said to indicate that he'd had knowledge of me before we met in the park—that he knew exactly who he was taking out to dinner tonight. A twinge of uneasiness struck unexpectedly. I'd accepted the dinner invitation fully intending to talk about the building, assuming he wasn't asking me out because of my delightfully grime-smeared clothes, lovely hair, and tearstained face.

Why the second thoughts? Why did I feel so unsure of this? I usually considered myself a good judge of people and an excellent judge of business. Now I felt like the insecure middle school girl again, all arms and legs and doubts.

You didn't even know your own mother, Whitney. And if it weren't for your overconfidence, the Bella Tazza 2 disaster never would've happened.

The voice of insecurity hit with paralytic force. I hated that voice—the one that had haunted me since I was old enough to understand what happened to my father. I'd learned to drive those whispers away with logic, with rational arguments. My father's suicide had been the result of his violent mood swings, most likely bipolar depression he was too proud to admit to—unstable brain chemistry that had gone untreated. There was nothing a little girl could have done to cause it or to stop it . . . or to deserve it.

But somehow this place, all the questions here, stirred old emotions. *I got this* had turned into *This has got me.*

Suddenly, I just wanted to go home.

"Something wrong?" Casey cast concern my way while the hostess seated a group of girlfriends enjoying an early season beach trip.

"No." Was I telegraphing my thoughts? "Everything's fine."

"You keep looking at the door." His mouth quirked upward in a way that said he knew I was thinking about bolting.

Fortunately, the hostess came back before I had to answer, and I pulled myself together on the way to our table. This was a business negotiation. Business negotiations, I could do in my sleep. One disastrously unforeseen situation with a restaurant did not negate that.

After we perused the menu and ordered, Casey slipped back to the conversation about the sea turtle charity and his pictures. He'd traveled all over the world on photography vacations. I'd worked in some of the places he was talking about. Bali, Curaçao, the Gold Coast. We actually had a lot in common. "It's really a shame that you haven't seen a turtle hatch. The logger-heads and the greens are just coming up to nest now. If you're still here in a couple months when they start, I'll take you down and let you see a boil."

"A *boil*?"

He laughed softly. "When the babies come up out of the sand. It's called a boil."

"Ohhh . . . I'd like that." I let the thought settle a minute, sank temporarily into a fantasy of life on this long strip of sand surrounded by sea . . . dating a guy who'd been all over the world, just like I had . . . except he didn't need a job to get there. He could simply buy a ticket. The fantasy whirled away as quickly as it had come, disappearing like a balloon with the string untied. "But I don't think I'll be staying that long. There's a lot going on with my restaurant right now."

"You could come back."

"Maybe . . . I'll have to see how things turn out. I'm really only here to take care of the crisis with my stepfather and see about the building."

There was a flicker of some involuntary response on Casey's part. It came and went too quickly for me to identify it, but clearly, a covert thought had slid past the perimeter of our conversation. Was all the talk about watching a sea turtle hatch just a way of gauging my intentions for the building and how long I planned to be in Manteo? Was he trying to charm me or romance me . . . or both?

"I heard you were cleaning out the second floor." He paused as the waitress delivered the mixed drink he'd ordered. She offered a shameless flirt along with it. He noticed, was polite, but didn't return the attention in a way that would've been insulting to a dinner date. I couldn't help taking note.

"I'm trying to sort a bit while I'm here—decide what to keep and what to get rid of."

Sitting back, he stirred his drink, extracted the little paper umbrella and offered it to me, our fingers brushing before he relaxed against the chair, crossing his legs at the knee and hooking an arm comfortably over the backrest. "I *might* be interested, if you've got things for sale. I'm a bit of an Outer Banks history buff. I like to include some of it in my properties, give the residents and the vacationers a feel for our heritage and what it means."

"That's nice." The davenport desk, the ship's manifest, the taffrail device, the ruby brooch with the crest, the scrimshaw and the carved bone necklace . . . How much might they be worth?

And what about Alice's letters? What about the family secret I was only beginning to piece together? I'd found the first letter hidden away with the ruby brooch and the bone necklace. Were the items and the letter hidden together for a reason? Did they tell parts of the same story? If I separated the elements, would I ever understand the whole?

Yet here was a man who would probably offer cold, hard cash. A way out of the financial mess Denise and I were in. An easy escape.

"I haven't found a lot yet." It wasn't exactly a lie, but it wasn't the truth either. "A few antiques that belonged to Grandmother, a little jewelry, some old letters that I'm trying to piece together. I don't know that any of it has much value, other than sentimentally speaking."

"I'd love to take a look. Be happy to give you an opinion. I've bought quite a bit of maritime memorabilia over the years. I'm a pretty good judge." He was using the hard sell now. Switching tactics.

Interesting . . .

"Sorry," he said, as if he'd noticed that I'd noticed. "I didn't mean to push. I'm sure you have emotional attachments there. It's not easy to think about cleaning out. My granny had a farm in the Smoky Mountains when I was a kid—my favorite place in the world. Trees to climb, creeks to wade, lakes to fish in. The view from the porch went for miles. Man, I loved that valley. Cohler House had been in the family since the mid-1800s. It was a tobacco plantation, back in the day. My parents sold the whole thing to pay for college for my sisters and me. That was about the saddest day of my life. I went back to see about buying it later on, but the coal companies had taken over the property and torn it up. None of it was there anymore. Not the house, not the barn. Nothing. Just slag heaps and coal roads and the pads from operations trailers."

"That's terrible. I'm really sorry." I felt the tug of sympathy between us and again realized that Casey Turner and I had much in common.

We talked about his grandparents' farm until the waitress came with our food, her visit changing the mood at the table—a little laughter, a little obvious flirtation. Her efforts were almost embarrassing. I got a vague feeling that she knew Casey.

"Well, anyway, if I can be of help with the cleanout, let me know," he went on once she'd left. "I could send some muscle if you need it. We run a program out at the resort where we bring in exchange students, keep them employed for a year, let them work on their English and learn about the country. When they're finished, they get the chance to travel. So . . . all that to say, there's always plenty of labor around, if you need any. No sense breaking your back."

I nodded, thinking of Mark's warning about involving Joel in the process. The more people involved, the more likely the word would get around. There was almost no security for the upper floors of the building—no alarm system on the stairwell, no one in the shops at night, just rickety locks on old doors that would probably collapse if someone leaned too hard.

Casey took a sip of his drink, studied me deeply, his eyes a seawater blue. "I'm not trying to pry. I just got the impression at the park that you might have a little too much on your plate."

A thistle bloomed in my throat, prickly and raw and unexpected. I swallowed hard. "Thanks. A lot. I'll keep it in mind. The problem right now has more to do with dealing with my stepfather than anything. He's not healthy enough to keep living in the residence alone, but so far he refuses to think about changing anything. He and I are not . . . close, so it's been pretty much impossible to even talk about options. I tried inviting his sons into the conversation, but they don't want anything to do with him."

"Bring him over to see our retirement colony at the Shores. It's a great assisted-living facility. He might really like it. Might solve your problem."

If only things could be that simple. "I don't know how I'd ever get him to come. Besides, Clyde doesn't have the kind of money a place like that costs."

Casey's gaze held mine, offered a host of hidden meanings I could only guess at. "We'll work something out."

Was he still talking in theory, or was he making the very offer I'd been hoping for . . . and fearing the most?

CHAPTER 9

MAY 1, 1936

Dearest Queen Ruby,

Happy May Day, Dear Sister! I hope you will find someone with whom to wind a maypole by the sea. Here in the mountains, I have yet to see one.

There could not be a more oddly beautiful and yet frightfully contrary mission than this which we have undertaken. Perhaps, having lived so many years within the staid and ivy-laced walls of the college, it was natural for me to believe that there would be order to this process of encountering the mountain folk and gathering their stories. I had (quite foolishly) assumed that word would be sent ahead of us, and upon our arrival in each town, zealous folk would rush to the door of whatever housing had been arranged for us.

How naive I was!

Thus far, not a thing has been planned on this journey, nor do the folk in these hills understand why, in the name of heaven and earth, we would be mapping their roads and documenting the goings-on in this hardscrabble country.

Yesterday, an old woman waved a finger at me and asked if I knew there was a Depression going on.

"Yes, I do," I said to her. "I lost my husband in the Crash of '29. He fell from a ferryboat that very evening and drowned."

She frowned at me as if she had not an idea of what I meant, and then she spat a plug of tobacco over the railing before shooing me off her porch. It is no help to tell them I am a Federal Writer, either. They mistrust the government all the more. These hill folk are a people unto themselves and wary of strangers. Generally, the outsiders they do see are sniffing about for untaxed liquor stills and illegal moonshine storehouses.

You can imagine, I suppose, the looks we draw as we claw our way up some treacherous road to a squat mountainside settlement or a ragged cabin teetering on the edge of the earth and sky and begin unpacking our camera and surveying equipment.

My companion, Thomas, is a country doctor's son, raised nearby in Tennessee, so this is not unfamiliar to him. "I can see you've never been far from the city, Mrs. Lorring," he observed today, upon finding me perched atop a woman's well house with my notepad, after having been chased away with a shotgun and set upon by her cur dog.

"For heaven sake, that creature would have tackled and maimed me, if it had caught me!" I protested to Thomas, at my wits' end. "And what if I'd had Emmaline with me?" I was quite put out with Thomas at that moment. He is a delightful lad, but much like the silly college chaps of whom I have oft warned the female students. He makes light of things when he should be taking them seriously.

"He doesn't look all that hungry," Thomas commented, after studying the dog, and then he lifted me down from the well (a good thing, for I was in a straight skirt and tailored jacket to look nice for the day's interviews, and I was wondering how to descend from the wellhouse without creating an embarrassing situation. I could not, at that moment, recall how I'd managed to scramble atop it, but thank heaven it was a covered well!).

"You don't look any worse for the wear, Mrs. Lorring," Thomas said, giving a full grin and struggling to restrain his laughter. "If that dog wanted to have you, believe me, he would've, though. Next time, be sure to stop at the edge of the yard and hail the house, so's to check that you're welcome. That's the proper way in these parts. You don't never just walk right onto someone's porch, unless you know you're sure enough invited."

Shifting the empty notepad under my arm, I brushed a mess of snarled red hair from my eyes, giving both Thomas and the house a good look and thinking he was again playing one of his silly pranks. "Just . . . stand at the edge of the yard and yell?" (Said most incredulously, of course, such a novice was I.)

"Yes'm."

"Thomas, for goodness sake! Do not say that word. You sound like a bumpkin. And 'don't never' is a double negative, by the by."

"Yes'm. I won't . . . never."

"Why must you annoy me so?" (I will flatly confess, Ruby, that he is a good boy and I am grateful for his guidance and protection, but he is no small trouble.)

"It keeps the days short, Mrs. Lorring." He moved aside to recover his tripod and transit from the grass. The dog, now

reclining in the shade nearby, had the gall to wag its mangy tail at him! "My pappy used to say, any day you don't find a reason to laugh is like livin' two days, neither one of them worth a whit."

"Your father," I corrected, as I was in quite the mood by then. "It is good advice, though, I suppose."

"Yes, ma'am, it is." His blue eyes fell to mere slices, like small slivers of sky, brooding over something. He cocked back his head, another question finding its way to his lips. He did not ask it, though. Instead, he bent to his instruments. "And, Mrs. Lorring, be sure you leave Emmaline in the car 'til you know you been welcomed in a place." He glanced to our WPA car, where Emmaline was napping. Fortunately, she had missed the entire incident involving the dog, but I will tell you, Sister, that she has held up very well these first days of our journey. She is such a brave little thing. She welcomes each new experience with vigor and anticipation, never the least bit afraid. Of course, this only means that I must be afraid for all three of us. Rest assured I am doing a fine job of that!

"The house there by the Mill Camp Store, that's the district nurse's place, I found out. Miz Merry Walker." Thomas started away again with his tools in hand, the ever-present mountain wind billowing his loose canvas shirt and pinning the brown trousers close around his legs. "Seems if you can get Miz Walker to favor you, she can tote you all over the territory and introduce you to the midwife women and the healers. She's about to travel the hills, telling the midwives about a teaching meetin' with a doctor from Raleigh next month." He sent a grin and a wink over his shoulder, like a boy who's certain he's answered the winning question correctly

in the spelling bee. "You might just get yourself somethin' to fill up that empty notepad, Mrs. Lorring."

I confess, I was still in a bit of a stew at that point, so I responded with a huff and a stomp of my foot rather than a thank-you, but as I have already conveyed, Thomas can use a bit of reining in. He tends to leave the ground first and then assess how high the jump may be.

After our many years of foxhunting together, Sister, you know the potential results of that! I would say it is a wonder that we haven't careened from one of these narrow, perilous mountain roads thus far, but I do not wish to worry you. Rest assured that Thomas has experience with the back paths in Tennessee, and he is quite the capable driver.

I will pause for now and add to this letter later. I've been watching across the way as I write, and I see that the district nurse has just arrived. I am off to make a friend, I hope. . . .

Ruby lifted her head and growled into the shadows, the noise slinging me from Appalachia to the Excelsior's second floor—from Alice's body to my own. I jerked upright, looked around, had the creepy feeling that I was being watched, but the salon was empty, the stairwell door still closed.

"What's the matter, Ruby?"

She hushed, rolled her eyes my way, then rested her head on her paws, like she was embarrassed for sounding a false alarm. I couldn't blame her. The place was murky and eerie so early in the morning, which was why I'd dragged Ruby down here in the first place. She probably would've rather been upstairs sharing Clyde's breakfast.

I, on the other hand, wanted to be anywhere but there, especially after my late night out, sitting on a pier under the stars with Casey Turner. We'd talked about the Outer Banks and about the Excelsior building. Casey appeared to be my one-stop solution. But the last time I'd jumped into something that seemed too easy, I'd ended up with a lovely mill building to convert into a restaurant. At an inexplicably low price, in a deceptively great location.

Maybe that was what worried me most. Casey made it all sound way too simple, almost elementary. I knew it wasn't. There were so many issues to be considered, so many potential ramifications. So many loose ends that seemed impossible to tie into neat little bows.

It was easier to turn back to the next page of Alice's letter. These pieces, I knew how to put together.

Hello again, Dear Sister. Let me go on with the story of my meeting with the district nurse and all that came of it.

As a side note, Thomas and I have discovered a bit of a mystery in the course of our duties today. I am determined to document and perhaps solve it while I am at work in these mountains.

I will leave the details to the end of this letter. First, let me tell you the story exactly as it happened, and it will be as if you were here with me:

Upon seeing the district nurse return to her home, I exit the car where I have been waiting and hurry to her porch, catching her before she lets herself in the door. I quickly explain my business and offer to help with the parcels she is juggling. Though she is only dimly aware of the Federal Writers' Project, she seems delighted to visit with someone from the city. Aside from that, she is a Roosevelt woman herself, so we have something in common.

I soon learn that, in '32, her Raleigh hospital went the way of bankruptcy, as so many did. Soon after, Mrs. Walker accepted this position as district nurse as a means of leaving behind the destitute city scenes and exchanging them for a different sort of desolation. "Here in the mountains," she muses as the door swings open, "the people are equally afflicted with crippling poverty, but they are prepared for it. They have always lived hardscrabble, surviving on what they can grow and produce."

The cities, she goes on to point out, are filled with the ugliness of this Depression. One can scarce turn a corner without observing the scourge of breadlines, hoboes wandering in search of food or work, ragged children playing like pack rats in sewer drains while their hopeless fathers succumb to liquor and their mothers sit at empty cupboards.

Yet the mountains provide a feast for the eye if not for the stomach. The mountains fill the senses in a way even money could not. Scenes of natural glory hide the ugliness of human deprivation. The people live firmly tied to their land and their traditions. They seem quilted by soft, even stitches to the sense that this is the natural way of life. Hard. Randomly cruel . . . and then, in the blink of an eye, possessed of great magnificence.

"This place will steal your soul and hold it captive," Mrs. Walker warns, gazing into the distance as we stand at the door.

A cloud shadow sweeps down the path and then dances up a ridge, disappearing into a smoky mist that comes out of nowhere. I am struck by the contrasts of this place, the suddenness of light and shadow, of storm and clear sky, of threat and welcome.

Mrs. Walker is, in herself, a contrast. The widow of a doctor, and quite clearly aristocratic in her speech and mannerisms, she is as plain as homespun cotton. There is not a fancy thing about her. Her graying hair is wound in a braid around her broad, German face. Her nose is a cheery bulb and her cheeks are naturally red and shiny. Framing her hazel eyes, lines lie deeply etched, and her hands are rough as a cob, the skin chapped and calloused. She does not seem to mind it. She is as utilitarian and practical as the gray nurse's uniform she wears.

She quite readily agrees to speak further with me. "I'll enjoy the company," she says, and quickly invites me into her square and trim white home. While the furnishings in the front room are spare, the china cupboards and velvet settee give evidence that Merry Walker once lived a grand life. The place is neat as a pin. The homemade bench placed along one wall, I assume, is for her patients.

"My daughter is with me in the car," I explain with some trepidation, hoping this will not change the tone of Mrs. Walker's welcome. "But she is no trouble. She is a very accommodating child and quite happy with her colors and her paper."

In truth, Emmaline has worn the colors down to the nubs already, and there is scarce enough to pinch between her little fingernails. I haven't an idea of what to do about it. I had imagined that they would last longer. We have been advanced our first month's salary, but I must make certain it lasts. Better no colors than no food or roof to shelter under. We have already spent nights in the car twice, while Thomas slept outside in a tent. There is often in this country no stopping point at which a room can be had.

"Nonsense," says Nurse Walker. "How can a girl grow into a woman, sitting in a car with colors? To understand life, one must experience it!" Her silver-flecked eyes seem to bore through me as if she is well aware that I have been keeping Emmaline away from these mountain people and their children, who are oft clothed more in scabs and vermin than in pants or shorts or dresses.

"Of course," I say to Mrs. Walker, and I move to retrieve Emmaline from the car, but Mrs. Walker catches my arm and says, "Come along inside. I've a patient I think you might like to meet after a while. You and I can chat until then. Able will go after your daughter."

She calls down the hall and out comes a tall, thin girl of perhaps twelve or thirteen years of age. She is wrapped in a knitted shawl, though the day is not cold. Long, curling tendrils of dark hair reach to her waist. Her skin is the color of burnished hickory, and her eyes are a striking pale blue. The closest thing I can liken her to are the gypsies we saw passing along the road on our trip to Ireland the year we turned ten. Do you remember them, Ruby, with their jingling bells and mysterious ways? This girl could be one of them.

Her shawl shifts aside, and I see that she is heavily pregnant. I cannot help but stare. She is only a child.

Does Nurse Walker approve of this, I wonder? Surely not!

Passing bashfully by, the girl nods at Mrs. Walker's instructions and then is gone before I can wonder whether Emmaline will be frightened by her.

"You must excuse Able," Mrs. Walker says regretfully. "She hardly knows a thing. A week ago when I made my

rounds, she followed me down the mountain. She won't say who the father of the baby might be or whether she's run away from a husband. I don't quite know what to do about her. Sweet, dear child."

"A husband!" I gasp, craning to watch the girl descend the porch steps, balancing her load. "Surely not." Yet I am sickened by the possibilities, either way. She is not so many years older than Emmaline! Who could have done such a thing to this child? What has she endured in her short life?

"It's not a rarity that I come across such things," Mrs. Walker admits. All she knows of the girl is that her name is Able and she is neither Negro nor Cherokee nor white, but another thing I will tell you of at the end of this letter. "Certainly, I couldn't just leave her on the mountain, but I'm afraid trouble may come of it."

Together, we peer through the window and watch Able and Emmaline making friends. Able seems quite interested in the car, and Emmaline invites her inside to see. They close the door, perhaps sharing Emmaline's colors and book.

Nurse Walker takes my hand and pats it between hers. "Looks like they're chums already. Come along and I'll brew some coffee for us. Tell me more about this Writers' Project. . . ."

Over coffee at a small table in the kitchen, I acquaint myself further with Merry Walker. I am also introduced to Jolly, a lop-eared brown hound that Merry laughingly refers to as her "resident assistant."

It isn't long before a knock comes at the back door and Jolly announces the visitor with a bark and a long, yodeling howl. Nurse Walker's patient has arrived, and I, in turn, have the source of my first story.

On the back porch this day is an old Negro man who has come here about trouble with his eyes. He has traveled quite a distance, Mrs. Walker being the only bona fide medical professional available in the area. The patient's granddaughter has brought him by mule cart, which stands parked in back. The mule is quite happily chewing the bark off Mrs. Walker's apple tree, which she sternly requests be stopped immediately.

The granddaughter hurries off to handle the mule, and I am introduced to Bass Carter, who is in his eighty-seventh year. He becomes the subject of my inaugural narrative.

"Don't know why you folks wadn't askin' 'bout them times long ago, back when they was more a us," he says to me after my purpose has been explained. "The gub'ment, you say? The gub'ment wanna know 'bout us peoples? Well don't that beat all!"

"Yes," I agree, and smile at him, and think of the many colored women who worked in Mother's kitchen and in Grandmother's. While we had a fine time vexing the help, it dawns on me now that we never asked any of them for their stories. In all those years, it never occurred to me to care.

Now my very livelihood depends on my ability to persuade Bass Carter to share his experiences with me. Suddenly, I see that Bass Carter's story matters as much as my own. Perhaps more. He has lived longer, being not quite three times my age.

There is an air of quiet dignity about him as he sits back in the rocking chair and speaks.

"I's borned on the Culberson plantation. Don' 'member it much. My mama's name Nessie and my daddy's Franklin. Both a them pick cotton and tabacee, minute the day come

up to when the day go down. By the light a the moon if'n was bright 'nough. But I don' 'member much 'bout that. First thing I 'members clear is Massa get my mama to clean me up, bring me to the big house. I know my Mama's sad 'bout it, and I don' know why. I's only five year old. The kitchen women gimme fine suit a clothes and they puts me in it. Shoes and ever'thin'! I can't even walk in them thangs! But that day, I's da birthday present for the massa's grandson. He three year old and need him somebody to play wit'. Massa give me to him fo' his property. I's gonna have a easy life now in a new house. No mo' pickin' cotton. Only trouble is, that house a long way off. . . ."

Onward goes Mr. Bass Carter's story, as I alternately listen and scribble notes and try my best to commit to memory the patterns of his speech, the rise and fall of his voice, the juxtaposition of words. Via our FWP leaders, we have been instructed to deliver "no ivory tower writing" but to bring "the streets, the stockyards, and the hiring halls into literature." This admonishment bids us to accurately record our informants and to make them feel that they are critical to our mission.

This is no trouble for me as I sit with Mr. Bass Carter, his granddaughter nearby, eyeing me with some wariness as her face rests against the nose of the dozing mule. Bass Carter's eyes grow cloudy and far away, and I am transported to the time before the War between the States, a time that is bred into our awareness as Southerners, yet most often lauded as a day of grace and grandeur. Mr. Bass Carter causes me to wonder . . . how different is that history when seen from the fields and the lowly slave cabins?

Now I walk in the shoes of this five-year-old boy, his very first shoes, as his bare feet are hemmed within leather and laces and he is offered as a possession, taken from his mother without a second thought.

I hear Emmaline inside the kitchen with Able, talking in their girlish voices and carefree giggles, and I am nearly overcome by my emotions. What if someone removed her from me, gave her away and I was powerless to stop it?

I pour the pain into ink and write and write and write.

The words paint pictures and I live Mr. Bass Carter's life through lines and pen. This, I know now, is story at its highest capability. It agitates us to genuine joy and tears. Within story, we are given a new soul, another's soul to try on like clothing, knowing we can shed it again should we choose.

"I been a long time fo' this world," Bass Carter says in the end. "Hard lotta years, I been here. Work hard plowin' and plantin' and harvestin' all my livin' days since the war. God done brung me through it. Don' reckon I knows nothin' to say that matters mo' than that."

I pose him for a photo and take it since Thomas is nowhere nearby, then jot the frame number and note the subject on our list, so as to later match it to Bass Carter's interview.

Merry examines him and gives drops for his eyes. "It won't stop the cataracts, but it will help you feel better," she says.

Bass Carter thanks her, and his granddaughter offers a basket containing bread and jam. The old man rises and bids us a pleasant good-bye, and we watch as he rattles off beside his granddaughter in the mule wagon. He turns his face to the hills, but cannot see them. Perhaps just the feel of the breeze is enough to remind him of the view.

I find myself strangely wrung out as we lunch in Mrs. Walker's kitchen and discuss plans to travel the mountain roads to hidden places where we will encounter the women who engage in midwifery. "We'll set out first thing in the morning," Mrs. Walker says and offers lodging for the night. "In the meanwhile, you might interview the Lundy sisters, who run the whistle-stop store along the track near Rice Creek. It isn't far, just over two miles each way. If you're amenable to it, I've a medication delivery for them. That will get you in the door. When you hail the house, tell them Merry Walker sent you."

I thank her, and she asks if I'd like to leave Emmaline here with Able. I'm leery of it, not knowing the place well, and tell her that I believe Emmaline had better come with me.

"I understand," she sighs. "I'd send Able along for the walk, but I must keep her close to home until I can decide what to do about her. Her kind aren't welcomed around here. Jolly might enjoy trotting along and chasing a groundhog or two on the way, though. Call her from under the house as you go."

We are interrupted, then, by the arrival of a boy with a kitten injured by a snare trap. Merry draws a hasty map and sends Emmaline and me off with a package, and Able watches sadly through the window as we strike out with Jolly at our heels.

Able is still waiting there, hours later, when we return. Emmaline is overjoyed and rushes up the steps with her golden curls bouncing as she offers up peppermints from the Lundy store. I've learned much about the valley from the sisters, who have run the whistle-stop all their lives. Neither ever married.

I spend the evening typing furiously on my Royal DeLuxe portable, writing and revising and retyping a clean copy of my first narrative interviews as Thomas, Merry Walker, and the girls play dominoes at the kitchen table. I suspect we've eaten food that can't be spared, but Mrs. Walker will not admit to it.

Finally, with the girls settled on a pallet for the night and Thomas bunking in a room that would normally house patients requiring overnight care, I am tucked into bed and writing this letter to you.

Ah, but before I stop, I had promised to share a bit of the mystery of poor little Able.

Do you remember our long-ago nights in Charleston, and the wild ghost tales we told in the lavender room at Grandmother's? You recall, I am sure, Old Juba's stories of the fearsome blue-eyed mountain Indians with their six fingers and brown skin and wicked ways? No doubt you can still hear Juba threatening that, were we to vex her enough, those Melungeons would come and steal us away in the night.

Ziltha, there are such people! The girl, Able, is a Melungeon. According to Mrs. Walker, her kind live high in the hills, but they are a reclusive, suspicious sort and do not warm to outsiders. Nor do outsiders warm to them.

I see no extra fingers on her little hands, but Nurse Walker assures me that, indeed, the sixth finger is not an uncommon thing among Melungeons. Ziltha, can you imagine? All these years, that which we thought to be mere ghost tales and fairy dust is real after all. A secret hides among the high peaks and hidden hollows of this place.

I cannot help but ponder these odd people and wish to know more. My curiosity is piqued. Is yours?

As always,
Alice

I ran a finger over Alice's signature, grounding myself in it, seeking some sort of . . . I wasn't sure what. Comfort, maybe? A promise that an uncertain situation could end up leading to something good?

Uneasiness hung over me this morning, and even after hours of losing myself in the letters, it was fresh and potent. I'd felt it the minute I'd come to consciousness. Before I'd even opened my eyes, the scents of my mother, of her threads and yarns, her bath spray and her favorite room deodorizer were waiting, reminding me that this building wasn't just brick and stone, it was a living thing, the keeper of my family's past.

I'd come downstairs, telling myself I would get serious about the cleaning and sorting, but instead, I'd found the next postmark in order and started looking for the pieces. Two separate letters had been sent in the envelope—ten complete sheets altogether, covered front and back. Fortunately, the paper wasn't water stained and the pieces were fairly large.

I'd put one letter together, and the second was waiting.

I could no more resist it than if it'd been a gold coin, just waiting for me to grab it up and put it in my pocket.

One more, I told myself. *One more and then I'll go upstairs and talk to Clyde.*

CHAPTER 10

MAY 4, 1936

Sister Dear,

Three days have passed since I was able to write, and this was most certainly a trio of days to remember! I have, by the glow of electric light and kerosene and coal oil lantern (whatever could be provided in the places we were lodging) completed no less than my first seven field interviews, and I have a slew more to write up. At this pace, I will more than make my quota for The Project.

Once again, let me tell you the story of my experiences with Nurse Merry Walker, as if you were here with me:

The morning after coming to her cozy home, we rise early while the mists still sigh from the mountain slopes and blanket the hollows. Thomas carries boxes to the car for Mrs. Walker.

"You ladies have a fine trip," he says, but he is worried that the journey will take us away for two nights. "I'll be back here for you on Saturday noon, Lord willin' and the creeks don't rise. Meantime, I've got plenty of work to do."

Merry Walker thanks him and then asks if he might stay the nights here, instead, and look after Able. "I don't dare take her with me, but I do worry, leaving her here alone."

Thomas agrees, though I think he'd planned for camping out, and then he is off. One more trip to the house, bringing water from Mrs. Walker's kitchen in rinsed-out Royal Crown bottles, and we are ready. Merry also presents both Emmaline and me with small bundles of goat cheese and bread, along with Bass Carter's blackberry jam.

"For our journey. It won't do to go hungry," she says.

We leave Able behind with an admonishment that she is not to venture out while we are away. "I must find a safe place for her soon," admits Mrs. Walker as we drive away in her car. "It's a complicated matter."

We pass by Thomas on our way out of town, and I am momentarily distracted by his enthusiastic waving and carrying on. He lifts his camera as if he means to snap a photograph of our departure. "Fill up that notepad, Mrs. Lorring! I'm not hauling that typewriter around for nothing!"

"I will, Mr. Kerth!" I call out in response, and then feel a blush stealing into my cheeks. Heaven forbid that Mrs. Walker think anything untoward is happening between us.

In back, Emmaline waves out the window and yells, "Good-bye, Mr. Thomas!" She is still unable to decide whether Thomas is a playmate or an adult, and though I have instructed her to address him properly, "Mr. Kerth" is not quite a fit.

Unhappy at being left behind, Jolly trots after the car, yipping and howling out a complaint.

"Here, here, Jolly!" Mrs. Walker scolds gently, for everything about this woman is gentle and kind. "You go home now!"

Finally, another half mile down the road, Jolly complies.

Our route from there takes us along winding and shadowed corridors that slither through narrow valleys and climb mountainsides like poorly stitched ribbon on a girl's dress, ruffled and shrunken, torn and folded. Wild rhododendron and spreading ferns brush fingers over the car as we pass. Gray fox and groundhog skitter for cover among the rocks. Dogwood and redbud spatter slopes with color, and the air is so thick with nectar, each breath is sweet.

I wonder, in all of our family travels when times were good, in the fields of Europe and the far-flung reaches of the South Pacific, have I ever seen a place more glorious to the eye and beguiling to the senses than this one? Around us, misted valleys and high mountain vistas offer fold upon fold upon hundredfold of myriad greens. All is dressed in a splendor of cloud shadows.

I have always been a woman of study and reason, rather than of evident faith, but suddenly I see with clarity that in doing what had seemed the worst thing, in taking away my university position, God has indeed done what is best for me. A thing that was needed. He has broken me loose from my perch. I sense that flight is only now beginning.

My travels with Merry Walker pause first at Log Hill. There we meet a woman of inestimable age, a midwife through five generations in some families now. Her body creaks and complains and her breath labors as she settles into a badly listing bentwood chair. She offers the better ones to us, smiles a toothless smile, and greets Mrs. Walker as an old friend. "Ain't none so good round these parts as Mrs. Walker," she boasts, then admires Emmaline, and finally says to me, "Hist over here and set a spell, child. 'Twas right nice of you'uns to ride by. You come up'n here fer hearin' stories, y'say?"

"Yes," I tell her. "And to document them—to write them down, so that others might read them."

Her eyes glitter and shine. If she is aware of the destitute nature of this cabin with the sagging spine, she does not show it. The place seems as if it may give a weary gasp and slide off the hill at any moment. "Well ain't that a right pearly thang!"

Onward she goes, with stories of births she has attended. The tales stretch far and wide, hill to valley, life to death. "Course ain't all of them is borned fat and healthful. Cress Temple's eighth boy come 'longside a lil' tiny twin that wadn't long for this world. Hooked together on the side a the body, they was. Ri'chere." Shifting in the chair, she points to her hip. "Listen, child, that was the poorest thang. One babe a'squawlin', the other'un still and pale as milk. Come from glory and gone on to glory in the same hour. Had to cut 'em apart. Wadn't nothin' else to be done over it. Put that little'un that was still breathin' inside a roastin' pan, we did. Kep' him in the basket part, all bundled up in a sheep fleece with a bit of warm water 'neath him. Land's if he didn't survive anyhows."

She throws back her head. Laughter jangles the air, and Emmaline tosses against her chair and laughs too.

I've written all of it in my notes, from which I compose first drafts, then edit and retype for submission to the state headquarters. We have been encouraged to retain our notes and rough drafts, in case problems should occur with the mail. For now, I am collecting them in the bonnet of my traveling bag, where they will be safe and dry. I shudder to think of such material ever being lost!

Something more has roused my curiosity, these last days as we have traveled about. In conversation, I have learned more of Mrs. Walker's trouble with the girl, Able. It is rather a grim story, I am afraid. Not a soul will take the child in. Mrs. Walker sees no option but to attempt a placement at an orphan school she has heard of. It is a place expressly for Melungeon children. It is said to be high in the mountains near the border, but finding the details of its location has been difficult. Nurse Walker hopes to know something soon and to arrange for Able to go there. She is, of course, concerned as to what they will say about Able's condition and whether they will be equipped to shelter the baby, but this is the only solution she can think of.

It is so very sad to consider . . . a baby not yet born and already with no place in the world to be wanted. Able is such a bright and beautiful thing, too. She sings like an angel and mollycoddles Mrs. Walker's hound dog, yet she seems to have only a cursory realization of the state she is in. She is more little girl than woman. What in heaven's name will become of her and of the baby?

When we return to the clinic, I plan to speak to Thomas about the Melungeons. Their stories do, quite rightly (as the midwives would say), belong in the patchwork of these mountains.

I intend to find those stories while I am here. . . .

The hallway door opened, a breeze blew through, and I bent forward over my carefully pieced pages, holding them in place with my body.

"Thought you might not be up here yet this morning." Mark Strahan was wearing a drysuit, the ends of his hair damp, as if he'd greeted the sunrise on the water, despite the spring chill that had me in a sweatshirt.

"Didn't sleep too well." That was only part of the truth, of course. The rest of it was that my late night with Casey Turner had left me with much to think about. Too much.

Now here was Mark, further muddying the waters with a strangely friendly greeting.

"Thought I'd see if we'd caught your little friend. If you'd rather not be present for the big reveal, there's coffee downstairs. I came in early to take care of some inventory."

Coffee? Mark was suddenly offering me coffee and morning pleasantries? Clearly he didn't know where I'd been last night. Or maybe he did.

"I think I'm willing to risk the big reveal."

"Gotten a little braver since yesterday?" he said with a slow, spreading smile.

"Working on conquering the phobia." All the same, as he moved toward the storage room door, I set a piece of cardboard over my hard work and backed away a few steps, preparing to bolt if necessary. "But . . . if he *is* in the cage, he can't, like, get out . . . until you let him out, right?"

"Depends."

"On what?"

"*Most* of them can't get out."

"What does that mean? *Most* of them?" Was he just messing with me, or was he serious?

"We do catch a few Houdinis from time to time." He turned the storeroom doorknob and I felt my skin crawl. "When we get one of those, they can. . . ."

"I'm sure this is just a *regular* squirrel."

He winked at me before going in. "Let's hope."

I paced the hallway, debated taking him up on the coffee offer, tried to angle a long-distance glance through the gap in the door. A head-to-toe shiver ran over me, and I remembered my mother taking me into a zoo bathroom and stripping my traumatized six-year-old self down to the underwear to check for squirrel bites and scratches as my aunts whispered about whether a series of rabies shots would be needed . . . and how horrible it would be if they were. The petting zoo attendant felt so bad about the mugging, he offered free tickets to come back another time. My mother couldn't talk me into it no matter how hard she tried.

The squirrel trap was dangling from Mark's hand when he emerged. He looked triumphant—Mark, not the squirrel. In the little wire enclosure, the bushy-tailed invader was checking walls and corners, his four-fingered hands reaching through the bars and groping air, gleaming black talons arching outward.

Mark held him up like Exhibit A. "Yep, one minute the world is offering you a stack of free peanuts, and the next minute you're stuck in a cage. I think I found your squirrel entry point in there. There was a hole in the ceiling around the old radiator pipe. I plugged it with a piece of mattress fabric, but I'll send Joel up later to do something permanent and check around a little more. In the meantime, you're safe to operate in your storeroom, but there's glass all over the place."

"Ummm . . . I think the squirrel is ready to go away now."

Mark laughed. He had a nice laugh. The soft kind that comes from deep in the chest. "I'll take him down to the park."

"What? I thought you'd give him to the wildlife department or something, so he can be released far away. Someplace where he won't break into any more buildings."

"It's a *she* squirrel."

I didn't even care to ask how he knew that. "Well . . . *she'd* probably like to live in the woods too."

A quick head shake and then, "She might have a nest around here. I'd hate to think of her kits starving to death, all *alone*. Wouldn't you?"

My conscience wrestled with my desire for a rodent-free building. It was a fairly even match. "Yes . . . I guess I would." Why did I have the feeling I'd be seeing that squirrel again?

Lifting the trap, Mark gave the animal a sympathetic assessment. "What about you? You somebody's mama?"

A long, slow Southern drawl stretched the last word, *mama*, in a way that told me he had one and he loved her a lot. "This is like a scene from the *Squirrel Whisperer*." The words came out sounding flirty, even though I knew that wasn't a good idea.

His little chug of laughter warmed the air even more. "Well, you know, when you get a chance to pay it forward, you should."

Curiosity niggled, making me wonder about the rest of his story. He really did seem like a decent guy, but then again, so did Casey Turner. They had opposite views of what should happen in and around Manteo. In Casey's version, the construction of condo towers taller than the six stories recommended by the city plan made sense. More housing meant cheaper housing, and moving upward rather than outward meant less overall acreage destroyed. *Smaller footprint on the land per resident,* as he put it. Increased housing in the area also created business for stores and restaurants and brought money into the local economy. For a town that had almost died in the seventies as the fishing industry waned, that was important. Given the tough economic aftermath of the hurricanes, the Outer Banks needed growth industries. Last night, *Casey* had warned me to be careful of

Mark. He'd backhandedly hinted at something in Mark's past, but hadn't come right out and said what it was.

Now I found myself trying to guess. What secrets were hiding behind the smiling exterior of the Rip Shack's owner?

He turned to leave, then hesitated a few steps away. "There's a meeting of the folks involved in planning for our version of Seaside House . . . tonight. Thought you might want to come and learn a little more about it." A slow appraisal took in the high ceilings and swept down the long hall. "This is a great space. Not right for retail, but it'd be perfect for the counseling center. We might even be able to rehab a couple rooms and use them as rentals—office space or maybe even tourist lodging. Let the place have its own source of funding, other than donations. Anyway, the meeting this evening might give you a clearer picture. Just casual. My house. Seven o'clock. We'll do a little Old Bay boil in the backyard, eat corn and blue crab, invite some of the incomers who've moved here with deep pockets. They've got an interest in keeping up the quality of life in Manteo too. Bring your stepfather if you want."

"Oh . . . I don't . . . think he'd come." I was completely at a loss for a longer response. Dealing with Mark was easier when he was a jerk. This new softer, kinder, squirrel-handling version worried me. "And I've . . . got so much to do up here."

He looked disappointed, maybe even a little crestfallen. "Well, if you can clear a couple hours, I'm easy to find. The two-story gray Victorian with the ship's-wheel gingerbread in the eaves. Turn by the white house with the blue trim on the way into town, then keep going until you get to the water. You can't miss it. There's a historical marker in the yard. *The Captain's Castle*."

Curiosity reared its stubborn head. Mark lived in a historic house? A place that carried the title *castle*? Maybe I could go check out the party for a little while. . . .

A text chimed on my cell phone, shattering the momentary temptation. One glance at the screen and the muscles in the back of my neck pulled so tight I could've plucked a tune on them. No way Denise would text me during the morning prep work . . . unless there was a problem. This was a food delivery day. She should've been running like crazy right now.

Call me, the message read.

The squirrel got restless, as if even she sensed the tension flooding into the room. Mark flicked a curious look toward my phone. "Well, think about it. I'd love to have you there." His gaze captured mine, intense, compelling, filled with secrets and questions.

A strange fascination skated through me, momentarily overpowering the questions about Denise's text.

"To meet everyone, I mean," he added, as if he thought the extra explanation might be important. Maybe he had a girlfriend . . . or even a wife? That hadn't occurred to me until now.

He started toward the door again. "By the way, Kellie's finally back in town—downstairs in the jewelry shop. If you're looking for information, or planning to sell some of your finds from up here, she'd be a good one to ask. Her shop deals mostly in artisan pieces, but she lists a lot of vintage stuff online. She'll give you honest information, and she might make an offer on some of it."

"Thanks. I appreciate that." I stood staring at the door after he left, waiting until he was well out of earshot before I called Denise.

"We've got a problem." She didn't bother mincing words. "The range hood over the grill needs attention. The fan motor has been smoking and squealing since you left, and *of course* it went nuts exactly when we had an unannounced health inspector visit. The guy wrote us up for it—said if the grill isn't properly vented, we can't run it."

"Oh *no*." We'd been trying to limp along with the old range hood in Tazza 1. Upgrading to a new one was an eight-thousand-dollar investment. "Is it toast?"

"The repair guy was nice enough to come first thing this morning. It looks like with a cleaning and a new motor assembly, we'll get by awhile longer. But it won't be cheap, of course."

Suddenly I was squarely back home, both feet planted in the mushy Michigan spring, my lungs filled with pungent scents of yeast and vinegar and garlic . . . and the lingering odor of smoke. "How much and when?"

"The estimate is twenty-five hundred, total. As soon as I call him, he'll order the motor, FedEx overnight for delivery tomorrow by nine. He'll come install it first thing even though tomorrow's Saturday. We can probably get by without the grill today. We'll just tell everyone it's out of commission for now. If we cook on it, we run the risk of being written up again and shut down."

"Do any of the employees know we got written up?" If Tagg Harper found out about this, it would be one more piece of ammo—a way to spread rumors. Our employees had families to feed, and after the shutdown of the other restaurant, they were understandably nervous.

"They know the range hood had issues, but they don't know we actually got written up."

"Good." *Twenty-five hundred dollars by tomorrow. Twenty-five hundred . . .* "Order the part."

I was already looking down the hall toward the davenport desk.

CHAPTER 11

Kellie separated off the taffrail device, the captain's book, the ruby brooch, and some silverware I'd found during a hurried sweep of the storage room. Pushing those items to one side, she positioned them near the scrimshaw and the ivory necklace. "These, you really need to take down to Hatteras. I have a feeling it'll be worth your trip. Considering that the manifest and the taffrail log are obviously connected to a Benoit ship, I'm guessing that the rest of these are too. The museum would be your best market—not that I wouldn't love to have them to sell, but given that your grandmother was married to one of the Benoit sons, the museum should see them first."

Sweat beaded under my T-shirt. Hatteras was well over an hour's drive south—if there was no traffic. It was almost lunchtime already, and I needed twenty-five hundred dollars by the end of the day. Did it show? Could Kellie tell how desperate I was?

She pointed to the tusk-shaped scrimshaw piece and the bone necklace, now lying on a square of velvet. She'd set them there as carefully as if they were made of china. "Don't sell these two without some *significant* appraisals and research. There are lots of fakes of these out there, so no telling if these are the real thing and if it's possible to determine the identity of the carver, but you can just see a maker's mark down here beneath the woman's dress. That's not unusual, especially if it's authentic. Many of the sailors who crafted these couldn't read and write, so a maker's mark or symbol would be typical."

Her fingernail traced the pattern etched into the rim of the necklace before she turned over the pendant. "See? It's here, too. This was done by the same person as the scrimshaw. Probably made around the same time . . . if it's authentic. Occasionally, items were forged to look like they were by well-known artisans. In the Victorian era, ivory carvings were a moneymaker, and of course reproductions have always been popular for parlor decoration, especially in coastal homes." Turning the pendant over again, she fingered the Maltese cross etched on the front. "I'd love to have it, but I just can't do that to you. I'd rather help you to do what's right with it. If it's real, it's out of my price range. Well out."

I blinked at her, shocked and temporarily speechless. What was her price range? What kind of value were we talking about?

"Thank you, that's . . . I appreciate the honest answer." Kellie's revelation was good news and bad news. I had a range hood to pay for. Now. "What about the other ruby necklace?" I pointed to the one Joel had found in the storeroom, thanks to Ruby-the-dog . . . and the squirrel.

"It's a lovely piece." Grabbing her jeweler's loop, she studied the necklace under magnification. "East Indian. These are natural AAA fine rubies with only a few inclusions. The color and cut are excellent. The adornments around the pendant here are small diamonds and sapphires. Also excellent quality. It's Victorian-era, so if it was given to your grandmother, chances are it was antique at the time. Many of these items came out of newly impoverished European homes after World War I. Anybody who was lucky enough to have money to spend could pick these up for a fraction of their actual value. It's very nice. I won't have any trouble selling it."

"How much is it worth?" I'd never, ever been reduced to something like this. I had worked my way through culinary school without any real difficulty, and after that I'd always made more money than I needed to live on. I hated this. It was humiliating. I felt like a drug addict, pawning stolen treasures from my mother's jewelry box so that I could go after my next fix.

"Today?" A worried look came my way. She was wondering about me, trying to figure out what was behind all the desperation.

"Yes." I shouldn't have even tried dealing with the shopkeepers right here in the building. It would only shore up the conclusion that I was squeezing whatever I could out of the Excelsior before moving on.

Kellie studied the necklace further, while I sweated and fidgeted, embarrassment crawling under my T-shirt on needle-sharp legs.

"I can give you fifteen hundred. That's a top-dollar offer, I promise. Retail on this will probably be about twenty-three, on a good day. That gives me some room to work with."

"I understand." It was all I could do not to collapse onto the counter, my muscles soft with sudden relief. *Over halfway there, thanks to Joel and the squirrel.* "That'll be fine."

"Is a check okay?"

How could I get a check to Denise in less than eighteen hours? "Would it be possible for you to wire it directly to my bank? I can give you the account and routing numbers. You'd really be helping me out." I'd never had to ask people for things, to beg for favors. I'd arranged my entire existence so that I wouldn't need to. "I know that's a lot of trouble. I'm so sorry."

"It's no problem." Resting both palms on the counter, she tipped her head to one side, her eyes narrowing slightly. "Listen, are you in some kind of trouble? Can I help?" Her expression offered both sympathy and acceptance from beneath a trendy crocheted cap in rainbow colors.

The truth was probably a better option than anything she was imagining. "Just a malfunction with the range hood at my restaurant, back home. It'll be expensive to fix. Not in the budget this month, you know? My cousin called me a little while ago."

The worry lines softened on her forehead. "A family business. That's nice. I didn't grow up with any family. Never had one . . . until I found one here in Manteo."

It was clear enough that she wanted to tell me the story. On a normal morning, I would've politely listened, but right now I just wanted to do this embarrassing deal and get out of here. There was still the question of traveling all the way down to Hatteras to get the rest of the money. "That's really nice."

She rested against the counter in a way that let me know the story was coming whether I wanted it or not. "I found out I had cancer right after I moved here. New place. Didn't know a soul, except a few of the other shopkeepers, and I'd only just met them."

Her revelation stung in the tender place that belonged to my mother. Kellie was a cancer survivor. Another woman who'd defeated the beast. "That must've been hard." *No more small talk. Just pay me.* "I'm glad you made it through."

"Your mom was a really sweet woman. She actually knitted

this cap for me during my second round of chemo. I didn't even know she was dealing with a diagnosis herself, until later."

Stop. No more. No more. No more.

Tears needled the underside of the mask I was struggling to keep in place. I swallowed hard. "She loved to knit."

Kellie fingered the thick brown braids hanging from the cap, perhaps reminding herself that the dark days were, for her, long over. "Sorry. I don't know how I got off on that. Yes, I'll wire the money. But please do something for me, okay?"

"Sure."

She lifted the ivory necklace again. "Be *very* careful what happens to this. These are in the news a lot now, especially around here. I can't tell you all the details. I don't watch much TV, and I don't do Internet except to take care of jewelry sales, but the museum will know. Don't take this anywhere but there. I realize that it's a drive down there and you're in a bind, but you need to know who you're dealing with on this one. Trust me."

"Okay."

"In fact, if you're going today, could I ask for a little favor?"

"Of course."

She edged toward a nearby desk, as if she thought I might bolt. "Sandy's Seashell Shop down in Hatteras Village makes all my sea glass jewelry. She's got a box ready, so I can stock up for the season, and I hate shipping that stuff. The cartons are heavy and the pieces are delicate. Benoit House Museum is in Fairhope, so it's not very much farther from there to Sandy's place. If you could swing by her shop and pick up the delivery for me, that'd be awesome. It'd save me fifty bucks in rush shipping too. In fact, I'll tack that onto the price of the necklace."

"Sure. I'd be happy to. But you don't have to add the

shipping cost. I'm going anyway." It felt good to do something for the woman wearing my mother's rainbow hat.

"Awesome." She wrote down the information and handed it to me, along with a business card bearing a photo of a little antique house by the water. *Sandy's Seashell Shop—An Ocean of Possibilities*, the card read. "Grab a chai latte while you're there. Sandy's lattes are like little cups of heaven."

I thanked her, shared my banking information, and we walked out of the shop together, Kellie telling me who to look for at Benoit House Museum. She thanked me again for picking up her shipment at the Seashell Shop, we shook hands, and I hurried upstairs to throw on some clean clothes.

I was in and out in ten minutes.

"I'm going down to Hatteras this afternoon" was all I said to Clyde as I crossed through the living room. "There's a sandwich and fruit in the kitchen."

A grunt answered.

My molars ground against one another. Why did I even bother? Why did I continue to hope that he and I could miraculously come to some sort of cooperative agreement? "There's milk and tea in the refrigerator."

"I ain't blind."

"Fine."

A narrow-eyed look came my way, framed by the clenched chin of a military man accustomed to staring down arrogant young recruits. "Whatever you got up your sleeve, just don't try makin' off with anything from in here and selling it."

"What?"

"I seen you down on the street with the hippie broad that's got the jewelry place. You think I don't know what you're doin'?"

I stood gaping, dumbfounded. Finally, I grabbed my stuff and walked out.

Driving away, I did my best to leave my stepfather and all thoughts of the Excelsior behind. The bright Outer Banks day was simply too beautiful to be spoiled. The bypass lay startlingly deserted again, mile upon mile framed by silent beach houses and tourist-trap stores with only a car or two parked out front. No racks of discount merchandise under the awnings, no knots of women in brightly colored beach dresses strolling by, only an occasional off-season guest bicycling down the sidewalk, enjoying the drowsy shade of live oaks and the bursts of spring color. Here and there, views of the ocean and the sound peeked in from left and right.

I found myself relaxing into the scenery, sinking toward the idea that I was just another escape artist, abandoning the real world for a week in paradise before the crush of vacationers crowded onto the islands. In all our years of visiting, my mother and I had never found time to travel any farther south than Bodie Island Lighthouse. When Mom did have her half days free from the Excelsior, we usually packed a basket and went to Nags Head, where Mom told me the stories of her first trip there with my father. Romantic stories. Wonderful stories.

Stories in which she was secretly wearing Clyde's necklace?

Driving south into unfamiliar territory, it was a relief to leave old scenery and the questions behind.

Near Pea Island preserve, massive dunes trickled onto the road, waiting for the highway department to do sand removal. I marveled at their size, their windblown shapes, their random beauty. Surely in a place like this, nothing mattered but sea and endless sky, the view only occasionally interrupted by a V of pelicans flying by. To my left, the tide roared. To my right, the Pamlico

Sound whispered into quiet expanses of marsh grass. Scenes like these were made to persuade you that your problems are smaller than you think, transient in the grand scheme of things. Sometimes, even when you've spent years ignoring God, there are places where his fingerprint and his intentions seem absolute.

Take a breath, look around, a voice seemed to be whispering. *None of this is here by accident, and neither are you.*

On occasion, when thoughts like this came, when they caught me unaware, I wondered if the seeds my mother had tried to plant in me years ago weren't completely dead after all. She'd wanted so badly for me to understand that my father's decision to end his own life had nothing to do with me and nothing to do with God making it happen. *We make our own choices, Whit,* she'd told me over and over again. *Sometimes we're weak in the moment. We make the wrong choices and it's too late to go back.* More than anything, I wanted to finally take those words to heart, know them as truth. My father had a weak moment . . . a *human* moment. He made a bad choice and he couldn't take it back. End of story.

Maybe this trip was about my finally coming to that understanding. If I let my father's decision dictate the rest of my life, I was only giving that moment endless power.

I'd given it enough already.

I imagined myself casting it into the breeze as the miles drifted by, letting it sail off into the ocean, where God could master it with winds and tides.

The National Seashore finally faded, giving way to the stilt homes and quaint shops of Rodanthe, Avon, Waves, and Salvo. I studied restaurants and stores along the road, idly speculating about real estate costs, rental terms, potential customer traffic, the unpredictability of hurricanes and nor'easters.

By the time I passed through Buxton, I'd almost lost myself in the fantasy that I was here scouting property for a new corporate start-up. I had the surge of adrenaline that came with ditching an old location and moving to a new one. The early stages of launching a restaurant were so chaotic that there wasn't time to think about anything else. I liked that. It was a comfort zone. A haven of busy white noise.

Reality crept in again as the little community of Fairhope appeared ahead, its marina glistening in the sun, boats lounging lazily in the early-season stillness. A small billboard invited passersby to the Benoit House Museum. *Dedicated to the Preservation of Outer Banks Maritime History,* the sign read. *Mansion tours, historical programs, weddings, meetings, and group events by appointment. Tour bus parking available.*

Turning off the highway, I passed the docks and Bink's Village Market, then curved left toward the steeple of a little white church nearly hidden in the trees ahead. A sign pointed tour buses toward the church parking lot and funneled cars into the driveway of a gorgeous Victorian home. Lounging beneath the shade of loblolly pines and live oaks, it seemed almost a part of the landscape. Its ornate gingerbread trim and two tiers of wraparound porches, the tall white turret clad in scalloped shingles and the rooflines pitching at all angles—all evoked the opulence of a bygone era when shipping tycoons amassed vast fortunes.

The parking area in front of a small caretaker's cottage, now marked *Office*, was empty. It wouldn't be for long, apparently. A tour bus was rumbling past, headed for the church.

I hurried into the cottage, where the museum director was giving instructions to a young assistant behind the counter. "The group will be next door checking out the church and watching the Benoit history film for about twenty minutes, then they're coming here. The caterer should show up any minute with the finger-food buffet for the ballroom."

"Ohhh-kay. I think I got it." The twentysomething helper exited the cottage looking frazzled and terrified.

My hopes sank. I'd shown up at a bad time. I wanted to turn around and walk out, but that really wasn't an option. There was the small matter of a commercial range hood repair bill to consider.

How would the museum director feel about my reason for being here? Did people often walk in off the street, looking to sell things?

I tried to appear confident as I offered my hand and introduced myself, but the heat of a blush was working its way up my neck.

Tandi Chastain smiled as if she knew me already. Dressed in slacks and a silk shirt, her dark hair smoothly fastened into a twist, she gave off a businesslike yet relaxed impression.

"Kellie called from up in Manteo and told me you were coming," she revealed. "Are you in a huge rush? If you can hang out a little while, I'll have the time to really sit down and look at what you've got for us."

I would've hugged Kellie-of-the-rainbow-hat if she'd been close enough just then. She'd done the hard work for me. I didn't even have to explain myself. "Oh . . . sure. That sounds fine."

"Sorry about the delay. I know you're in a hurry." Tandi touched my arm sympathetically, and I wondered what else Kellie had told her about me. Did she know I was desperate? "Why don't you go on over and check out the museum for a few minutes while I make sure Lily's got things under control at the church? She's new here, on a mini-mester internship from college. Good kid, but about as green as they come. She loves history, though, and she's got a fascinating research project going, involving what happened to the Lost Colony survivors up on Roanoke, so we're glad to have her."

"Nice place to have an internship—Hatteras Island, I mean . . . and the museum. The house is gorgeous."

"Thank you. We're really proud of it." Snatching a clipboard and keys off the counter, she angled toward the door. "Enjoy. There's a volunteer docent there if you have any questions. If you see the caterer, tell him the food goes to the ballroom—just kidding. The docent knows what's happening. Check out the exhibits. Some of the pieces have been gathered over time, but most of the collection was left behind by a very special lady who lived here almost all her life. She loved the house and the Outer Banks and wanted to see the history preserved for future generations."

Preserved for future generations. By contrast, I was selling off the family heirlooms piece by piece and contemplating ditching the Excelsior so that a condominium tower could take its place. What would Tandi Chastain think of me if she knew? "She must've been someone special."

"Oh, she was." Tandi led me through the cottage door, then closed it behind us. "There's still a lot of her in that house."

CHAPTER 12

In the upstairs turret room, I sensed the legacy of the house's former owner. The room had the feel of a holy place. Beneath the fresco ceiling, blue and ivory paneled walls stretched upward, whispering with framed pages and quotes from writings Iola Anne Poole had left behind. Her words brought to life the Outer Banks and its people. Theirs was a struggle through storms and rebuilding, economic disasters and recoveries, losses and gains, heartbreak and hope. The unpredictable journey of an existence by the sea.

Suddenly it struck me that so many of the things I'd thought of as world-turning and earth-shattering probably weren't. Life is a process of storms and rebuilding, of fires and regrowth, of loss and gain.

Wandering the room, I read Iola's letters, felt them touch so many parts of me.

She lays her tired head on my shoulder and looks through the shell with me, into the great mystery. I think again that heaven must be like this place, and I say that to Isabelle. I wonder, When she is in heaven and I am not, how far away will she be?

"It's just another journey," she whispers. . . .

I thought of my mother, of how desperately I wanted her to be here a little longer, a lot longer, forever. Sometimes it seemed that I should be able to change things, to alter the course of events, just by wanting it badly enough. But I couldn't. Iola's observations said as much.

We, in our humanness, cannot help but foolishly desire eternity in this life.

I was standing in the blue room, contemplating the thought, when Tandi Chastain came to find me. "Well? What do you think of it?" Bracing her hands on her hips, she gave the room a visual sweep.

"The museum? It's impressive." The house itself was a feast for the eyes, the walls framed with elaborate gold-leafed cornices, the ceilings adorned with clouds and angels, the leaded-glass windows filling the rooms with tiny rainbows.

Taking a long breath, Tandi looked around the room. "There's so much history here. It's a shame for visitors to come and go from the Outer Banks and not learn about it. The past shouldn't be lost."

I had a feeling that last part was for me—that Kellie had briefed her on the shopkeepers' concern about the Excelsior and its contents. But instead of thinking about the building, I thought of Alice, of her journey with the Federal Writers' Project. Perhaps her story shouldn't be lost either. Maybe it had as much power as the one preserved within these walls.

"Let's go over to the office and see what you've brought." Tandi ushered me toward the stairs. Below, a few visitors had already begun wandering over from the church. She waved at the guests as we crossed the lawn, the two of us making pleasant chitchat about the differences between life on Hatteras and farther north on Roanoke.

"The museum gave us tickets to the Lost Colony drama up there last year," Tandi offered. "Paul and the kids thought the amphitheater was a neat experience. The show was spectacular, especially with the water in the background. It was good information as well. We have a bit of the Lost Colony mystery here, too."

The intern interrupted before Tandi could fill me in on the rest. Catching us in front of the cottage, she cast a wild-eyed look at her boss. "Okay, I finally got everyone outta the church. Sorry I didn't make it over before they showed up at the house. It's like herdin' barn cats. They don't all go the same place at the same time."

Tandi laughed. "Take a breath, Lily. It'll be okay. You don't have to be everywhere at once. There's a docent inside and the caterer's there. They both know the drill."

The intern fanned her flushed cheeks. "They kept askin' me questions. I thought I'd studied a *lot* to get ready to work here, but I'm gonna have to study some more."

Tandi looked pleased. "The questions mean you had them interested. Just wait until they get upstairs to the Benoit brothers' papers."

Lily's face brightened. "*That* I do know somethin' about."

"True. Now, you just keep that thought in mind and wow them with your expertise on the brothers' exploits and all things Lost Colony."

"Well . . . I'm not *really* an expert." Lily blushed.

"You're the closest thing we've got. Go entertain the folks with tales of expeditions, archaeological digs, arrowheads, and of course the signet ring that was found here on Hatteras. Oh, and don't forget the scrimshaw necklaces and the boat in the Great Dismal Swamp. That can't help but fire up some fascination . . . and fascination does . . . what?"

"Brings in the money." Lily giggled, then turned and started toward the house.

Tandi watched her leave. "I love these college kids. Without them, we'd have a tough time affording all the staff we need around here. Lily has read literally everything there is on Sir Walter Raleigh's Lost Colony. She has a particular interest in it—long story—but when we were renovating the mansion, we found an old metal box full of arrowheads, pipes, and other artifacts. There were also bits of what seem to be the wood and hand-wrought metal from a boat, and a woman's carved ivory hair comb of the right period to have been Lost Colony. That's part of the research project Lily and our other interns will be working on this summer. We think it's possible that the Benoit family history may hold some clues to the mystery of what happened to the Lost Colonists after they vanished from Roanoke Island."

"Really?" Having spent so many summers in Manteo, where everyone had a theory about what had become of the colonists, I couldn't help but catch a bit of Tandi's enthusiasm. I'd never heard that my ancestors had some connection to it, but then I knew so little of the Benoit family history. Grandmother Ziltha didn't like to talk about it.

"This house originally belonged to Girard Benoit, who'd made a fortune in shipping. His sons grew up summering here and developed a fascination for shipwrecks and other historical sites. As young men, Stephen and Benjamin were famous for spending extravagant amounts of money while chasing after Blackbeard's cache and Lost Colony relics, but they kept the locations of their explorations secret. We know they dug around here, and that they journeyed up the Great Dismal Swamp in Virginia. Unfortunately, we don't know exactly *where* they found the items they uncovered. All we have are notations from Benjamin Benoit's personal journals, and he was more of a romantic than a scientist."

"I always thought Benjamin was primarily a ship's captain." My mind was whirling, calling up lines from Alice's letters—mentions of Ziltha's dashing husband. My grandfather was a treasure hunter? He grew up here, in this house?

Tandi gave me a meaningful look. "When Kellie called to tell me you were bringing some things from the Excelsior building, I was hoping you might have a few pieces to our puzzle. If we can find *anything* that further documents the Benoit brothers' expeditions, we want it. We actually discovered some love letters in the wall of the caretaker's cottage here when we redid the plumbing. Stephen Benoit had a secret romance with a Creole servant named Esther. When the Benoit brothers went on expeditions, she traveled along as a cook, and it looks like there was something of a love triangle involving the beautiful Esther. Eventually, the family sent Stephen to sea and arranged a respectable marriage for Benjamin, in hopes of squelching the scandal. The Excelsior Hotel was purchased as a wedding gift, to settle the new couple into happy matrimony. In reality, though, Benjamin's wandering ways continued. He spent more time in the field and at sea than he did at home with his wife. Esther was only one of several women he strayed with before he drowned at Diamond Shoals."

I realized we'd stopped on the porch, and I was just standing there staring at Tandi, my thoughts rushing through a wild web of connections. *The family arranged a respectable marriage . . .* "My grandmother Ziltha was Benjamin Benoit's wife."

Tandi blinked. "Your *grandmother* was Ziltha Benoit? I figured you were farther down the line somewhere."

"I was a Benoit before I married. My dad was Ziltha and Benjamin's only child, Arthur Christian Benoit, but he was in his forties when I was born, so my grandmother was old, from the time I can remember. She resented the Benoits, and all I really knew was that there was some kind of long-standing family feud. She and my father had been disinherited sometime after my grandfather's death." Benjamin Benoit had mistresses? *Multiple* mistresses? Was my grandmother aware of that?

The Ziltha I remembered—stoic, sour-faced, aloof, critical—underwent a rapid metamorphosis in my mind: starry-eyed young girl, heartbroken wife, devastated mother-to-be, lonely widow forced to raise her son alone. Old, long before her time. "Let me go . . . get the box out of my car. I don't know if any of it will help answer questions, but now I'm definitely curious." I left the porch, my thoughts suddenly crowded with the hidden details of my grandmother's life.

Clearly Alice hadn't even begun to understand her sister's situation. She'd spoken of the marriage with romantic fascination, as if Ziltha were living a fairy tale, married to a dashing sea captain many a young woman would have swooned over.

Could it be that Alice had abandoned Ziltha just when Ziltha's life was spiraling out of control, when she needed someone the most? Was that why Alice's letters had been discarded unread, why I'd never known that my grandmother had a twin sister? Was destroying the letters a form of retribution . . . or a desperate attempt to survive the painful disappointments in her life? Suddenly I could relate to her in a way I never had before. I knew what it was to have a husband cheat and lie, to have a marriage fall apart, to discover that the future you'd imagined wasn't the future you would get.

Taking the box from my car, I stopped, looked at that opulent white house my grandmother might have visited as a young bride. The house my father might have inherited, had circumstances been different. How would they feel about my coming here, inadvertently releasing skeletons from the family closet?

Tandi was waiting at the counter in the front room of the cottage when I entered. She gave the box a look of anticipation.

"So, let's see what you've got here." She put on a pair of thin gloves, and I thought about how carelessly I'd handled my finds. She'd probably be shocked if she knew. Once again, I felt like a down-and-out Vegas gambler, stumbling into a pawnshop after a night of drawing unlucky cards.

Tandi focused on the box. "I appreciate you bringing these things for us to look at first. So often, stuff ends up on eBay and from there it goes into private collections, and we never have a chance." The top sheet of paper clung to the side of the box, seeming to resist the pull as she lifted it. "Now, I won't be able to talk prices with you today, other than to tell you if we might be interested and maybe give you a rough estimate, depending on the item. Everything here has to be verified by historical experts, and I'm *not* one. Those approvals can take a little while. I hope Kellie explained that."

A brick clinked against my ribs and landed in my stomach. "Oh . . . how . . . well, how long might that be?"

Gingerly, she took out the ship's manifest and opened it. "A couple days, maybe a week, depending on the item and who we have to call in for authentication. Of course, that's only if it's something the museum can use, and quite frankly, if we can come up with the budget for it. We're funded by historical grants, private donations, and event rentals."

"I see." What if this trip to Hatteras was a total strikeout? On top of the range hood issue, payroll was due and so was my rent.

"Oh, this is nice." Tandi unearthed the taffrail device and dangled it by the cord. "They used these to calculate how fast the ships were moving, back in the day. This one is especially ornate, with the scrollwork . . . and yes, that's the Benoit crest. Chances are, this belonged to one of Benjamin Benoit's ancestors and was given to him. We'll see if we can match it to any of our existing documentation from the shipping company. Anyway, it's beautiful. We've paid as much as three thousand dollars for similar artifacts, and given that these have a Benoit history, we might get clearance to go a bit higher. Where did you find them, exactly?"

"In an old davenport desk in the Excelsior building. I was always told that the desk had belonged to Benjamin."

"Wonderful. That helps establish the chain of ownership. I'll need you to write down what you know about the items. You can e-mail it to me later."

"Okay. Sure." But the *later* part had me concerned. While the dollar figure sounded like a gift, the process here would obviously be lengthy.

"We might be interested in the davenport, as well." Tandi was already moving back to the box. She drew out the ruby brooch, unwrapped it. "Oh, look at this. This is beautiful! And it's made in the form of the Benoit crest. This is definitely a family piece. Possibly a wedding gift to your grandmother. We have photos of the wedding, but they are in storage right now. The ceremony happened right here on the property and was quite the grand affair. Reports on the bridal showers and whatnot made the newspapers as far away as Richmond and Charleston. It's possible that we'll find this brooch in one of the photos. It's older than that, though. I'm not an expert, but just comparing it to some other things in our collection, I'd guess that it might be early eighteenth century. It was most likely something that had been in the Benoit family before their emigration from Europe in 1736. I have no idea of the value, I'm sorry. But I know we'd be interested in it for the museum."

"That's good." Once again, it was and it *wasn't*. If these items were that old, their price alone might buy Bella Tazza's way out of impending disaster and allow us to continue the fight against Tagg Harper. There was nothing in the world I wanted more than that.

Except . . . range hood money. Today.

So far, that wasn't looking promising. "There are a couple more things down in the bottom of the box. Could you look at those?" Based on Kellie's reaction in Manteo, I had a feeling the answer on the carved pieces would be much the same—*Probably valuable, but wait and see. No money today.*

Was there still time for me to make it all the way back to Roanoke, tear the storeroom and the salon apart, and see if I could find anything else to quickly sell off? Maybe I needed to break down and have the antique store owner come look at what was left of the furniture on the second floor . . . including the davenport desk.

The idea left me hot and nauseated. I wanted to *keep* the desk, to retain that small connection to my father's history.

Tandi lifted a stained hotel towel from the bottom of the box, set it on the counter and opened it carefully, then hitched a breath. "Oh. Oh my word! These are incredible." Grabbing a magnifying glass from the drawer, she leaned over the necklace. "We're working on a special exhibit. . . . We've been given a small grant for it. There's been a lot of interest in these necklaces over the past year, and since we found one among the Benoit brothers' hidden treasure trove, we're diving into the mystery of whether these are related to the Lost Colony survivors. I'll have to send this and the scrimshaw to the University of North Carolina to have them looked at."

Her brows rose hopefully as she set aside the glass and turned back to me. "If you're willing to leave them with us, we'll keep them secure and handle them carefully, I promise. We haven't even seen anything as large as this scrimshaw piece, so that makes me wonder about authenticity . . . well . . . that and the condition. For sixteenth-century items, these seem in awfully good shape."

"I don't think these *could* be fake, or at least not recently made, anyway. Someone must have put them in Benjamin Benoit's davenport desk over twenty years ago . . . before my grandmother died."

Carefully picking up the necklace, she studied the center pendant. "Please don't take it as my doubting your story, but we have to verify *everything*. Our funds are so limited, we can't afford to make mistakes." Pulling off one glove, she pinched a small brass peg between her fingernails, carefully wiggled it loose, and opened the back of the pendant, revealing carvings inside. "This one is amazing. We've only seen one other that has the relief carvings of Mary and Jesus inside—one other *authentic* piece, I mean. These increase the necklace's value *if* it's real, but they also make it more suspect. Fakes, especially the fancy ones, are hot items in the tourist stores around here."

The door burst open, zinging inward so fast that it struck the wall and bounced back. Lily skidded into the room, looking red-faced and panicked. "Mr. Muggins sneaked into the house and got in the food! The caterer's cussin' a blue streak. The people are still upstairs, but I don't know where Mr. Muggins went."

"Oh *no*." Tandi closed the pendant and pushed the holding pin into place. Her attention shot from the jewelry to Lily to the door. "That stupid cat. One of these days, he is going to find himself on a slow boat to . . . someplace else." Bracing her hands on the counter, she took a breath. "Okay . . . all right . . . Lily, go back in the house and try to talk the caterer off the ledge. See if he knows for *sure* which platters of food the cat got to. If there's no way to tell, we'll have to remove it all. He won't have time to go back up to Rodanthe for more food. I'll call Sandy's Seashell Shop and Boathouse Barbecue and see if they can help."

"Yes, ma'am. I got this. I'm gone." The intern spun around and dashed out the door, her footsteps clattering across the porch.

"I really hope you're all right with leaving these here with us?" Tandi reached for her cell phone. "I'll put them in the safe, I promise. As soon as I'm able to get assessments on them, I'll let you know. Most of this, we can probably have wrapped up by early next week. On the carved pieces, it could take longer. Those are more complicated."

I vacillated between doing the right thing—agreeing to her terms—and doing the desperate thing. If the museum was this interested, other people probably would be too. "Okay. Yes, that's fine."

"Thank you. You had me worried for a minute there." Carefully, she began wrapping the pieces and placing them back in the box. "I'm so sorry you caught us on a crazy day. I'd love to talk with you more about your grandmother and what else is in the Excelsior building. Maybe we can do that next week."

Grabbing a business card from my purse, I laid it on the counter. The picture of Bella Tazza underlying the text was a quick and stark reminder of the real purpose of my visit here. "My cell number and e-mail are on there. Can you call or message me as soon as you know anything? I have some ongoing business issues in Michigan, and I'm just not sure—" *how I'm going to pay the massive bill that's due tomorrow*—"how long I'll be here on the Outer Banks. I need to wrap things up quickly."

"Absolutely." Tandi whisked away down the hall, the box of my grandmother's treasures in hand. "If you'll trust me to send you an acknowledgement of receipt on these items a little later, I'd really appreciate it. I'll text it to your cell."

I agreed, and we were out the door in a few short minutes, Tandi locking the cottage behind us. I didn't bother asking her how far it was to Sandy's Seashell Shop. I figured I could find it easily enough. Hatteras only had one road in and out. The store couldn't be too well hidden.

I dialed Denise's number on my way down the island, the prospect of the phone call spoiling the view of sleepy soundside harbors, craggy live oaks with hanging curtains of Spanish moss, salt-weathered homes dozing in the sun, and fish markets with colorful stacks of crab traps, kayaks, and inner tubes piled out front.

The scenery should have been a nice diversion, but as soon as I heard Denise's voice, the beauty was overshadowed by the reality of what I had to do next. I started out with, "How's the afternoon looking?"

"A little slow. I think we'll end up slightly below average today." That wasn't good news. I'd been hoping for a phenomenal report—one that would yield about a thousand dollars that could be used to pay the rest of tomorrow's repair bill. "We can't do steaks with the range hood like it is, so the grill is down, of course. Most of the customers are being good about it, but you know, there are always those few stinkers. Had a guy think we should give him a discount or a free meal for his trouble. Seriously. People sometimes!" I could almost see Denise's blonde bangs poofing upward as she huffed. "It's like dealing with third graders again. Anyway, so fifteen hundred showed up in the bank account. What are we doing for the rest of it? How's the cash hunt going?" She was trying to sound laid-back, but her edginess was unmistakable. She needed good news from me.

I didn't have it.

"On the upside, the museum is seriously interested in the rest of the stuff from the desk, and it sounds like we could come out with enough to catch up on the bills and float Bella Tazza 2 until our hearing. That'd make Tagg Harper shake in his loafers, wouldn't it?" Just the mental image was delicious. I savored it a moment before dropping the bomb. "But . . . on the downside . . . the museum has to authenticate everything, and that takes time. Several days, maybe a week. It doesn't help that today is Friday."

Denise groaned. "I'm sorry, Whit. I know you're doing the best you can. Maybe I can talk to a couple of the girls . . . see if they'll wait a few days for payroll."

The air in the car thinned, losing oxygen. I rolled down the window. The breeze was cool, perfect, scented with sand and salt and sun, but it burned my throat. "*No.* Denise. They're already sacrificing enough." Somehow we had to solve this problem without making things any harder on our employees. "Listen,

I want you to go to my cabin. I'll call Mrs. Doyne and tell her to let you in. I need to talk to her about the rent, anyway. On the dresser by my bed there's a little heart-shaped trinket box. There's a ring in there. A white-gold diamond solitaire. Take it and do what you need to with it." I swallowed hard, biting back emotion. Maybe Denise wouldn't remember where the little solitaire had come from.

But I heard it in her horrified gasp. She knew. "No, Whit, that was your mother's *engagement* ring. You are *not* selling that. I'll figure something out."

"Mom wouldn't care. You know she hardly ever wore her jewelry." Now I couldn't help wondering if the ring my father gave her meant anything to her at all. Perhaps when they'd made hasty promises to one another, she was still dreaming of Clyde. Maybe that was why she'd never worn my father's ring after he was gone, yet she'd continued to wear Clyde's cross.

"I am *not* selling that ring." Denise's answer was the steely rebuke of a girlfriend trying to save you from yourself. "If *you* want to sell it when you get home, fine. I'll find another way for now."

"Just go get it. Do *not* ask the employees to wait for payroll. The ring is just a hunk of rock and metal. A *thing*. People come first." If Denise didn't sell the solitaire, I knew whose pay she'd hold out first. Her own. She or Mattie or Grandma Daisy would go without something that was needed while a diamond ring sat by my bedside.

Stubborn silence held the other end of the phone, which was typical of our arguments. Wherever she was right now, Denise was standing with her head tipped upward and her pointy little chin in the air.

"Promise me you'll take care of it." I'd never been good at

playing the silent game. Denise was a master. "Denise? Denise, cut it out, okay? I need to go. I just pulled into Sandy's Seashell Shop. I'm supposed to pick up some things for the woman in the jewelry store at the Excelsior."

"I'm *not* selling the ring." Her singsong voice made my teeth grind.

"Yes, you are."

"No, I'm not."

"Are too."

"Not happening, and you can't make me." She hung up, leaving me to growl into a dead phone.

CHAPTER 13

The Outer Banks had a magical ability to be a place apart, a haven where other problems couldn't reach. The women of Sandy's Seashell Shop seemed to understand that allure. While they were getting Kellie's box ready to go, they gave me a chai latte on the house and invited me to browse the merchandise or sit on the deck and enjoy the view of Pamlico Sound. Lulled by the effects of the chai, I could almost put the day's strange events out of my mind.

"So, Kellie says you're from Michigan." A fan of wrinkles creased Sandy's round cheeks as she finger-brushed spiky salt-and-pepper blonde hair. Her remark came with a curious look that said either Kellie or Tandi had talked to her about me. Sandy seemed particularly interested in figuring me out.

"Yes, I am. Not too far from the Upper Peninsula."

"That's a pretty area. I'm from Bay City, myself. Came down here twenty years ago on an empty-nest vacation. My husband and I saw this little house for sale, and we fell in love and decided to turn it into a seashell shop. Been here ever since. Sometimes your heart just takes a turn and the next thing you know, you're headed in a whole new direction."

"That's nice." I did my best to make innocuous conversation. But Sandy was clearly the type to work her way into other people's business. Here in her shop, she not only spun out a great cup of chai but created beautiful stained-glass art and spent time chatting with whoever came through the door. I liked her immediately, but I could also tell that an assessment was under way. She'd probably be reporting back to Kellie as soon as I was gone. Was there no place on the Outer Banks where the local info network didn't reach?

Despite the soothing atmosphere of the building, with its well-loved sofas, old lamps, and wall art bearing phrases like *Sand castles or seashells? That is the question* and *Sandy feet always welcome*, I couldn't get out of there fast enough. As soon as the box was ready, so was I.

Driving Highway 12 up Hatteras Island, I felt the whispers about me traveling along, trailing me all the way back to Roanoke Island as the shadows grew long, the sun slowly leaning toward the sound, the dunes casting shade over the road. I turned on the radio and cranked it up loud to block out the gossip, real or imagined.

A six o'clock news brief interrupted the music as I turned toward Manteo. The gathering at Mark's place would be happening soon, the party-slash-planning-meeting getting started in a little over half an hour. . . .

I pictured him in the backyard, his bare feet deep in the lush grass by the shore as he stoked an outdoor kettle, preparing for a New England boil. I had the strangest urge to turn off the road, go by and see what these people were all about. What if they really *could* come up with the funds to take over the second floor of the Excelsior, start a charity, do renovations, pay rent? Should I write them off so quickly, just because I was in a hurry to solve my own problems?

Something I couldn't explain drew me toward the idea. What difference would it have made in my life, if I'd had a place to go when I was a teenager—somewhere I felt accepted and understood? The question seemed to come from both outside and inside all at once. It came from the person I wanted to be—someone who tried to do the best thing for the most people.

Passing the turn to Mark's house, I glanced in the mirror and confirmed that, after working all morning and driving all afternoon with the windows down, I was a wreck. Aside from that, I hadn't checked on Clyde in hours, and Ruby undoubtedly needed a walk. I could go by the Excelsior, take care of things there, clean up, and then . . . see if the urge to go to Mark's party was just a passing thing.

Maybe I'd get over it.

But the idea of seeing where he lived, of untangling the seemingly unrelated threads of who he was, held an undeniable fascination. Why would an athletic, good-looking, fortysomething guy who still owned at least part of a business on the mainland and was obviously making a lot of money, suddenly decide to cash it in and move to the Outer Banks to open a surf shop?

Business failure? Divorce? Premature midlife crisis?

The lure of a girlfriend, maybe? Did he live alone in the Captain's Castle? He'd referred to it as *my house*, not *our house*. Hadn't he?

I'd made up my mind by the time I hit downtown Manteo. I was definitely going to the party. *It's research,* I told myself. *If the things you took to the museum are as valuable as Tandi indicated, any number of possibilities might open up for the future of the Excelsior. You need to be looking at the potential options.*

But I felt a little like a high school girl with an unexpected invitation to the prom—sort of giddy and strange. What did I have in my suitcase that would look good for a waterside yard party? Nothing, but at least I'd finally done my laundry.

Should I take food to the party or arrive empty-handed? I hadn't asked whether the guests were bringing anything.

I had ham and cream cheese in the kitchen. I could whip up ham rolls and throw together a platter. I'd bought a bag of spinach at the grocery store. It would do as a garnish. I could leave ham rolls and a salad for Clyde. He wouldn't thank me for it, but it would be gone when I came home.

The idea was just starting to jell, to seem like an interesting possibility, when I rounded the building to park in the alley and my little fantasy blew away like smoke. A gold BMW convertible sat along the curb on the side street, and I knew instantly whose it was.

I had the urge to drive right on by, which didn't make sense, really. Casey and I had shared a nice dinner and a pleasant chat last night. We had a lot in common. He hadn't been pushy, businesswise or romantically. At the end of the evening, he'd held my hands in his and given me a chaste kiss on the cheek, with a warm smile afterward and a look that said he'd like to do more. He probably wouldn't be nearly as friendly tonight, if he found out I was contemplating going to a party at Mark's house.

I circled the block and sat in the alley parking space a moment before getting out and walking around the corner.

Oddly, the stairwell door was hanging open a smidge, swaying slightly in the breeze. I'd locked it before leaving. The store owners had keys so they could get to the industrial vacuums, floor polishers, and extension poles for changing lightbulbs, all of which were kept in the porter's closet Old Dutch had used for luggage.

Casey Turner wouldn't have a key to the stairwell door. How had he gotten in, and why was he here?

I heard him on the stairway as I moved closer. He was whistling as he came out the door. When he spotted me, his smile was quick, friendly, and familiar. Genuine. Not guilty of anything. "Well, just the woman I was looking for. It's not every day a girl bolts to get out of a dinner date." The words ended in an expectant pause, as if he were waiting for an explanation of where I'd been today and what I'd been doing.

"Dinner?" I didn't have to pretend to be confused. I was.

"Sure. We talked about it last night. Don't you remember? Fisherman's Wharf? The docks? You said you'd never been down to Wanchese."

"Ohhhh." I did vaguely recall that part of the conversation, but we hadn't made firm plans for tonight . . . had we? "I'm really sorry. Today got crazy and I had to drive down to Hatteras."

His reaction told me nothing. It was merely pleasant. "Shopping?" He motioned to the Sandy's Seashell Shop cup in my hand.

"A little. Sandy's makes a good chai latte."

"Love the place. Great little store. Great people." Why was I not surprised he knew of it? "Gave one of their stained-glass prayer boxes to my mom last year for Mother's Day. Now I'm a hero around our church. Never would've thought of the idea if it hadn't been for Sandy and her crew."

Hmmm . . . So, Casey shopped for his mama and spent time around a church? Nothing I'd learned about him fit the depraved image Mark had tried to convey. "It sounds like you're a good son."

"If mama ain't happy, nobody's happy," he joked, then paused to cast a narrow glance at a group of tweenaged townies zipping by on bicycles. "At least *my* mother didn't let me wander all over the place unsupervised." He turned back to me, smiling again. "So . . . anyway, here you are and here I am." A blondish-brown eyebrow lifted hopefully. "Dinner? There's still time to drive down to Wanchese."

I thought about ham rolls, Mark's party, Clyde and the dog. And condo buildings.

Then I thought about my desperate, awkward, silent pleas throughout the day. Maybe Casey showing up just when I was about to go over to Mark's party was an answer. Could Casey's interest in the Excelsior, and his ability to provide a retirement housing solution for Clyde, have been the answer all along?

Clyde would be so much better off in a place where he could get the help he needed and have some interaction with other people. "Is there a rule about pets at the Shores?" I blurted, and then realized I was talking from the conversation in my head, not answering Casey's question about dinner. "Sorry. I was thinking maybe we could drive over and see the retirement village after dinner—if you've got time, I mean. It just crossed my mind that if Clyde thought he could keep the dog, he might be more likely to consider the Shores as an option. Ruby is such a sweetheart and surprisingly devoted to Clyde. She deserves a good home. At her age she probably wouldn't have much luck getting adopted from an animal shelter."

Casey smiled approvingly. "Sounds like you've been thinking it through. I'm glad." A sympathetic look followed, and for the first time I felt like someone understood—really understood—the struggle here. Designing and operating senior communities, Casey had probably seen generational push-pull in all its gritty forms, especially in this new age of fractured families. "Pets are no problem in the assisted-living apartments. Residents can even book pet services as à la carte items on their monthly plan. We've thought of everything." His eye traveled the exterior of the Excelsior, the look both expert and calculating, as if he were measuring the square footage of the footprint, just by giving it a quick scan.

Or picturing something else in its place.

Which bothered me in a way I couldn't quantify.

Stop, I told myself. *Stop looking a gift horse in the mouth. This could fix everything, even the issue with the dog.*

"And don't worry about Ruby." Casey was still taking in the Excelsior, his head tipped back. "We'll find a place for her, I promise."

His kindness poured over me like warm water. I felt myself falling into it, falling into *him*. Not many guys on his level would devote time to worrying about what happened to sea turtles and stray dogs.

"Thanks." A thin, choked sound hampered the word and I cleared my throat to hide it. This day had wrung me inside out and suddenly I was feeling it.

"So . . . yes to dinner . . . if you're not in a rush, that is." No matter where I was going this evening, I needed to change clothes and take care of things upstairs. "And a restaurant on the water sounds nice, but I have to get the dog out for a quick walk and make sure Clyde has something to eat for supper. Otherwise he just sits in his chair and broods."

A dark, heavy feeling fell over me, as welcome as a lead cloak on a summer day. It was the same feeling I always had when I entered the residence upstairs. The combination of Clyde, my mother's belongings, and the pileup of unanswered questions was like a gut punch.

Casey craned away. "Whitney, there's no one home up there. I just knocked. Nobody answered and all the lights were off."

"The door at the top of the stairwell was unlocked too?" It couldn't possibly be . . . unless Clyde had gone through it. Even the shopkeepers didn't have keys to the upstairs doors, and I'd locked both when I left. "The dog didn't bark?" Ruby always barked . . . even when *I* came to the front door, she barked.

"Not a sound."

I turned, looked toward the park, then up and down the street. Where would Clyde *go*? Had someone come to pick him up? Maybe he'd had another episode and called 911? Would the first responders have left the doors unlocked? Could they have taken the dog because no one was there to look after her?

Surely Clyde would've given them my number . . . if he were able to talk.

Maybe he fell and hit his head . . . but then where's the dog?

Clyde wouldn't have . . . done something to himself . . . would he?

I turned and ran for the stairs, vaguely conscious of Casey calling, "Whitney? Whitney, what's wrong?" I'd made it up the first flight before I heard Casey pounding along behind me, climbing the steps two at a time. He overtook me at the front door as I fumbled through keys, trying to sort out the right one.

"Here." He took them from my hand. "Which key is it?"

"The gold one . . . with the . . . cutouts in the top."

He unlocked the dead bolt, pushed the door open, and I hurried past him, flipping on the lights, chasing away the shadows of the evening. I checked bedrooms, bathrooms, and even the larger closets as Casey waited in the living room. No sign of

Clyde or Ruby. Where could they have gone? I reached for my cell, stood staring at it for a moment. Who could I call? Maybe Joel and his social-worker girlfriend? Would she know if Clyde was back in the hospital?

I dialed Joel's number, caught him at someplace chaotic and loud. A party maybe.

"Whitney? Hey, I'm in . . . minute . . ."

The background noise quieted, but Joel seemed only partially tuned in as I rushed through the explanation. His answer came in slow motion. "Dude . . . whoa . . . that's totally off the chain. I dunno . . . I could, like . . . help you . . . help you look or somethin'. . . ."

Casey touched my shoulder, drawing my attention to the table between Clyde's recliner and my mother's. The light on the answering machine was blinking.

"Hey, Joel? Joel?" The background noise had intensified again. "Joel, listen. I'm going to check the answering machine here, and I'll call you back if I need help looking."

Casey was already taking charge, pressing the button before I could get there. A woman's voice came on, the message sharp with a Jersey accent. "Hi. I hope I'm calling the right place. I don't want to cause any issues, but there's an old guy here sitting on the bench near our boat, and he seems a little . . . out of it. He's been there a couple hours, and when he gets up, he's not too steady. I'm afraid he'll end up in the water. We asked if he needed anything or if we could call somebody, but he wasn't interested. I think he should have some help. I checked at the restaurant on the corner, and they gave me this number. You might want to come get him. Even the dog looks worried. She keeps getting between him and the water."

A similar message followed a couple hours later. The woman

had again asked Clyde if she could provide help, food, or a glass of water. He'd told her to leave him alone; it was public property.

I snatched one of his jackets from the hall tree. "What in the world is he *doing* out there? What's he trying to prove?" Was this Clyde's newest weapon in the war? His latest way of making things so unpleasant, I'd finally leave?

Casey grabbed my arm, not hard but just enough to stop me. "Whitney, calm down a second. Listen to me. I'm going to give you a little advice, and it might not be something you want to hear, but it could be important."

"In a minute, okay? I'd better go get him before someone calls the police." The last thing I needed was a public scene between Clyde and me. Word would get around.

"It might be best if someone *did* call the police; that's my point." Casey's voice was calm, gentle, but matter-of-fact. "Someone *other* than you."

"What?" I gaped, confused. "Why would I *want* someone to drag the police into this?"

"A conservatorship." The word sank in slowly. He allowed it to marinate a moment. "It'd be easier to seek a conservatorship of your stepfather if his sons were willing to participate, but even if they won't, you could still begin the process. To do that, you'll need proof that he's incompetent—a danger to himself or to others." Casey pointed to the phone. "Save those answering machine messages; they could be useful later. Let me call the police to come and do a welfare check down at the dock. If Clyde won't cooperate with returning home or he decides to get violent, they may go ahead and remove him to the hospital immediately and institute a temporary psychiatric hold."

The suggestion hit me with mind-numbing force. How would my mother, tenderhearted teacher and rescuer of lost cats, the woman who'd worn Clyde's necklace her entire life, feel about that? I knew before even asking myself the question. "Casey, I can't."

His grip held me where I was. "You may end up very sorry you missed this opportunity."

"I just *can't*. It's . . . I can't do that."

"I'm not saying you necessarily have to make the decision right now, either." His hand shifted to rest reassuringly on my shoulder as he leaned over the answering machine to save the messages. "Just that, even if you're not sure yet, you'd be wise to begin preserving the evidence. Whitney, you have to remember, if you go the conservatorship route, you're doing what is in his best interest. If he were thinking straight, he wouldn't be tottering around by the water, in danger of falling in. People can be too stubborn for their own good."

"He is *that*." I looked at the recliners side by side, my mother's pink slippers and one of her sewing baskets still resting between them.

Still, I couldn't fathom doing what Casey suggested. Obviously, he'd seen this kind of situation before and knew the ins and outs of it—but I didn't want to force Clyde *or* become his legal guardian. I wanted him to come to his senses and realize that he *needed* to leave.

"Let's just go get him off the dock. I'll think about the rest of it later. Thanks for saving the messages." I turned and started toward the door, Casey following behind. A breath hissed through his teeth, indicating that he thought I'd end up regretting this.

CHAPTER 14

. . . and happy to say that, due to our delay of two additional days at Merry Walker's home (caused by the weather), I was able to complete my first field report and send the packet by mail to the FWP office. After a rocky start on The Project, I am far ahead of my quota. In the packet were several interviews conducted on Nurse Walker's back porch, including Bass Carter's recollection of living as a slave. Also in the envelope were several stories from the midwives, along with Mrs. Walker's own account of her work in the Blue Ridge. She detailed so eloquently the delicate balance that must be practiced when challenging age-old mountain superstitions with modern scientific knowledge and current medical practice. I wish you could have heard her!

To say that my submission packet was filled would be a grave understatement. We had, indeed, stuffed it to the gills, requiring almost none of the newspaper filler Mrs. Walker provided us. She receives the Charlotte Observer by mail, so as to keep abreast of happenings in the old homeplace. I inquired of her, as we sat watching the last of the sun disappearing over the mountains, if she was not lonely for the daily routines and friendships she knew back home.

Her response was a bit of well-spoken advice that I cannot help but share with you, Ruby. "The most important skill in life is to learn the acceptance of that which you have not planned for yourself. Discontent, if watered even the slightest bit, spreads like choke weed. It will smother the garden if you let it," advised Mrs. Merry Walker. "We must always continue to grow beautiful and useful things. My father named me Merry, I do believe in the hope that I would be a happy person. He often quoted these lines to us from a poem he loved: 'Whenever the way be filled with doubt, look up and up, and out and out. . . .'"

The rest of the letter was water-spotted, rippled, and missing some of its pieces. The ink ran in streams and splotches, the mutilated pages stuck to each other, so that only some of the text was readable. I pried the scraps apart, trying to piece together more of Alice's journey.

. . . concern over our plan to seek out the Melungeons and attempt to gain their favor, so as to document their stories.

"I don't mind telling you that the nurses have had no luck with those people," Mrs. Walker warned. "They've long tended to marry among themselves and keep to themselves . . . unless they've chosen to move off somewhere and try to 'pass,' which many of their young people do if they're pale-skinned enough to get by with it."

"Oh, I see" was all I could dream to say. Certainly "passing" is no small thing, as we are all aware of the laws

against it, both written and unwritten. Mrs. Walker cited a push in Virginia to qualify all persons as either colored or white, the "white" designation being only for those with no proven native, Negro, Mediterranean, Oriental, or mixed blood of any sort. The Melungeons and many others are quite concerned about this, of course. Mrs. Walker's opinion of such a thing was as difficult to discern as, quite frankly, my own. In the past, I most certainly would have said, "Well, of course, people should obey the law," without a second thought of it, but what if the law is . . .

Alice's handwriting faded into a smear. I carefully peeled away fragments of the next page, slid the pieces together, found more of the story.

. . . troubled by members of the Ku Klux Klan, which according to Mrs. Walker has dealt harassment and violence upon them, driving the Melungeons from one county to another over the years. Nurse Walker herself has been given some harassment by men associated with Klan groups, which locally are gaining strength of late, as in so many states.

The Klansmen and their sympathizers do resent, in general, the district nurse's propensity for offering equal priority to the whites, the Negroes, the Cherokee, and on occasion, the Melungeons. "I suppose," she said, "they believe that if a baby or a child is to die, and one is white and the other colored or Cherokee, it should be the white baby who is saved. If the third of the group were to be Melungeon, well, they'd not shed a tear over letting it perish."

So, Ruby, you can see why the Melungeons do not trust outsiders. They find no welcome from any group. The pastors here preach against Melungeons as being witchy and devil-fired, so no God-fearing people are likely to stand in defense of them either. Of late, Mrs. Walker has found threatening notes pinned to her door several mornings in a row. There are those who do not want Able in the house, and should she have the baby here, they have vowed to . . .

I held the scrap of paper to the light, trying to make out the next words, but they were hopelessly lost. The only option was to move past the smeared ink and find what I could. Alice's story had grabbed me by the throat.

. . . Thomas and I sat long on the porch last night as Emmaline and Able chased fireflies and tucked them into pharmacy jars. We discussed at length Mrs. Walker's request. Neither of us is reckless enough to believe that it would not amount to a risk. . . .

Nothing more was left but the faint shape of Alice's signature trailing from the bottom. I sat staring at the water-spotted scraps. What had been written there? What had been lost? What words? What experiences? There was no one left to answer the questions. Alice, this great-aunt I'd never met, had been stolen by water and time.

How was it possible to feel so deep a connection to her? I couldn't say, but for some reason—maybe the unmoored feeling I'd had since losing my mother, or perhaps the similarities between Alice's life and mine—I *wanted* this part of my family's history. I wanted to understand it. I felt the need to remedy the wrong my grandmother had done. The effort Alice had put into these letters had been wasted. Rather than sharing her sister's life, Grandmother Ziltha had rendered it insignificant. Had she simply done it out of anger, or could the bouts of depression that had troubled my father have also plagued my grandmother? Was discarding the letters a vindictive act . . . or a hint of madness?

Or maybe she really was just . . . trying to hold on when the world seemed to be sliding out of control.

Maybe that's what Clyde is doing.

The last thought surprised me, but it didn't come out of nowhere. When we'd finally dragged him home from the docks last night—which had only happened after I'd warned him that people would call the police if he didn't come with Casey and me—Clyde had let something slip. Yesterday had been his and my mother's special day—both the anniversary of their marriage and the anniversary of the day they first met, when she was a seventeen-year-old high school girl. My mother and Clyde would've been married nine years as of yesterday.

He'd gone to the bench by the water because that was one of *their* places, the spot where they'd often sat and watched the boats and the waterbirds.

He'd stayed there for hours, trying to be close to her.

In reality, Clyde and I wanted the same thing. We wanted my mother back.

Neither of us could have what we wanted.

I turned to another letter and began arranging the pieces atop the intricately appliquéd quilt in her craft room. After being unable to sleep, I'd braved the trip downstairs despite creaking rafters, mice scampering through the walls, and nagging questions about whether squirrels were nocturnal. I'd gathered Alice's letters and brought them upstairs, so as to spend the sleepless hours piecing more stories together, while also keeping one eye on the hallway in case Clyde tried to leave again.

I didn't really think he would. I had a sense that we'd crossed some invisible barrier last night, that we understood one another a bit better now. At least, I hoped so.

Outside, the security lights flickered and the moon slipped below the rooftops as I focused on pieces of the next letter. Searching through the box, I separated fused-together pages, matched up seams. A noise in the hall testified to the fact that Clyde was out of bed, probably about to begin his morning round of tennis ball toss. The normal time—4:30 a.m. On the way to down the hall, he passed by my doorway, stopped a few steps beyond, and wandered back, teetering slightly and once again not using the cane I'd given him.

"Did you need something?" I glanced up from the letter.

He looked tired and disheveled, his thick gray hair sticking out in all directions. "Saw the light on. Thought maybe you'd left."

His tone made it obvious that he didn't mean *left* as in *a quick run down to the convenience store*; he meant *left* as in *gone for good.* Maybe we hadn't bonded after all. Maybe yesterday's fiasco had been another attempt to get rid of me.

"No, Clyde. I just went downstairs to grab something. I couldn't sleep."

"Hard to believe that." Somehow in those four little words he managed to convey that I was a lazy ne'er-do-well who slept all the time.

"Whether you know it or not, I do have things on my mind." The snarky remark slipped out before I could stop it. I didn't want to descend into an argument. What we needed was a calm, logical conversation about possible next steps. Even though I'd been forced to give Casey the bum's rush yesterday, I fully intended to call him later and talk about touring the Shores. I hoped to convince Clyde to come along.

"I know what you got on your mind."

Emotion and exhaustion bubbled to the surface. "I'm trying to do what's best here. My—" I bit back the rest of *my mother would have wanted me to.* It'd only dredge up yesterday's pain, and what good would that do? I had nothing to gain by hurting Clyde. Maybe that was one thing I'd learned from these letters, these scraps of a sister bond that had been torn, and torn again, and discarded in the trash. There was nothing but loss here. Terrible, heartbreaking loss. Alice's temporary departure from Ziltha's life had somehow become a permanent one.

"There are bagels and fruit in the kitchen." Maybe I could divert him with food. Get rid of him.

I turned back to the letter.

Dearest Queen Ruby,

I write to you today from a lovely rock bluff high atop the waters of a majestic, tumbling falls, where Tom has stopped us for lunch. We are enjoying a picnic given to us by a Mrs. Esther Mae Powers, a delightful woman whose interview will be submitted in my next packet. Honestly, Ziltha dear, I'd worried that my eighty dollars per month might amount to starvation wages for myself and Emmaline, but I have learned that it is possible to survive on much less than one might think. The mountain folk are so very generous, once you've come to know them. Though they are often suspicious of our purposes at first, I have found that merely mentioning an acquaintance with this mountaineer or that one a hollow or two hills away will . . .

I looked up, and Clyde was still skulking in the doorway like the proverbial toad atop a toadstool. His chin poked outward, his bottom lip pressing frog-mouthed into the top one.

"Your coffee's in there by now. I set the timer." *Come on, it's too early for this.* Anytime was too early. I wanted to close the door, turn the skeleton key, and spend the whole day with Alice's story . . . and without Clyde.

I'd just noticed that in the time since the last letter, *Thomas* had suddenly become *Tom*.

Interesting . . .

"Whatzat?" Clyde's whiskery jaw bobbed toward the scraps of paper lying in strategic piles on the quilt.

"It's not from up here. Don't worry, I haven't touched anything of my mother's."

Despite the barbed assurance, he didn't leave.

I stopped what I was doing, sighed, rested my elbows on my knees. "What, Clyde? *What?* You know, I just want to sit here and work on these letters and be left alone. For a while, at least. Okay? We'll talk later, after I've had a shower." *And called about the retirement home and looked for anything else downstairs that can be sold quickly.* I'd talked to Denise last night, and as predicted, she hadn't taken the ring from my cabin. She wouldn't tell me where she'd gotten the rest of the money for the range hood bill.

"Letters?"

"Yes. They're letters. To my grandmother Ziltha. I found them in the storage, but somebody's torn them up. I think they were probably in the trash at one time or another. I'm piecing them together the best I can."

"What for?"

"To see what they say. They're interesting."

Silence, finally. Teetering sideways a bit, he caught himself against a dresser, then wobbled a few steps in the door, eyeballing the bed. I focused on the papers, felt myself locking into defense mode. Clearly, the agenda was to pick a fight this morning.

If Clyde tried hard enough, he'd get it, and I was afraid the fallout would be epic. I was just so . . . tired.

Clyde, these letters were not my mother's and they're not yours. Just leave me alone and go drink your stupid coffee. It was on the tip of my tongue, but Clyde spoke first.

"Like workin' a puzzle."

I swiveled a tiny scrap of paper, slid it into place, feeling a strange sense of calm as the edges met. One torn piece of the world suddenly right again. Real life should be so easy. "Yes. A little."

"Your mama liked puzzles."

A tender memory rushed in, and I felt Mom there behind me, her shoulders leaning over mine, her chin resting on my head, her breath stirring my hair, my body momentarily enveloped by hers, as if she'd taken me into the womb again, making us one. She'd always kept a puzzle on the two-seat breakfast table of our Michigan kitchen. We'd never worked hard on it—just added a few pieces here and there, during breakfast, during supper, late in the evenings sometimes as we popped popcorn or stirred cocoa, getting ready to watch a movie together.

Even when we were arguing, or I was sulking, or she was too

exhausted to deal with my teenage angst, we could always put together a piece or two of the puzzle.

She'd walk by, tap a finger, say, *This one goes there, I think.* She had the benefit of having looked at the picture on the box, but she always hid the boxes from me. *This way it's a mystery,* she'd say.

"Yes, she did," I whispered, then closed my eyes over the memory and quickly tried to lock away its tenderness, to protect the vulnerable space before Clyde could use it to wound me.

"She kep' one on the table here in the kitchen. Worked on it while we had our coffee in the mornin'."

I pinched my lids tighter, trying to ignore the vision. I didn't want to think about my mother doing puzzles with Clyde. That was *our* space. *Ours.*

"Your mama cleaned 'em up whenever you come to visit. She wanted ever'thing to be nice." The floor groaned as he shifted from one leg to the other, hobbling closer and leaning his weight against the bedstead. The small bit of effort brought a low moan. I still couldn't imagine how he'd made it all the way to the park yesterday, but the trip had taken a lot out of him.

I heard Ruby sidle to a position nearby. She let out a whimper, as if she felt the air in the room changing again.

"I just wanted to see *Mom*. I didn't care what the house looked like." But after her marriage, things had been so different. It was as if she felt the need to put on a June Cleaver performance whenever I came around—to fill our time with scheduled activities and four-course meals and shoreside shopping trips, during which Clyde would sit on a store bench, looking grumpy and bothered. Ruining everything.

"She wanted you to like it, so's you'd come more."

That stung. "I came as much as I could, Clyde." I pressed my fingertips to the sudden throb between my eyebrows. Tears needled.

"Your mama knew that."

"If I'd realized how sick she was . . . I would've come for good . . . for however long it took." A rush of breath followed the words. On its heels, I sucked in air, slid my hand to my mouth. I wasn't doing this right now. I wasn't.

How dare Clyde use my mother as a weapon in this war.

"She didn't wanna bother you."

I snapped upright, felt my nostrils flare in preparation for breathing fire. "She was my *mother*, Clyde. Of course I wanted to be *bothered* if she needed me. I would've dropped *everything* to come take care of her." Whirling my feet around, I hit the floor, looked down at my sweats and sleep shirt. I needed clothes. I had to get out of here *now*.

The clean clothes were lying beside my suitcase. I snatched up a T-shirt and jeans, threw them on the desk, then added socks, underwear, and a bra, hoping the unabashed display of feminine underthings would chase Clyde away.

Instead, he shuffled back to the doorway, leaned heavily on the frame, he and Ruby blocking my exit. I had the ridiculous urge to go in the closet and dress, then barrel past Clyde and make my escape.

"I tried to tell 'er."

Stopping midstride, I gaped at him. "What?"

The skin beneath his eyes drooped, his lower lip hanging slack on one side, as if he had a plug of tobacco in it—a habit my mother had insisted he quit after their marriage. His eyes, old, cloudy, gray, found mine. "I tried to tell your mama you'd wanna know. But your mama wouldn't listen."

I searched his face, felt myself hovering on a tightrope between anger and horror, struggling to know which way to fall. Which was the softer landing? "My mother *wanted* to keep me in the dark? That was *her* idea?"

I studied him, watching—*pleading*—for some hint of deception, some evidence that he was lying.

There was none.

"She knew you'd drop ever'thing and come. She didn't want to mess up that new restaurant of yours, out there in Dallas. She was so glad you'd quit all the flyin' around the world for that big-deal job. She thought those people had just took advantage of you, never paid you near what you was worth. It made her glad that your restaurant was a great big goin' thing, and she knew you'd been workin' night and day to get it that way. She told people all the time about it. Whenever she'd meet folks out here who come from Texas, 'Go eat at my daughter's restaurant,' she'd say."

I collapsed against the lowboy dresser, stood looking at the face in the mirror—my mother's, except for the dark hair and blue eyes. It'd been so much easier to blame Clyde than to accept any of the blame myself. Every time Mom had called, it'd seemed like I was in the middle of some crisis or other, half-listening to her on my Bluetooth as I dealt with incorrect orders from the vendors or helped the cooks catch up or talked to some customer who was dissatisfied and wanted a free meal. *Mom, can you hang on a minute?* Or *Mom, can I call you back?* These were as common as *hello* and *good-bye* in our conversations.

"I never wanted her to feel that way."

"You cain't do nothin' about what other folks decide for theirselves. Your mama had her own mind, and she thought it was best that way." Clyde seemed to offer me absolution, but I couldn't grasp it, especially considering that it was coming from him.

I closed my eyes again, let my head fall forward, tamped down the swell of emotion. Maybe Clyde would move on now, go to the kitchen for his coffee.

But his labored breath hovered a few feet away along with Ruby's soft panting.

"I could do them things. I was good with your mama's puzzles."

When I looked up, he was backhanding toward the scraps on the bed. I could only blink at him, fairly certain that the earth had suddenly reversed its rotation. "You . . . want to help me reconstruct my grandmother's letters?"

A soft, sardonic puff of laughter and then, "I got time on my hands. What d'you hold 'em together with when you're done? Scotch tape?"

Everything tilted again, in a different direction this time, like a ship sloshing around on a storm tide.

Clyde, offering to *help* me with something? "I haven't been doing anything to hold them together. I've just been reading them and then keeping the pieces stacked in order. It didn't seem like a good idea to put tape all over them." Beneath my immediate curiosity about my grandmother and our family secrets, there was a sense that the letters should be preserved. Alice's story, whatever it turned out to be, shouldn't be lost to time. But I had no idea how to properly restore a torn piece of paper.

"Seems kinda stupid. What if ya wanna read 'em again?"

"I guess I'll piece them together then."

He hobbled closer, grunting as he moved. He'd probably gained well over fifty pounds since I'd seen him at my mother's funeral. *Mom wouldn't be happy with the condition he's in.* The thought was both unexpected and unwanted.

I replaced it with, *At least at the retirement home, he'll get proper care and whatever physical therapy he needs to regain his mobility.*

"Them plastic pockets," he blurted out of the blue.

"What?"

"Them clear plastic pockets, like you put a thing in and hold it in a notebook? We used 'em for our maintenance schedules in the Army, to keep the papers clean and dry. You go on and get me a big box, over to the Walmart. And a stapler. A good stapler."

"Clyde, I don't see—"

"I know how to do things. I ain't useless as you think." His chin jerked upward. His jaw clenched. Sinew hardened beneath sagging skin.

"I never said you were useless."

"Then you go on to the Walmart." The words were issued like a military command. No room for argument or discussion. I was being given my marching orders. "And get me that card table in the hall closet first. Set that thing up by my chair. I need someplace to work." He was already perusing the collection on the bed, curiously thumbing one pile and then the next.

"Oh . . . okay . . . I guess." Clutching my clothes, I started toward the nearest bathroom, still glancing over my shoulder to make sure I hadn't imagined Clyde altogether. I half expected him to vanish, but there he was, still hovering over the bed.

Like it or not, my project with the letters had just taken on staff . . . or been assigned a new general.

CHAPTER 15

I heard the noise at the bottom of the stairs before turning the corner from one landing to the next. The soft moan echoed against the walls and wound its way upward like a curl of smoke. Stopping, I peered over the rail, saw someone—a man in a dark sweatshirt and muddy jeans—sitting in the shadows with a hood pulled over his head. My heart slapped against my ribs, then fluttered upward. I'd locked the alley door last night . . . hadn't I? In all the excitement over bringing Clyde back from the marina, maybe I'd forgotten it after Casey left. . . .

Who would be down there at this hour? The street was still quiet. The shops wouldn't be open for a long time yet. Silently rounding the landing, I moved closer, stood balanced between two steps, ready to turn and run.

His head rolled sideways against the weathered wooden banister, long strands of sun-bleached blond hair sifting from beneath the hood. Something about it was familiar, even in the dim light.

"Joel?" What in the world would he be doing in my stairwell at this hour?

Mark's warnings whispered in my head. *He doesn't necessarily hang around with the most savory people.* Had he sneaked in here last night to see what he could find on the second floor? Surely not. Joel was such a nice kid—smart, helpful, interested in the antiques. He wouldn't do something like that.

Huddled on the bottom step, he looked sick or . . . really hungover.

"Joel, are you okay?" I stopped just out of reach, uncertainty creeping in. He'd been at some kind of a party when I'd called him last night. He could be under the influence of . . . who-knew-what right now.

He rolled his head upward, using the banister for support. One eye opened in a thin slit. The other was bruised, puffy, and swollen shut. "Huh-uh. I mes-s-s-sed u-up. . . . I did-didn't mean. . . . Mark's g-gonna kill umm-me. . . ." The words were a thin muddle, echoing up the silent stairwell.

I moved closer, squatted beside him. He didn't *sound* dangerous, just confused and fairly out of it—like a kid who'd overdone the partying, maybe even tried the hard stuff. This wasn't my first go-round with teenagers who'd been on a bender, then gotten scared and ended up at work because work was the only stable place they could think of to go.

"What happened last night?" The shiner and the dried blood were evidence that it was nothing good. The arm dangling between his knees was cut up too. I took his hand, turned it carefully. Just nicks and scrapes. Not life-threatening.

"Mark's gon-n-nna kill ummm-me," he moaned again. "Oh, man . . . I s-s-screwed up. D-did we umm-mess up the sh-shop?"

"What shop? *Mark's* shop?" A sense of doom slipped in. I'd been through this scenario too—had seemingly random restaurant break-ins end up being traced to employees. "Were you in *Mark's shop* last night?"

He bobbed forward with sudden ferocity. "Oh, ummm-man . . . g-gotta go s-s-see about the sh-shop. Somebody had s-some stuff las' night. At the p-party. We got s-so ummm-messed up. The car's toas-toast."

"Joel, why would you . . . ?" The idea of him trashing his future this way was sickening. There was a good heart inside that confused teenage skin.

"Man . . . s-somebody wreck . . . wreck the. . . . g-got . . . n' ran-n-n f-for it . . . didn't . . . w-whatdda do." He sank against the banister again, closing his eyes.

"Stay here a second, okay?" Stepping over him, I hurried out the door and around the building, afraid of what I might find there. But Mark's shop looked fine. Quiet. Untouched. The store was locked up, everything in place. The morning shadows reflected peacefully against the plate-glass windows, streetlamps still competing with the dawn light.

Maybe Joel had hallucinated or dreamed a break-in? Maybe he'd been talking about it with someone but hadn't gone through with it? Now what? Call the police? Call Mark? If Joel were my employee—one I'd been trying to steer in the right direction—I'd want to know. But the only number I had for Mark was his shop phone. That wouldn't do any good so early in the morning.

I *did* know where Mark lived. If I could get Joel into the car, I could take him there. At least then, Mark could figure out what should happen next.

Unfortunately, Joel wasn't keen on being relocated. "Umm-man. . . . I feel-l-l like . . ."

"Let's go, buddy." I dragged him to his feet and moved him out the door, staggering under his weight. This reminded me of some nights out with coworkers in foreign countries—times that I now regretted. I hadn't been much smarter than Joel when I'd first left home. I'd let people talk me into things—including David Monroe, which was how I'd ended up in a beachfront wedding chapel with a guy who still had eyes for other women.

The difference between Joel and me was that I'd had points of reference to fall back on when I'd eventually landed face-first in the dirt, brokenhearted and confronted with the inevitable truth. David didn't love me. He didn't even really understand what love was. But I *knew*. Examples had been set for me, growing up. My mother had shown me what love really was. At my best or at my worst, my mom was always ready to wrap her arms around me and love me, no matter how rebellious I was. From what Mark had said, Joel didn't have that to rely on. He was trying to figure things out all on his own.

Driving over to the Captain's Castle, I listened to mumbled explanations as Joel tried to sort out the last twelve hours or so. He was worried about what his boss would say, and whether Mark was going to kill him, and whether he might finally lose his job this time.

"Jus-just ta-take umm-me home, 'kay?" Moaning, he threw the bloody arm over his eyes. "I jus . . . I jus needa s-sleep awhi . . . while."

"No, Joel. I'm taking you to Mark's house." In the distance, the sun crept through the live oaks, spraying light over shadowed yards and dark windows as we wound through a neighborhood of gorgeous, graceful old homes. Any other time, it would've been beautiful scenery. I remembered riding one of the hotel's loaner bicycles through neighborhoods like these when I could sneak away from my grandmother. "He's not going to kill you. He *cares* about you. He cares what happens to you."

But as I pulled to the curb in front of a three-story white

house with a rose-draped picket fence and blue Adirondack chairs on the porch, my confidence flagged a bit. This place was not only huge; it was immaculate. It didn't look like the sort of house that had time for other people's issues. Somehow, I had expected Mark's home to be a . . . well . . . bachelor pad maybe—also a bit more modest in scope, despite the *Captain's Castle* handle. This place wasn't quite a mansion, but it wasn't far from it, and everywhere I looked, stem to stern, the Captain's Castle showed evidence of a woman's touch.

I exited the car and hurried up the porch steps, my nerves jangling as loud as the doorbell in the early silence. I prepared to explain myself to the lady of the house, if there was one.

Behind the glass, a silhouetted form moved down the stairs, a shadow at first, finally coming into view on the last few steps. Pulling a turquoise T-shirt over his head, he pushed his arms into the sleeves, and rolled the shirt into place over a pair of sweatpants. I didn't mean to stare, but I couldn't help myself.

A golden retriever cut him off in the entry hall. He and the dog tangled feet, the dog yelped, and Mark staggered forward several steps, catching himself just short of nosediving into the front door. By the time he finally looked through the window, we were almost face to face, the beveled glass like a fun-house mirror. He blinked, understandably confused. A slow, surprised smile followed, and I was temporarily mesmerized by it.

"The party was *last night*," he was saying as he opened the door, his hair still wet and slick, as if he were fresh out of the shower.

I had the bizarre urge to giggle and tease, even flirt a little, but the real reason for my visit quickly stole the air from the balloon.

Mark's smile dropped. "What's the matter?"

I served up the short version of Joel and the stairwell. "I'm still not sure exactly what happened, or what kind of trouble he's in, or if he's in trouble *at all*, other than that he made some really stupid decisions and he's pretty beaten up. I just thought you'd want to know first."

"Thanks." He was already starting toward the car, his face grim, his jaw rigid.

I trotted to keep up. "Listen, he's really worried about what you're going to think. He's afraid you'll kill him for screwing up."

"I might."

I understood that urge. I really did. "Take it a little easy on him, okay? Whatever was going on last night, he *did* decide to finally run out on it. He came to the building because he was looking for a place to hide. A safe place. He's pretty lost and definitely confused . . . and he's ashamed of himself."

Mark stopped at the gate, yelling at the overeager golden retriever as it tried to cram its body through the pickets. "Rip, cut it out. Stay!"

I grabbed Rip and pulled him aside, which I had a feeling might save lives right now. There was fire in Mark's eye, and I hadn't even told him the part about Joel worrying that he'd damaged the store. What if this ended in Mark deciding Joel wasn't worth the risk as an employee? What if he fired Joel? Where would Joel go from here?

Probably nowhere good.

Rip dragged me forward, standing on his hind feet and bracing his paws on the gate as it swung shut behind Mark. A worried, whiny yip warbled toward the car as Mark tore open the door. Inside, Joel lifted his arms, blocking his face and sheltering his head the way a kid does when he's used to being smacked around. A torrent of slurred explanations flowed out. A dog barked somewhere nearby, and Rip issued a deafening answer. I couldn't make out Joel's words—only the rise and fall of his voice, broken by an occasional gut-wrenching sob.

Mark grabbed Joel's shirt in handfuls, lifted him from the car like a rag doll. Rip lunged again. I heard the metal gate latch click, felt the gate fall into my knee. For an instant, I considered letting Rip go, but in the street, Mark just stood there while Joel sobbed against his shoulder. Nudging the gate closed, I took Rip back to the house and sat with him on the polished wooden stairs in Mark's entryway, waiting.

When they came inside, Joel had pulled himself together a bit, but Mark was still holding him by the scruff of the neck. Rip and I tramped quietly after them from the entry hall, through a parlor, and into a cavernous living room with an enormous fireplace mantel. The house was decorated in antiques and, like the yard outside, flawlessly neat. The bookshelves and artwork rivaled Grandmother Ziltha's collections back in the day. I caught myself listening for noises, again wondering if anyone else was upstairs.

But there were no women's jackets on the umbrella stand. Only one coffee cup and cereal bowl sat on the breakfast table when we finally ended up in the kitchen. Done in retro black-and-white octagon-shaped tile, the place was still littered with trays, glasses, and paper plates from last night's party. A stack of flyers about the plans for the charity project sat on the counter. I caught myself twisting so as to read the headline.

MANTEO COUNSELING AND ACTIVITY CENTER
A DEDICATED FACILITY FOR YOUTH AT RISK

Mark hung Joel over one side of the double sink, then rinsed the scraped-up arm in the other. Meanwhile, Joel babbled semicoherent apologies and dry-heaved into the drain. Snatching a dish towel from the countertop, Mark doused it with water, wrung it with one hand, and laid it over Joel's neck and head.

"Sober up, hotshot. You need a shower, and I'm *not* putting you in there. You're going to have to handle that yourself."

"I screwed up. Ohhh, umm-my h-head," Joel moaned.

"Yeah, that's what happens when you're at the wrong place with the wrong people. You can't hang out like that and live a normal life. If your uncle's got a party going on at home, don't *stay*. You *know* you can always come here. You're lucky you're not dead or in jail. You get caught again for drugs, or somebody wrecks the car and you're under the influence, if you *don't* end up dead, it's *not* juvie and parole this time, Joel. It's *prison*. You're over eighteen."

"I know, th-that's why I r-ran. Ohhhh . . . mmmhhh . . . owww . . ."

"You can't be around it. Even a little." Mark braced a hand on the counter, anguish forming deep lines around his eyes, giving evidence of a deeper sorrow. His head shook slowly back and forth.

What? What was behind that expression?

Letting out a long sigh, he turned to me as if he'd suddenly remembered I was there. "There's Bactine spray or something like that in the bathroom cabinet, down the hall, by the door to the deck. Could you go grab it?"

"Sure. Yes, of course." I hurried from the kitchen, wandered through more of Mark's house, found my way to the little half bath by the back door. The Bactine was right where he'd said it would be, in an antique, arch-shaped medicine cabinet with a gold-leafed frame. When I returned to the kitchen, Mark had moved Joel to a chair, the injured arm resting on the breakfast table. Damp pink stains slowly colored a clean white towel.

Mark treated the scrapes, then wrapped the towel around Joel's arm. "Doesn't look like there's any glass in it. You'll have a pretty decent shiner on the eye by tomorrow."

"You should see the other guy." Joel's lips twitched upward, then he winced and his smile fell. "It hurts."

"I'm sure everything does."

Head slowly sagging to the table, Joel settled his cheek next to the injured arm. "Thanks, Mark," he groaned, tears seeping from the swollen eye and falling to the cloth.

Mark didn't answer, just stood looking out the window, an index finger tapping out a Morse code of frustration as Joel's breaths lengthened.

Frowning apologetically, he finally turned my way. "I'm sorry he showed up at the Excelsior and got you involved in this."

"It's okay."

"It's a long way from *okay*, but I'm glad you were there. I'm sure this wasn't what you had in mind for your morning."

"No, but it's not a big deal. I was just making an early-morning Walmart run. Guess I should get on with it."

"I'll walk you out." He waited for me to cross the kitchen, then followed. Our footsteps echoed off the high ceilings as we passed through the living room. Somewhere in the house, Rip barked. A moment later, he raced past with a squeaky ball, ready to play. Scampering around the room, he tossed the ball, then caught it, then grabbed a stuffed moose from a toy basket and abandoned the ball. Ducking and diving, he tried to tease us into a game, ignoring Mark's command to knock off the racket.

I had the strange thought that Rip reminded me of Joel on a good day—boundless enthusiasm, interest that quickly flitted from one thing to another, a cheerful, hapless personality you couldn't help but love. Yipping and whining, the dog followed us onto the porch and bolted down the steps, stirring a sparrow from the dewy grass, then chasing it, then spotting a squirrel on the electric line and stopping to watch.

"That squirrel looks familiar." I tried to lighten the moment, then realized I probably shouldn't have. Mark looked like he was carrying a hundred pounds on each shoulder—as if Joel's weight were still resting there, plus some.

I wondered again about the *some*. What else was going on here?

The screen door fell closed behind us, and Mark stopped at the steps, so I stopped too. "Thanks for what you did for him, Whitney. He's a good kid—better than what you saw today—but he's lived off and on with three or four family members, and it's never a stable situation. If teenagers around here want a party, they can find one. Tourists come in, they've got money, they like the idea of hanging with the locals, finding places everyone doesn't know about. It's an ugly side effect of the resort culture. When I moved here, that was the last thing I thought about. I was looking for the perfect place to leave everything behind, and thought I'd found it, but if you stay awhile, you realize that there *is* no perfect hideout. There's a set of realities, anywhere you go."

"Joel's lucky he has someone who cares this much about him. That's not always the case when you're dealing with kids and minimum-wage jobs. Most businesses are just interested in taking on labor, not people and certainly not issues."

He nodded, still looking grim as he combed damp-dry curls from his forehead. "When he sobers up a little, I'll get the details out of him . . . as much as he can remember, anyway. If there's anything we need to report to the police, we will. Don't worry. But if he was just in the wrong place at the wrong time with the wrong people, at least he gets the chance to not make the same mistake next time."

"I think he might've learned a lesson."

"Let's hope." The stubble around Mark's lips made his disappointed smile look wan and sad. He was afraid Joel *hadn't* learned a lesson. "Listen, Whitney, I know you feel like I've been harassing you since you came here. And I know you've got enough on your plate with your stepdad's health and the problems with the Excelsior . . . and you have a business of your own to run. I'll understand if you do what you have to do with the building. I won't be happy about it, but I'll understand it. I'd still like you to meet the whole crew of the youth project and at least hear what they have to say, but I get it that you have your hands full."

And just like that, I was off the hook. Free to go about my day, my week, my *life*. My disposal of the family property. No more guilt trip? No more bargains made in squirrel-induced hysteria?

I was free. . . .

I descended two steps, then stopped, caught the railing with one hand and turned around, clutching a heavy finial that had seen years of salt air and seasons passing. "How did you get involved with the charity project?"

I'd opened the door, and I knew it. It wasn't a smart thing to do, and I knew that too. I should've been getting out while I could.

Meeting Mark's gaze wasn't smart either. Something wildly electric sparked, then crackled through me.

"Would it make a difference?" The cagey answer went a short

distance toward convincing me I should mind my own business and head for the gate.

"I don't know."

Leaves parted overhead, sliding a patch of sunlight over his tanned skin. He closed one eye against it, studied me narrowly through the other, as if he were deciding whether to offer up the truth or something that would brush me off and get rid of me.

Finally, he rested against the porch post, crossing his arms and his bare feet. He watched Rip climb the steps and lie down on the top one. "I lost my daughter to a drug overdose. She'd just turned fourteen."

He watched me intently, searching for my reaction. No doubt, he caught it. Shock and confusion hit me like a wave, smacking hard and then penetrating, pouring salt water through muscles and veins. I felt cold all over. A daughter? A fourteen-year-old daughter? Everything I'd thought about Mark Strahan suddenly didn't fit.

"I'm . . . I'm sorry. I shouldn't have . . . ," I stammered, lost.

He nodded in a weary way that told me he'd been here before. "I know. There's no easy way to tell someone."

I understood it then—the exact position he was in. It was always hard to gauge the timing when someone new came into my life. How long do you wait before you say, *My father committed suicide when I was five*? How long do you maintain an acquaintance before you show your scars? What do you do with the surprise and sympathy that come afterward?

"I'm sorry," I said again. "For your loss." *What was her name? What happened exactly?*

A house finch flitted through the yard, its crimson feathers catching the early light. Both of us watched it, grasping at its startling lightness of being.

Mark motioned to the golden retriever, who'd lifted his head to listen. "Rip was Hadley's dog. A birthday present when she turned twelve. Straight As on her report card. You know, divorced dads go big on that kind of thing."

I nodded mutely. How long ago had Mark lost his daughter? Rip wasn't young. He'd started graying around the muzzle. Seven or eight maybe?

Mark seemed to know the usual questions. He went on with the story . . . without my asking. "Laurie and I were young when we had her. Laurie was the preacher's daughter and I was the deacon's son, and it was like we'd read the script from some bad made-for-TV movie. We messed up. She got pregnant. We tried to do the right thing, but we weren't very good at it. We weren't good enough to each other. I was busy with my undergrad degree, and then law school, and then getting a toehold in a firm."

A car drove by. He waited for the noise to wane before finishing his story. "Sometime in there, Laurie decided she wanted a different life . . . with somebody else. That was that. She and Hadley moved halfway across the country. Things were never good between Hadley and her stepdad. Hadley just started . . . looking for stuff to do, and she found some of the wrong options. The wrong guy to date. The wrong party with the wrong kind of powder to slip in a drink, and that was that. Sometimes one mistake is the only mistake you get."

He was matter-of-fact about the details, as if he'd steeled himself against the telling of this story—prepared for it. But the muscles in his neck tightened and he swallowed hard, an instinctive reaction he couldn't control. "You never picture yourself at your little girl's funeral. And it's the strangest thing, because you're standing there looking at the grave, and part of you still feels like you're watching a movie, and you should be able to just . . . flip a switch and turn it off, but there is no switch."

"I can't imagine. . . ." That was the truth. I couldn't fathom the pain that was in his history. How was he still standing, still walking, still working, still thinking about the future, still taking risks on kids like Joel? Wasn't he afraid of being hurt again, disappointed again, *broken* again?

In the midst of that thought, there was another one—something that had struck me yesterday in the Iola room at Benoit House, the very thing Alice was learning as she traveled to the mountains.

How wonderful the days when all was well.

How necessary, also, that we must release them now. It is fine enough to glance at the past, but one must never focus there overlong. Don't you think?

Here was Mark, with an unthinkable past, still looking forward, still seeking after today's purpose, still taking chances on other people.

I *wanted* to understand him. I *needed* to. I'd walked too long in the shoes of a child who was still waiting for her daddy to magically come home and fix everything. But the truth was, I had to fix myself. For too long, I'd harbored a five-year-old's broken heart, one that was terrified, deep down, that no one could really be trusted. I was always ready to leave but never ready to really love. I told myself it was better that way, safer.

I have lost the carefree girl I once was . . . allowed the cutting blades of fear to whittle me down to nubs. I dearly believe it was not fate that brought me here, but God himself. This is the place I will finally find courage and breath and voice.

What I'd witnessed as I'd watched Mark tend to Joel was the work of love. I needed that like I needed air.

"It's been six years, and still sometimes when the phone rings, I pick it up expecting to hear Hadley's voice on the other end. I'm ready for her to give me the play-by-play of her latest softball game or complain about something her mom won't let her do or ask when I'm going to fly out and pick her up for a visit." His voice held a combination of sadness and resignation. "It's just so . . . random. You never know when it's coming."

Without even intending to, I laid a hand on his arm, felt muscle and skin beneath my fingers. Warmth. Life. "I know." The connection between us was soul-deep in that moment, the kind of shared bond that no one wishes for. "I still walk into the Excelsior and think I hear my mom singing in the next room, or I catch the scent of her bath spray and feel like she's just passed by. It's so *real* in that moment, I almost create it for myself. And then in the next moment, it's not real, no matter how much I want it to be." It was the first time I had confessed that to anyone. "That's not what my mother would've wanted. I *know* that on one level, but on another level, I'm afraid that if I let her go, I'll forget who she was. I won't be able to get her back."

"Yeah. That's it, I think. But on the other hand, life has to go on, one way or another. I'm still Hadley's dad even though I can't see her or pick up the phone and talk to her. I came to Roanoke looking to get away from all the things that were constant reminders of what'd happened, of the ways I'd failed my little girl. I just wanted some . . . peace. I put a bid on this house with everything in it, then bought the shop in a different location and eventually moved it uptown to the Excelsior. I thought I had things set. I thought I'd found my escape—a place that was so perfect, trouble couldn't touch it. Instead, what I got were nosy neighbors who wanted to know why a lawyer opens a surf shop, townie kids with issues, and two local congregations looking to start a center for teens and young adults. I didn't want anything to do with it at first, but then I realized, I can do for other kids what I didn't do for Hadley. If there's anything good that can come from her death, it comes from letting her life stand for something. From convincing another kid not to make that one stupid mistake. Hadley didn't get a second chance. Teenagers need to know that sometimes, they won't. It's been a way of finally dealing with the pain and starting to let go."

I stepped away, breaking the flesh-to-flesh bond between us, suddenly uncertain. Anger and blame were so much easier to manage than acceptance. They were hard and solid. They made good walls. Acceptance was soft. It let everything in, including the pain.

The conversation flagged. We watched Rip as he rolled onto his back and stretched all four legs into the air, twitching in a dream.

"Surfing," Mark whispered and motioned to the dog. I chuckled, relieved at the change in topics, and Mark added, "Don't laugh. He's pretty good at it."

"He surfs?"

A smooth grin and a wink answered, and Mark was *Mark* again—charismatic, in charge, comfortable. He reached for his wallet, but then noticed he was still in sweats. "I was going to give you a business card. It's got Rip's picture on it. You can check him out on the Rip Shack YouTube channel, though. He's a surf bum. Loves the water. Never let it be said that you can't teach an old dog new tricks."

"Now this I've gotta see." Inadvertently, I'd cast the net for an invitation. I caught myself holding a breath, wondering if Mark would pick up on it, and then he did.

"Come watch him this afternoon. I'm only in the shop until

twelve thirty today. If the weather holds, I thought Rip and I would hit the water after that." He glanced over his shoulder toward the house, added an apologetic wince as an afterthought, his honey-brown eyes narrowing. "Sorry . . . I forgot I had the little party animal in there to deal with."

It reminded me that I'd been on a mission of my own before I found Joel curled in the stairwell. "I probably shouldn't leave Clyde alone in the building for too long, anyway. He had an *incident* yesterday." The real world pressed in with the force of a D9 bulldozer, plowing over tentatively built bridges and haphazardly strung lines of communication.

I felt foolish, standing there on Mark's porch, talking about surfing and . . . well . . . flirting with him, because that's what it was now, really. It wouldn't in any way help solve the problems with the building or pay the bills at Bella Tazza or get me back to Michigan to take some of the stress off Denise. It would only complicate things.

Guilt weaseled back to its usual space. There was no time for a personal life right now . . . and Roanoke Island, a thousand miles from home, certainly wasn't the place to start one.

"I should get going." I shrugged toward the car.

"Tell you what. Let me grab a business card for you. Text me later if you think you've got time to go to the beach, and we'll see where everything's at. Maybe we can still work it into the day."

No was in my mind, but *yes* was in my mouth. "Okay." I knew better. I did. But I was flattered, or fascinated, or both. I could watch surfing dogs on YouTube, but it wasn't the dog who'd piqued my interest.

I waited for Mark to retrieve the card, then admired Rip's surf photo before saying my good-byes and walking to the car.

On the way to Walmart, I called Clyde to let him know I'd be a while yet—I'd gotten caught up in something unexpected. He couldn't shuffle me off the phone quickly enough. He was busy with the letters.

"And you're *staying* there today, right? *In* the building?" I added at the end of our conversation. "You're not going to try the stairs again?" I imagined him falling in the stairwell and lying there until I got back.

"I ain't going AWOL, if that's what you're gettin' at. Buy me plenty of them plastic sleeves. I'm good with these letters, but there's a lot missin' here—some pieces I can't find and other parts that's been wet. Hard to make out enough to understand what they say."

"You're actually *reading* the letters?" I tried to imagine Clyde following the tender story of Alice's journey into the Blue Ridge.

"Well, you ask me to put 'em together—how am I s'posed to do that without readin' what they say?"

"Clyde, if you don't *want* to put the letters together, you don't *have* to. I can just work on it as I get time." It was petty, I guess, trying to force him to admit enthusiasm for something that had to do with me. "Or I can take them back to Michigan with me when I go. There's no big rush." That wasn't true, of course. I was desperate to know the rest of Alice's story. I was even more convinced now that, in some way, I *needed* it.

My stepfather growled like a bear coming out of hibernation. I pictured him shifting forward in his seat, that scraggly chin jutting out. "Well, I hadn't got nothin' else to do."

"You can watch your TV shows."

"Can't go nowhere. Got me locked up here like a pris'ner. You at least gonna bring me some breakfast? Duck Doughnuts. I like Duck Doughnuts."

Sighing, I relaxed in my seat as Roanoke Island faded in the rearview mirror. "You know, Clyde, you could just admit that the letters are interesting."

"I didn't say they wasn't interestin'. Don't put words in my mouth."

"I wouldn't dream of it." A laugh chugged out, punctuating the sentence. This was so ridiculous, it was funny.

"Brought back some mem'ries."

"Memories?"

"Them Melungeons."

The word stopped me short. I'd never heard it spoken before. "You *know* about Melungeons?" It hadn't occurred to me that, at his age, Clyde probably remembered some of the things Alice was describing in her letters.

"I knew some once't. My daddy was a Navy man. Was a recruiter in the mountains when I was little—Blue Ridge and the Smokies. North Carolina, Tennessee, on up into Virginia some. We'd tramped all over the country by the time I graduated high school. Had a Melungeon family down the road a piece in Tennessee. They was Mullinses and the mama was a Collins. A lot of them Mullinses and Collinses was known to be Melungeon. Local folk didn't cotton to them much. Sort of thought they was odd and trickish, but my mama didn't mind it. She was German, herself. After the war, she knew what it was to be looked at sideways by folks. She didn't believe in doin' it unto others. She let me run around the woods with little Henry Mullins. He and I knew enough to mostly keep it to ourselves. You could get in real trouble with that kind of thing back in them days. Once in a while, my daddy found him a recruit from the Melungeons too. A lot of them was dirt poor, didn't have too many prospects, so the Navy pay looked good. And they had a natural-born likin' for the water. Even though they mighta spent their whole life in the mountains. Was a peculiar thing."

"That's really fascinating." My mind raced to Appalachia, conjuring images of two boys running the mountain hollows, aware yet unaware of all the things that separated them.

I'd always loved Appalachia. At the end of every summer on the Outer Banks, Mom tacked on a few days in the North Carolina mountains—our reward for having worked so hard at the Excelsior. Together, we camped under the stars or enjoyed the sense of history in old cabins, hotels, or bed-and-breakfast houses. We hiked trails to waterfalls and climbed rocks and cataloged wildflowers. We collected pretty rocks, acorns with perfect hats, and hickory nuts to use as the faces for Mom's handmade Christmas angels.

Had my mother's fascination for that area started long before I was born? Perhaps with stories Clyde had told her?

"Guess I got lots of them mem'ries." His voice took on a faraway quality. "Didn't figure anybody cared to hear them tales. Never woulda thought of it, except for the letters. Here these two young folks are trekkin' all over the mountains, lookin' for Melungeons. And the thing about a Melungeon is, ain't no point in lookin' for him. He don't want you to find him, you won't."

CHAPTER 16

Dearest Ruby,

With any good fortune, by the time this letter reaches you, we will have discovered the Melungeons and begun to win their confidence, so as to record the history of these maligned and elusive people. Indeed, their origins in these mountains seem as ancient and mysterious as the hills and hollows themselves. By all accounts, these blue-eyed, dark-skinned people were here to greet the first European explorers in this high country. Even the Cherokee cannot say exactly when and how the Melungeon people came to be. An old Cherokee woman, Alva Rainwater, whose manner of speech was as musical as her name, imparted to me during her interview that even her great-great-grandmother, a medicine woman of the tribe, did not know of a time before the Melungeons.

Such is my fascination that lately I have come to end each interview with these two questions: "What do you know of the history of the Melungeons?" and "Have you any information that might help us find them, so as to document their stories?"

Invariably, the question brings wary glances. Several people have hushed me over it and then looked with great suspicion at Able, whom we've been compelled to bring along with us after leaving Nurse Merry Walker's. There was no other choice. A bloody chicken foot and a live timber rattlesnake were found hanging from a string on Mrs. Walker's porch the morning of our departure. These folk symbols portend the coming of death, and indeed could have caused one, as Nurse Walker bumped into the snake while opening her front door.

A crudely scratched note had been nailed there as well, and the threat was made clear enough—Able was to be kept no longer at Mrs. Walker's home nor allowed to birth the child there. That same morning, Able awakened from a dream of crossing water, which in mountain superstition also indicates sickness or death.

Thomas and I simply could not leave her behind. At Mrs. Walker's instruction, Able will travel along with us until we either find relatives to take her in or discern the exact location of the Melungeon orphans' school and can settle her there. Finding that information may not be such a simple thing. As we travel, the mountain folk do not look kindly on Able. They eye her as if they expect her to vanish into vapor or throw a hex upon them. What a strange thing that in this modern age when man can traverse the oceans by plane and a telephone wire can carry our voices almost instantly, such superstitions still exist, but such is the case.

Indeed, we have experienced our first run-in with a Klansman, who was quite proud of his affiliations. It was my own doing, I suppose. I went looking. Those were our instructions, as per our leaders—that we field reporters would write about all spheres of life. In some way, perhaps I had been under the belief that our official status with the government held us separate from whatever local prejudices and old battle lines still exist here. I was disavowed of that illusion this very afternoon, by a man at a small vegetable stand near a crossroads. Upon hearing his unabashed conversation with the proprietor, I asked if I might interview him. He was quite willing to speak with me and was most candid—dare I say splendidly proud—in regards to his missions with the Klan and his own beliefs. During the interview, he produced several postcards bearing photos of lynchings.

Ziltha, I suppose we might consider ourselves sheltered, but even having heard of such abominations, I could not imagine something so obscene as a photograph of white-hooded hooligans with their guns, pitchforks, pickaxes, and their little children, posed beneath a tree with the bodies of three lifeless Negro men hanging like sacks of grain. I would have done well never to have seen such a thing, for it is the sort of sight that drops your spirit to its knees and causes you to silently cry out, How can this be? How?

I remained as impassive as my newly practiced reporter's face would allow, but inside I was prodded like a sleeping dragon. Had Tom not been off with his camera and equipment, and the girls playing with kittens behind the barn, I would have closed the interview then and there. But Tom was nowhere in sight, and by then the proprietor of the vegetable stand had gone away as well.

I had barely begun to pray that the girls would not reappear when, of course, they did. They had found the company of two children belonging to the Klansman, and together, the girls were giggling and sharing the kittens. The four of them were upon us before I knew it.

The Klansman withdrew his daughters roughly by the arm, backhanding the eldest girl hard across the face and admonishing her that they would quite likely catch some terrible malady now. He cast eyes at me in a way that chilled my blood. "She your'n?"

When I understood that he was referring to Able, I was aghast! The man then grabbed me by the chin, asking, "You some colored's whore?"

Never in my life have I experienced anything of such a nature, and I hope I never shall again, Ziltha! One always hopes that, in the face of evil, one might be bold and courageous, brandishing the sword of truth and the shield of justice. I know that, had it been you in that situation, the man would have quickly had cause to regret his behavior, but I don't mind telling you that I was more toward shrinking violet than roaring lion. I thought I might faint.

Only when Emmaline called out, "Mama?" and started my way did something within me rise up. You must protect the children, it insisted. I yelled to the girls to go back to the car, where I hoped they would be safe, though I was well aware that the Klansman could move past me if he chose. Able, fortunately, had the good sense to gather up Emmaline, who was agog, and beat a hasty retreat.

I then tore myself from the man's grasp and slapped him full across the face, saying, "Sir, I am an employee of the United States government, a Federal Writer, and you will mind yourself, or you will find the law at your door!"

He seemed quite undaunted, an acidic smile showing tobacco-browned teeth (what remained of them). "Ain't no law nowheres near here what can't be counted kin to my fam'ly, one way or t'other."

"The federal law," I ground forth. "And if you doubt that I am able to bring that to bear, you just try me out, sir!"

The man then snatched the pad of paper right from my hand and began tearing away the sheet notes. He shredded them, his beady eyes pinned to me with such hatred as I have never seen from another human soul. Before all was through, he had stomped the pad into the mud, which was just as well for me, as I did not want it after his ugly mitts had touched it.

His face was suddenly inches from mine, and I stood my ground, but oh, Ziltha, if you could have heard my heart hammering!

"You mind yer bid'ness, gal. Y'ain't in no big city, n'more. You'uns come to my mountain. Git on the wrong side a us, you'll find yerself down t'holler where ain't no fed'ral gov'mint ner nobody'll never find what's left of ya." He promptly disappeared into the woods from whence he'd come, dragging his daughters with him. The vegetable man then returned, and I realized that he had been hiding during my peril, unwilling to become involved. He seemed quietly regretful about the issue, though we did not speak. I went to the car but was too shaken to sit with the girls. Instead, I paced back and forth outside, and that was where Tom found me.

He knew that something was terribly amiss, though I attempted to keep the story from him. "I am merely in a yank to be on the road," I said. "You disappear into the woods, Thomas, and I am left waiting and waiting. You promised to be back within twenty minutes." Tom had been gone so long, I had begun fretting that he and the Klansman had run across one another in the forest and had an altercation. I was relieved to see him back at the car.

"I spent a bit longer than I thought," he admitted. "There's a confluence of springs and a waterfall down thataway. I took the time to stop a fella fishin' and ask about it. I wanted to get the name so it could be in your notes for the guidebook." He paused to look me over closely then. "But that's not why you're nervous as a long-tailed cat in a room full of rockin' chairs, Alice. What happened while I was off yonder? And don't think of lying to me over it. I'll ask the girls, and you know they'll give me the story anyhow."

I had no choice but to relate the tale.

He was incensed, just as I had feared he would be. His impulse was to go after the man and come to fisticuffs with him to defend my honor.

"Don't be foolish, Thomas," I scolded, once again feeling more like a parent than a colleague. "The man assured me that there isn't a law officer on this mountain he cannot count as a relative. We'll end up hanging from a tree, pictured on one of those despicable postcards."

All that had happened then came back in one crippling blow. The photographs from the postcards swirled before me, along with the Klansman's words, his touch, my own imaginings of the terrible sensation of a rope snapping tight, cutting off air, suffocating life. I began weeping and covered my face, collapsing in on myself.

Tom gathered me up as I sobbed against man's inhumanity to man. If Satan has toeholds that allow him to claw and climb from the underworld to this one, they lie in our failure to see ourselves in others.

I had no concept of how long I wept. When Tom finally helped me into the car, I was limp and wrung out. The girls were silent as little birds sensing something dangerous near the nest.

"Your mama's just tired," Tom said to Emmaline. "Don't you worry about it a bit. She needs some rest and she'll be shipshape again. You girls keep quiet awhile and watch out the window, find what's pretty to see."

I thought of the Apostle Paul's words to the Philippians: "Finally, brethren . . . whatsoever things are pure, whatsoever things are lovely . . . think on these things."

Sleep came, taking me all at once and consuming me. For the first time, I wanted to leave this place and know no more of it. Even amid the dream mist, there were the sweet mews of newborn babies as Merry Walker's midwives delivered them in the ancient ways, and then the groaning for breath as ropes tightened and feet dangled, nothing to hold them but air.

We camped that night in a glen by a stream, and even after pitching the tent and listening to Tom tell stories by the fire and catching fireflies to make lantern jars and tucking the girls into the rear seat and floorboard of the car to sleep, I lay staring out the window, sleepless. Above, a myriad of stars glittered between the dark circles of tall pines and maples. I attempted to ponder their beauty, but instead I found only a question, one I could not answer. How can God allow such abominations to flourish unchecked in this world?

The answer came in a question, Ruby.

God, in reply, asked, "How can you?"

If I had thought that my purpose in the Writers' Project was to record the grandeur of this country, and to document ordinary lives, I now understand that my purpose here is at once much greater and much smaller. As small as the tale of one human life. As great as the moment when one man finally understands what it is to walk in the shoes of another. So many of the world's ills could be cured if only we knew the joys and hardship of others' paths.

It was in that thought I finally found solace and through the dark hours of morning drifted into a ragged sleep, lulled by the girls' breathing, but awakening at every sound outside the car. The Klansman's threats lingered with me, and they must have haunted Thomas as well. In the morning, I noticed that he'd slept with a pistol nearby. He was hollow-eyed and weary in a way I'd never known him to be. He seemed older than himself, his carefree step gone as we cooked a camp breakfast and made ready to travel. Before departing our little resting spot, he insisted upon giving me lessons with a pistol and his rifle.

"You oughta know how to use 'em both, Mrs. Lorring." He delivered a long and stern look.

"I suppose I should."

Ziltha, you're aware, of course, that I have never touched a firearm in my life; Papa would not have considered such a thing either genteel or proper, but indeed, I wanted to learn. Given the unpredictable nature of our work here, it seemed prudent.

Perhaps I should not have shared so much with you, Sister Dear. Forgive my need to discuss these events with someone. Having no womenfolk of my own here, my letters are my only confidante. I feel certain that, living with an adventuring husband such as Benjamin, you will view my revelations with a practiced and practical eye. Please do not worry over me. I am well, and I am determined. I have been given a great commission in these mountains and I intend to fulfill it.

I am also, as it happens, a crack shot.

All my love,
Alice

"So what'd you think?" Clyde asked, and I suddenly realized he was leaning across the end table between his recliner and my mom's. "How's that for a tale?"

"Wow." I lowered the plastic sleeves that held the letter. Clyde had insisted on sealing up the rebuilt pages before letting me have them. It was a slow process, so I'd worked downstairs a bit and then taken care of lunch while I waited, but instead of eating his sandwich as I read, Clyde had been finishing up another letter, all the while grumbling about how hungry he was.

"It's interesting, but it's . . . sad at the same time," I admitted. "You know, when I read these things, it feels like it should be a couple hundred years ago, not just two generations back."

Like Alice, I'd lived a fairly sheltered life, closeted in a safe, working-class neighborhood and attending a private school. I'd occasionally experienced prejudice in other countries as an adult but not the kind of blind hatred Alice described in her letter. I'd certainly never had to look it in the eye.

Clyde repositioned in his chair, letting out a *harrumph* as he returned to his process of painstakingly tweezing shreds onto one side of a plastic sleeve, then laying the other side over the top and stapling carefully around the paper's borders to hold the letter together without the aid of tape. The floor around his feet was littered with maintenance-manual documents he'd torn from his old notebooks, so as to experiment with sleeves while I was gone.

"Not even a couple generations." He eyeballed a shred of paper through his bifocals. "I remember that sort of thing. Colored fellas come home from World War II and figured they oughta have it better after that. They'd got some respect while they was in the service, had kinfolk die, earned a military paycheck, seen the world. They come home, and they wanted to be treated like soldiers. Over in Europe, they didn't have to go to the back of the bus. They'd got a taste of livin' like men.

"Some folks thought they'd gone real uppity. There was a way things'd always been, and a colored man who expected different or wanted to use the GI Bill for college . . . well, he flew in the face of it. I ain't sayin' everybody was thataway toward the coloreds. There was plenty, includin' my daddy, who thought them Jim Crow laws was bad. There was plenty who'd seen the pictures and the films of the death camps over in Europe and couldn't abide things they might've turned a blind eye to before."

Peering over his bifocals, he picked up the box of scraps, shook it, searched for colors and textures that matched his current letter in progress. "I know my daddy wrestled with it in his job. In '48, Truman desegregated the army, and that made folks real edgy. If my daddy recruited a young colored kid and that kid's family had been somebody's sharecroppers since slavery days, like as not that farmer would show up on our doorstep, hotter than a pistol over it. He could see how it'd squeeze his own family's livelihood if Daddy took them boys away for a stint in the service.

"There was a time we was livin' down in Robeson County—Daddy was a recruiter there, too, and he was doin' pretty well with the Lumbee Indians, but there'd been some problems with the Ku Klux Klan over the Indians race mixin' with the whites. Daddy'd heard that Catfish Cole hisself was settin' up a KKK rally right in the heart of Lumbee territory. Daddy was afraid there'd be bloodshed over it, and he went there to try to bring home some of the boys he'd signed. Turned out, Daddy ended up right down there in the middle of five hundred mad-as-spit Lumbees with guns and about a hundred Klan marchers. I remember that night my mama kep' us all huddled in one room. She was scared to death Daddy wasn't comin' home."

Leaning over the card table again, Clyde added another scrap of paper, then reached for his tweezers to maneuver it into place. "My pap was the kind of fella other men knew not to trouble with, though. They were scared of him. To tell the truth, I was too. You didn't question him. You sure enough did mind what he said, though. Was a different time, back then. You knew better than to go around cryin' about whether your daddy took you fishin' or hugged you enough. You respected the man, and if he supported a family and didn't drink and didn't beat your mama, you thought you was a pretty lucky kid."

He rolled a look my way. "How about you leave me be awhile, so's I can eat my lunch and finish up this letter? Some afternoon coffee sounds good. Usually, this'd be my naptime by now, but you got me workin'."

"All right. Sure. I'll go take care of some things." I purposely sidestepped Clyde's comments about fatherhood. I had a feeling those were aimed at his kids.

If he knew I'd tried communicating with them, we wouldn't be sitting here happily putting letters together.

The future was a slippery slope I wasn't ready to approach again. For now, for this one rainy day, I wanted to enjoy the temporary cease-fire in the Excelsior war. The issue of Clyde was so complicated, it tied my brain in knots. It was easier to wander off to my room and call Denise to see how things were going at Bella Tazza. She still wouldn't tell me where she'd come up with the rest of the money for the range hood, but things at the restaurant were back to normal.

"Listen, Whit, I've gotta run." She shuffled me off the phone before I could dig down to the truth about the money. "We're slammed with Saturday traffic, and I mean *slammed.* Looks like it'll be a rush day." She sounded more weary than excited, which only made me feel that much more guilty as we said good-bye.

I sat in the chair by the window, staring out at the water-slick rooftops of Manteo and thinking about Mrs. Doyne. I still needed to contact her about the rent. Closing my eyes, I tried to compose an explanation in my head. Maybe I'd tell her that the range hood had put us behind a little—would it be all right if the rent was just a couple days late?

This was so unfair to her. I hated taking advantage of her kindness.

With any luck, the museum would have some decisions for me soon . . . and some money.

My thoughts drifted, wandering back to the Captain's Castle. I saw Mark on the porch and Rip in the yard . . . Joel's arm wrapped in a white towel . . .

I imagined a teenage daughter who wasn't there anymore . . .

The next thing I knew, I was waking up and three hours had flown by. I pushed to my feet, logy and confused, slowly remembering the morning, the plastic sleeves, Clyde.

When I returned to the living room, he was napping in his chair with Ruby at his feet. Another letter lay atop the table, completed.

I went to the kitchen and made coffee. The noise woke

Clyde, and he gave the cup I brought him a curmudgeonly look. "Slowest coffee I ever had."

"You looked like you were sleeping, so I left you alone."

He handed the new sleeves to me, matter-of-factly. "There's the next letter."

"Thanks." I turned again to Alice's story, letting it carry me into the past, into what had been written long ago.

Dearest Queen Ruby.

"One of the times we was movin' from place to place, I seen them doors in the mountain, like the ones that's in the letter there," Clyde interrupted before I could read any further. Knobby, red knuckles indicated the letter I was holding. "Don't 'member where we was goin', but I looked up the mountainside—it was someplace in Tennessee—and there was doors built right into the side of the mountain. I piped up and asked what was them doors."

"Doors . . . in the mountain?" I couldn't decide whether I was more compelled by Alice's latest letter or the bait Clyde had just tossed out. The letter, I decided, could wait. Later, Clyde might not be in the mood to talk. Our cease-fire might be over.

"Sure enough. Way up high, a boy come out of one. There was no house there, just the mountain, with a door in it. That boy stood there watchin' us go past. But then, when I tugged my sister's sleeve and pointed, the boy was gone and there was just the door. My sisters joined in on the questions too. We were all tired of bein' piled in the backseat of that old Packard by then. Daddy was in the mood for tale tellin' that day, I guess—sometimes he got that way at home, but mos'ly he kept his talkin' at the office, where it could win him recruits.

"'Back in Depression days, folks lived in them caves,' he told us. 'If the bank took their house, they went out and found a cave someplace. They'd build doors on the front to keep out the critters and the cold.'" A bushy gray eyebrow lifted. "That's somethin', ain't it? Folks livin' in that way?"

"Yes, it is." All those times my mother and I had driven through the mountains . . . somewhere hidden beyond the trees, were there caves with doors on them?

"Hadn't remembered about my daddy tellin' that story in years, either . . . not until Alice's letter come along. I 'member, back then, I thought it'd be real fine to make a house in the mountain. I told my daddy we oughta try it, and my mama got the shivers. Her family had hid out in a cave at the end of the war in Germany, and they pretty near got buried alive when the bombs dropped. I didn't talk about the cave houses anymore after she gave us that tale."

Watching Clyde, I saw the young boy in the back of that car. I imagined all the history he would live in the coming years—history that deserved to be preserved and shared with his sons and the grandchildren he never saw anymore. Maybe if they knew what he had experienced, they would understand him better, be able to forgive. "You really should take time to write those things down. Or record them on a digital recorder. Those memories shouldn't be lost."

"Nobody cares about them old things." He went back to work and left me to read Alice's letter, but for a moment, I only stared at the words, my mind preoccupied with my stepfather's life. I let my thoughts drift again to the crowded Packard as the breeze blew through and a boy stood on the side of a mountain, watching a car snake along an old two-lane below. That wouldn't have been so very long after Alice and Thomas discovered those mountains with Emmaline and Able curled together in the backseat.

What had Alice learned about the doors in the mountain?

Dearest Queen Ruby,

It is a fine day, indeed! A miraculous day, and though you know me to have been generally more pragmatic and routine in matters of faith, I cannot attribute these recent events to anything other than divine providence. We have discovered the location of some Melungeons.

I do believe it was by God-given appointment that Able and Emmaline noticed two little girls playing in the river in their white chemises. We were proceeding slowly, as a man with a horse cart had the road. The trees were thick on both sides, a sharp peak to our right and a drop-off to the river on our left. I had threatened Tom with his life, should he try to bypass the horse and cart under these conditions, so we were creeping along, with Tom not in the most famous of moods.

This was the reason, this and the warm day, that the girls noticed the children in the river and the doors on the mountainside across the way. Had we not rolled down the windows, we would never have heard the little girls singing below.

"Look, Mama!" said Emmaline, pointing with great excitement, her arm dangling from the car. "Mama, there's doors in the hill!"

I followed her line of sight, and in the next gust of wind I saw the doors and then the two girls in the river, splashing about like pixies. As we were making no time anyway, we pulled off the road at a covered bridge just down a bit, left the car parked in a wide spot, and hiked back upwater with

Able and Emmaline in tow. Tom was afraid we could be disturbing a bootlegger's camp, but with the children present and their clothing not the least bit ragged, I doubted that they were any such thing.

So, of course, they were not. What was found, when we had labored along the creek and then been led uphill by the children, was a village built into the hillside, not unlike the ancient pueblos you and I once admired in the mountains of Colorado. Ziltha, some forty souls live in the caves here! Various families reside two per cave in the larger ones, and some caves hold only one family. They have built doors across the openings to hold away the rain, snow, and wildlife, and this is how they stay.

Having lost their homes, farms, or employment in other places, they have found their way here and formed a community of survivors. They hail from many walks of life—some Cherokee, some mountain folk who were born in these hills, some who have gone away and come back. They live off the land, and what the land may provide. They fish, hunt, trap, and dry meat. They have, between them, two cows, which give eight gallons of milk per day. These are divided among the families.

"We tell the children it is a castle and they are fortunate to have the adventure of it," said the father of the two girls we had seen at the river. In another life, he'd owned a car sales business in Greenville. Their clothing makes it evident that they have seen finer days and were once quite well-to-do. When the bank failed, they lost everything. "I wanted to lay my head down somewhere and never wake up," he admitted, and his confession brought thoughts of my Richard, of the fate he chose for himself that day on the

ferry when he could not face that the stock market crash had taken everything.

I was, at that moment, so very angry with him again, almost as if the wound were still fresh. Here before me was a man who had brought his family to the mountains where he had once vacationed in fishing and hunting camps. Here was a husband who had not abandoned his wife and children, but fought for them. They had come here by hoboing the train as far as they could before the railroad bulls caught them and threw them off. After that, they hiked for days through the mountains. They were the first to take up housekeeping in these caves and build a door. The others have joined as time went on, but Mr. Ross is the clear leader of the community. He keeps the peace and decrees whether or not newcomers will be allowed to stay.

He is quite a learned man, and he travels the mountains by mule from time to time to trade for supplies or medicines, as needed. It was he who told me of a small settlement of Melungeons some forty miles from here, around the mountain and across another valley. Though it will take us off our tour route, Thomas and I have made plans to travel there tomorrow, to record the stories of the Melungeon people and to see if Able might have family among them. If no kin can be found, we hope they can give us the exact location of the Melungeon orphans' school.

I have also learned a bit more about the Melungeons, courtesy of Mr. Ross. A well-read mind does not cease its hunger because physical circumstances change. Mr. Ross has devoted his time here to documenting the native plants and how they are used medicinally and as foodstuffs. As a result of his dealings with the Melungeons over this matter, he has studied their history and believes that the bloodcurdling rumors of their communication with spirits and practice of witchcraft are unfortunate falsehoods, partly perpetrated by those desiring to claim the Melungeons' land and partly caused by the innate reclusiveness of Melungeon families.

"Can you blame them?" he asked as we sat talking. "From the time they were first discovered in these mountains, the Melungeons have been treated terribly. They've been pushed from their lands and farms, labeled as Free Persons of Color, and stripped of their rights. Prior to the War between the States, they were subject to being kidnapped and pressed into slavery. It's certainly no wonder they've kept to themselves."

He shared with me the stories he had heard from several families whose ancestors had once hosted Miss Will Allen Dromgoole, a journalist who came to the mountain country and penned several newspaper articles about the "Lost Tribe of Blue-Eyed Indians" in 1891. The content of Miss Dromgoole's articles on Melungeons was considered to be quite derogatory to the very people who had welcomed her into their homes. To be fair to Miss Dromgoole, perhaps this was a product of the time in which she lived and wrote.

Mr. Ross has warned me that many among the Melungeon families have not forgotten Miss Dromgoole's work. They are still smarting over it, now forty-odd years later, and I might have my work cut out for me in winning their trust. My letter of introduction from the Federal Writers' Project will do no good with them, he assured me, and suggested that I invoke his name instead. He has shown me a small, strangely carved bone pendant roughly the size of a silver dollar. The piece bears an etching on the front and opens via a small brass pin, revealing a tiny compartment.

Mr. Ross claims that the pendant came from the Melungeons, and that, indeed, several of their women possess similar items, which they wear tied on strings around their necks. These are considered sacred. They are passed down from generation to generation, following the line of eldest daughters. The items are used in prayer, and often the owners will place scraps of paper inside, bearing written needs, pictures, or small pieces of Scripture.

Whereas last night found me sleepless with worry and fearful of the Klansman, this evening I lie settled into a cozy log-and-rope bed vacated by the Ross children. I am filled with anticipation as I write to you by kerosene light! My thumb rubs back and forth across the smoothly worn surface of Mr. Ross's bone locket, and I am once again overtaken by the conviction that, above all else, I was meant to gather the stories of the hidden people. Had I not come here, had my life remained in all the familiar rhythms, I would never have found this calling that gives me new purpose.

How sad, I think now, to live an entire life blinded by the ordinary, when the path to the extraordinary waits just beyond the well-meaning prisons of our own making.

It is no accident that the small pendant, shaped much like a watch case but carved from polished bone, feels so very holy as I hold it in my hand. It bears on its front the etching of a Maltese cross.

I know it is true that God has brought me to these mountains.

All my love,
Alice

CHAPTER 17

"This . . . is amazing." I turned over the last sheet of Alice's letter and set it on the card table.

Clyde slid his bifocals down. "Must've been somethin' else, seeing all the people livin' in cave houses. Young folks don't understand how it was back then, but of course, I grew up with people who'd lived through the Depression. My mama and daddy saved ever'thing from bread wrappers to chicken livers. I didn't know there *was* such a thing as clothes or toys that hadn't been somebody else's first. Folks didn't just run out and buy, buy, buy. They knew to save for a rainy day. Now if people have a little trouble, they go crawlin' to the insurance company or some government program, or they file for the welfare. Back in Depression times, you had to pull yourself up by your bootstraps. Daddy used to tell us how ever'body was broke. Was no place to get a job when he was a boy. Even the military got cut back to bones after the First World War. My daddy's folks were farmers in the Blue Ridge, and that's how they survived. Daddy used to say he didn't know what a real dollar looked like 'til he went into the service durin' World War II."

Listening to Clyde, I was reminded of how much of my own

family history had been lost, especially on my father's side. "The story about the cave houses is fascinating. But this necklace she's talking about, the ones Alice says the Melungeons wore . . . I found something similar downstairs. I wonder if she might've sent it here to my grandmother? Maybe Mr. Ross gave it to her to keep?"

But why would Ziltha have saved the necklace, while throwing away all the letters? If she had broken ties with her sister, why hide the necklace and Alice's original letter in the desk? Or had Lucianne done that? Had she hoped that one day I would find these things and search out the rest of Alice's story?

Clyde worked his lips like he was chewing cud. "Maybe she thought it was worth somethin'." He returned to his task. "I get the rest of these letters together, they might answer the question for us. Near as I can guess, we got less than ten more."

"Only *ten*?"

"That's the *most* there is, and some are pretty fouled up with water stains and pieces gone. I don't think we'll be gettin' the whole story, but maybe we can find some of it. Might be we can figure out the rest another way."

"The museum . . ." I was thinking about the card Tandi Chastain had given me. She'd been so interested in the bone necklace. . . .

"What'zat?"

"I need to go check something on my computer." If fakes of those necklaces were so popular, surely I could google around a bit and find out why. What was I missing here? Tandi had mentioned a research project having to do with the Lost Colony. What potential connection could there be between that and Alice Lorring's travels in the Blue Ridge Mountains almost eighty years ago?

Real-world problems battled with that question. I'd once again burned up the day, researching Alice. In reality, it didn't matter *where* the necklace had come from or what Alice's story was, aside from whatever way that affected the price. My getting emotionally involved wouldn't help.

But I already was emotionally involved, and I knew it. I felt the ties to Alice, and the more I learned about her, the more they deepened.

"It's about time for some supper." Clyde's complaint followed me down the hall. "Can't expect a man to work on an empty stomach!"

Ruby caught up to me as I turned the corner into the bedroom, her expression apologetically saying, *If somebody doesn't take me to the park soon, we're gonna have troub-ble.*

"Ruby . . . *now*?" My laptop was right there . . . within reach.

A whimper, a hangdog look, a cowering body. Ruby's answer was easy to read.

"Okay . . . okay, I'm sorry." I patted her head. Tucking the cell phone and some money into my pocket, I grabbed the dollar-store leash, hooked it on Ruby's dollar-store collar, and slipped into my tennis shoes. The dog panted and lunged, dragging me down the hall, nearly choking herself as we moved through the living room. "We have to make a park run. I'll grab some supper at the Full Moon while I'm out."

"I'll be here." Clyde was fully engrossed in a letter. "Go on, git. Stop watchin' me work a'ready." He didn't even look up as Ruby and I hurried off.

On the street, Mark was just closing up his shop. Ruby skimmed past him in a rush, wrapping his legs in the leash, so that Mark and I almost experienced a *101 Dalmatians* moment. He side-straddled the dog in one quick leap.

"You two are dangerous." A wink gave the words a double meaning.

A strange, glittery feeling fluttered through me. "I think she's a little desperate to get to the park. She's been cooped up all afternoon."

Nodding, he assessed the roiling clouds over Creef Park. "Been that kind of a day. Looks like it's moving on now, though."

"Guess it didn't cooperate with your plans to go to the water." The murky weather offered a convenient excuse for the fact that I hadn't been in touch about taking Rip to the beach. It was probably a good thing the storm had come through. *You do* not *need to get involved here,* the voice of reason was telling me, but at the same time, Mark was smiling *that* smile, and I felt it in the pit of my stomach. I'd never experienced anything quite like that before, and living the resort life, I'd crossed paths with some hunky men.

I was vaguely aware of Ruby tugging her way around the corner of the building, but it was a moment before I realized she'd just befouled the Rip Shack's flower bed. "Sorry." I winced.

Mark's soft laugh was warm and familiar—the kind of chuckle that's traded between friends who make allowances for one another. "Don't worry about it. She's not the first dog to get that idea."

"Rip would *never* . . ."

"He's probably the reason she did that."

The mention of Rip brought to mind the revelation about the dog's original owner . . . Mark's daughter. I remembered the sensation of standing with him this morning, the connection I'd felt, the sharing of things that were honest and raw. It was so unlike me. I usually kept my junk to myself and didn't invite other people to reveal theirs. Things were easier that way. Less complicated.

Mark was a risk in so many ways.

"How's Joel?"

"Better. His girlfriend, Kayla, came to stay with him at the house. She's a good kid. Has her life together. Twenty-three and out of college, working, so she's older and wiser. She's pretty stuck on Joel, but she wants him to clean up his act. To grow up. She's convinced she can change him."

"What do *you* think?" It was a deeper question, one that went far beyond Joel and his decisions about life.

Mark took a moment to consider his answer. "I don't think people change unless they want to. I told him if he'd get his stuff from his uncle's house, he could come stay with me awhile, as long as he keeps clean, stays out of trouble, and shows up for work. The guys he was with at the party last night rolled somebody's Jeep. That's where Joel got the scratches. Apparently they all walked away, but the vehicle is totaled. Some vacationing college student has an unhappy phone call to make to Mommy and Daddy, I guess."

I thought of Joel, of all that potential hanging on the thin thread of a nineteen-year-old's decisions. Someone like Mark could make the difference. "I hope Joel takes you up on it."

"Me too."

Overhead, the Excelsior moaned in the wind, as if it were adding to the conversation, pointing out that it, too, could have a purpose. This place could change the future for kids like Joel. Depending on the value of the bone locket and the other things I'd left at the museum, so many options might open up. If replicas of the lockets were sold around here, Mark might know about them.

"Hey, I've got a question for you. Are you in a hurry right now? Can you hang on a minute while I take Ruby across the street?"

"I'll walk over with you." He started off without waiting for agreement.

I fell into step with him, Ruby lurching ahead, tugging me like a tetherball as I tried to relate the story of the letters and the necklace and what I'd learned at the museum. "The director there said she was afraid the necklace was fake because there are so many reproductions around now, that they're a tourist item. I was about to do a little googling about it, but Ruby decided it was time to make a trip to the park."

Mark mulled a moment. "Sounds like you might be talking about the story keeper necklaces."

"The what?"

"The story keeper necklaces. Your museum director is right—there's a flood of them being produced in China and India. Stores and gas stops from here to Nashville carry them. Once the movie comes out, I'm sure they'll be hanging in novelty shops everywhere."

"What movie?"

He blinked, blinked again, looked at me as if my head had suddenly popped off my body and danced a jig. "Where have *you* been for the past year? Under a rock?"

"Sort of." Usually after a day in the restaurant, I came home exhausted, and the last thing I wanted to do was turn on the TV and take in the news. There were times when it was all I could do to get out of bed, make the drive into work, and face the staff and the customers . . . and Denise. Failure is a miserable feeling, especially after you've tried so hard.

There were other times when I told myself I needed to quit being such a wimp. Today was one of those. Compared to what

Mark had been through, my business problems were minuscule. I hadn't lost anything that hard work couldn't replace. Mark's daughter was *gone*. He wouldn't see her grow up, graduate from high school, go to college. He'd never walk her down the aisle. . . .

The dose of perspective hit me hard. I'd made the restaurant business life or death.

It wasn't.

Mark was eyeballing me. "Time Shifters? Evan Hall? The writer? You work around young people. That must ring a bell."

Snapping my fingers, I pointed at him. "I do know that one." *Thank you, hot-line cooks and lovesick waitresses.* For years, I'd been listening to twentysomethings prattle on about their latest entertainment obsessions. "So the necklace I found in the Excelsior is somehow related to . . . a book?" Perplexed didn't even begin to describe me right now.

Mark chuckled. "You really are out of the mainstream. His last book, *The Story Keeper*, stirred up a huge hoopla, especially around here because there were some ties to the Lost Colony. I'm sure that's why the museum down on Hatteras has such an interest. Supposedly parts of the book came from a true story—an old one. There are people who dispute whether that's fact or fiction, but all the press makes for good business. No doubt that's what the museum is thinking."

Ruby tugged on her leash, and I let her go. She never wandered far when we were outside; she was too afraid of being left behind. "Okay . . . so, clue me in a bit about this whole thing. I'm not all that up on pop culture. I just learned what *YOLO* meant, like, a month ago. I thought the kids at work were saying *yo-yo*. My cousin's six-year-old daughter had to finally explain that it meant 'you only live once.'"

A playful *tsk-tsk* answered. "All work and no play . . ."

"Sad, I know. Long story, but it's been a complicated year. We're fighting a legal battle over our second restaurant. The other side is as crooked as wet linguine and just about as slimy. But they're *not* going to win."

Thick lashes hooded his thoughts. Something passed by—something deeper than chatter about books. Was he registering the fact that I had reasons to sell the Excelsior—reasons that couldn't be ignored? "All right. Here's the quick version: When the book came out last year, the press nugget was that it was based on a turn-of-the-century journal and an old manuscript that had been written about the journal. Both were supposedly rediscovered recently. One of the carved bone necklaces was found with them. The author of the manuscript claimed that the necklaces originated with people who were marooned here on the coast long before other Europeans came—before the Pilgrims and so forth. If that's really true, those people could have been Sir Walter Raleigh's Lost Colonists. That might challenge some of the theories about how they vanished from Roanoke and where they went."

"Okay . . . I see." Now the conversations at Benoit House made more sense, and so did Tandi Chastain's intense fascination with the scrimshaw piece and the necklace.

"You can imagine what a hot debate the subject is."

"Wow." Without even realizing it, the Excelsior and I had stepped into a local news hotbed. Somewhere in there, Alice's letters niggled too. What had she learned about the necklaces and the Melungeon women who wore them? "So, do *you* think it's real—this whole story keeper thing, I mean?" Mark seemed like a practical man, not the kind to succumb to wild theories or Hollywood hype. He was a lawyer, after all. Lawyers dealt in facts. Things they could prove.

His lips pulled to one side, and I caught myself watching in a less-than-platonic way. That massive house he lived in had a woman's touch because he'd purchased it fully furnished, not because there was a wife or girlfriend involved. But it seemed to be . . . waiting for something. For some*one*.

It wasn't the kind of place a guy bought and kept as a bachelor pad.

It was a home for a family.

What did the owner of the Rip Shack really want from life?

"I think you have to be careful of taking things at face value." He frowned, and I had the sense that those words referred to *me*, not the necklaces. "The whole setup has high theatrical value. It could've been manufactured to hype a book and a movie. Word is that, so far, they've found nothing to corroborate the journal, and nothing about Louisa Quinn, who wrote her manuscript based on the journal. If you ask me, it smells like a publicity stunt. But again, it's good for the Outer Banks, and after all the hurricanes, we need it. The cheap Chinese knockoffs of the story keeper necklaces are cheesy, but that's not all bad either."

"I guess not." I imagined Alice stroking the Maltese cross as she fell asleep beneath the flickering kerosene light in the cave house. Her letters were real enough, and she'd had one of those necklaces in her hand in 1936.

Mark leaned in, catching my gaze. "So . . . what's going on in there, Whitney? You went somewhere else for a minute."

"I did?" *Evade, deny, hide.* The reaction was instant.

"See now, if I had you on the witness stand, I'd be drilling down, looking for what's underneath."

"Good thing I'm not on the witness stand, then . . . right?" We were playing at this back-and-forth banter, yet we *weren't*. In some sense, I was on trial with him, but that went both ways.

I couldn't quite decide what to think of Mark. All the evidence seemed to add up to one thing—that he really was a decent guy. The kind you didn't meet every day.

But I couldn't trust the evidence.

He rested his hands on the waist of his jeans. "Sorry, once a lawyer, always a lawyer. I'm still in recovery."

I couldn't help laughing. "I get it. I can't go in a restaurant without analyzing the food, the flow patterns of the waitstaff, and the plate time. I'd be back in the kitchens checking those out, too, if I could do it without getting arrested."

"You must be a tough dinner date." The warm tone and a glance toward town said he was thinking about it. In reality, I was too. I wanted him to ask even though I didn't need the distraction, couldn't spare the time, and Clyde was upstairs waiting for sustenance. *Plus there's the dog. You can't take Ruby to dinner with you.*

Excuses, excuses, excuses . . .

There were plenty of reasons why not. And one reason why.

Him.

The phone rang in my pocket. I took it out and looked at who it was, felt my chest seize up. "I have to take this. I'm sorry." And I was, in a way, but another part of me was relieved. I had the feeling that comes with realizing you've narrowly avoided something potentially dangerous, like a car accident.

Turning a shoulder to Mark, I answered the phone and asked what was up. Denise didn't leave me in suspense for long. "Nothing good, I'm afraid, Whit."

"Oh no . . . *what*?"

Mark politely wandered a few steps away, checking on Ruby.

Denise's answer came in a rushed whisper. "Tagg Harper and a group of his buddies are sitting at table number six. He just

. . . walked in here like he owned the place. Amber was running the front end, and she didn't have any idea who he was or not to seat him. Melissa took his order. She didn't know who he was either."

"*Tagg Harper* is in our *restaurant*?" I couldn't even give her time to finish the story. I was livid. I wanted to grab Tagg by the scruff of his neck, drag him to the door, and throw him into the parking lot, then kick him across it until he was off the property. Right now, I felt capable of doing it—evicting all three hundred pounds of him. "Well, tell him to get out. Tell him we're not cooking him *anything*. Tell him *I* said it, if you want to." Sometimes Denise was just too nice. Too passive. It drove me crazy.

"Calm down, Whitney."

"I *am* calm, Denise. But you do *not* have to serve that jerk. Showing up there is just one more way of trying to intimidate us. He's gloating because he's so sure he's won. He thinks he can force us out of business." I sank onto the bench, trying to breathe.

"They'd already ordered, and their meals were half plated by the time I even knew they were here. I was working in the back. Kenny's home sick with the flu. I'm just hoping no one else catches it."

"Well, if you think anyone else has symptoms, have them plate up Tagg Harper's food." Every muscle in my body tightened and burned.

Denise gave a weary groan. "Thought about it. But I guess the good news is, for the most part, the Tazza 1 staff doesn't seem to know who Tagg is, which means the Tazza 2 staff have kept it quiet, like we asked them to."

"I *guess* that qualifies as good news." I rose from the bench, paced, sat down again. "Ohhhh, I wish I were there."

"If you *were* here, I don't think he would've come in. It's *you* he's wondering about. He asked Melissa a whole bunch of questions about where you'd gone. And you know Melissa—if she thinks there's a tip in it for her, she'll spill almost anything. Fortunately, she hasn't a clue why you left or where you've been. It's pretty clear that Tagg is worried about it, though."

"I'm sure he's trolling eBay every five minutes, waiting for us to put the equipment from Tazza 2 up for sale. It's probably driving him crazy that we haven't."

"Yes, that's pretty much the impression I got. He's seriously desperate for news."

"Well, it's nice to think of Tagg Harper as desperate." Thank goodness I'd asked Mrs. Doyne not to tell anyone about the phone message that had brought me to the Outer Banks.

"Yeah, true." Denise sounded shaky, obviously nervous. There was something more that she wasn't telling me.

"Denise, what else is wrong? You don't sound good." How much pressure was Tagg laying on? With me gone, was he working even harder on Denise? "Did Tagg Harper threaten you?"

"No . . . I don't know . . ." She was still deciding whether or not to burden me with whatever was burdening her.

"Denise . . . *what is wrong*?"

"Mattie said there was a man outside her window the other night, that's all."

"She *what*? There was someone outside Mattie's window? At your *house*?" I felt dizzy and sick, my heart pumping. "Did you go look? Was someone there?"

"Mattie was home with Grandma Daisy. Grammy just thought Mattie was making excuses not to go to bed, so I didn't find out about it until I got her up for school in the morning.

She'd slept in my bed, and I asked her why. She told me it was because of the man outside."

"Could you see any evidence that someone had been prowling around your place?" What now? Was this just a stunt? A way of getting me to resurface? Or was it a genuine threat? Everything pivoted on one central balance point, the most important one of all: what was Tagg Harper really capable of?

"I looked, but I couldn't tell anything. Her bedroom does face the park, though. It would definitely be possible for someone to walk across. But . . . then again, the whole thing really could be Mattie not wanting to sleep in her own bed. Anyway, I put the old nursery cam in her room and pointed it toward the window, just in case. She's sleeping in my bed for now."

"Denise, if you even *think* someone's been stalking your house, call the police. Promise me. If it's Tagg or one of his guys, they're probably just trying to scare us, or maybe to see if I'll show up at your place. But if Tagg *is* worried that we're mounting a new defense for the code commission hearing, there's no telling what he might try."

"I *am* being careful. But if I can get his face on the nursery cam, we'll have—"

"I mean it, Denise. Do *not* take any risks to catch him."

"Yes, I heard you. Hey, Whit, I need to go. I just peeked out and orders are stacking up." That was probably true, but she was also brushing me off.

"Okay. Listen, I'll try to check with the museum tomorrow. If I can get in touch with anyone on Sunday, I'll ask whether they can speed things up, and I'll get back home."

Denise and I said good-bye, and I started formulating plans. I needed help finishing my search of the Excelsior's second floor. Maybe it would be worth asking Joel, despite Mark's concern about the company he kept. After what'd happened last night, and especially if he was staying at Mark's house, Joel would hopefully be keeping his nose clean. Working with me in the building would give him something productive to do in his off hours.

"Sorry about that." I walked to where Mark and Ruby were mirror images, watching a tree squirrel watch them. There was no point pretending that Mark hadn't heard my entire conversation with Denise.

"That didn't sound good." He frowned.

"No, it's not." I was about a scant half inch from cracking apart and dissolving into a weeping, moaning, ranting basket case. Instead, I ran the practical next steps through my mind. "This does mean that I need to step up my time frame here in Manteo. Before I go back home, I have to at least finish a thorough search of the second floor. I guess you can see why that's important." *The cat's out of the bag, but what does it matter? Reality is reality.*

What was he thinking? What, exactly, was behind that concerned expression?

"I know it sounds mercenary, Mark, but the things in the hotel building, they're . . . I realize that some of it is historical, and I want to do the right thing with whatever we find, but I'm out of time, and . . . it's not like I have an emotional attachment to any of it." That wasn't true. I *was* attached. I just couldn't let myself be. "It's only *stuff.* Just . . . possessions. I have employees depending on me at home . . . and my cousin. I was the one who convinced her to go into the restaurant business in the first place."

Could he see that I wasn't some horrible person? That I was just desperate and doing the best I could to thread my way through the minefield of a horrible situation? "Do you think it'd be okay if I hired Joel to help me for a few days? I know almost no one here, and I need to wrap this up, and there are still boxes and closets and dresser drawers to dig through."

A skeptical look darkened Mark's face, and I rushed on before he could answer. "I just thought . . . if Joel's staying with you right now, he wouldn't be out running around with . . . whoever. . . ."

Mark watched a boat idle toward its slip, letting the idea perc a minute. "That's the tough part, to tell you the truth, and that's the reason it hasn't done a lot of good when Joel has moved to my house before. I'm gone a lot. I still own an interest in a law firm over in Norfolk, and there's the Rip Shack. I'm not home to watch Joel, and Joel doesn't do too well on his own. His girlfriend works odd hours a lot. You leave Joel by himself for the evening and he wanders off, looking for something to do."

"The building could definitely keep him busy for a few days." Even as I said it, I realized there was no way I'd be out of here as quickly as I'd led Denise to believe . . . whether I had Joel's help or not. I could put off decisions about what to ultimately do with the building, but I still had Clyde and the dog to worry about.

Two tons of bricks descended again. I felt their crushing weight.

Mark's expression turned sympathetic. "Listen, Whitney, I know you and I got off on the wrong foot when you came here, but I might be able to do something to help. I don't really practice law anymore, except for handling a few corporate clients who've been with me a long time, but I'd be happy to take a look at the situation with your restaurant, do a little research, see if I can come up with any angles for you."

My instinctive reaction was to pull back, to be careful, to question. Why would he offer to do that? What did he want in return? Lawyers didn't give away their services for free. Of course, he *did* want to keep me from making hasty decisions about the Excelsior. . . .

Maybe you should be leaning in instead of pulling away. The urge hit me completely by surprise, so foreign I didn't even recognize the voice whispering in my head. It came from someplace outside the person I knew. *Maybe there's a reason that phone call came while he was around to hear it.*

"You're wondering what my motives are," he preempted.

"Stop that."

"Stop what?"

"Stop trying to read me." Hugging my arms close, I looked away, felt the wind of new possibilities pull against the mooring lines of old habits. Did I have the courage to cast off the ties to the life I'd been living since I was five years old and trust had become a liability?

Mark shifted his weight, tucked his hands loosely in his pockets—a patient, unhurried posture. "You're hard to read," he admitted, "and I'm usually pretty good at that."

His observation left me briefly triumphant, then sad. "In business, you have to be careful . . . about people."

"In business, or in life?"

"Both." The admission was so close to the core, I couldn't believe I'd let it come out. I looked away, watched some kids laughing and joking, daring each other to bail off as they crossed the arched bridge to Festival Park.

Overhead, a pair of grackles raised a ruckus in the trees. Mark waited for them to quiet. "Then I guess the question you have to ask yourself is, 'What's he really after?' Maybe I'm just trying to make sure you have time to really think about the future of the Excelsior."

I turned back, and he was watching me intently, his warm brown eyes pulling me in, a slight smile toying, as if he were enjoying the attempt to decipher me . . . as if he relished the challenge. "But maybe I'm after something more."

CHAPTER 18

I held the letter closer to my face, then farther away, then closer again, trying to make out as many of the water-stained words as I could.

"That one's not easy to tell much about." Clyde paused across the card table. The remains of two takeout dinners were stacked between us, slowly drying into sculpture, and we had dragged in floor lamps from everywhere, trying for better light as evening dimmed the room. I'd lost track of how long we'd been sitting there, but my rear end and the chair had slowly become one. My clothes felt itchy and tight. For hours now I'd been vaguely conscious that I'd be much more comfortable if I'd just get up, walk down the hall, and change into my sweats and T-shirt.

But there was a sense of magic in the air, and if either Clyde or I moved, the spell would be broken. I could feel Alice and Thomas there with us, or perhaps *I* was with *them* as they struggled through unfamiliar country, forced off course by rains that had flooded the only available river crossing. The main bridge was out of service until WPA workers could build a new one, stone by stone.

Even here, so far from the cities, Roosevelt's controversial

New Deal was in evidence. There was talk of the ongoing construction of the Appalachian Scenic Highway, which would traverse the Blue Ridge from Virginia through North Carolina. In the tiny theaters of mountain hamlets, newsreels lauded progress and the ability of the country to "tighten its belt a notch" to survive hard times. Thomas had insisted on stopping to take the girls to the matinee showing of *Captain Blood*, featuring Errol Flynn and Olivia de Havilland. Able had never seen a picture show, a theater, or the ocean.

Neither Thomas nor Alice had realized that, before the main feature, a newsreel would explore the tragedy of the Dust Bowl in Oklahoma, Texas, and Kansas. The filmmaker had recorded not only skies blackened by blowing dirt but the shack camps filled with refugees. There, he'd interviewed hopeless families and filmed bone-thin children dressed in rags, their hair hanging in brittle, dirt-encrusted mats, their expressions hollow and bleak. Their eyes were haunting, their skin sunbaked and scabbed by the effects of pellagra and other diseases of malnutrition.

Alice's letter had described the somber mood in the theater, making me feel as if I were there.

> *Oh, Ziltha, you cannot imagine how sad the moment when adult realities land hard upon your child. Emmaline threw her hands over her face and wept, and Able leaned close to my ear. "Them folk be a far piece off yander, you reckon, Miz Lorrin'?"*
>
> *"Yes, Able, Oklahoma is quite a distance." I dabbed at my eyes, silently questioning whether I should be collecting relief pay for my writing when the funds could be used to feed starving children. There are those who say that make-work*

projects like ours steal food from the mouths of babes.
Perhaps they do.

Beside me, Able startled in her chair as the tail of the film whipped loose, the projector flipping light, then dark, then light, then dark, until the theater worker caught and stilled it. "There be a train there like that'un the fella livin' in the cave rode hisself on with his woman and young'uns?"

"Yes, Able, they do have trains in Oklahoma. Although there may be such sand drift over the tracks that the trains no longer run."

Able nodded, her lips set resolutely. "We oughta git us a big ol' basket'r two, and hist us on up the mount'n. I can find some cottonwood bud and boil a Gilead mash fer them scabs. If'n you got a lil' whiskey, it'll make up right pearly, even. The pawpaws is a ripenin' now too. I seen some not fer off from here. Reckon we can find us a big ol' mess and send 'em on that train to them folks over yander? Pawpaws is good eatin, 'n' keeps purdy awhile too."

Alice had lifted an arm to hug Able, but the girl shied away. Thomas took Alice's hand instead, and she didn't stop him from it. Later, she reprimanded herself. As they left the theater, she told herself that she shouldn't encourage him. In her letter, she confessed to her sister that she knew Tom had taken a fancy to her. She referred to it as "a schoolboy crush" and spent paragraphs analyzing the difference in their ages, pointing out the fact that he was just a boy, and she a widow and a mother. He was the age of the college students she'd helped in the dean's office.

She reminded herself that she and Thomas were colleagues, hired to perform an important job. That they must set a good example for the children. That nothing could happen between them. But, reading her letters, it was clear enough that something was happening. . . .

The card table creaked as Clyde leaned my way. "Keep tryin', you'll make it out. You got younger eyes than mine. You could borrow my lookin' glass." He held up the large, square magnifier that my mother had used with her fine needlework. While I'd been down in the park with Ruby and Mark, Clyde had gathered up a few new tools.

"I've got it. Thanks, though."

"Be stubborn, then. Sometimes, you could just take somebody's help."

"Look who's talking." A laugh pushed out, and Clyde snorted in response.

"Just like your mama."

I glanced up, and he shook his head, then went back to work, his lips moving like he was chewing gristle . . . or trying not to smile.

Just like your mama. Was I anything like her? My mother was the best person I'd ever known. She had a nose for potential. She found it in pieces of sea glass and driftwood, and in people. She always wanted those around her to see the greatest possible versions of themselves. That passion made her a fantastic teacher.

I wasn't anything like her. But I wanted to be.

"Thanks, Clyde."

Shrugging away my gratitude, he put the magnifier back in its stand, peering through it as he tweezed tiny scraps of paper onto a piece of double-sided tape. Some of the letters, corroded by liquids or food acids, had disintegrated to the point that nothing else could be done with them.

I returned to the one Alice had written after the visit to the theater. That evening, storms, more flooding, and a flat tire had trapped them at the farm of a friendly old couple. Alice took advantage of the opportunity to collect the family's stories of life in the mountains before the turn of the century. Thomas spent time in the barn working on the car, which had been pulled from the ditch by the farmer's mule team. The girls enjoyed brushing and riding a Shetland pony, kept for the entertainment of twenty-four grandchildren.

I read the letter in bits and pieces, making out what I could between stains and ink runs.

Mr. Higgs knows of the Melungeons and says that we have made out the map given us by the cave dwellers quite correctly, despite our enormous detour caused by the flooded water crossing. Even though we'd had slow going, with two flat tires the day we stopped to see the picture show, it is good to know that we are still on roughly the right track. I have explained to Mr. Higgs that it is our intention to find the mission school that was Merry Walker's hope for Able. Poor child, she is round as an apple in the middle, though the baby isn't due for two months yet.

Mr. Higgs was reluctant to talk of the Melungeon school in the beginning, but has since admitted that, though he has never seen it, he has heard of the place. He has directed us to go from here to the home of Mrs. Ida Mullins, a Melungeon woman living an hour's drive around the mountain, though less than a mile across the hollow, as the crow flies. The location is quite remote, the last part of the trail traversable only by mule or on foot. He is confident that she can direct us to the orphan school. He has warned us, though, that it is unlikely the place will be equipped or willing to take in Able's baby. Not many schools are prepared for orphans so young. We've told him we will cross that bridge when we come to it.

On our route to the home of Ida Mullins and then hopefully to the school, we will cover some of our requisite tour territory, albeit not by the prescribed path. The national headquarters has decreed that all tour descriptions for the guidebooks must run from south to north. Thomas says that the bureaucrats in Washington do not understand the nature of mountain roads and flooded bridges. With Thomas's skills and mine, we will piece together the information needed to keep up my quota and ensure that field reports go in more or less on time. As we've been able between the storms, Thomas has worked at his mapping and photography, and I have collected narratives and have written descriptions of several nearby rock bluffs and waterfall sites that will be included in the North Carolina State Guidebook.

I have begun to worry, if only slightly, what the headquarters' reaction may be when I submit the Melungeons' narratives, assuming I am so fortunate as to gather them. Indeed, I have been shocked at times by how venomously the residents here speak of the Melungeons. There are those who find their inclusion in the project to be a threat to the reputation of the mountains.

Even Mrs. Higgs, who is part Cherokee herself, does not speak well of these people. She has not refused shelter and food to Able, but she will not allow her to sleep inside either. We've been forced to put Able on the porch. When Mrs. Higgs sat us to dinner, she sent the girls to the kitchen, claiming the space at the main table for her grandchildren, who had walked over from the nearby farm in the rain. Though they were big boys, they were quite afraid of Able, and I gathered that, like many children, they had often been threatened that the Melungeons would spirit them off to some devilish fate, were they to misbehave.

What a sad and strange thing that, having herself suffered some amount of injustice over the years for her Cherokee blood, Mrs. Higgs would not find the stench of it unpleasant. Indeed, her husband is loosely aligned with local Klansmen, having friends among them and occasionally attending their rallies and parades, in his words, "for the good o' my bid'ness."

It does cause me to wonder if we have not been quite the same over the years ourselves, Ziltha, but I did not speak up about this to Mrs. Higgs. As we were staying beneath her roof and dependent on her husband's kindness to repair the car, I thought it polite not to press the issue. If I am completely honest, perhaps I was merely lacking courage. I did allow her to put Able on the back porch on a sleeping pallet, pregnant as the child is, rather than insisting Able be given the bed with Emmaline.

Upon our preparing to leave when the car was ready for travel, Mr. Higgs delivered a stern warning to me that, if we valued both our health and our souls, we would deposit Able as quickly as possible, either with Ida Mullins if the woman consented or at the orphan school. Mrs. Higgs admonished me not to inquire about the eventual fate of Able's baby, should the school be willing to take her in.

"Goodness," I said. "I couldn't leave her without knowing that the baby will be cared for. Able is hardly prepared to raise a child. I do not think she has fully grasped what will soon happen to her."

"Ain't yer worry what'll come of it," said Mrs. Higgs. "No tellin' what man that gal's been with. Could be her

babe might pop out blacker'n coal dust. Be better if'n it died birthin', then. The gal's just honey brown. She could be took for Injun if'n you bind up that nappy hair, but saddle her with a colored whelp and ain't no man gonna want her, never. Best hope she's ever got is if'n some fool feller might take a fancy to her."

"Able is just a child, and the baby only an innocent," I protested, at once horrified and terribly aware that Mrs. Higgs was only acquainting me with the reality to which I had conveniently turned a blind eye thus far. Whatever future we may find for Able, there was scant chance of a future here for her child. In this hard place, in these lean times, little ones die every day. The rough mountain graveyards are filled with tiny bones.

I thought of Emmaline when she was born . . . so small, so helpless, so dependent upon me to protect her and care for her. My heart ached for the babe nestled within Able's body. What might happen to that fragile little life?

Mrs. Higgs took me by the arms then. She held on hard. "And don't dally there among them people, neither. Any sorry man 'r woman what goes to Melungeon country is liable to come home carryin' some ailment what can't be cured in the old ways ner the new. . . ."

Alice's story vanished into a water wash of ink, the bottom of the page, both front and back, completely unreadable.

I turned over the plastic sleeve, read the top part of the back.

. . . fear that, for all my worrying about the Ku Klux Klan, and how the state FWP office may receive my narratives, in the end, this may be my undoing instead.

I have spoken to Tom of it several times, but he is young and carefree, and he considers these matters with his heart and not his mind. He does not yet know the weariness of the world, Ziltha. He practically still believes in fairy stories!

I told him last night it was only a youthful crush he had for me, and that one day when he sat happily at his kitchen table, settled into a fine home with a family of his own, I would be but a distant memory. I would be only a woman he knew in another time and another place, merely a friend with whom he had shared an adventure in the early part of his life. No longer someone who mattered a bit.

He insisted quite firmly, his blue eyes clear and earnest . . . painfully so, "There won't be a life for me without you in it, Alice. I'll marry you one of these days. You just wait and see."

"Mrs. Lorring," I corrected again. "Thomas, please. I have been married. I have lived a life. I've a daughter to raise and guide. You are a very sweet boy, but I do not intend to marry again. Not ever. Not to anyone." And though I knew it to be unwise, I bridged the space between us, touched his face as he turned away from me, hurt. "Thomas, you are so young. . . ."

"I'm old enough to know my own heart, Alice." He was as firm as can be, and just then, it was as if I could see into him, as if I could feel what a fine, good man he was, and how rich will be the woman who one day becomes his wife. I imagined seasons and years, mornings and nights, and babes with his soft blue eyes, his blond curls, his dimple embedded in their tiny chins.

I know I could never commit such a wrong upon him. I could never deny him all that he truly deserves, all that his mother back home undoubtedly has dreamed for him. "I'm broken, Thomas. I am."

I told him of Emmaline's father then, of the choice he had made to hurl himself from the ferry's bow, his death by all accounts no accident. Not a tear came from me with the story. None ever have. There was only the hollowness again. "He never even knew his daughter. Three months after he passed, Emmaline came. Perhaps it was my grief, or the nerve tonics the doctors prescribed to me, but there were problems with Emmaline's birth. I can never have another. . . ."

Her confession disappeared into an ink run at the bottom of the page. I held it to the light, trying to make out anything more. How had Thomas answered her? Where had the conversation gone from there?

"Won't find it." Clyde eyeballed a vacant spot in his current project, tried one tiny shred of paper, then another. "No way to tell what his answer was. She's a stubborn woman, that Alice. Silly, bein' so worried about . . . whatever it is . . . ten, twelve years' difference. That was part of the trouble with your mama and me. She ever tell you that? She was just barely seventeen when I went to Michigan to visit my aunt and uncle. I was twenty-seven. I had some leave time before headin' overseas, and my cousins ask' me up there ice fishin'. I met your mama one night at a dance hall—not the sort of place they have nowadays. This was a respectable deal. We two danced all night long, and that poor fella she come there with, he finally just give up."

Clyde took off his glasses, sat back and rubbed his eyes, then gazed into the darkness beyond the room. "Next day, I ask your mama out to go snowshoein' in the north woods, and she said sure, she'd like that. Hoo-eee! That was some day! Just quiet, the spruce trees all aglitter and the ground lookin' like somebody'd sprinkled sugar over it. It shined ever'where. Your mama had on a red coat and a hat to match, and curls tumblin' over her shoulders. I can still see her, clear as yesterday. She told me she knew how to snowshoe, but truth was, she had never been, not even once. I spent the whole day catchin' her, and the two of us laughin'. She had the sweetest laugh, your mama. Just like harness bells, jinglin' soft over the snow the way they do on a winter morn."

I sat perfectly still, lost in Clyde's story now, imagining the scene. Imagining my mother: young, vibrant, seventeen, her auburn hair long and thick. No bald head, no tired eyes, no heavy disappointments in life yet.

If only I could talk to her—that girl in the woods. The one I'd never known. If only I could understand who she was . . .

Now I saw a truth I hadn't before. *Clyde* was the only way I could. He held a piece of my mother I'd never experienced. That piece would be gone when Clyde was gone, unless I asked him to share it with me.

"What happened?"

"After eight days, it was time for me to ship out." Clyde told the story matter-of-factly as he worked, as if he'd already made peace with it. "I was headed to 'Nam for a yearlong tour of duty. But your mama and I knew it was love. We walked down the lakeshore that day and promised we'd wait on each other, however long it took. What I didn't know was that she hadn't told her folks what was goin' on, at all. They thought them dates was with a boy from school, not some soldier. When they found out the truth, and that I was ten years older and headed off to Vietnam, they said no—we had to end things."

"Your mama and I wrote letters while I was in 'Nam, and we traded 'em through my cousins, but her parents got wind of that and made it clear I'd better stop. So I did. I couldn't blame 'em, much. If I had a daughter, sixteen, seventeen, I wouldn't want some grown man chasin' after her neither. Once I come home on leave, I wrote her a letter and told her I was gettin' married. Not too long after that, I did."

The seams of the story came together like one of Alice's letters, ragged edges slowly fitting in, changing what I'd always believed. I'd never asked my mother about Clyde after they'd reunited. I didn't want to know. She probably wouldn't have told me anyway. She'd done everything she could to protect and repair the damaged memory of my father, believing that by doing so, she was protecting and repairing me.

"So . . . you broke my mom's heart?" *Seventeen.* That would've been around the time she'd been awarded a scholarship by her dad's employer and gone to college—the first one in our blue-collar family to do so. She'd finished her music education degree in less than four years and taken an inner-city teaching job because it came with a grant that would pay off the rest of her education and allow her to start graduate work. She was almost through her master's degree when she'd met my father at his concert. She always said she'd fallen in love with him over Lord Byron's poem and Tchaikovsky's Violin Concerto in D Major, a piece once deemed unplayable.

Ironically, Tchaikovsky wrote the concerto after a disastrous three-month marriage and a suicide attempt. Perhaps that had been a harbinger of things to come. My mother had no idea that the euphoria of new love was only one of my father's many long-lasting moods.

". . . did what I thought was best." Clyde was still telling the story—his and my mother's. "I thought your mama'd get over me, and I thought I'd get over her, too. In some ways we did and in some ways we didn't. That's how life goes. Nothin's all true and nothin's all wrong. You make choices, and you guess at how they'll turn out. Little bit like these letters. It don't come with a map, and only some of the print is on the pages. The rest, you gotta figure out yerself."

The doorbell sounded. Ruby stood up and barked, and Clyde and I looked at each other. I had the odd sense that my mother was out there in the quiet darkness, finally home and waiting for us to let her in so we could clear the air between the three of us, once and for all.

You see, she'd say in the patient, managerial teacher voice that tamed classrooms full of rowdy music students, beating on instruments. *There's no sense in getting upset. When you're upset, you don't think clearly. Just take a deep breath and try again. . . .* Years of working with kids had taught her not to be too reactive about anything.

"Who d'ya reckon is downstairs at this hour?" Clyde checked his watch. "It's after nine thirty in the evenin'."

"No idea." After last night's incident in the stairwell, I'd made sure to double-check the lock when Ruby and I had come home with supper. Softshell crab was on special, and I'd splurged. Following the conversation in the park with Mark, I'd felt giddy and impractical . . . and relieved. A good lawyer could make all the difference in our situation with Bella Tazza, and I didn't doubt that Mark was a good lawyer.

Rising from my chair, I had the silly notion that Mark was downstairs—that he'd come by to . . . I couldn't really conjure a reason he'd stop over at nine thirty at night, but the thought was appealing. I paused at the long, gold-framed mirror in the hallway, wiped away the mascara stains under my eyes, whipped the ponytail holder from my hair and let it fall in loose, dark waves around my shoulders.

Not good . . . but not horrible, either.

I'd done all that before I even realized how dorky it was. Of course it wasn't *Mark* down there. He wouldn't just show up at my door without calling. And he had my cell phone number. He'd put it in his phone right after he'd opened a whole new—and confusing—door during our conversation in the park. I was afraid to step through that door. I think we both were. But I couldn't resist taking a peek, thinking, *Maybe I'm after something more. . . .*

What did he mean by that, exactly?

A message on his cell phone had reminded him that he was late leaving for a dinner meeting, so we'd parted ways hurriedly, and with the question unexplored. Mark had hustled off while I'd stood in the park with Ruby, inconveniently theorizing as to what sort of dinner meetings happen on Saturday nights. Maybe he had a date.

Curiosity still niggled, even hours later, as the doorbell rang again.

"You gonna get that, or do I gotta?" Clyde prodded.

"I'm headed down." *Come on, Whitney, get a grip. It isn't Mark.*

But I did a last once-over, just in case.

When I reached the bottom landing and opened the door, Joel was on the other side, not Mark. He had a purple-red shiner on one eye, and his arm was wrapped in an Ace bandage. He looked like he was probably wearing some of Mark's clothes. The orange surf shirt and sweats were too big on his bony frame.

Oversize togs couldn't hide the sag of contrition. He

blubbered out a long and clumsy apology before I could even speak.

"Joel, you didn't have to come by here tonight. It's okay." I touched the bandage and lightly turned the arm over. "That looks like it smarts. Did Mark take you to the doctor?"

"It's not broken or anything." He slipped his good hand into his pocket, then withdrew it clenched in a fist. "I brought you somethin'. I didn't even remember it was from here 'til I looked at my stuff sittin' on the table at Mark's a while ago."

I opened my palm, and he dropped a coin into it. The design around the rim was hard to make out in the dim light of the doorway. I hoped he wasn't returning some contraband he'd lifted from the place while he was upstairs helping with the squirrel incident. Surely not.

"It's, like, a saloon token. Del, over in the antique mall, says there was a speakeasy here for a while during Prohibition. I dug that coin up in the flower bed one time when Surf Dude had me puttin' in pansies. I been carryin' it in my pocket for luck."

I turned the coin over, felt the warmth of Joel's body still on it, understood its value. "Maybe it worked last night."

"Guess it did . . . kinda."

"You're okay at least, Joel. It could've been worse. A lot worse."

Sighing, he slumped lower, his head dropping forward. "You don't gotta give me the lecture. I already heard it from Mark, *big time*, I promise."

"Did it sink in?"

"I hope so."

"Don't *hope* so, Joel. Make it true. You have so much going for you. Don't waste it on stupid people and stupid things." Mark's daughter came to mind. Despite the calm exterior, Mark had to be scared to death that Joel would make the same mistake. "You don't have to give me this." I tried to hand the coin back, but Joel wouldn't take it. "I'd so much rather you just be good to yourself . . . and listen to Mark. He really cares what happens to you, you know? He's not trying to limit your fun; he's trying to show you the way to a good life. Sometimes when people are older than you, they know a few things." Suddenly I felt so mature, so settled, so completely unlike the mixed-up girl who'd wandered the world, recklessly trying on different locations and relationships. These last few years in Michigan had changed me—I hadn't realized how much until this moment. "That's the lecture. You got it anyway. Sorry."

"Okay." He pushed the coin back. "I want you to hold on to it. Like . . . collateral. If I don't do better, you can keep it."

Making a fist over Joel's gift, I swung at him playfully, tagging him on the chin. "Then I'm counting on not having this for very long."

"Yes, ma'am." He looked at his ragged, blood-spattered boat shoes again.

"Don't call me *ma'am*. It makes me feel ancient. That's one of my rules around the restaurant. No one gets to call me *ma'am*." Maybe I could take Joel back to Michigan and put him to work in the kitchen. Kenny, the kitchen manager, would be such a good influence. Kenny came from a tough upbringing too, but he'd left it behind, changed the pattern.

As quickly as the thought came, I realized how silly it was. We were barely keeping our own people employed. I didn't have anything to offer Joel.

But there he was, still hovering on the stoop like he wanted something.

"Yes, ma'am," he said, then smiled impishly. "Sorry."

"Did you need something else?" Each shift of weight seemed to bring him closer to the door.

"Well . . . Surf Dude told me about maybe workin' for you. Helping you finish up on the second floor? He said you, like, might need to leave for home pretty quick because of stuff with your restaurant?"

"Yes, that's true." Fear and faith instantaneously went to war inside me. What if I really *couldn't* trust this kid? There was no way I could supervise him every minute—not while looking into a place for Clyde, trying to wrap things up with the museum, and worst of all, attempting to convince Clyde that, at a retirement condo, he would have the help he needed and wouldn't be so lonely.

Why did I feel guilty for even thinking about that?

And now, here stood Joel, stoop-shouldered on my doorstep with a black eye and his arm in a bandage, complicating things even more. The image of him weeping against Mark's shoulder, broken and remorseful, tormented me.

Forgiveness given is forgiveness gained. It was a proverb I'd learned while opening a corporate-owned restaurant in American Samoa, widely known as the happiest place on earth. If Mark could take the risk on someone who'd disappointed him before, so could I. It was time I stopped protecting myself and started taking risks. A life lived with everyone at arm's length wasn't really a life.

Maybe Joel hadn't ended up in my stairwell by accident. Maybe all of this was meant to happen.

"Sure. Definitely. I do need the help." A small leap of faith. A beginning. It felt good.

Joel sidled toward the door.

"Okay, Joel . . . well . . . thanks." What else was there to talk about at nine thirty at night, standing on the threshold? A mosquito the size of a B-1 bomber had homed in on my head. It really was time to end the conversation and close the door.

"Okay." He looked past me toward the stairway.

"Oh . . . wait . . . did you mean *now*? You wanted to work now?"

A quick sigh and a shrug. "If it's cool. I'm kinda, like, a night person? Kayla's working, and Mark had to drive over to Norfolk. So . . . it's weird-quiet at the Captain's Castle, y'know?" He swiveled toward the street, then back. "Rip's in the car, though."

Swishing at the mosquito, I leaned around the corner, and yes, there was Rip happily panting out the window of the Rip Shack's pickup truck.

The thought process that might have led Joel to my doorstep at almost bedtime, with Mark's dog in tow, was anyone's guess. No point trying to make sense of it. "Well . . . all right then. Let me run upstairs and tell Clyde what we're doing and grab my gloves, and . . . we'll work awhile."

"Cool." Joel added a sheepish look. "It's okay if Rip comes too, right?"

Was there an alternative plan in his mind? "Yes, of course it is. You and Rip come on in. Ruby will probably enjoy the company."

CHAPTER 19

"I checked all the mattresses, and I mean, like, I *really* went aggro on it. There's nothin' left but bones. I bagged the old rotten stuffing and all. Man, some of it was gnarly. Only thing I found inside were some acorns." Joel mopped his forehead with the bandaged arm, now brown with dust. "Then I thought, *dude*, maybe it wasn't a person who put that red ruby necklace in the mattress. Maybe it was the squirrel."

"The *squirrel*?"

"Could be. My uncle had one livin' under his trailer house, and there was a box of pecans on the porch, and we're still findin' shoes and coat pockets jammed with nuts." He scratched his head. "Wait . . . maybe that was a rat. But I bet squirrels do it too."

"Anything's possible, I guess." But no squirrel could've hidden the Benoit brooch and the story keeper necklace in the davenport desk. That was still a mystery, and meanwhile, Joel and I were burning up time. We'd worked until midnight last night, while Rip and Ruby stood guard against crickets and marauding mice. First thing this morning, Joel had shown up at the stairway door again.

I looked around, yawned into my hand, watched dust

drifting through the window light. Outside, the sky was a clear, fathomless blue. A perfect day to be by the water. "Joel, why don't you go ahead and start on some of the boxes in the salon? There's so much stuff junked in there." Stopping and taking stock was depressing. Despite all the time I'd spent on the second floor, the place still looked almost as disorganized and clutter-filled as it had to begin with. The painstaking process of watching for any scraps of paper with handwriting on them had slowed things down immensely. Even the containers of library books had to be unpacked and the books inspected one by one in case letters were hidden inside. "Unless you need to go to work, I mean. I don't want to keep you from anything you're supposed to be doing."

He pulled a face. "Mark took me off the schedule at the Rip Shack until I look a little better."

"I can't say as I blame him. You'd probably scare the customers."

A chagrined huff, and then, "That's what Mark said."

"And you told him it wouldn't be a problem anymore, right?"

"Yes, ma'am . . . I mean, not *ma'am* . . . but yes. Me and Mark talked a long time after he got back last night."

"That's good."

Joel wandered off to the other side of the salon, and I watched him go. When I'd finally kicked him out last night, I'd texted Mark to let him know Joel was coming and where he'd been all evening. It felt a little like *informing*, but I'd done it anyway. I didn't want Mark to think the kid had been out partying, and if I were completely honest with myself, I might've been looking for a wee excuse to see what Mark was up to after we left the park.

If I were totally, completely honest . . . I was fishing for information as to whether or not the appointment that had pulled Mark away last night was a date.

The problem was, I couldn't tell a thing. He'd been at some kind of gala in Norfolk, apparently, and at midnight when I'd texted about Joel, Mark was on his way home. Business dinners didn't usually last that late.

This morning, I'd awakened bleary-eyed and half-dead after staying up until after three, researching the story keeper necklaces, the Federal Writers' Project, and Alice Lorring. I'd found plenty of information on the first two. The mystery of the story keeper necklaces was all over the Internet. Interest had skyrocketed since the publication of Evan Hall's blockbuster book, and just as Mark had indicated, there was a new firestorm of controversy about the fate of Roanoke's Lost Colonists and whether the carved necklaces might in any way provide clues.

The Federal Writers' Project was fairly easy to investigate as well. Plenty of photos and narratives from the massive collection had found their way online in university libraries, in museum collections, and on the Library of Congress website.

But nowhere, not *one* place, was there a reference to Alice Lorring as a member of the FWP staff, nor were any of her FWP narratives available online.

There were a few postings of narratives recorded in areas where Alice and Thomas had traveled. Many of the manuscripts had been scanned in, showing the yellowed pages and the author's markup notes. But the handwriting wasn't Alice's and she wasn't listed as the interviewer. Perhaps the manuscripts she'd turned in to the Writers' Project had been, as she'd feared, rejected for political reasons? Discarded maybe, or lost over time? Or could they still be gathering dust in a vault somewhere, along with tens of thousands of unpublished pages from the FWP?

On a historical website, I'd discovered a grainy image of Alice in an old college newspaper article about the financial problems at the women's college. The photo had been taken less than a year before she'd sent the first letter to Ziltha, announcing her intentions to join the ranks of the writers' project and travel to the mountains to collect stories.

Staring into the faraway face of the woman in the photo, I'd thought, *Where did you go? What happened to you? You didn't just disappear. . . .*

"Hey, your phone's buzzin'." Joel caught my attention from the other side of the salon. "Here, you want it?" He'd picked it up and pretended to toss it my way before I remembered that not only had I recorded a message on the museum's answering machine this morning, I'd called Casey Turner's cell and left a voice mail.

My heart hopscotched, and I jogged over to grab the phone. "Thanks." I glanced at Joel, checking his expression as I headed for the stairway door. No sign that he was suspicious of anything.

"Morning." Casey was cheerful on the other end. "You sound a little out of breath."

"I've been working in the building." I moved down a half flight of stairs, watched the door to the second floor click shut. Still, the walls seemed to have ears . . . or perhaps mouths, because I heard the nagging whisper of guilt. Guilt and indecision. I could only hope that once I had all the options, the answers would become clear.

Casey's package deal was definitely the easiest choice—wrap up the sale of the building and provide a place for Clyde in one fell swoop. Casey had seemed so confident when he'd talked about the Shores. *A lot of older folks come for a visit, and they're reluctant to move out of the homes they've always lived in, but they see the facility and the amenities and the view from the upper floors, and they fall in love. If that doesn't work, we ply them with food. The restaurant is first class. . . .*

"Got your message. So, are you busy right now?" he asked. "I thought I'd check while I was in the neighborhood."

"In the *neighborhood*?" A pipe wrench tightened around my neck. The Rip Shack would be opening in a half hour. Was Mark down there yet?

"I can be at your door in . . . ten minutes. Let's go grab a cup of coffee, and I'll take you over to see the Shores. I think you're really going to like it."

I searched for an excuse. "Oh . . . you know what . . . I'm a wreck. Rain check? I could drive out there later today." The *last* thing I needed was Mark and Casey in one place. I could just picture how well that would go.

A pause followed . . . the complicated kind that said Casey was either analyzing my answer or recalculating his day. "Well . . . I hate to tell a pretty lady no, but I might be leaving town later. I'm in dealings on a property in Virginia Beach. I'm not sure how long that'll take. Once I head over there, I could be gone a few days." He ended with an expectant pause—let it float like bait on a hook. Whether or not he really had a business trip planned, he knew I couldn't wait several days to make decisions. I'd told him that in my message.

"Thirty minutes," I rushed out. Was it safe to leave Joel here alone? Did I have a choice? The work needed to be done. "Give me thirty minutes, and I'll meet you over at the Shores, okay?"

"Perfect. Got the top down today. Sure you don't want me to just wait on you?"

Yes, I am. Really sure. "Thanks, but I need to make a grocery run, so I was planning to get out anyway. Clyde's complaining about the lack of milk this morning."

A soft *tsk-tsk*, and then, "One more great thing about the Shores. The residents have their own little market, right in the building. He'll never run out of milk again."

The way Casey said it bothered me a little—as if we'd already done the deal. "Sounds good. See you in a bit."

I hurried back to the second floor and gave Joel instructions to continue sorting through the boxes in the salon. "Remember not to throw away anything that has handwriting on it. Clyde's working on putting Alice's letters back together upstairs, and every little scrap helps. Just leave whenever you feel you need to . . . if I'm not back, I mean. I'll set the doors to lock behind you when you go. I'm not sure exactly when I'll be done with my errands."

"Aye, aye, Cap'n." He saluted me and offered a bruised, lopsided smile. It only served to add to the guilt, considering where I was headed.

Upstairs, Clyde's enthusiasm heaped stones onto the pile. For once, my stepfather was excited to see me. He had things he wanted to share about the letters. Unfortunately, I didn't have time to listen. "I have to go take care of some errands. I'll be back in a little while, okay?"

His face slowly lowered, the folds of skin settling like mud. He turned back to his work. "Guess I'll be here when you get home."

"I'll try to hurry. I want to know what you found in the letters. Joel's working downstairs. I told him if he uncovered anything with handwriting on it, to save it for you."

Clyde answered with a grunt, and I didn't have much choice but to disengage. I washed up, slipped on yellow capris and a black T-shirt—the only two decent things I had that were clean. The girl in the mirror looked like a bumblebee. Then I realized I didn't care. Other than in relation to questions about the building, I hadn't had a random thought about Casey since our first dinner date.

Yet I entertained random thoughts about Mark all the time—actually, they came whether I entertained them or not.

What did *that* say?

Driving out of town, I tried not to overanalyze it. Today's meeting was about business, and on the personal front, I *had* run across Mark a whole lot more than I'd seen Casey. Of *course* Mark would be on my mind. . . .

But even as I thought it, I was remembering the way Mark had looked at me in the park, and those words that had hinted at something and remained a misty bridge between us. *Maybe I'm after something more. . . .*

I'd analyzed that one short sentence every way it could be analyzed. Even so, I thoroughly dissected the possibilities again on the drive to the Shores.

Casey was waiting on a bench by a trickling marble fountain when I drove up to the retirement village. The place was gorgeous. Pristine. A brilliantly planned miniature community. To my right, a small group of retail buildings mirrored the architecture of a New England fishing village along the waterfront. To my left, tennis courts and a swimming pool offered entertainment. All around, the gardens were immaculate. Cabbage palms swayed over brightly colored cabanas; docks offered kayaks, canoes, and water bikes.

Exercise trails waited with racks of bicycles. A wide sidewalk circled a small lake. The grass was thick and green, meticulously edged along curbs. Every window trim and shutter was freshly painted. Glittering brass plates offered the names of each building. Signs on decorative posts pointed toward streets filled with exclusive townhomes and duplexes. Under the sprawling portico of the main tower, a valet stand awaited arrivals.

This was retirement living at its finest. Luxury everywhere. But the glitz couldn't hide the monstrous glass towers jutting skyward. They loomed over the driveway, blocking the sun as I pulled up.

Mark was right. Despite the efforts to give the place a village look, the towers were an eyesore. I tried to picture something similar shooting up in place of the Excelsior. I couldn't.

"So, let me show you around." Casey was as friendly as ever, greeting me with an easy smile, his blue eyes lingering with a flattering amount of interest. "You look nice." He leaned in and kissed me on the cheek.

"I look like a bumblebee, but I only brought a small travel bag when I came here, and with all the dirty work on the Excelsior, I keep running out of clothes." I wasn't sure why I felt the need to tamp down the illusion of romance; I just did.

Pulling away a little, Casey smiled again, undaunted. "We have stores here on the Outer Banks."

The comment was a quick reminder of how vastly different our financial situations were. In better days, running out and buying more clothes might've been my first thought too.

"Too busy to think about it, so far."

"Finished sorting through the building yet?" He closed my car door, whirling a hand abruptly at the valet.

"Working on it. Everything's such a mishmash. I'm just trying to make sure I don't throw out items of value—sentimental or otherwise."

Slipping a hand against the small of my back, he guided me

up a ramp toward a pair of brass doors that looked like they could've come from the dining room on an old luxury liner. The *Titanic*, maybe. Potted jasmine lined the walkway, the scent syrup-thick on the air. "Sounds like you could use some help with that. I know of a good estate service. I've used them before when we've contracted on old properties. I could call and make some arrangements, take the burden off."

I was momentarily at a loss. Casey had an answer for everything, and all of his answers sounded good. That was what worried me.

He pointed out the virtues of the village's design as we strolled in. "Each of our entrances is ramped for convenient handicapped access. The residents have key cards to automatically open the doors, but any uncarded visitors have to go through the office. No unauthorized access to the facility. Our clients don't have to worry about a thing, including solicitors showing up on their doorsteps, kids selling Girl Scout cookies, and politicians looking to shake hands."

"That's nice." *Too bad for the Girl Scouts. This place could be a gold mine.* The people sitting on the conversationally grouped lobby furniture, the ones coming and going from the elevators, those passing by with golf bags and tennis rackets in hand, definitely had the look of money. I couldn't help wondering where the Shores hid the income-assisted apartments that Casey had mentioned during our dinner at the Black Pelican. The apartments that Clyde could afford . . . with a little help. None of these people looked like they needed government assistance to pay for their waterside condos.

We stood in the rotunda and looked upward, Casey pointing to the second-floor library on the balcony, the private movie theater, the doorway to the game room. Strolling on, we passed the indoor pool and spa, saw happy retirees swimming and chatting. They looked like they enjoyed it here, like they'd been commissioned as extras in a commercial about luxurious retirement living. In fact, everywhere we went on the tour, people gave the appearance of contentment. The facilities were clean and well-managed, even though much of the staff did seem unusually young. Kids from foreign countries, I quickly gathered—Russia, Ukraine, Malaysia.

Casey picked up on the fact that I'd noticed. "I think I told you that quite a few of our employees come through a work-study program. They're with us for a year, which gives them the chance to develop language skills and international business knowledge that will be valuable to them after they go back home. When they finish with their work tour, if they've saved the funds to do it, they have a month left on their visas to travel before they return to their own countries." He pushed open a kitchen door, giving me a view of a crew washing dishes while cooks worked the hot line nearby.

The place was poorly arranged, doubling the strain on the employees. Workers were scurrying everywhere, threading past one another with trays and serving dishes for the dining room buffet. I glanced around at the various supplies and cans on the shelves. Cheap ingredients. I never would've allowed that stuff in one of my restaurants, but it probably passed in a retirement village where a meal plan was part of the fee. One thing I'd learned from our corporate eateries in all-inclusive resorts—when the food was complimentary, the people were easily pleased.

We wandered on, looking at a sample apartment, more common rooms, and an upper balcony that afforded a view from land's end. All in all, by the time we finished the tour, I couldn't really *fault* the Shores for anything. The place was clean. It seemed generally well-thought-out. The residents appeared to be satisfied with it. Other than the fact that the towers were out of step with the landscape and there were some rather sad restrictions about residents having grandchildren and other minors stay with them, it seemed like a pretty good life.

I kept trying to picture Clyde in it, to imagine what he would actually *do* here. I couldn't, quite. But then, I didn't know Clyde all that well. I had no idea what he'd been interested in, or how he had typically spent his time before he'd slipped in the bathroom and ended up in the hospital. The apartment Casey had shown me—the sort he was offering to Clyde—was efficient, if small. Unlike others in the complex, it lacked a balcony, which made it feel more like a room in a low-budget extended-stay hotel, but it had everything that was really needed.

Maybe this could be just the thing to break him out of his rut, I told myself as Casey and I stood by the jasmine, waiting for the valet to hustle after my car.

"So. What do you think?" Rocking back on his heels, Casey crossed his arms over a well-toned chest. He looked like a kid presenting the teacher with a crayon sketch he'd worked on long and hard.

"It's nice. The people seem to like it here." I wasn't sure about the employee program. It bothered me that I hadn't seen anyone local. Literally from top to bottom, the staff—other than the guard out front, the activities director, and the people in the office—came from some other country, yet Mark had talked a couple times about the need for solid, nonseasonal employment for young people growing up here, like Joel.

No telling what the Shores actually paid the imported workers, but it probably wasn't much beyond their room and board. Not that it would really affect Clyde, but . . .

Casey was pleased. "I'll run up some figures for you, balance out our offering price for your building, the buy-in on an apartment for Clyde, plus the assisted-living maintenance fees for . . . say ten years or so. I'll need Clyde's tax information so we can get him approved for the rent-assistance program, but it shouldn't be an issue. We can always work it, one way or the other. Fortunately, he doesn't *own* the Excelsior building, so it's not an asset, as far as his financials go."

I felt the proverbial wall, suddenly cold and hard against my back. "I'll have to sit down and really talk to him about all of this." *When? How?* I couldn't keep putting it off. I had to get home to Denise . . . to take Tagg Harper's target off her back.

"Are you sure you want to go that route?" Casey's concern was lightning-quick and obvious. "You know, considering the shape he was in at the docks the other day and his recent history of ill-advised behavior at the hospital, a conservatorship could be more efficient. Once you start discussing the Shores, you lose the opportunity to arrange all of this without his fighting the process as you go."

"You mean do it without telling him *anything* about it?"

He laid a hand on my arm, slid it slowly downward and held my hand, looking at my fingers. "Listen, Whitney, I know that sounds harsh. I know you're having a hard time with it . . . because of the kind of person you are. You think about everyone else first. You care about whether they're happy and okay. But you have to realize that you're doing this *for* him, not against him. A person who's not making rational choices is a danger to himself and possibly to other people. And like I told you earlier, I've seen clients come here in his kind of shape and quickly brighten up, with some interaction and activities around. They do a whole lot better than they would have at home. It's a win-win."

I watched a retired couple stroll by with their golf bags, chatting happily. Did Clyde like golf? Had he ever tried it? "Maybe you're right. . . ." But the options were as much a muddle as the second floor of the Excelsior.

Casey squeezed my hand, his face tender and sympathetic. "Let me work up a deal that will take care of cleaning out your building and the storage of whatever you want to keep. It'll make things much easier on your end. We've done that before in cases where we're buying a property that's a teardown."

I paused, gaped at him, that single word replaying in my mind. *Teardown.*

The idea came heavy and unwieldy, the weight of it cutting off oxygen and everything else.

CHAPTER 20

There was a missed call waiting on my cell as drove away from the Shores. The museum was looking for me. I hoped this was good news.

Please, please, please. This has to be good news. . . .

What I needed right now was a break. A big one. Something that would let me delay the decisions about the Excelsior. As attractive, as easy, as Casey's package deal sounded, that singular word had gone down like a lump of dried, day-old bread, the edges sharp and painful to swallow. Now it was sitting in the pit of my stomach, completely undigested, a pool of acid swirling around it.

Teardown.

The Rip Shack, Kellie's shop, the upstairs residence . . . gone. The massive marble cornices and gargoyles would end up in an architectural salvage shop somewhere. . . .

Clyde would be forced to accept a new life, most likely against his will. A conservatorship . . . could I face that? Would it be good for him or would it break him? Yet, something terrible could happen to him, alone at the Excelsior. Something probably would sooner or later. I couldn't live with that possibility either.

Mark . . .

The charity and the Rip Shack were his vision, the dreams in which he'd found solace after surviving the unthinkable. How could I make a choice that might take away those hopes? Something about Mark tugged at me in a way I didn't have words for yet. But I was afraid of it too. Could I trust it? Could I trust him? What if he was doing the same thing Casey was doing—trying to play me because I had something he was after? What if it wasn't *me* he wanted, but the building?

What if it *was* me he wanted? What if he felt the same mysterious, undeniable connection I felt?

There had to be some way of postponing this, of taking time but not losing everything back home and letting Tagg Harper win. The story keeper necklace could be the solution.

Taking a breath and holding it, I returned the museum's call.

The phone rang, then rang again, a third time, a fourth. A recorded message came on. "Thank you for calling Benoit House Museum. We're not in the office right now, but if you'll leave a message . . ."

I waited for the tone, left a call-back request, and then hung on the line, hoping against hope that someone would answer. Of all the times to be playing phone tag. I even tried Tandi's cell, but it rolled to voice mail.

Finally, there was no choice but to give up. Throwing myself back against the headrest, I rubbed the burgeoning ache in my forehead. I needed to *know* something. I'd promised Denise that I would figure this out, that I'd be heading home soon.

I hadn't even checked in with her today, and I knew why. I didn't have any answers, and I couldn't hold up under the load of one more stone. If Denise reported bad news, if there had been another incident at her house, if Tagg Harper had shown up at the restaurant again . . .

It was easier to just assume everything was all right.

Sometimes self-delusion is the only thread left to keep you hanging upright. But delusions are slippery things to hold on to. I felt my grip sliding as I parked in the alley behind the Excelsior and walked around.

Mark was casually washing his store windows, whistling to himself. He smiled when he saw me, but the expression faded as I came closer. He read me, just as he had all along. The way he saw into me was both compelling and disturbing, as always. I could never decide whether to step in or run and hide.

"What's going on?"

"Nothing." A complete lie. Could he tell? Probably. "It's just been a . . . complicated day."

"How's your partner doing?"

Panic dealt a sudden blunt-force blow. Blood prickled up my neck and into my cheeks. Did he know about my meeting with Casey Turner?

"What?"

"In Michigan. Your partner." He squinted at me. "Whitney, are you okay? Is there something I can help with?"

Yes, I wanted to say. *Yes, there is. Stop being such a great guy. This would all be so much easier if you weren't.* "Sorry. I'm just a little out of it right now, I guess. I haven't talked to Denise today . . . but she would call me if there was any problem." Such a lame-sounding excuse. About now, Mark was probably wondering if I was concerned about my cousin at all.

He moved a few steps closer, his head inclining a bit. "A little short on sleep last night? Sounds like you've hired one of my employees out from under me."

It occurred to me that I hadn't even talked to Joel about actually paying him for the work he was doing. That was stupid. Of course he'd need to be paid. "He said it would be fine with you. He told me he was on temporary furlough from the Rip Shack." The tone came out sounding passive-aggressive. I felt like I needed to defend myself, but not for any reason Mark would've understood.

"Well, of course it's fine." A pause, and then, "Whitney, are you sure you're okay?"

"Yes." No wonder he was confused. Yesterday, I'd been melting all over him in the park. Today, he probably felt like he'd run into my frigid alter ego. "Thanks, though. And thanks for being fine with Joel working upstairs. I can definitely use the help."

"I'm glad. He needs good people around him. He's had a lot of disappointments over the years. He may be nineteen, but there's still a little kid in there who's desperately trying to convince people to want him around. He'll mature out of some of that . . . if he can stay out of trouble long enough."

"He's good help." And on top of everything else, I could send Joel off the deep end if I ditched the Excelsior. I'd be one more person who'd let him down.

I offered Mark a lame excuse about needing to go check on Joel's progress. He seemed confused and a little surprised when I didn't invite him along. "Thanks, Mark. I'll see you after a while." I couldn't do this conversation anymore. I really couldn't.

"Sure." Folding his hands over the squeegee handle, he leaned on it like he intended to ponder me as I walked away. "Talk to you later." A *come hither* look warmed his brown eyes, and I felt myself responding to it.

"Yes. Definitely." I hurried off before things could lead someplace that would only muddy the waters.

"Whitney . . ."

I stopped with one hand on the stairway door, turned, and saw him standing there, the old metal canopies of the Excelsior silhouetted behind him. There was an openness in him that I hadn't seen before. A vulnerability. For some reason—I wasn't sure why—my mind took a snapshot.

The kind of image you know will haunt you at some point later on.

"I meant what I said yesterday in the park."

"Thanks." I hurried through the door, pulling it shut behind me. Closing my eyes, I leaned against the porter's closet and tried to think.

Could Mark really help me find a way out of the mess with Bella Tazza? Tagg Harper had, no doubt, been counting on the fact that we couldn't hire legal help for our code commission case, even if we *could* keep ourselves afloat financially for that long. But now Tagg was getting desperate, wondering where I was and what sort of plan I might be hatching. What would happen if we brought big guns to the fight?

One thing at a time. Just go see how Joel's doing upstairs.

But the second floor was empty when I reached it, the stairway door unlocked. Maybe Joel had run out to grab something to eat and left the doors unlocked because he was coming right back?

The tennis ball thudded overhead. *Whack, whack, whack.* Apparently Clyde and Ruby were having a recreation break. She probably needed to be taken to the park.

I left the second floor and trotted upstairs, then stopped on the balcony, surprised.

Voices drifted through the screen. Joel and Clyde? Talking . . . and laughing . . . and throwing Ruby's tennis ball? I slipped silently inside, hesitated in the hallway.

"But . . . so . . . like, what'd you do then? Did he shoot the dude?" Joel's voice.

"I was just a young fella, stuck on the far side of the world, first time in my whole life. All a sudden there I was, starin' down the muzzle of my sergeant's pistol and thinkin', *This thing could happen and not a soul but him and me is ever gonna know it.* Then I thought, *If he don't shoot me, he'll sure enough throw me in the hoosegow, and when my daddy gets wind of it back home, I'll wish I'd got shot.* But every once in a while—and y'all young folks can mark my words on this, because it's somethin' that'll be true as life goes on—every once in a while, you hit a minute in your life when you know the Almighty is standin' right over your shoulder, and he's expectin' you to be true to yourself—to the moral fiber you got inside. And if you don't stand up for that, you're gonna be less of yourself tomorrow than you was today. You gotta make your decision in the blink of an eye. Who you gonna be? You gonna be *less* or *more* when you wake up tomorrow?"

"That's really profound, Mr. Franczyk." There was a girl's voice too. One of the other clerks from the Rip Shack? Or maybe Joel had invited his girlfriend over?

Clyde snort-laughed. "I ain't ashamed to admit, it didn't feel real profound right then. Truth told, I was a half step from soilin' my standard-issue drawers. But I did what I thought was right. I stood there in front of that shrunk-up old man who was clutchin' them two blankets he'd stole off our line, and I said, 'Sir, Sergeant, sir, you ain't gonna shoot this fella over a couple blankets? You're just tryin' to sure enough shake him up a bit, sir, ain't ya?'" Clyde sniffled and coughed. "Was a long minute, the sergeant stood there lookin' right through me, crazy-eyed like. Then, little by little, the crazy cleared up, and when it was gone, the sarge just seemed wore out. He went hollow and walked off without a word. Seemed like the tiredest man I ever seen. That Vietnamese fella went to babblin' and gettin' rid of them blankets, and he scampered off, checkin' over his shoulder all the way."

"Man," Joel breathed.

"You saved somebody's life that day." The girl's voice again. "Did you ever tell anybody that story before, Mr. Franczyk?"

"Quit callin' me Mr. Franczyk. You seen me half-nekked with my rear end hangin' out a hospital dress. No sense bein' formal after that."

"Well, now, there's a picture," I said and entered the room.

Joel, Clyde, and a petite, pretty blonde girl abruptly turned my way. Joel quickly made introductions. As I'd guessed, the girl was Kayla.

Clyde cleared his throat, embarrassed at having been caught in a tender moment.

"So, what's going on up here?" A pizza box balanced on the arm of my mother's chair, and three to-go cups sat on the end table. The pizza was mostly gone, the remains starting to solidify. Joel and Kayla had been up here for a while.

Joel slanted a self-conscious look at the mess. "Kayla called and asked if I wanted her to, like, grab a pizza for lunch and bring it over to me, and I told her, 'Heck yeah, I'm hungry' . . . and . . . ummm . . ." He shrugged overgrown straw-colored curls from his eyes. "I hope that was cool. I had her bring enough for the dude upstairs too."

A warm feeling slid over me. "That's nice, Joel, thanks. And of course it's okay." The scene was calming, a little oasis of kindness in an otherwise-confusing day.

"Anyhow, don't think we ain't been workin'." Clyde deployed the lecture finger and wagged it at me. "Joel here found another handful a letters stuck in a old peanut can downstairs, and he carried it up to me. These ones hadn't been tore up, so I skipped over the last of the ripped ones and we been readin' these. You're gonna be surprised what's in 'em. Alice and Tom found Ida Mullins and a little town of Melungeons. But when Alice and Tom got there to the settlement, it wasn't a nice, warm reception. Them Melungeon families—a couple dozen of them livin' in shanty houses up an' around a long holler—was shy of outsiders. But folks would talk to Able a bit—ask her who her people was and such.

"Alice started to takin' Able around when she'd interview folks, and little by little she got a story or two—some about the families, and some about the old times, and the plants and roots they knew to use for healin' sickness and such. Her and Tom stayed there a week, Tom gettin' them Melungeons to let him take pictures, and Alice travelin' around in a mule wagon with Ida Mullins. They stayed with Mrs. Mullins in her little shack. Alice wrote quite a picture of that place."

I stood spellbound as Clyde thumbed through the letters, his head tilted back so he could scan the words. "And . . . then there was a little romancin'. Thomas hadn't given up yet. . . .

"And there's some in here about the necklaces. Alice was findin' here and there that the Melungeon women had 'em. She also learnt that Able had one, but the cord was broke. Ida Mullins fixed it for her with a buckskin string. Every one of the necklaces was a little different, but all the women who had the necklaces, folks called them the sea keepers, not the story keepers. They said the necklaces proved that their people come over the water on a ship, a long time in the past, all the way from England."

Pausing, he leafed through several more pages, skimming the

words and summarizing. "Tom and Alice found out where the orphan school for Melungeons was. . . .

"Thomas traded with a man and got a little carved walrus tusk that was s'posed to be from them sea keepers. It didn't belong to the man's family. He'd found it in a cabin where the people died from dysentery. . . .

"I got one letter left." Clyde stopped offering highlights as he opened the seal on the last envelope. Meanwhile, Kayla, Joel, and I waited, breathless.

"Let's see what it says," Joel prodded, leaning over Clyde's shoulder.

Clyde's forehead lifted behind his bifocals as he read. When he'd finished, he slowly handed the letter to me. "Y'all might oughta read this one for yourselves. It tells where they went next." Joel and Kayla repositioned, so as to read along with me. Turning to Alice's words, I caught a glimpse of my stepfather shaking his head as he sank deeper into the worn corduroy chair. "I'll warn ya, this story ends in the middle."

CHAPTER 21

Dearest Ruby,

We've come into a spot of trouble, and I've found it prudent to package the collection of my rough drafts into one of my smaller suitcases, which I will be sending to you via post very soon. I know that you will hold the originals in safekeeping, so as to preserve them, should any of my finished pieces fail to reach the state office or be rejected there.

Upon leaving the home of the Melungeon woman, Ida Mullins (an experience which I will no doubt sit up late to tell you of in detail someday), we passed through the small community of Towash, a place Ida and the Melungeon families scorn, as they are most unwelcome there. The Melungeons will, in fact, travel over twice as far around the mountain to do their town business and shopping elsewhere.

Our intention in Towash was to purchase some supplies at the small general store and post my latest packet to the state FWP office. Tom also planned to speak with the man at the Gulf station as to the possibility of trading his beloved Kentucky rifle for new tires. The WPA car was not in good condition at the outset, and now we have been repairing three to four flats per day along the rocky upland roads. The situation at this point is fairly desperate. Even so, the reception we received in Towash sent us onward in no small hurry, I will tell you. The man at the Gulf informed Tom that he had no tires for sale, even though there was a full rack visible in front and a sign advertising the price. All were presold, the proprietor claimed. In the general store, the girls and I were accused by two local women of "stinking like Melungeons." Imagine!

I refused to buy a thing there, and we left. A pair of young rounders followed us out the door, making cattish conversation. I was midway between perturbed and petrified, as Tom was still over at the filling station, arguing with the man. I had Emmaline clutched on one hip, and Able close by, and I was thinking of the little pistol Tom had insisted I carry in my satchel. (Please do not worry, Ruby. I refuse to even keep the bullets in it.) Of course, I could only imagine what would happen to us here, were I to brandish it on the street. The local constable himself was on the porch of the jailhouse, pretending not to notice our harassment.

Finally, I turned to the boys, getting Able and Emmaline behind me. I imagined those scruffy young mountain lads as rowdies, chasing after my college girls, and I gave them a red-faced scolding, also letting them know I had the pistol and I would surely not be worried to make use of it.

"Both of you run along now, or you'll find yourselves in a bushel of trouble!" I told them.

The larger one, a sorry lump who looked as though he had not missed a chance at the trough in quite some time, said,

"I y'ain't worriet. Anybody's been wit' them Melungeons ain't welcome in Towash. I heared the Klan's gonna put yew down in a holler where ain't nobody'll never find ya."

Ruby, I must tell you that when one has never been the target of injustice, it is as jarring as a sudden slap. I thought of the man who had accosted me at the vegetable stand and wondered whether word of us was traveling these hills in whispers, moving faster than we were.

"Young sir," I said, "I am under the employ of the United States government. You would do well to tell whoever might be making threats that should we meet the slightest trouble here, there will not only be federal agents to deal with, but an occupation by the National Guard. We Federal Writers have been tasked to travel this country by none less than President Roosevelt himself, and we shall visit all parts of it, including the portions occupied by both the Negro populations and the Melungeons."

"My pappy says ain't nothin' them'uns gotta say needs'a be toldt in no book, nohow," he stammered out, but his skinny friend was already backing away. "Nobody'd ought'r be thinkin' the mount'n folk is back'ard as them Melungeons that lives up to Rooster Hill, that's how my granny told't it. Said a long time back, some woman put them Melungeons in the Tennessee newspaper. Spoke agin' the mount'ns, she did! Them Melungeons witched the woman, was what they done. My granny 'members."

He was, I knew full well, speaking of Miss Will Allen Dromgoole and her reporting, some forty years ago.

"I assure you that I write only the truth, young man. In fact, I would write your story, if you would tell it. Or your granny's if she would like to speak with me. We haven't come

only to talk with the Melungeons, but to document the lives and histories of all mountain folk."

"Y'ain't witchin' me. . . ." The boy began backing away. "Y'ain't comin' on our place stinkin' like Melungeons, and with that'un carryin' devil spawn in 'er belly, neither. Be better if it was dead 'fore she can birth it." He gave Able a hateful look as if he would have beaten her right there, if he could. It chilled me to the core.

"You will move along, young man!" I insisted and advanced with a finger pointed right in his face. "Shame on you!"

Perhaps he could see that I was incensed, for he retreated, following his bony friend across the street to the porch of the brick jailhouse. The girls and I hurried on to the post office, only to have the postmaster request that I take my business elsewhere.

"To be truthful, ma'am, your mail might not make it out of here if you leave it." He was a young fellow, polite and cleanly dressed, but painfully honest. "There's lot of folks round this area have got Melungeon blood someplace back in the family, and they don't want that fact told, nor any discussion of it. They don't even want folks pointing out that there are Melungeons round these parts a'tall. If you look a little, you'll find there were plenty of white fellas who'd married a pretty Melungeon gal, back when womenfolk were scarce. Truth is, there's even Melungeon blood in some fine families in the North Carolina statehouse, and they don't want that sort of thing told neither."

He leaned close across the counter, beckoning me to him as if the very walls might be listening in. "You'd be wise to take my advice and let the Melungeon issue lay. Don't be scratching up old bones, if you take my meaning. You're likely to find that the politicians you're figuring will send in the troops might be just about as unhappy as the folks round here. Every so often, there's rumbling about how the Melungeons and the Cherokee and the free coloreds were chased off their land back in the old times, and with no payment for it. Some want reparations made. That's not an issue the governor cottons to. Just the other day on the radio, I heard that Roosevelt was talking about eventually mixing the military. Colored fellas bunkin' right next to whites. Can you figure? I don't have a thing against coloreds, nor Melungeons. I'm a God-fearing man, and I figure the Almighty doesn't ever meet a stranger, but it's not easy to bend old minds around new times. There's many here who're barely scratching out a living themselves. They're good folk, but they like things the way it's always been. You'd best keep that in mind, is all."

I thanked him for his counsel, and we hurried off to meet Tom. When I related the details of our encounter, Tom was as upset as I, and we departed from Towash as quickly as possible.

In the next town, we left Able in the car and quietly mailed my field report and final drafts to the state office. I thought it prudent to wait and post my suitcase with the rough drafts from a different location yet. When I can, I will send it to you. Please keep the stories safe for me. So many people do not wish these to be told. Perhaps political pressures will cause the Melungeons to be omitted from the state book altogether, but I must try.

When I return from these wanderings, perhaps you and I will edit these works together and find a publisher for them, if need be; however, I cling to the hope that right will prevail in the state and national FWP offices. I simply cannot believe that we will not print the truth. We have, after all, been charged to record all of the stories, and the Melungeons do have quite a tale to tell.

I have penned this letter during our stopover for lunch at a small white church with a lovely new picnic park built by the relief workers. Upon leaving, we will travel two hours (but only fifteen miles, we've been told) up a mountain, as close as we can come to the Melungeon mission school. From there, we will walk on foot the rest of the way in, finally crossing the rope bridge, if you can imagine!

The school is quietly ignored by others in the area, and none care to speak of it. Our information is scant, but Thomas feels confident of finding the trail. We can only hope they will provide a safe place for Able, despite her condition. Otherwise, I do not know what we will do with her. All Able will say of the child is that she has no means of raising it and she plans to give it away. To whom, I cannot imagine. Parents here cannot feed the children they already have.

I pondered her situation long and hard as the girls ran and played in the field, as carefree as newly hatched butterflies, the sunlight outlining the arc of Able's stomach. In that moment, I decided that when we do reach the Melungeon children's school, if it is necessary in order to secure a place for Able, I will offer to return following the birth and take the baby myself.

Please, before you form a reaction, Ziltha, know that I did fully consider the implications that such a decision might harbor for Emmaline and for me. The idea left me no small bit afraid, so much so that I felt compelled to fall to my knees and ask for guidance. No one was nearby our little church in the wildwood, so I went inside and knelt in one of the pews, thinking of Able and her people. In the way of the Israelites, they have wandered in the wilderness. Not for forty years, but for hundreds.

This poor baby will be born in hostile country, just as was the infant Christ. I feel as though I have been called to the manger, much like the shepherds, frightened and unprepared, but I simply cannot abandon the little foundling to a place where so many would rather see it dead.

Peace descended upon me there in that chapel as I prayed, and I knew that my decision was as it should be. I am meant to save this child.

After rising from the altar, I found Tom sitting in the doorway light, holding his hat in his hands. "I didn't mean to intrude," he said. "I just thought it'd be good to come in and talk to the Almighty, all things considered. It's stayed in my head a bit, what that boy in Towash said to you about Able's baby."

"Tom . . ." I went to him then, intending to assess whether he had overheard my prayers about the baby. I could see that he had. Would he attempt to dissuade me?

I looked into his eyes, so fair and so blue beneath his tawny curls, and he took both of my hands in his, and I fell into him, weeping for all that is wrong in the world. "Tom . . . the baby . . ." was all I could muster.

"We'll find a way, Alice." His voice was thin and choked, his head inclining over mine, holding me protected. "I promise you, we'll find a way. With any luck, the father is white and the race won't show, but if it does, we'll do what

we have to. We'll go to Europe, or out west, or to Alaska . . . or Timbuktu. We'll make a life. I'd walk to the ends of the earth, Alice. For you, I would."

Only when I had cried myself out did he lift my face to his and kiss me and taste the salt of my tears. The bitterness fell away and became as sweet and glorious as summer fruit.

I do not know why I confess this to you now, Ziltha. It is so private a matter, and troublesome for all the reasons I have already mentioned. But, Dear Sister, you and I have always kept one another's secrets. Were you to see me in person this moment, you would know the truth in less than a heartbeat.

I have come to life again and found myself, quite impossibly, in love.

Your sister,
Alice

I stood for a moment, staring at the letter. "This is it? This is the last one?"

"Whoa," Joel whispered.

Kayla sniffled and wiped her eyes.

Clyde cleared his throat. "That's all we got so far. That one was in the peanut jar. Feels like you been left danglin' in the wind, don't it?"

"Yes." I scanned the last page from beginning to end again, as if somehow by rereading it, I could make the paper stretch, grow new words, tell me more of the story.

But paper doesn't *know* the story. People do. If only I could've found these letters when my grandmother was still alive. Had Alice ever come to Roanoke after her work with the Federal Writers' Project was over? Had Ziltha refused further contact . . . or had Alice run away with Thomas and the baby and never returned? Perhaps they'd moved overseas or out west and started a whole new life?

Could my grandmother have told me what became of her sister?

"There has to be something more down there." I set the letter with the others.

Joel nodded, blond hair falling over his eyes. He finger-combed it and held it in a ponytail atop his head.

"Don't know how you can find anything with that mop over yer face." Clyde searched the mess on the card table and snatched something up. "Here, I got a pair of scissors. I can fix that real quick."

A smirk answered, making it evident that some sort of discussion had gone on before I'd arrived. Joel and Clyde were actually teasing one another. Go figure. "Yeah, that's okay, Old Dude. I think I'll spend the eight bucks on Great Clips. I don't wanna come out lookin' like I joined the Army."

Clyde pointed the scissors, a twinkle in his eye. "Tell the barber to give you somethin' that makes you look like a respectable young man, not some hippie boy. Never woulda let any son a mine in the door lookin' like that. Neither would my daddy. Fella wants to be taken for a man, he's gotta look like a man."

"Yes, sir." Joel awkwardly tucked the hair behind his ears.

I pictured the kind of relationship Clyde must've had with his own sons—authoritarian, dictatorial, demanding. A boot camp for mini recruits. Resentment, resistance, cross-purposes.

Kayla caught my eye across the table, gave me a look that said, *Well, miracle of miracles, they're bonding.*

"We can, like, go downstairs and look some more," Joel offered. "Kayla said she'd help."

"How much is left to search?" Maybe Alice's suitcase of rough drafts was still here. Had I seen anything like that? Not that I could remember. Maybe my grandmother had thrown it away when it arrived, or emptied the letters from it. Perhaps it failed to show up here at all?

It could've been discarded when the third-floor apartment was cleaned out after my grandmother's death. . . .

There were so many possibilities, and probably the least likely one was that the suitcase was still here, but if it was, I wanted it.

Joel's cheek scrunched around a purple-tinged eye. "There's three hotel rooms we haven't touched at all, but it seriously just looks like dishes and old furniture in those, and some more boxes. First pass, I'm guessing clothes and stuff. I dug up a couple old suitcases—just empty ones, though. I scoured those suckers—even the linings, in case somebody hid stuff there. Or the squirrel. I found a few old peanuts that squirrel dude had stuck in a coat pocket. Bet he's really burned he can't get in anymore. I heard somethin' in the shop ceiling downstairs the other day. There were these two old chicks in lookin' at the swimsuits, and they're like, 'What's that noise up there?' And I'm like, 'Ummm . . . oh, that's just the pipes.' And the one lady says, 'Son, my daddy was a plumber. That's not pipes.' And—"

"Okay, time-out. I do *not* want to know any more about the squirrel," I warned.

"We catch him, I can make a pretty good squirrel soup," Clyde offered.

"We got a squirrel trap down in the shop, Old Dude." Joel shrugged toward the door.

Seemingly pleased with himself, Clyde rocked forward in his seat. "No sense lettin' good meat go to waste."

"Ewww!" Kayla squealed. "Joel Coates, if you catch that squirrel and eat it, I am *never* kissing you again. *Ever.*"

"Ffff!" Clyde snorted. "Squirrel's good eatin'. In Vietnam . . ." He launched into a tale about grilled rat and other things I didn't want in my mental queue.

I took the opportunity to slip off and change clothes for the search downstairs. When I came out again, everyone was ready to go, including Clyde, who'd donned a cap and a pair of sneakers that still had beach sand clinging in the seams. He was sitting on the edge of his chair, the card table pushed away.

"Are you sure you're all right to be down there?" I questioned.

"Joel's gonna help me wrangle the stairs." Clyde reached for the cane that had generated more than one sniping match between the two of us already. "And just to make y'all feel better, I'll take this blasted thing."

My mouth fell open. I couldn't help it. "Ohhh . . . okay."

"The boy can bring me boxes and I'll go through the insides with a fine-tooth comb. Be faster thataway. You two girls can check dresser drawers 'n' such. We'll work it like a grid. That's how we done it in the Army."

Joel clapped his hands, his long arms dangling loose. "I'll shoot Boss Man a text. Dude was just askin' what we were doin' up here. Might be he'd come after he's done at the shop."

A jolt of anticipation traveled from the tips of my toes to the ends of my hair. Warmth prickled into my cheeks. Could anyone see? Did it matter if they knew? Suddenly, I was primed and ready for Clyde's grid search. "I guess we should get going, then."

Joel clicked the backs of his flip-flops together and saluted. "Operation hotel blitzkrieg commencing, Cap'n."

Kayla rolled her eyes. "You're such a dork, Joel."

"I'm gonna have to teach you how to salute like a soldier." Groaning, Clyde pushed to his feet, made a slow shuffle-turn, and limped to the coat rack for his jacket. Properly attired for the project, we started down the hall, moving toward our own Mission: Impossible.

CHAPTER 22

By the time Mark came upstairs after closing the Rip Shack, we were sweaty, dirty, and fairly hopeless. He arrived bearing gifts in the form of supersize slushies from the creamery. I updated him on our progress as he surveyed our mess. Kayla was searching the last of the old hotel dressers, and Joel had just carried the final few boxes to Clyde.

"We were hoping," I sighed, "but we haven't found a thing. If there were more letters, or a suitcase with Alice's rough drafts in it, it must be long gone." That fact was hard to accept. Alice's journey to the mountains, her nights of pecking out stories by kerosene light, her experiences, her thoughts . . . all that remained were the bits and pieces that had survived someone's attempts at destruction. "Of course, her official copies could still be stored in a file room somewhere, but I don't know how we'd ever find out. I read up on the FWP. Literally thousands of pages of source material were packed away after the project lost funding."

Mark seemed almost as disappointed as I was. "How about a little comfort food?" He handed me a drink. "If there's any chance of getting at those documents, I think Benoit House

Museum is probably your best source. They might have the contacts to pull some strings."

Gasping, I glanced at my watch. After six. I'd gotten caught up in the treasure hunt again, and the things that were supposed to happen this afternoon hadn't happened. "I'm an idiot. I meant to call the museum again today and see if I could get any kind of update on the necklace."

Toasting me with his slushie, he turned away. "Go ahead and do what you need to do. I'll check on the crew. Who knows, maybe we'll find what we're looking for in the last corner of the last box. Where there's an unturned stone, there's still hope of a gold nugget." He winked, one tea-colored eye twinkling at me.

My mind went as blank as a summer sky. I just stood there, watching him walk away. What was this *thing* that came over me when he was around? I didn't have a name for it. I'd never experienced anything like it, but in a strange way, it seemed as if we'd *always* known one another—as if we'd been waiting all these years to end up in the same place at the same time.

Was this the sort of whirlwind that had caught my mother as a seventeen-year-old girl, meeting a soldier who was from a completely different background, too mature for a schoolgirl like her and headed into harm's way? Was this the hold that had continued to grasp her as the years went by?

Was it possible for people to just *know*?

The idea was like a handful of Mexican jumping beans. Explanations and emotions bounced everywhere at random, but the clearest one I could grab was, *Whitney, if you walk out of his life without seeing if this is for real, you really are an idiot.*

He glanced over his shoulder, caught me looking, and thick lashes narrowed over the light fan of smile lines. He pointed to his watch, lifted an invisible phone to his ear, then gave me a thumbs-up.

A tingly feeling traveled the length of my body and came to rest just below my ribs.

I walked into the stairwell to make my phone call, afraid that if the news about the museum offer wasn't what I'd hoped, the reality would hit hard. Everything rested on the price that my few found items might bring. With a good report from the museum, things could still work out for me, for Bella Tazza, for the Excelsior, for Mark, and maybe even for the charity project.

I moved down a half flight again, leaned against the railing, and looked up the stairs, taking in the soft light from the windows above.

"Here goes." Hope fluttered and landed and fluttered again, skipping along as uncertain as a butterfly as I dialed the number and waited for the call to connect. What were the odds that someone might be there on a Sunday after business hours? If nothing else, I could leave another message, just letting Tandi know that I didn't want to be a pest, but I really was running out of time.

The phone rang, rang again. I composed a message in my head—polite, yet somewhat insistent. *Business will be taking me back to Michigan even sooner than I thought. I was wondering if you've had any news about the items I brought in? I know you said next week, and it's only Sunday, but I was hoping you'd heard something. I really would like to wrap this up before . . .*

Tandi Chastain was out of breath when she answered. I took the opportunity to tell her I was calling to check in.

"I'm sorry for not getting back to you earlier." She sounded frazzled. "We've been swamped all day. I'm hoping you've called because you found something else of interest in the Excelsior?"

"Nothing like the items I brought in earlier." I thought of Alice's story, about the clues it provided to the necklaces and the people who called themselves the sea keepers. "But we did come across a little information about the carved pieces. There were some old letters here, and we found a new batch today."

"Ohhhh . . . really? Tell me more."

I hurried through an explanation, then finished with, "I think Alice may have sent the necklace and the scrimshaw carving here to my grandmother. Maybe she wanted Ziltha to have them for safekeeping, or maybe they were a gift. From what I can tell, though, Alice and my grandmother had a falling-out. I never even knew my grandmother was a twin. Honestly, I wish I had more time to look into it, but there are some business issues I have to tackle in Michigan. Do you have *any* idea what the pieces I brought in might be worth? It's just . . . I have decisions to make before I leave Manteo. I can't wait much longer. I'm sorry, I know I'm putting you in a tough spot."

"That's okay. I'm glad you called me. I know that our museum board doesn't want to lose the chance at what you have for us, and I know that our historical specialists would love to take a look at exactly what's in those letters. I'll work like crazy to get a meeting set up for tomorrow. Is that doable for you?"

Relief spiraled through me. "Yes, definitely. Thank you. Monday sounds good. Just let me know what time."

A strange pause held the line just long enough to dim the euphoria, and then she added, "Whitney, I do need to be honest with you about something. When our university guy looked at the necklace and the scrimshaw, I thought his eyes were going to pop out of his head. It's an exciting find, but there's no way the museum foundation can make an outright purchase on something of that magnitude. Not right now, anyway. Your other Benoit items—the ruby brooch, the taffrail log, the manifest—are in a category we can handle. Somewhere between fifteen and twenty thousand dollars, total, from what I hear. They haven't come right out and told me, but I know from experience that the board will ask you to commit the necklace and the scrimshaw to our collection on long-term loan, so they can be scanned and studied and compared to the other artifacts that've been found. The board hopes to eventually purchase all of these pieces, but we can't yet. It's hard to get funding when you're still trying to establish the historical significance of something . . . and you can't establish the significance without enough pieces to study. It's a catch-22."

"Oh . . ." *What now?*

"I know that's not the news you were hoping for, but I'd really like you to consider agreeing to the loan. Adding your pieces would be huge for us. We're working with the foremost authorities on the potential Lost Colony connection, but there's a very wealthy collector from overseas who is after these pieces. We can't study what is locked in some billionaire's vault. America's history belongs in America. End of soapbox, but please give it some thought."

"What about the value . . . if the pieces are authenticated?"

A sigh, and then, "Similar items have sold in the six figures, but like I said, please give it a good think. Seven of these have surfaced so far, largely thanks to all the publicity from Evan Hall's book last year. We've been able to bring three into our collection, but we've lost three, also. There's actually a reason I have a strong personal interest. The project here started with a necklace that was found in my family. So when I ask you to consider committing the piece on loan, I *know* what I'm asking. Believe me, I'm not rich and I understand that the money is tempting."

"I'll think about it. I will. But there are so many factors involved here." She couldn't possibly imagine how many. With that kind of money, a myriad of possibilities could open up—for me, for the Excelsior, for Bella Tazza, for Mark and his charity . . . for Clyde. If I could use some of the money to at least begin renovations and repair the elevator, maybe Clyde would be able to come and go from the building. Maybe we could hire live-in help for him.

"Thank you for giving it honest consideration, Whitney. I know our specialist would like to see the letters you found too. Would you be able to bring them to the meeting?"

"Sure. Yes, of course."

"Text my cell if anything changes." She meant, of course, *if you decide to seek a buyer elsewhere.* "One more favor I'd ask is that you keep word of our meeting quiet. Gossip travels around the Outer Banks, and there's so much random interest in the story keeper mystery right now."

"I understand." We wrapped up the phone call with a promise to communicate first thing in the morning. Meanwhile, Tandi would move heaven and earth to bring important people to Hatteras Island by tomorrow.

I hung up the phone and stood trying to take it all in, comparing two completely different options, weighing the benefits and sacrifices of each. What mattered most? The value of history preserved? The lives of the people who were here now? The good we might be able to accomplish if we were able to restore the Excelsior? My restaurant, my cousin, my employees? Finally defeating Tagg Harper?

Could there be a compromise, an in-between solution? With the money from the ruby brooch and the Benjamin Benoit items, Denise and I could keep Bella Tazza limping along until the code commission hearing. If Mark was willing to help on the legal end, we might win the case. . . .

What about the Excelsior? Where would the money for full renovations come from then? Unless I won the lotto soon, I didn't have the funds to take on a project like this.

I forced myself to put the brakes on my runaway train. One thing at a time. First, I needed to talk to Denise. These decisions would affect her more than anyone.

Dialing her number, I tried to mentally organize the information, to lay it out like a well-planned presentation, but presentations led toward an end goal. In this case I didn't know what the end goal should be. Hopefully Denise could lend a clearer perspective.

But Denise didn't answer. All I could do was leave a voice mail and fill her in, then walk back up the stairs, as confused as ever.

On the second floor, Mark was alone in the storage room, picking up the bits of shattered glass and mattress stuffing still strewn around the floor. I stood outside the door and watched him a moment, tried to decide whether to cross the threshold. Should I share the news from the phone call? Should I keep it to myself until I'd made my plans?

He turned as if he felt my presence there, sent a quizzical look my way. "What's up?" Maybe he sensed the ongoing war inside me. The battle between old habits and new possibilities.

"I just . . . got a little news from the museum." A small surrender, a tentative step.

He glanced at the cell, still dangling in my hand. "Good news?"

"Yes and no, I think." *Tell him? Reveal? What if you're only giving him ammo he can use to win the building? What if that really is all he's after?*

Then again, what if it isn't?

"Sounds serious." He wandered closer, pulled off his gloves and tucked them in the back pocket of his jeans. "Want to talk about it?"

I closed my eyes. Decision time. *Yes or no? Yes or no . . . ?*

"Yes. Yeah, I do."

"All right, shoot." Hooking a leg over the corner of an old dresser, he relaxed in a way that said he'd stay there and listen all evening, if that's what it took.

I pulled a breath, started out with the news from the phone call, but then everything else came spilling forth—the financial implications at Bella Tazza, the possibility of renovating the Excelsior, the uncertainty that could come with committing the necklace and the scrimshaw to museum loan. "And the thing is, my heart tells me it's the right thing to do—letting the museum have those pieces. It honors Alice's work. She wanted the stories of the Melungeons to be told, and the best way to do that is to give the museum access to her letters and the story keeper pieces. . . ." I paced the room, kicking aside pieces of broken hotel china left behind by Ruby's battle with the squirrel.

"But . . . ," Mark prompted.

"But my gut tells me I could end up needing the money. For the restaurant, for this building, for who knows what else? So many people are counting on me."

"It's your decision to make. The things you've found in this building are yours. You get to decide what to do with them."

I turned his way, blinked at him. Was he telling me I should sell the necklace . . . or was he just testing me? "I'm stuck. I don't *know* what to do." There, I'd admitted it.

"You want to know what I think?"

"Yes, I do."

"I think we have a good shot at the code commission hearing on your restaurant. I've looked into it a little bit and talked to a few people, based on the information you gave me in the park. As for the Excelsior, with a little time and a lot of volunteer hours, I really do believe that we can get the funding to refit the second floor for the charity's use. That leaves you with the question of the rest of the work that's needed here. There again, I think we can bring in grants and historical preservation dollars. I know the Excelsior is in bad shape, but it's one of two downtown buildings to survive all the waterfront fires in Manteo over the years. That makes it historically significant . . . and valuable to the town."

I chewed my lip, tried to think. I wanted to believe him. "How confident are you?"

"Pretty confident." He looked down at his hands, slowly rubbing his palms together, considering the implications. "Does it amount to a risk for you? Yes, of course it does. Selling the necklace to a private collector is a sure thing." He stood up, came closer.

I felt his nearness, had an electric sense of it. I had no idea what to do with that, but it pulled me in.

"Whitney, sometimes the things that matter most involve the greatest risk." He reached across the space between us, his palm skimming my cheek, a shock at first, and then I leaned into the pull, turning away from the window and toward something I'd imagined more times than I wanted to admit.

When Mark kissed me, it was as if I'd already known how it would feel, as if he were made for me and I for him. The scent of his skin, the curve of his body felt natural and perfect and right. There was no fear, just the sense that this was not only worth the risk . . . but worth *any* risk.

CHAPTER 23

A flock of seagulls flew by, leaving Shallowbag Bay for their nighttime roosting places. I tipped back my head, watched them soar over the Excelsior and disappear. Taking in a deep draft of air, I listened to the harbor sounds, exhaled all the way to my core. This place that had both repelled and terrified me only a week ago was slowly beginning to feel like . . . home?

I let the thought twirl in the breeze, looking at it from all directions as I caught a few breaths of solitude while Mark, Kayla, and Joel helped Clyde down the stairs. We'd sat for a bit on the second floor before deciding that it was past suppertime and our discussion could be moved to the restaurant down the block. There were details to work out, but we'd kicked around the idea of Joel staying at the Excelsior with Clyde for a while after I headed back to Michigan. There was plenty of space. Clyde needed companionship, as well as physical help. Joel needed someone to keep him out of trouble. The two seemed as though they might be good for one another, and with Joel there to do doggy care, Ruby could stay.

I hoped it wasn't all just wishful thinking. I needed this to work out, at least for now. I couldn't hang on here much longer, which was part of the reason I'd moved ahead on the slow trip downstairs. I wanted a moment to gather my thoughts. Gazing down the block, I thought of Clyde and my mother, having their Sunday dinners and their walks around the marina. She must've loved those quiet, peaceful strolls. She must have loved this place, and him.

And even though she had, that didn't mean she'd loved my father, or me, any less. The heart is a wellspring. It has infinite capacity to manufacture love. The only barriers are the ones we put in the way.

I'd been wrong to oppose her seemingly impulsive marriage to Clyde, to try to spoil it by withholding my enthusiasm, to put conditions on my love. If only I'd known their story, maybe we could've made peace between the three of us while there was still time.

The thing about mistakes is, they become valuable when you learn from them. I wouldn't live my life that way anymore, always holding back, always protecting myself, always clinging to the fear that love would end in pain.

It was time to let go of the damaged little girl inside the woman, and I was finally ready.

The hotel door opened, and I realized how much I was going to miss everyone once I was back in Michigan. I'd *found* myself, here in this little town by the sea. As always, the Outer Banks had a magic all its own. I didn't want to leave it behind. Would things be the same between Mark and me when he flew to Michigan in a couple weeks to talk about the legal case?

Yet the real world was rattling its chain, growling and snapping and demanding attention. After my meeting at Benoit House tomorrow, I would spend one more night in Manteo before saying good-bye, crossing the bridge, and leaving Roanoke Island behind.

As I watched our motley crew exit the hotel, the time for good-bye loomed far too near.

Clyde shook Joel off his arm, taking his cane and insisting that he could proceed on his own, now that they were on level ground. "Calm down, son. I can make it. I'm just slower. Trouble with you young folks is y'all think everythin's gotta happen this minute."

Mark looked back at me as they jaywalked across the side street. "Whitney, you coming? Dinner's on me."

Grabbing my phone, I snapped a picture of the group, a memory to keep when I went home. Michigan suddenly seemed so very far away as I turned to cross over and catch up with them.

A honk stopped me with one foot dangling over the curb. I lost my balance, had the sudden flash of myself facedown on the pavement. The moment hung in freeze-frame for an instant before I stumbled back to the curb, then blew out the tension. *Look both ways, Whitney.* I was so busy worrying about the future, I'd almost gotten myself run over in the present.

Rolling my palms upward, I sent a chagrined look across the street. *What can I say? I'm a doofus.* Mark might as well know now. Hyperfocus was definitely one of my issues. It wasn't the first time I'd almost stepped into a street without checking.

Oddly, Mark didn't laugh or shake his head. He wasn't even looking at me. Instead, he was just . . . watching, his head tilted, his chin slightly forward, a finger running along his bottom lip.

What . . . was going . . . ?

The moment seemed to stretch again, take on the quality of

a slow-motion film. I swiveled, followed Mark's line of sight, saw the gold BMW convertible pull up to the curb. Casey Turner exited, a breeze fanning the stack of papers in his hand.

Every ounce of blood in my body drained to my feet and oozed onto the curb. I'd forgotten all about Casey as the rest of us sat, heads together in the Excelsior, making plans. Other than a vague thought that I needed to call and tell him not to bother working up a deal—and that I'd better be prepared for the hard sell, because he wasn't going to like that answer—I hadn't dealt with this issue. I'd had no idea he would rush the paperwork through and show up here tonight. How was that even possible?

Because he had the paperwork ready before you ever talked to him. He was confident he could get you to go through with it.

Casey Turner was always confident.

"Hey there, pretty lady!" In three short steps he was planting a kiss on my cheek in a way that felt—and undoubtedly looked—intimate. "Glad I caught you. I've got your contract all set, just like we talked about this morning. Curbside service." His voice traveled down the street and drifted toward the water, out of place like a tornado siren disturbing the peace of what had been a perfect evening.

I was conscious of one thing in the pause that followed. Utter silence. Not a sound. No voices chatting, no ribbing between Joel and Clyde, no *pop-swish-pop* of the rubber grip on Clyde's cane grabbing the sidewalk, then releasing.

Everything halted as Casey slid closer, holding the clipboard so that both of us could see. Licking a finger, he turned the page. "I went ahead and bundled it all into the contract—the offering price on the Excelsior, the pay-in on the retirement apartment for your stepfather—I assume you had *the talk* with him when you got home. Of course we hope to get him approved for housing aid, which would reduce that. But it's not a problem. We can rebate the difference, post-contract. We've also included the charge for an estate service to clean out the building here, as well as transportation of the containers and an estimated one-year rental on an appropriate climate-controlled storage facility. Basically, they'll take care of everything, just as we discussed, before the teardown begins. Completely turnkey. Simple as pie."

"Casey, I . . ." My brain was still reverberating, shell-shocked. I tried to shake it off, gather my wits, but all I could think about were the spectators just a few feet away on the opposite curb. They'd trusted me. They'd believed in me. They were *hearing* all of this.

Casey glanced at his watch. "Thought we could get it signed and still have time for dinner. How about our old spot at the Black Pelican?"

"Casey . . ."

"Another walk on the beach afterward? Who knows? Maybe we'll get lucky this time and see a turtle wandering up to nest. Either way, it's perfect weather for—"

"Casey."

"Some time under the stars. A little moonlight." He leaned close again, whispered the last words against my ear. "A little champagne to celebrate."

"Stop. Just *stop*." I stepped away, noticed Kellie standing by the door of her jewelry shop, openmouthed. She slowly turned her attention across the street, and I did as well, but I knew what must be happening there.

The expressions on those faces were exactly what I'd expected to find. Horror. Shock. The burn of complete betrayal.

I turned back to Casey, angry, numb, embarrassed. Caught in

my own web of deception. *Lies with the best intentions still break trust.* My mother used to say that to her students. "I had no idea you were coming here with paperwork."

Whether Casey was genuinely surprised or putting on a performance, I couldn't tell. He was a man accustomed to having deals go his way. He was good at what he did, obviously. "Don't worry about a thing. A touch of cold feet is perfectly natural. But you and I had a verbal agreement, Whitney. None of this should be coming as any surprise."

"We . . . what? We did *not*."

Chin cocking back, he gave me the fish eye. The expression dissolved into a knowing grin. "Ohhh . . . now . . . don't tell me you've decided to play a little last-minute hardball. This offer is everything we talked about and *more*. It's an *outstanding* offer. Let's go out to dinner. We'll walk through it piece by piece again, give you a chance to ask questions."

"I'm not ready to do *anything* with the Excelsior." I took another step away, putting distance between us. "And I *have* dinner plans."

"Whitney, don't be shortsighted. I know there's some emotional attachment here, but this building is an albatross. Think about how much unhappiness it's already brought you. And there's no way you can afford to renovate it and get it up to code. It'll bleed you dry . . . and that's *if* nothing catastrophic turns up when you start knocking down walls. Black mold, structural damage, rot, termites, asbestos . . . there are any number of issues that could keep this place from ever passing muster."

I stared at him, my mouth gaping. Did I hear a veiled threat hiding in there? This was like dealing with Tagg Harper. "*The*

Excelsior. It has a name, Casey. And it's mine. I'm not signing any papers."

Pulling away from him, I stepped off the curb and waited for a car to drift by. All of a sudden, there was traffic.

On the opposite side, Kayla and Joel were clustered around Clyde, supporting him as he hobbled down the sidewalk, gaining as much distance as he could. Mark squinted at me as if he were eyeing a stranger.

"Mark, wait! Just let me explain."

"I think we've heard enough, Whitney. Nice move. Really nice. Way to subdue the opposition while you were making your own plans." Shaking his head, he turned and started after the group.

"Stop!" I called again. "We need to talk."

But when he paused, turned back to me, the change was undeniable. The look in his eyes was stone cold. "That was actually very clear. Great job on playing everyone. Congratulations on that, I guess. You could've just been honest from the beginning. It would have at least given us a few more days to decide what to do before you take a wrecking ball to the place." His hand sailed rapidly through the air, indicating the hotel.

"Your mama would be ashamed!" Down the street, Clyde tottered as he shook a fist at me. "You ain't worth a plug nickel. And you ain't gettin' me outta that buildin' til they *take* me out in a box."

He stumbled, and Joel caught him by the arm. "Come on, Clyde, let's just go get dinner." He tried to guide my stepfather toward the restaurant, but Clyde shrugged off the help and struggled on alone. Mark turned to follow.

Casey was coming toward me, his hands outstretched, palms

and clipboard up. "Whitney, for heaven's sake, let's go somewhere and sit down. We'll talk it through."

I wheeled around, stabbing a finger in the air. I wanted to deliver a right hook to the jaw, but this whole thing was as much my fault as anyone's. I couldn't just trust. I couldn't just have faith that, like Alice's journey in the mountains, my journey here had a reason, a God-given plan that was beyond my understanding. I had to craft a backup strategy—something *I* had control of.

"Just leave me alone!" I didn't wait for an answer. Instead, I turned and started running, the streets of old Manteo—houses, racks of rental bicycles, fences, flower beds—passing in a blur.

I ran until I couldn't anymore. Until I was winded and boneless, my legs rubbery and heavy as I staggered along sidewalks, sweat-drenched, my mind faltering and falling, trying to find someplace to stand firm. This felt like an old waking nightmare, like all the times I'd tried to sort out why my father had chosen to abandon us, why he didn't love us enough to stay . . . and how, after all these years, I could still be so broken by his decisions.

Maybe I'd been fooling myself when I thought I could change, become something new. Maybe something in me was damaged beyond repair—God's or anyone else's. Maybe I would always choose the wrong relationships, trust the wrong people. Mark and Casey were nothing more than two sides of the same coin. They both wanted what I had, and they were *using* me to get it. With Mark, it was worse. I'd let my guard down, fallen for it all the way. I shouldn't have.

I wouldn't make that mistake again. Ever.

They could forget it. *All* of them could forget it. If *ruthless* was what they expected, then they'd find out just how ruthless I could really be. . . .

By the time I returned to the hotel building, anger and mosquitoes had driven me half mad. I wasn't in the mood to deal with anyone, but the lights were on upstairs, which meant that Clyde had come home. Just the idea of starting into the battle was almost more than I could face.

I circled the block, walking stiff-armed, shoring up defenses, trying to center myself and firm up my resolve. *You don't owe Clyde anything. Not one thing. He's already gotten far more than he deserves.*

But in the back of my mind, there was the image of my mother and Clyde as young lovers on a wintry day, laughing as she tripped over her snowshoes and tumbled into the drifts. I didn't want that picture. But it was there. It shared space with Joel's lopsided smile and Ruby-the-dog, her hip bones and ribs still poking out beneath saggy skin. Her big, sad eyes. There was Mark. With the kiss. With *everything*. Everything I wanted . . . and in one careless, crazy moment, thought I could have. Now the door that I'd opened wouldn't close again. Not neatly, anyway. The wood had swelled in the salt air. It no longer fit into the old frame.

Somehow, I had to plug the gap, to remind myself that I had been doing just fine without any of these people a week ago, and I would again. Mark was just one more man who couldn't be trusted.

I gathered my resolve as I went upstairs. Clyde, of course, was waiting in his favorite chair, loaded for bear.

"You get outta my house," he growled. There was actually a shotgun propped beside him. What he intended to do with that, I couldn't imagine.

"You can *bet* I will." I marched into the room, stood across from him, started gathering the plastic sleeves that held Alice's letters . . . and Clyde's hard work. *Our* hard work. Those long hours of discovering the past together seemed light-years away now. We were right back where we'd always been. *I hate you and you hate me.* Simple. Easy to understand. "I'll be out of here first thing in the morning. And these letters are going with me. They're *mine*."

"That's all you're takin'. I'll make sure of it." A hand slid toward the shotgun. For a moment, he seemed serious in the intention.

"Like I *really* believe you're going to use that thing, Clyde. And you know what? I *am* taking some of my mother's keepsakes with me. There was nothing in the will that said you got to hold those things prisoner. And as far as this building goes, you and your friends can have it for now. Let it fall in around your ears. It's one less thing for me to take care of, and so are *you*."

Whether my shot hit the mark or not, I couldn't say, but it ricocheted and struck me. *Stop, Whitney, this isn't who you are. Just let it go. Let* them *go. Move on. Don't sink to their level.*

Fingernails bit into my skin as I pulled the reins on my runaway temper. "I'll be gone in the morning."

Clutching the letters, I left the room, not waiting for him to offer any more threats. My plans had solidified while I was walking around being eaten by mosquitoes. I'd decided on a few mementos I wanted to claim. I'd mentally packed my bags. Depending on what time Tandi Chastain set the meeting tomorrow, I would either stay on Hatteras overnight afterward or start my trip home. If I needed to, I'd scrounge up the money for a hotel, maybe hang out and sip coffee on the back deck of Sandy's Seashell Shop. Forget that this nightmare in Manteo even happened. As soon as my business here was done, I'd shake the dust of this place from my feet. I wouldn't be coming back until sometime in the future, when Clyde was finally gone from the building.

I called Denise once I was safely in my bedroom with the door closed. I needed to talk to someone. It wasn't until she answered, sounding haggard and tired, that I realized a depressing information dump from me wouldn't help lighten her load. I swallowed my rant and instead told her I'd be starting for home Monday or Tuesday, depending on the meeting.

"I'm glad," she sighed. "Whit, I know you've had a hard time there, and I haven't wanted to make it any worse, but I *really* do need you here. Jason and his girlfriend broke up, and he ditched work all week. Luckily, I called some of the crew that chose not to come over with us from Tazza 2, and Eric's new job hadn't panned out, so I hired him. Then, of course, Jason shows up yesterday and asks for *his* job back. The fact is that Jason's better and faster, and he never gets the plates wrong. Eric's not good about looking back at the tickets and he'll try to cheat on the sauces. But I can't *fire* Eric. He dropped everything and came when I was desperate. So I just had to tell Jason that, as soon as I've got a space, I want him back."

She paused, waiting for input. I tried to concentrate on the problem, but I felt like someone had wrapped piano wire around my brain and was slowly pulling it tight. "That sounds reasonable. If my meeting tomorrow goes like it's supposed to, hopefully it won't be too long before we can take on help again." But the by-product of today's disaster was that we wouldn't have Mark's help with the code commission hearing. We'd have to fight the battle ourselves, with whatever money I could get from the museum pieces. Disaster here in Manteo might spell disaster for Bella Tazza, as well.

Maybe I needed to reconsider what to do with Alice's necklace. Given that my future and Bella Tazza's were now hanging in the balance, selling the necklace and the scrimshaw made the most sense. But the idea felt like a betrayal of Alice and Thomas, and even Able, whose story was connected to the Melungeon people Alice was searching for in the mountains.

"Wait. There's more." Denise went on talking, oblivious to my whirlwind of indecision. "Tonight, Amanda tells me that Jason just went to work for *Tagg Harper*. You *know* that's not coincidence. Word is, Tagg's been all over the place trying to ferret out why we still haven't started breaking up Tazza 2."

Welcome home. "Great."

"I've got a really bad feeling, Whitney. Jason knows *everything* about this place. He has all of our recipes. He's probably even got some idea of our cash flow at Tazza 1. There's no telling what kind of information Tagg could get from him. On top of that, Grandma Daisy just called, and Mattie's running a fever. If she's coming down with a cold, the asthma will kick up. . . ."

The tumble-in of issues accomplished at least one thing—it properly reorganized my priorities and put my mind squarely back home where it belonged. Suddenly, I couldn't wait to get there and help out.

I would've packed my bag and left right then, if it hadn't been for the upcoming meeting at Benoit House. That was one last appointment I had to keep before leaving the Outer Banks behind for good.

CHAPTER 24

The lightning and thunder still hadn't let up. I stood at the window, stared into wind-folded sheets of rain glittering against the streetlamps. If this didn't stop by morning, I'd be drenched before I got everything loaded in my car. I'd been watching the storm for hours, first from the rooftop, where I'd hidden out with one of my mother's quilts, curled amid the scents of climbing roses and the sea. The clouds slowly stole the stars, and the lightning came too close, and there was no choice but to go back inside. I was thirsty, and hungry, but the lamp was still on in the living room, which meant that Clyde remained staked out in his chair.

I'd tried to sleep, but only managed short fits and gasps. Time and time again, I dreamed that I needed to run, but my legs wouldn't function, needed to get to my car, but the waves were slowly carrying it to sea, needed to find my way out of the Excelsior, but suddenly there were no doors, only hallway after hallway and room after room. I couldn't free myself, no matter how hard I struggled.

The dream was a fitting metaphor for this night. It seemed

endless. I wanted daylight to come and the storm to stop pounding—both outside the window and inside my head.

Finally, in the refuge of an old wing chair, I closed my eyes, let my thoughts drift and drift and drift.

I was on the beach at Nags Head, walking along the tideline, the sea's foamy fringe caressing my feet, then pulling away. My mother was there, standing on a narrow finger of sand well out into the ocean. I stood and looked at her, in her yellow dress, her auburn hair flowing over her shoulders, the way she'd worn it when I was young. I remembered how soft it had always been against my skin when she'd hugged me. Like satin ribbon.

I called to her and she turned my way. She was speaking, but I couldn't hear over the tide. Her hand stretched out, the palm turned upward, the fingers curling and opening, beckoning me nearer. I ran through water that grew deeper and deeper until suddenly there was no bottom and I was sinking, a riptide dragging me out to sea. A hand grabbed mine, pulled me up. The eyes looking down were those of my beautiful mother. My mother with her cheeks rosy, and her hair thick, her smile vibrant. No sign of cancer. No sallow skin over jutting bones. No evidence of all the horror that disease could bring.

"Mom!" I sobbed. She was sun-warmed and strong. Here by this sea, she was alive again. Well again. "I'm sorry," I whispered. "I'm sorry I didn't stay. I'm sorry I wasn't here when you were so sick. I'm sorry, I'm sorry. I didn't know. Mom, I'm sorry."

"Ssshhhh." I felt her lips close to my ear, her chin cradling my head as I stood at the edge of the water and she on that glittering shore where the disease could no longer conquer her. "Don't cry, Whit. There's so little time. Stop running from things and *to* things. Be happy where you are."

Then something was pulling me away. A wave. A wave of

sound, a flash of light, a rumble beneath my feet. I clung to her dress, clutching fistfuls that only slid through my fingers as if she were draped in sand.

Her garment slipped away from me, and then her arm, wrist, hand.

"Mom, no!" I cried out, afraid I'd never see her again this side of heaven. Her gaze caught mine in the last instant our fingers touched, and without speaking, there were words. Her words. *No tossing everything in the closet, Whitney. Sort things out. Don't let them pile up.*

How many times had she said that to me over the years when she caught me stuffing messes in corners, to deal with them later?

What was she trying to tell me now?

She was gone before I could ask, and I was whirling away like a Chinese kite, traveling skyward, and then spiraling down and down and down, into noise and light, and then utter darkness.

My phone was ringing when the thunder died. The room was as black as pitch, the power out. The only source of light was the call flashing on the screen.

Denise?

The vague anxiety of the dream's ending turned sharp. It stabbed inward, finding tender flesh. My cousin was already babbling out a story when I answered.

"It's gone, Whit . . . burned . . . it burned."

Horrible images overtook me—Denise's small brick house consumed by flames. "Denise. Is everyone okay? Is everyone out?"

"No . . . yes, we're all right." The words ended in a sob. "There was no . . . nobody was . . . Thank . . . oh, thank God. Eric almost spent the night. He lost his apartment and he didn't have anywhere . . ."

"Eric was spending the night at your *house*?"

She sniffled, took a breath. Coughed and wheezed, pulled in air again. "No. The *restaurant*. The restaurant is gone. They call . . . called me, and b-by the time I got here there was nothing . . . nothing left."

"Wha . . . what?" The flame leapt across the miles and ignited inside me. All I could think was, *Tagg Harper. Tagg Harper did this.* "What are you saying? The mill building *burned*? They burned Tazza 2?"

"N-no." Denise's voice was only a scrap of sound. Hopeless. Thin. "Not the mill, Whitney. Tazza 1. It's . . . it's gone."

The words didn't make sense. I couldn't form the image. "Denise, what do you mean it's *gone*?"

"I got . . . I got a call a little after 3 a.m. The police. They told me . . . they wanted me . . . to come. That there'd been a fire at the restaurant. I thought . . . at first they meant Tazza 2. I went to . . . to the wrong place, but the mill building was fine. I was so . . . relieved. I thought . . . maybe . . . maybe a prank? Then I thought maybe they were trying to get me away from my house. I panicked. Then Melissa called. Her husband had caught it on police scanner. They were already here at Tazza 1. I just got here. Oh, Whit . . . we . . . this just can't be happening."

Denise echoed my thoughts. I stared into the darkness outside the Excelsior window, closed my eyes against it, told myself, *It's only the dream. This is just part of the dream. This is not real. It can't be. It can't.*

"Whit, I have to go. I'll call you back in . . . when I know something more."

"Denise, wait. I'll head for the airport. I'll get a flight as soon as I can and . . ."

"Just . . . just stay put, okay? Let me find out what I can. I need . . . I need everyone safe where they belong. Just . . . give me a little time. I have Melissa and Doug here, and Eric just sh-showed up. Whit, we'll have to lay off the whole crew. Amber's dad lost his job two months ago and she's helping to pay the house payment and the bills, and . . ." The sentence trailed away half finished. "I need to go. Just stay there by the phone."

She couldn't have made a more difficult request. Everything in me wanted to grab my things and run. My suitcase was already packed and ready for a quick departure.

Instead, I sat in the darkness, feeling hollow and sick. Outside, the wind howled and lightning outlined the rooftops of Manteo, illuminating the shape of a cross atop the bell tower of the old Methodist church. *How?* I wondered. *How can this be happening?* Just when we'd finally found some hope . . . to have it snatched from us, to have hope become disaster . . .

The storm inside me raged again, as violent and defiant as the one beyond the window, as filled with angry rain—enough to extinguish any spark of faith. If this was part of the plan, it was the *wrong* plan. The good people got hurt, and the bad people won? Not in my world. Not if I could help it. . . .

I sat, waited, allowed the anger to boil. I made plans, let the metallic taste of revenge galvanize everything. If I could've gotten to Tagg Harper in that moment, I would have made him pay, but before this was all over, I'd find a way to even the score.

The electricity finally came on, and outside, the clouds separated from the horizon, traveling inland over the marshes. With enough light to see by, it was time to gather my things and go home, where I should've been in the first place.

The meeting. The museum.

I'd have to call as soon as it was late enough, let Tandi know what had happened. Maybe I could phone in for the meeting, or come back once things were straightened out in Michigan. When would things be *straightened out*? If Tagg Harper was willing to burn down my restaurant, how would having money to fight our case at the state level make any difference? He could just set fire to the other building, destroy it as well.

When Denise called back, her mind was on much the same track. "Whit, they're saying it looks like it started in the range hood. The one we just had cleaned, serviced, and *inspected*."

"You've *got* to be kidding."

"No, I'm not."

Frenetic anger rose and buffeted me from all directions. "I just want to wrap my hands around . . . I want to find Tagg Harper and . . . Why don't you tell them that Tagg Harper has friends who would know a whole lot about setting a fire and making it look like an accident? He fishes with a fire marshal."

"Whitney, you *know* we can't just come out and say that. There's no proof. And we're going to tell one fire marshal that another one helped burn down our building? The next thing, Tagg will be hauling us to court for slander, and he'll drain us dry that way. We can't give him any more ammunition. Believe me, I've been thinking this through as I'm standing here looking at our life in ashes."

I took a deep breath, tried to see reason. "You're right. I know you're right, but I just want to . . . I want it so bad I can taste it."

"I know. I know. Me too. But we've got to be smart. We have to get Tazza 2 through the code commission hearing. *Whatever it takes.* Otherwise, none of us will have jobs. You and I both know that the insurance company will drag their feet, investigating the fire. And even if they cut us a check tomorrow, it would take too much time to rebuild. There's no choice. We have to save the second store, but for now, maybe it's best if we let Tagg Harper think he's gotten away with it."

"You're probably right." Accepting the truth was like swallowing poison. I wasn't sure I could keep it down without killing myself. "I'm headed home this morning. I need to be there. I'll figure out some arrangements with the museum after I'm on the road." But I was exhausted from an entire night of no sleep. I wasn't sure how I was going to make it through the trip.

I wasn't sure of anything.

Denise and I said good-bye, and I tried to find my feet in this alternate reality—to locate some reference point that still made sense. There were none. I'd never felt so completely, utterly lost, so broken and hopeless. So shatteringly alone and defeated. Movement was the only solution—movement toward . . . someplace else. Throwing the last of my belongings together—clothes, phone, computer, chargers, the box filled with Alice's letters—I tried to scroll logically through the rest of the details.

There were still things on the second floor I'd planned to hang on to, and keepsakes from my mother I'd intended to gather this morning, whether Clyde liked it or not. Should I take the time now? Should I leave them and trust that they'd be here whenever I could come back?

The davenport desk. I wanted it. Moving it by myself would be impossible, and it wouldn't fit in my car anyway. It'd have to wait until next time. Everything here would have to wait.

Loaded down with as much as I could carry in one trip, I opened the door as quietly as I could and started up the hallway. In the living room, Clyde was mercifully absent, but Ruby lay curled in my mother's chair. Lifting her head, she whimpered. What about *her*? Should I take her with me? Leave her behind and trust that Clyde would make arrangements for her? After I was gone, would Joel move in here as planned?

"Ssshhh," I whispered. "It's okay." *Please. Please don't bark.*

But she simply watched me go, then come and go again. Her soft, low, sad sounds followed me in and out as I made trips to my car.

For once, Clyde hadn't gotten up at promptly four thirty, thank goodness. Maybe all the emotion last night had tired him out. Maybe, if we talked this morning, he would stop accusing me long enough to listen to what I had to say.

I didn't have it in me. Not right now. I just wanted to be home, fighting for what was mine. Finding some way to summon a phoenix from the ashes . . . and to serve up a dish of vengeance, when the time was right.

On the last trip, I stopped in the living room, scratched Ruby's head and kissed her, then laid my cheek against the corduroy cushions of my mother's chair, took in her scent, thought, *Bye, Mom.*

Tears prickled, and I clenched against them, then straightened my back, walked out the door, and left the Excelsior behind.

On the side street, the rain had finally faded to a drizzle, the pavement glittering in an eerie, wet hush, as if Manteo were holding its breath, waiting for something.

Perhaps waiting for me to leave?

The door slammed hard behind me, knocking me forward. I stood for a moment under the metal awning, listened to the *drip, drip, drip* of water splashing into a pool and the tiny rain-river of a gutter burbling farther away. Beyond that, a cold wind whipped froth off normally placid Roanoke Sound.

Go. Don't think about it. But something seemed so . . .

strange. So wrong. Perhaps it was the news about Bella Tazza, but this felt like *forever*—as if I'd never see this place again. Things here were so unfinished. Once again, I was running away, leaving a mess behind, doing exactly what my mother had cautioned me against in the dream.

I had to go. Over the harbor, the sky was brightening toward a new day. If I didn't get out of here now, the town would come to life. I didn't want to see anyone. There wasn't enough fight left in me. I could call Joel from the road and tell him to go check on Clyde and Ruby. Maybe sometime today, I'd get in touch with Kellie from the jewelry shop, just to make sure things were taken care of upstairs. Hopefully she would be willing to help, as a kindness to my mother's memory, if for no other reason.

In the alley, a stray kitten perched atop my car—half-grown, cinder black, bone thin with one ear drooping sideways. It shivered and mewed as I unlocked the doors.

"Better get down. Unless you want a ride to Michigan."

The stray inched closer, the sad characteristics of rejection and helplessness painfully evident.

"Shoo. Now go home." I pulled the door latch, set an overstuffed box on the backseat.

The kitten only whined, wrapping its tail over its paws for warmth and casting soulful green eyes at me. I thought of the dream, of my mom standing by the ocean, beautiful and free, fully healed.

My mother would never leave a shivering kitten in an alley. *It's one of God's creatures,* she'd say.

"Come here," I sighed, finally. "I'll let you into the stairwell." I could call Joel later and ask him to figure out something about the cat. With any luck, it was just lost and someone would come looking for it. For now, at least I could give it shelter.

Quickly. The sun was rising. Monday was rushing in.

The kitten mewed, rubbing its wet head under my chin and shivering as I snuggled it against my jacket. A ragged purr chugged out, like an engine starting after sitting idle too long, the sound intensifying as we went inside. The vibration was soothing and pleasant, something normal in an otherwise-upside-down morning.

Maybe I could find an old blanket or a painting tarp or a box in the porter's closet—something for the cat to curl up in and warm itself.

Unfortunately, the closet door was locked, the keys upstairs, so I settled for grabbing a sweatshirt from my duffel bag and bundling it on the floor. The kitten purred happily as I set her in the middle and wrapped the sleeves around her. "You behave. I'll call somebody about you after a while."

Rubbing her head, I waited until she relaxed wearily against the fleece. Mom would be proud.

"Gotta go," I whispered into the quiet stairwell, then gave the kitten one last look before walking out the door.

Around Manteo, there were signs of morning activity now—the squeaky sneakers of a jogger out running, a door closing, a shout from the direction of the marina, a car passing the alley as I walked into it. At six thirty, the town was ready to greet a new day, but I wasn't—not in this place, anyway.

Even so, my stomach sank as I opened the car door. I hesitated again, thought, *Keep moving. Just keep moving. Let it go.* The Excelsior and the crazy dreams I'd hatched here had to become things of the past. Once I was away, once this place wasn't looming over me with all its memories and secrets, its power would be gone . . . wouldn't it?

"Leaving so soon?"

I knew the voice, even from halfway down the alley. It ripped through me like an arrow, the tip molten, easily cutting flesh, then searing off the blood flow. He was standing with his back to the gray dawn light, a hood pulled over his head, but he was easy to recognize.

"I come down here to check for hail damage, and look what I find."

"Yes, Mark, I'm leaving. I'm getting out of your way. You, Clyde, Joel . . . all of you can figure it out from here. Make sure someone takes care of Ruby this morning, because Clyde *can't*. And there's a kitten in the stairway. It was on top of my car." I turned back to my vehicle, my *escape*, grabbed the driver's door, tightened my fingers around it.

"So . . . you got what you wanted and you're gone?"

My heart squeezed. He couldn't have been more wrong. I felt like I'd lost everything I wanted. "I did. You're right. I did. Good-bye, Mark. Have a nice life." *Don't look his way. Don't.* Yet my senses strained toward him, trying to determine . . . was he coming closer?

Get in the car. Be done with it. The whole stupid fantasy. This thing I'd created in my mind—Mark, me, a charity in this building—was ridiculous. Careless. Foolish, and I was the fool. *He's just Tagg Harper in a surf suit, and you fell for it.*

"Not even going to tell me how long I have to find a new location for the shop? How many months before the condos go up?"

"If you weren't such an idiot, you'd know."

He gave a soft, rueful laugh. "I was an idiot, all right. I thought we had . . ."

Something, I wanted him to say. *I thought we had something.*

Instead he finished with, ". . . an agreement."

"Our agreement, which *you* let me out of anyway, was that I wouldn't sell the building without telling you thirty days in advance. Well *there*. You've been told." It was a lie, of course. I had no idea where things would go from here, nor could I think about it now. But the words were meant for impact. The rage that had been brewing inside me needed a place to go, and Mark was a worthy target.

"Don't spend the money yet. There will definitely be a legal challenge. This is a historic building, for starters. But I'll think of something more." He was closer now. Only a few feet behind me.

Don't do this. Not now. Please . . .

"I'm sure you will. But the fact remains. It's *my* building. I can do what I want with it."

"We'll see."

I whirled toward him then, emotion welling up. It shifted without warning when I saw his face. He'd pushed the hood back. The light caught him, turned his eyes a bright, golden brown.

Tears swelled in my chest, pressing upward, dousing the anger. "Just leave me alone, Mark. I don't have anything more to say to you. I *wasn't* making a deal with Casey, but . . . You know what? You can believe whatever you want. I don't . . . I don't even . . ." The sentence died in a whimper, a strangling gush of emotion.

I felt the tears spilling over, hot and rapid.

He pulled a breath to retort, stopped, studied me. "Whitney?"

"I don't . . . I'm . . ." But I was already sobbing, the last bits of my resolve, of my pride, washing away in the tidal flow. "Everything's . . . the restaurant . . . the restaurant . . . burned."

I threw a hand over my face, ashamed, overwhelmed, lost. I wanted to sink down to the wet pavement, finally surrender. Just give up. On everything.

"Hey . . ." Whether Mark caught me or I folded into him, I couldn't say. I felt the warmth of his arms, the curve of his chest against my forehead, the strong ridge of his chin over my hair. I smelled surf wax and musky cologne, sand and the rainy night clinging to the fibers of his sweatshirt. He didn't ask questions. He just held me while I cried. By the time I was finished, the mist had turned to rain again. We went to his Jeep to escape the weather. Rip was waiting in the back. The dog moved carefully to the console, sniffed me, and then licked the salt from my skin.

"Rip, cut it out." Mark elbowed him aside, then reached across to comb back the hair Rip had disturbed. I felt his fingers brush my ear and then my shoulder. They stayed there.

"So . . . what's going on? There was a fire in your restaurant? The one that's in dispute right now?"

He handed me a leftover restaurant napkin, and I wiped my eyes, brushing back the mass of damp, dark waves I hadn't taken the time to bind that morning. "No." I swallowed hard, gulping down the swell of grief. "Not the new restaurant, the old location. The one that was open. It's gone."

"*Gone?* How? When?"

"A few hours ago. They're saying they think it could have been the range hood. We just had it cleaned and fixed and fully tested. It *wasn't* the range hood. It doesn't matter, anyway. With the old store gone, we're finished. I just need to get home and . . ." *Do what? Do what exactly?* "And see what I can figure out."

I gathered my hair in my fingers, tugged it hard and held it, tried to think. "I need to go . . . to . . . to get on the road. It's a long drive."

Mark caught my hand. "Whitney, just hold on a minute."

"I want to get home."

"You're in no shape to be taking off. Talk to me. Let's think this thing through." His was the voice of reason, but it was hard to hear. Everything in me was screaming, *Run, fight, do something!*

"I *know* this was Tagg Harper's doing, and when I see him . . ."

"That's exactly why you don't need to be there right now. Judging from what you've told me, he'd probably love to have a legal reason to go after you. And what about the museum and the necklace? I thought you had a meeting today?"

"I'll tell them I can't be there. They'll have to understand." The gears were grinding inside me, pushing forward while Mark stepped on the brakes. "I can't leave my cousin to deal with all of this on her own."

Maybe I should fly . . . drive to the airport and catch a plane after all. I could be home by early afternoon. But I'll need my car when I get there. There's no money for a rental. There's really no money for a plane ticket. Who'd pick me up at the airport? Mrs. Doyne might be . . .

"Let me make the trip to Michigan instead." Mark's request was somewhere outside the din of my own thoughts. "Let me tell them you sent your lawyer to look into the situation. That'll help, both on the criminal end and on the settlement end. It never hurts to hit the insurance company from the initial stages. You go down to Hatteras. Do what you need to do there. Let me handle Michigan."

I gaped at him, dumbfounded. "What . . . but . . ."

Conflicting urges warred—two instinctive reactions. I needed to rely on someone, but relying on people was dangerous. At any moment, people could decide to just . . . not be there anymore. I'd always relied on myself. "Why would you do that?"

He leaned closer, stared into me in a way that held me against the seat. "You really haven't got a clue, do you? I didn't come here this morning to check for hail damage. I came because I couldn't sleep. I was thinking about you—about the way you looked when Casey drove up. I wanted to see you before you left for Hatteras, to at least hear what you had to say about it."

His fingers brushed my chin and sank into my hair, and he pulled me near, his lips meeting mine softly, gently at first and then filled with an intense need that mirrored my own. The feel of him, the taste of him, eclipsed the racing in my head. I gave myself to it, let it take me over.

I felt the ebbing of one tide and the swelling of another, this one as powerful as the sea itself. There was a knowing in it, the sort of knowing I'd never felt before.

To love and be loved is the very thing our souls scream for from birth and every moment after, the urge to need and be needed as natural as breathing, as life-giving as breath. For the first time since childhood, I felt as though I was no longer fighting for air, but instead sailing through it with no fear of where I might land.

CHAPTER 25

Benoit House was strangely quiet this late in the evening. No tourist crowd, no charter buses, no docents or caterers wandering around. The one-eared cat who'd terrorized the caterer last time now lounged in a window of the grand ballroom, looking harmless and comfortably at home. By contrast, I was as nervous as . . . well . . . a cat.

Letting Mark go to Michigan, my coming here instead, had been a shaky, clumsy leap of faith. The decision still had me on pins and needles, but I'd learned something in my time on the Outer Banks. I'd seen the difference between Alice's choices and my grandmother's. In opening herself to an unplanned future, in taking the risk, Alice had found her way back to life and joy and hope.

By closing herself away, my grandmother had gained nothing. She'd withered within her own walls long before her death. She'd worn misery like a cloak and covered those closest to her in its suffocating fabric.

Living, really *living*, wasn't about clinging to control but about giving it away.

Closing my eyes, I took in a long breath, exhaled, wiped

sweaty palms on my pant legs and tried to relax. *Breathe, breathe. It's going to be okay.*

More than okay . . .

I positioned my hands here and there around the chair, trying to decide which would look best when they entered the conference room. Tandi had stepped out to meet the board president and the historical specialist at the front door. I'd been kept waiting most of the day as travel snafus and other issues prevented them from reaching Hatteras. The board president had insisted we not go forward without him. I knew why. He was coming to give me the strong arm about leaving the necklace here on loan.

I'd been silently tossing the question around all day—*yes, no, maybe. Do the easy thing? Do the right thing and trust that our struggle with Bella Tazza will work out?*

The choice had eclipsed even the aftermath of the restaurant fire. Selling the necklace and getting the money would assure me the means of serving up the ultimate revenge against Tagg Harper. Denise—who right now was handling things much more sanely than I would have—could relax, given the kind of muscle the money could provide. On the other hand, Denise had assured me that Mark was quite an intimidating force all by himself, when in lawyer mode. She'd also texted, *Holy cow! You didn't tell me he was drop-dead-flipping gorgeous.*

My phone chimed in my purse and I scrambled to turn off the sound. Footsteps echoed in the hall—the *click, click* of Tandi's heels, the *slap, slap* of Lily's flip-flops . . . another set of heels . . . and a man. Wearing boots, maybe. He was tall, his footfalls even and far apart.

I stood up, then sat down, then stood up again and moved around the corner of the long, claw-footed mahogany table, braced my fingers on it, trying to appear cool, calm, confident.

Voices drifted through. "We've kept this meeting very quiet, for obvious reasons," Tandi was saying. "I have my fingers crossed for the best possible outcome, of course."

"I hope it's worth the trip." The board president sounded older, professorial, somewhat impatient—like a man who wasn't accustomed to being told no.

Sweat beaded underneath my shirt as they entered the room and Tandi made introductions. The board president's appearance matched his voice. Gabriel Sorenson was a mountain of a man, midsixties, bald head, neatly trimmed beard, one of the state's foremost authorities on North Carolina's precolonial history. Along with him came his historical specialist, Kay Harper, a middle-aged prof from NC State.

Sorenson didn't mince words or waste time. "Let's see what we've got." He motioned toward the table, and we moved to our chairs, Tandi sitting at the head, the board president and historical specialist across from me. Lily, the intern, hurried to the nearby buffet and retrieved a black plastic briefcase. My heirlooms had found better housing since I'd left them here.

"These are so amazin'." Lily looked like a kid at Christmastime. "If we could ever prove for sure that these carvings were done by somebody who was on one of the Lost Colony ships, that'd be beyond huge. It'd prove that at least one group of survivors got all the way to the mountains and lived there. It'd be the biggest Lost Colony story since the Dare Stones." She cast a furtive glance my way as she opened the briefcase and turned its foam-padded interior toward the newcomers.

Guilt and apprehension settled heavily on my shoulders. If I ended up selling that necklace and the scrimshaw to a private collector, I would be Public Enemy Number One around here. Word would spread on the Outer Banks. The next time I came to Manteo, the reception would be bitter. Mark, Clyde, Joel, Kellie . . . everyone would be disappointed in me.

I'd be betraying Alice just as completely as my grandmother had when she'd destroyed the letters.

Could I live with that?

Could I live without the security and self-reliance the money could provide?

The questions cycled silently as Sorenson and Harper leaned over the case, their chins dropping.

Sorenson slipped on exam gloves and lifted the scrimshaw carving, held it to the light. "We haven't seen anything like this."

Pulling a file from the front pocket of the briefcase, Tandi slid it his way. "We've had three different historical experts look at it over the weekend, as well as an art history specialist. All four concluded that the scrimshaw was done by the same carver as the other story keeper necklaces."

Sorenson's fingertip traced the image of the woman at the ship's wheel. "Is there anything that ties these to the Outer Banks, other than the fact that they were found here, that is?"

Everyone turned my way, and suddenly I was the focus of the meeting again. "I don't have proof, but there are some old letters that were written by my grandmother's sister. She describes finding things like this in the Blue Ridge Mountains and learning the story behind them, which seems to tie them to the coast. My guess is, she sent the necklace and the scrimshaw carving to my grandmother." I hurried through an explanation of Alice's story. "I brought along her letters for you to see, but there are so many parts missing. . . . We can only guess at the rest." Reaching into the dried and crackled leather attaché I'd borrowed from Clyde's closet, I pulled out the faded military binder that held the plastic sleeves filled with his work.

Sorenson was already nodding before I even handed them over. "Let's see what you have."

"We put the letters back together as well as we could." I slid the stack toward him. "They're still a mess, so it's slow reading, but Alice does mention encountering necklaces like this one among a group of Melungeon people in the Blue Ridge, and she talks about being given a scrimshaw carving shaped like a tusk. It's obvious from the last letter that she was becoming more and more obsessed with the topic, but it's also clear that there were people who didn't want the stories of groups like the Melungeons to be told."

I waited while he thumbed through the pages, the historical specialist anxiously reading along. "These are incredible," she whispered.

"I wish we had more, but we don't. It's possible that Alice's original manuscripts are somewhere among the volumes of stored material from the Federal Writers' Project, but I don't have the first clue how we'd find out. Alice was just starting to learn more about the Melungeons and that's where the letters stop. If there were any more, they're gone."

Sorenson's attention turned my way. "Would you consider committing the letters to our collection on loan as well? If not, we'd like to at least have them long enough to transcribe the contents. These may not be a complete solution to the puzzle, but they could provide some critical context."

Expectation tightened the air. My moment of truth had arrived. Now or never. "As far as the letters go, I haven't decided what to do with them, but I'd be happy to let you take them long enough to transcribe what's there. I think Alice would have wanted that."

She would've wanted the necklace and the carving to be here too. . . .

"How long?" I could barely force the words out. Fear had me by the throat. *Be careful,* it was saying. *Protect yourself.* "How long are you asking me to leave the necklace and the scrimshaw on loan to the museum?"

Do what's right, another voice whispered. *Look at everything else that has fallen into place since you came to Manteo.*

Blessings aren't fully realized until they're passed along. How many times had my mother said that to me? Alice had written almost the same thing in her letters.

"We'd like to ask you to commit to the loan for a term of one year." Sorenson braced an elbow on the table, bushy eyebrows lowering as he leaned toward me. "During that time, we hope to secure further funding for our studies here and for the exhibit. Our end goal would be to be able to bring your pieces into the collection permanently. In the meantime, the artifacts will be housed properly, studied, and kept safe. Your other pieces—the ship's manifest, the taffrail log, and the Benoit ruby brooch—we're prepared to make an offer on today."

He lifted a folder from his briefcase and slid it my way. "Here's the yellow sheet with our assessment of those pieces. I can promise you that we're offering top dollar. Because they're tied to the Benoit family, they're worth more to us than they would be to anyone else."

"That makes sense." I sounded surprisingly clinical—as if my hands weren't trembling and my nerves weren't vibrating like overcharged electrical circuits. My heart was sounding off like the Energizer Bunny clapping his cymbals. Surely everyone else could hear it.

I opened the folder, took in the sixteen-thousand-dollar offer. Enough to keep our heads above water until the Bella Tazza hearing. Not enough to single-handedly rescue us from the storm. If I went this route, I'd have to believe that Mark could do what he claimed he could—win our case so we could reopen Tazza 2, as well as somehow arrange grants and volunteer help for the restoration of the Excelsior.

Tandi leaned in slightly. "It is a very fair offer, I promise. And there's the side benefit of knowing that these are back where they belong and the public can have access to them for years to come. They won't end up on someone's mantelpiece."

"I know." My thoughts were moving in such a rush, I couldn't grasp any of them. One big breath, and then, "It's the right thing. I want to do it. All of it . . . including the commitment to the loan."

Things happened in a blur after that. I signed papers. I said things. They said things. We laughed. We smiled. I tried to imagine how Joel and Clyde would react, what Mark would say, what the future might hold for the Excelsior, for Bella Tazza . . .

For Mark and me?

The meeting ended, and we walked through the shadowed halls of Benoit House to the front door. Sorenson thanked me, and Kay Harper invited me to come visit the university. She was currently in the process of scanning the necklaces in 3-D, so that the etched motifs could be studied and compared to markings found on stones in other parts of the state.

"The artifacts you've allowed us to study are invaluable, as are the letters. It's still a puzzle, the story of who these people were and where they came from, but every piece brings us to greater understanding," she said.

We shook hands in the doorway, and then she and Sorenson disappeared into the night. I waited while Tandi moved through the nearby rooms, turning off lights. Around me, Benoit House creaked and groaned, the walls sighing and settling into evening slumber.

I thought of my grandmother, coming here filled with hope as a young bride, anticipating an advantageous marriage and an exciting life. How could she have ever imagined that Benoit House was hiding devastating secrets? How could she possibly have known that Benjamin's marriage to her was only a convenience? That her husband didn't love her and wouldn't be faithful?

Maybe in some way, my journey back here with Alice's story was redemption, an end to the anguish that had been passed silently from generation to generation. Now there were no more secrets, nothing hidden, nothing to hide *from*. There was only the future, and I was ready. It was time—well past time—to shed the dark legacy my father had left me and step into a life that was wholly my own.

CHAPTER 26

She was in my dreams again, my mother. She stood on the shore, on a jetty, just out of reach, yet so real. So filled with color and life, her auburn hair tumbling on the breeze like liquid.

"I miss you." The words didn't hurt this time. I didn't feel my heart breaking along with them.

"I'm here," she answered.

I wanted to touch her, but I didn't. If I stayed where I was, maybe she would stay too.

"You are loved, Whitney. You're always loved." Her smile was radiant, washing like warm water over my skin. Turning, she looked over her shoulder toward the water. "It's so very beautiful there." And then she was moving away, not walking, but moving farther from me.

"Mom, no!" The wind rose. I could see it swirling toward us, whipping the dunes.

"Take care of the baggage, Whitney," she shouted, laughing. Then she tipped back her head and let the wind take her, and she was gone.

I jerked awake, blinked into a night sky that was slowly

surrendering its stars to dawn. For a moment, I couldn't place where I was. Then I remembered rambling around the Excelsior after having supper with Clyde and telling him about the meeting at Benoit House. Sometime around midnight, I'd wandered to the roof deck with a quilt and called Mark to see whether he was still stuck in an airport on his way home. He'd been thinking about getting a hotel and starting fresh in the morning. "Let me at least pay for the hotel," I'd said.

"Nope." He'd sounded remarkably cheerful for a guy with two flights canceled so far. "It's all covered under the retainer agreement."

"Mark, I gave you a *dollar*."

"Still counts."

"You're sort of impossible, you know."

"That's what your old friend Tagg Harper thinks. He's quite a piece of work. I'm going to have some fun with him."

He'd laughed, and I'd laughed with him. Who could've imagined I'd ever find humor in any sentence that had *Tagg Harper* in it? "Just don't do anything illegal, okay?"

"I wouldn't dream of it."

We'd said good night, and he'd told me to have sweet dreams, his voice soft, familiar. My mind had drifted ahead, imagining things it probably shouldn't have, before sleep had finally stolen me away.

Now the first shades of morning had begun to lighten the dome of night sky. I sat up, looked around, breathed deep.

A faint, clear music floated on the gray-misted air. Whistling. Perhaps the reason I'd awakened so suddenly?

I threw the quilt aside, felt the dew gathered on its surface, stood up bent and stiff from the chaise longue, then wobbled toward the edge of the roof deck. The whistling was drawing closer, and with it, another noise—one that pulled me back to my teenage summers in this building. Footsteps on the fire escape's metal treads.

Someone was coming up, and I'd only heard one person around here whistle like that. . . .

A giddy pulse fluttered as I leaned over the railing. What was he doing here . . . *now*? And why was he climbing the fire escape? I couldn't imagine, but there he was, trotting up the second flight of stairs. Even in the shadows, there was no mistaking Mark Strahan. He'd parked his truck underneath the bottom landing, used it to make his way up.

"Hey," I called down in a laughing whisper as he rounded to the third flight. My voice carried on the mist—eerie, otherworldly. He stopped whistling, looked up, smiled.

Was I dreaming? Maybe conjuring all of this . . . and him? "You made it home," I said anyway.

"It wasn't easy." He was up the last of the stairs and over the railing quickly.

I backed away a step and let him in, stood suddenly uncertain as to what should come next. He seemed to be debating the same thing. One hand still held the metal safety bar. His gaze swept the roof, taking in the smattering of old lawn furniture and the ragged string of patio lights. "I called your cell phone. Clyde answered. He said you were up here."

"*Clyde* answered my *iPhone*? I had no idea he knew how." Techno gadgets and Clyde were really the last two things I wanted to talk about, but that's what came out.

"He knows more than you think." Mark's slowly spreading smile was visible even in the glow of the vintage camp lights my mother must have rescued from some rummage sale. Mark was standing under a green one, so that the smile was green and so were his eyes. Deep, dark green. I felt myself falling in.

"Clyde told me to come find you. He offered to let me in through the third floor, but . . . this felt like a better idea."

"It feels like . . . a really good idea." The fortress tumbled, the old walls falling away. What was the point? They weren't needed anymore.

Mark reached for me, and I slipped into his arms. I felt . . . *safe*. I was so ready to be safe with someone. To be safe *for* someone. Tipping back my head, I gazed up at him and said, "Thank you. For everything you did."

"All part of the retainer." He was as cavalier as if he rescued people every day. I leaned into his palm, let my eyes fall closed.

I was lighter than air. I could float off the rooftop and sail away. . . .

Maybe this was the very lesson my dream was meant to teach me—to stop clinging to the baggage, just let go.

"It was *so* worth the retainer," I teased, looking up at him again.

"We aim to please." He frowned contemplatively, adding, "But you do owe me for some luggage. After this trip home, I may never see my suitcase again. I checked it through when I left Michigan because I knew I'd be cutting it close on the connections. Bad choice. No telling where it is right now."

There was something undeniably sweet about the fact that he'd rushed home without worrying about his things. "I'll buy you a new one. Or if you'd rather have a classic, we can probably find a replacement downstairs." Thumbing toward the stairway door, I laughed. "There might be something really snazzy down in . . ."

Take care of the baggage, Whitney.

Take care . . . the baggage . . .

Fireworks went off in my head, and this time they had nothing to do with Mark's close proximity. My thoughts raced like flame along a newly lit fuse, sparks flying everywhere. "The peanut can," I whispered. The second batch of letters had been found in a *peanut can.*

Baggage.

I caught a breath, pushed out of Mark's arms, drew a confused double take from him.

"What?"

Blood was thrumming in my ears now. "Old Dutch!"

"The *what*?"

"Old Dutch . . ." *Lucianne wasn't the one who ate peanuts; Old Dutch was.* "The porter, back when this was a hotel. He ate peanuts and he saved the containers and stored things in them. He always had peanut jars and peanut cans. We found the second batch of letters in a peanut can."

Suddenly so many things made sense. Lucianne wasn't the only one who'd loved books. Old Dutch's small first-floor bedroom had been lined with homemade shelves. They were filled with volumes he'd salvaged from trash heaps and library book sales. Maybe the encyclopedia set downstairs hadn't quite seemed familiar because it *wasn't* familiar. Maybe it wasn't Lucianne's at all, but Old Dutch's. Maybe he'd been the one to rescue the letters. That was the reason so many pieces were missing. Old Dutch wouldn't have had access until the wastebaskets upstairs were emptied into the old rubbish chute. By then, everything would've been mixed together, including the hotel trash, but Old Dutch didn't mind trash. He was always coming up with treasures he'd salvaged from garbage bins. He used those things or he repaired them and gave them away.

He was clearly fond of Alice and her daughter. Emmaline had sent drawings to him.

"The *porter's closet.*" The words and the thought came in unison. "What if there *are* more of the letters? What if the suitcase Alice planned to send to my grandmother is hidden *there*? Old Dutch would've never let a perfectly good suitcase be hauled away with the trash."

Mark blinked, blinked again. "The *supply* closet? The one downstairs? There's nothing in there but tools and floor polishers. A couple rusted steam radiators nobody ever bothered to get rid of. I've been in there a million times, Whitney. There's no space for anything more."

"But it *used* to go way back under the stairwell. They closed it off and built shelves over that part when they shut down the hotel and remodeled for retail downstairs, but what if there are still things *in* there? What if they never cleared the crawl space . . . or maybe even left things stored there on purpose?"

Mark's mouth slowly dropped into an O. "It's possible. . . ."

He bolted for the fire escape, and I followed him over the railing, the two of us rushing down the stairs together. At the bottom, an agile jump landed him in the back of his pickup. He reached for me, but I was already swinging off monkey-style and dropping to the pavement.

"I get a feeling you've done this before."

"Just a few times." We'd reached the street door before I realized I was in my sweats and didn't have a thing with me. "Please tell me you've got keys?"

"In my truck." He jogged off while I paced under the awning, trying not to let my hopes go wild, but I couldn't help it. After all this time, could a miracle be waiting in Old Dutch's domain? Nobody else ever went into that closet, back in the day. The place had smelled of partially used paint, polish, grease guns, oil, floor wax, and customers' stored luggage. It would've been a safe hiding spot for something Old Dutch didn't want my grandmother *or* Lucianne *or* any of the hotel staff to find.

When Mark came back, we were like bumper cars going through the door. Mark's store keys gave us entrance to the closet, and we haphazardly piled cleaning equipment against the stairwell and wheeled floor machines into the landing. The shelves along the back wall of the closet were even more work. They were filled with spray bottles, outdated cans of wax, and assorted leftovers from the building's slipshod operation over the years.

"I actually don't think the unit is attached to anything." Mark grabbed a board and seemed to rattle the entire back wall. "Hang on." Lifting the plywood grid in one piece, he manhandled it around the corner and propped it against an adjacent wall. Where it had been, the Sheetrock from the renovation was unpainted, the seam tape curled and peeling. Mark rapped on it with his knuckles. "Sounds hollow in the middle."

I hurried to the hallway, grabbed a hammer and a garden spade. "Let's knock it down."

"You sure?"

"Yes, I'm sure. If there's anything back there, I want to know."

"It's your building." Mark laughed.

The wall gave in easily, but even so, an eternity seemed to tick by as the dust settled and the light reached in. Slowly, bit by bit, the remnants of Old Dutch's hoard became visible—peanut jars filled with salvaged nails, bolts, rubber bands, bits of string. Faded bobbers and crab pot buoys, rolls of fishing line rescued from the tide. Bottles frosted by time in the sea. Wooden crates, plumbing supplies, wire bins holding the pads for floor polishers, old scrub brushes, wringers, and dust-covered rags.

Three empty crates sat neatly stacked in one corner. A small suitcase rested on top, an innocuous brown tortoiseshell leather, twine wrapped around it and the remains of a disintegrated mailing label clinging to one side. The handwriting was familiar even in the half light. At this point, I would've known Alice's penmanship anywhere.

Staggering clumsily over the boxes on the floor, I tried to reach the case. Rotted cardboard collapsed underfoot and I felt Mark grab the back of my sweatshirt in a handful. "Easy there, Sherlock."

"I've almost . . . got it. . . ." One more stretch and the edge of the handle was within reach. I flipped it upward so that when it fell back, it landed against my palm. A quick tug and the whole thing slid free. I toppled forward with it, unprepared for its weight.

"That's not empty." Mark reeled me in, dragging both the suitcase and me by my sweatshirt.

"No . . . oof . . . It's not. I think I might've . . . found . . . what we were looking for." But in the back of my mind, there was a nagging worry. What if this suitcase had been emptied out long ago? What if Old Dutch had used it to store something else?

If Alice's manuscripts weren't here, it would be a dashed last hope, a final, crushing disappointment.

Stumbling out of the closet, I sneezed and coughed, puffs of Sheetrock dust falling in my eyes, turning my hair gray as it tumbled into my face. I pushed it out of the way, saw Mark grinning at me in the stairway light.

"You look like you've been playing in the dirt pile. Here." He wiped the smudges away with the sleeve of his crisp, white lawyer shirt. "You can buy me a new one."

"Deal."

We moved to the staircase together. Settling in beside the suitcase, I smoothed a hand over the label, took a breath. This small container was all that remained of Alice and Thomas's journey. It had survived these many years, thanks to Old Dutch. Inside, hope would be either lost or found.

"Here goes." I flipped the latches, lifted the lid, watched the shadows recede, saw Alice's manuscripts meet the light for the first time in almost eighty years. The bundles lay carefully stacked and tied with brown packing twine, the pages surprisingly pristine.

Lifting the closest one, I read the heading on the top page:

PROJECT #1721
ALICE LORRING
LA BELLE, NC
JUNE 10, 1936

The Narrative of Ida Mullins, a Melungeon Woman of the Mountains

The echo of Ida Mullins's laugh must surely travel mile upon mile over the crisp morning air as we sit by grass-covered foundation stones that seem as ancient as the mountains themselves. Nearby, a graveyard rises along the hillside. There are no granite markers here. Little commemorates the passing of these lives, save for rough, brown stones selected from mountain slopes. Some have been carved with names and dates, carefully etched by relatives, the carver spelling his sentiments to the best of his ability.

Ida rests a hand upon the foundation stones. She pats them for me to sit with her. The grass rustles near her feet, and she grabs at it, tossing something away. Her discard writhes in the air, then lands hard and slithers off. A snake. Ida pats the stones again, and I am loath to sit down, but I do.

"This 'ere be the oldest place I knowed'a. My mama knowed it, and her mama afore her. Was built a long, long time back yander, the way my granny told't it. Doubt she had any call to lie over it.

"Granny told't the story that the folks what made this place come to the mount'ns, back when there was none but the Cher'kee hereabouts, back before any white man ever laid his eyes on this country. The sea keepers, my granny used'a call them old-time folks, 'cause they told't a old, old tale of comin' over the sea and settlin' first by the big water. Was their women what was the keepers of their story. Was their job to always hold tight to the past, to tell it to the young'uns. The valley, their men farmed in it, and the hills, they hunted 'em. They was friendly with the Cher'kee and married up with the Injuns some too. They lived right pearly here, I reckon."

Her hand moves in the rhythm of slopes and valleys, peaks and folds. Those bent and curled fingers know the mountains, even from a distance. "This 'ere be their church." She pats the stones again, giving them a good hard thump, hard enough that it would seemingly hurt, but she does not wince. "Knowed the Lord, them folks that come o'er the big, wide sea. Brought him with 'em to the mount'ns.

Come to the fer country, like 'em old-time folk in the Good Book."

She stops, tucks her hands into her apron, squints against the sun to see me. "That's what my granny said 'bout them keeper women. They was Melungeons, but not all them Melungeons was sea keepers, and that's how it were. There's lots a old tales round here, though. Cain't tell ya all of 'em. All the old ways."

I know it is true. We could sit together for days, weeks, months. We could, indeed, watch the seasons change and the winter come, and still I would not hear all that Ida Mullins knows of this rough upland country. I must settle for what little I can learn today, the minutiae I can capture with paper and pen.

"Can you tell me if there were others who knew stories about this place?"

The trees overhead shudder and Ida looks up as if she's hearing their voices. A breath fills her, and I know another story is coming. I feel it brushing over me, like the change in breeze that portends a storm. My heart quickens with anticipation.

"Reckon I might could," she says and laughs into the wind. "Reckon I sure 'nuf might."

Overhead, the trees go silent, listening too. . . .

Letting the bundle rest against the suitcase, I lifted the corner of the paper without untying the twine binding. "This is incredible." A sense of wonder and joy filled me, overwhelmed me, pressed tears into my throat. Alice's stories had survived. After all this time, they could still be told.

I set down the packet, picked up another, began reading.

PROJECT #1735
ALICE LORRING
LA BELLE, NC
JUNE 21, 1936

La Belle School for Children of Melungeon Blood

Subject: R. A. Camp (Alias of Randolph Champlain. Name to be withheld by request of interviewee).

His skin is leathery and worn, as folded and lined as the bed of a mountain stream. Its characteristics have been shaped by time, experience, and the brushing past of other lives. Thick, silver-white curls neatly adorn his head, yet his eyes are stark, piercing blue, quick and acute. Even now, well into his sixties, R. A. Camp is a strong figure as he stands beside me on the slope, watching the children cavort in the playground below.

His wife, Sarra, is among the children, directing them in a game of Hen and Chicks. Thick, gray-dusted dark curls are piled atop her head, otherwise she could quickly be mistaken as one of the children. They are easy with her, and comfortable. She is of their own Melungeon blood. She was, her husband tells me, an orphan herself by the age of fifteen, given into the hands of reprehensible men at a trading post after the death of her Cherokee grandmother.

R. A. was the one to rescue her. They have now been married for forty-six years.

R. A. is a learned and cultured man. He begins our interview by politely asking that I not use his birth name in this narrative, as his family can be counted among fine Southern folk. Even after these many years, his marriage to Sarra is considered a blot on the family name, unforgivable by some, and illegal in the view of others. Formally educated in his youth, and self-educated in his adulthood, he recognizes the value of learning for these children, and for all children of the mountains. He and Sarra have long advocated for the well-being of workers in mill towns and coal settlements. They have fought for new laws that would prohibit the employment of youngsters at the helms of machinery and in other dangerous tasks.

"Here in the mountains," he says, "it is not an uncommon thing to find children as young as six or seven working ten hours per day in the mills. There's much to change yet." He speaks as if he intends to live a long while, but I have been told that he suffers from a slowly degenerating heart. There is no treatment for it.

Sarra attempts to heal him in the old ways, with roots and herbs, but even she feels the numbering of their days together. She is protective of him.

"For years, I helped to build those mill towns, but when I traveled to them later, the conditions I saw were akin to slavery. It sickened me, and Sarra as well. In places, we saw orphans kept as veritable chattel, either by mill companies, mining brothels, or adopted into families who used them cruelly. There were so few safe havens for unwanted children, and in particular those of mixed blood. Neither the coloreds nor the whites nor the Cherokee were warm to the Melungeon children. It was Sarra who concocted the idea for the school. . . ."

I stopped at the end of the page, took in the suitcase with a sense of awe. This small container wasn't only the hiding place for one life, but for many. I wanted to open each bundle, to read every story, but these manuscripts deserved careful handling. It shouldn't be done at the bottom of the stairs with dust, grease, and equipment scattered around.

"It was here all along." I looked at Mark, but he was engrossed in something he'd pulled from the suitcase. A letter.

He offered me the first page, shook his head, his mouth a grim line that made me pause with my hand in the air, think twice about accepting it. Finally, I did.

The handwriting was thick and angular, pressed hard into the page. It wasn't Alice's.

I glanced at Mark.

"It's from Thomas." His voice caught, and he cleared his throat. Dread clenched inside me. I prepared myself for something, but I didn't know what.

Dear Mrs. Benoit,

It's with a heavy heart that I send you Alice's belongings, which my father retrieved some time ago from the La Belle Orphan School, along with my own cases and the FWP equipment. I realize that you and I did not get on well during those tumultuous weeks at the hospital in Asheville, and that you wished no further communications from me. Yet I simply do not know what else to do with Alice's things. You should be finding a shipment of three pieces, two large suitcases with a smaller one. As soon as I have the money for it and know that you have received these items, I will send along a fourth item, a small wooden chest.

To be honest, I can't look at them any longer. I know you have your burdens as well, but a body and soul can only bear so much. I've left the FWP and returned home to my parents' farm in Tennessee to heal the shattered leg, and in hopes that time and familiar places may in some way mend a shattered soul.

Even here, I'm reminded that I had dreamed of bringing Alice, Emmaline, and the child we'd planned to raise together to meet my family one day. I still struggle to believe that they will never lay eyes on this place. It may be difficult for you to hear, but I loved your sister to the depths of my soul, and in spite of the difference in our situations, she loved me in return. I don't know if life will ever hold so dear and tender a connection for me again. I fail to see how it could. . . .

Mark handed me the last two pages, then leaned on his hand, stared at the wall, and sighed.

I turned back to the paper.

I respect your family's request not to have me at the funerals and to conceal Alice's employment with the WPA. I suppose in your position, it's a matter of reputation, not wishing it known that a member of the family was on government relief. Let me assure you, though, that Alice was devoted to the work of the Federal Writers' Project and very proud of it. She had fallen deeply for the mountain country and its people. She wanted to do well for them.

I implore you, if her works are edited out of the final volumes approved by the state and national offices, if politics and prejudice do prevent their publication (as is sadly becoming common, given growing accusations of Communist sympathies inside The Project), please publish her writings in some other way. Alice wanted to see that those stories were told. Possibly they could be printed under the pen name she'd selected for the manuscript she was so feverishly trying to finish in those last glorious weeks before our tragedy.

To cover our prescribed tour route during that time, we'd been fanning out from the orphanage, but returning each day or two, so that Alice could continue to write the story of Randolph Champlain and Sarra, his Melungeon wife. It was Alice's intention, before ever seeing the piece published, to alter their names and her own, so as to avoid any disparagement of the Champlain family or conflicts with Randolph's relatives. This was at Rand's request, and being aware of the Champlains as old and important Charleston people, Alice understood it. This is not to say that she did not find it sad, a man living apart from his family all these years, due to the blight of prejudice.

When I'm able to send along the wooden chest, you'll find the beginnings of Alice's manuscript, along with Rand's journal and Sarra's necklace (which Alice was allowed to take, as Rand and Sarra have no children). Alice had selected the pen name Louisa Quinn. She decided it had a ring to it, and she felt that anonymity for herself was best, given the current state of politics and racial affairs.

You should know that we had on several occasions been threatened as we went about our business for the FWP. Alice was concerned that publication of the Champlains' story could endanger Emmaline's safety in the future. There are those groups, and even many men in high political positions, who feel strongly against anything that offers a soft view of the mixing of the races. They do not want change, and as we well know, some groups will go to violence over it. I do deeply wish I'd had greater respect for that horrible potential. Youthful confidence made me far too flippant about what we'd undertaken there.

I could not say this to you at the hospital, in deference to your own grief, and in fear for Able and her child, but your sister and little Emmaline were murdered. I have no doubt of it. We did not veer off the road by accident or careless driving on our journey back to the orphan school that last day. Suddenly, and for no good reason, the steering was gone in the car. "A worn-out part," the sheriff said afterward, but he knew and I knew that the tie rod did not dislodge on its own. This will never be proven. They took the remains of my car to the scrap heap while I lay in the hospital those weeks, with Emmaline and Able still fighting for their own lives. The car is gone and along with it any proof that tampering caused Alice's death on that horrible day and eventually little Emmaline's as well.

I thank you for what you have done for Able and for the orphanage. It's on their behalf that I didn't go forward with taking Alice's manuscripts to a publisher myself. Rest assured that I will adhere to our agreement that I not intrude on your life or on Alice's reputation from here on out, but I will also expect you to keep your part of the bargain. I will, from time to time, make trips to the orphan school to see about Able and to make certain that her fees are being paid as promised, until her eighteenth birthday.

I wish you a good future and that your grief will be eased. I pray that you will let Alice share her stories with the world. Though she lacked confidence in it, she was a fine writer. Even more, she was a spectacular soul. The angels in heaven have gained back two of their own in her and little Emmaline.

I loved them dearly and think of them moment by moment. I always will.

Yours respectfully,
Thomas Kerth

Setting the letter back in the suitcase, I closed the lid, leaned across it into Mark, and cried for the death of a woman and a little girl I never knew.

And a story that had too long gone untold.

EPILOGUE

"I think you'd have to say it's been a smashing success." Denise rests her hands on her hips and looks across the park toward the amphitheater. Overhead, our blue canvas awning rustles in the sea breeze. The scents of deep fryers, hot skillets, batter, spices, and seafood hang in the air, and the last jazz number of the final act drifts over from the amphitheater.

"I think you're right," I agree and sink into my chair, boneless and brain dead, but content. There's still so much cleanup to do, but it can wait a few minutes. The pots and warmers and hot plates and spatulas and the plethora of utensils aren't going anywhere.

"We sold a lot of cookbooks." Denise measures what's left of the stack, then checks boxes and finds them empty. *Tales and Tastes of the Outer Banks*, both the cookbook and the festival, couldn't have met a better reception. "Next time, I think we should do one thing or the other, though. Sponsor a food booth *or* sign cookbooks."

"By next year, the cookbook will be old news." Although, with all of Manteo behind it, who knows? And now that Alice and Thomas's story is on its way to becoming the next big Evan

Hall novel, by next year, the tourists here may be thicker than crabgrass. A second edition of *Tales and Tastes of the Outer Banks* could be an even more successful fund-raiser for the charity, which has been officially named Excelsior House, in honor of the hotel's history and the inspiration from the Seaside House down on Hatteras. Manteo's version is soon to open its doors on the newly renovated second floor of the hotel building.

At this point, I wonder if I would survive one more fund-raiser, but it's all been worth it. The charity will commence operations fully staffed and offer programs for teens through young adults. With an ongoing income from the publication of Alice and Thomas's story, Excelsior House will make a difference in many lives, both here on the island and in pushing for legislation to aid family members of people struggling with addictions. "If there's another festival next year, someone else is going to have to be in charge. I'm hanging up my event coordinator hat . . . forever." But the truth is, Mark and his Excelsior House people drove this undertaking like a force of nature. They've made so much happen in slightly over a year. Mountains have moved.

Too many newspaper and magazine articles have tried to give me the credit for it, but the creation of Excelsior House is far beyond the ability of human hands. If I had doubted that, with divine intervention, a mess can become a miracle, this project is proof. From imperfect offerings, something perfect has been born.

When I'm not quite so exhausted, I'll appreciate that even more than I do at the moment. I'll take time to give proper thanks for the success of this day, for all the changes in my life over these past thirteen months.

Denise sit-stands on the edge of a folding table.

"Watch the grease." I toss her a towel. There's a little river running her way.

"Thanks." She drops the rag over it, but doesn't look. Instead, she picks at her fingernails and sighs. "Listen, Whit . . . about next year . . . I've been meaning to talk something over with you."

"Can it wait until we get to the beach house?" I'm hearing a loud *wah-wah-wah* inside my head, like it's swelling and shrinking . . . but in a good-tired kind of way. "I'm ready to stick my toes in the sand and just chill."

One of the backers of Excelsior House has loaned our crew a massive place up past the pavement in Corolla. We'll stay there for a week, going over every last detail before the charity officially opens its doors. We'll also have *a little celebration*, as Mark referred to it. The beach house has twelve bedrooms, and wild horses graze outside the front door. It's paradise. I could get used to living like that. As much as I love Michigan, it's going to be hard to get on the plane to go home after the grand opening of Excelsior House. Even harder to say good-bye to Mark, but he'll fly up for a visit as soon as things here settle down again. We're pretty good at this long-distance-relationship thing, even with all that's been going on.

Denise shakes her head. "No . . . it really can't. I have to tell them something by Monday."

"Tell who . . . what?" Denise and I are supposed to be hanging out on the Outer Banks for a week yet, walking on the beach and watching the wild horses, recapping the success of the *Tales and Tastes* fund-raiser. Back home, Bella Tazza 2 is in good hands. Even with the rush of summer tourists, the staff has it under control. The plate time is so fast and the food is so delicious, we've driven Tagg Harper completely out of the Italian food business. He's quietly gone into cheap hamburgers instead. I still don't know what Mark did to him, but we haven't heard a peep out of Tagg in months.

The look on Denise's face pins me to my lawn chair and all thoughts of Michigan fly from my mind. "Denise, *what*?"

"I've been offered a teaching job."

"Huh?"

"I have to let them know by Monday." She pulls a face, swallows hard, looks down at the food-spattered ground. Sugar ants are having a field day. "I want to take it."

I'm dumbstruck. Several minutes pass while I flounder around. I feel like a fish dropped on a hot sidewalk, unsure which way the water might be. "But the . . . Bella Tazza, and we finally got the insurance claim all settled . . . and we can build a second store again. . . ." Even as I say it, there's a little whirlpool of panic smack-dab in the center of my soul, as if someone is stirring the boiling pot too fast, creating a vortex. With the Excelsior, and Mark, and the cookbook, and the charity, I've been worried about taking on one more thing. Life is a blur right now.

If Denise isn't there to help keep the balls in the air . . . they'll all come crashing down. The juggling act will be over.

Her head falls to one side, and she gives me the parental look that I both love and hate. It means she thinks she knows more than me. It also means she loves me. "Whitney, here's the thing. It's time to make some decisions, and I *know* you've got this phobia about commitments, but to tell you the truth . . ." She takes a breath, waits for a woman to pass by with a baby stroller and grab samples off the tray of leftover food we've set out.

The customer dallies forever, complimenting our artichoke-stuffed mushroom caps and sun-dried-tomato panelle.

I'm about to explode by the time she leaves, but Denise is calm. She resumes her position and speaks before I can. "I think you need to move here, Whit. You and Mark are good together, but dating back and forth between Michigan and North Carolina is stupid. There's plenty of room for you at the Excelsior, and now with Joel ready to move from community college to NC State, Clyde's going to need help again. Or . . . maybe you and Mark should just stop beating around the bush and *take the plunge*, settle in at the Captain's Castle . . . have a nice life."

Before I can react to the bluntness, she lays a splay-fingered hand on her chest. "I am just plain *tired*. I'm *tired* of the restaurant business. I'm tired of the hours. I miss my classroom and the kiddos. I want to be *home* when Mattie gets there in the afternoons, and I want to be with her in the summers. We could even come here to visit you during semester breaks. If you start a restaurant in Manteo, whenever I'm off, I'll come help in it."

She finally stops, keeping a dead eye on me as she waits for an answer, but I'm like a deer in the headlights. I'm completely locked up.

"Say something," she nudges.

"S-something."

"Cute. Now say something meaningful. Give me your thoughts. I talk, then you talk. That's how this works, Whit."

She sounds so much like my mother, I'm temporarily lost in time. This is a kitchen table counseling session from back in the day. I'm being led by the nose, and part of me is aware it's for my own good, but part of me still doesn't like being *told* what's good for me.

Tandi and the crew from Sandy's Seashell Shop wander by,

providing another distraction. Denise and I slip into food-vendor mode again. The girls twitter about the chow and the festival and how well things went at their booth.

"We were close enough to the stage, we had music all afternoon." Sandy lifts her arms and gives a spunky senior hip wiggle. I can't imagine why she's not tired. "We just danced our way right through it. And it's for a good cause. I feel like Excelsior House is part ours, since Seaside House inspired it."

"I'm glad. Thanks for everything you did to help." We share hugs and trade a few anecdotes from the day. Sandy boasts that she got the headliner band to autograph CDs, which she'll sell in her shop.

Denise waves after the Seashell Shop crew as they move on. "I like them."

"You know she moved here from Michigan too, right? She just wanted to have a store by the sea. It's a really cute place. They make some beautiful jewelry, and . . ."

Denise clears her throat and delivers a thin lip that says, *That's not what we were talking about here.* "And? The *restaurant* plan? With my part of the money from selling Tazza 2, plus the insurance check from Tazza 1, Mattie and I can be sitting pretty, and you'll have more than you need to start a place here, without even tapping into your reserves. Besides that, if the museum ever does put together the funds to actually *buy* the sea keeper artifacts, you'll be rolling in dough—the real kind, not the kind we whip up at the restaurant."

"I'll just have to . . . think about it." Another groundswell of panic. That's what I feel. But I've grown up enough to know that Denise is right about me. This is my knee-jerk reaction to commitment. It doesn't necessarily mean anything.

I think about being here with Mark all the time, about finally making the plans we haven't quite gotten to in the rush of the last thirteen months. Panic slowly finds itself wrapped in a thick, warm blanket.

"You have until Monday to mull it over." Denise emits a huff to let me know I shouldn't *need* that long.

"That's the day after tomorrow."

"Don't overthink it, then."

"You're being a jerk." She knows I don't mean it . . . but at the same time, I do. If she's been pondering this long enough to apply for a job and go to an interview, *and* get an offer . . . She could've told me sooner, given me more time to think, to plan.

"I'm *tired*. I'm a jerk when I'm tired." She isn't flinching.

"You're really that unhappy in the restaurant?" Is she, or is all of this just a way of cutting me loose because she's convinced that she should?

"Yeah, Whit, I am."

There's no way to tell for sure. Denise has her poker face on.

"Okay . . ." I stand up. Mark is headed our way, weaving through the crowd of exiting festivalgoers. In the amphitheater, the last notes of an encore song have died.

"And look what you have to gain," Denise leans down and whispers in my ear before she slips out the back of the tent.

I maneuver around the table and start across the green, letting the fresh breeze off the water cool the heat of emotion.

"Success!" Mark cheers, pumping a fist. When we're close enough, he scoops me up and spins me around. I throw my head back and revel in the overwhelming flood of joy. Denise is right. Look what I'm missing every time I pack my suitcases and head home to Michigan . . . every time I let that last little bit of insecurity nudge me back to the same old place.

Sometimes you've gotta take a big leap to get over the hump.

Clyde's words to Joel about going away to college. *But once you're there, it's a whale of a ride down the hill.*

"I missed you all day," I say, and smile up at Mark. I've caught glimpses of him from a distance, hurrying here and there, people whispering in his ear and grabbing at him from all directions. He's so cool under pressure, it's impressive. He'd be good in a restaurant. . . .

One dark brow lifts. "Whitney, why are you . . . looking at me . . . that way?"

"What way?"

"In a way that scares me."

I wonder what he'd say if he knew I was thinking about the Excelsior and whether the space in the corner could be outfitted for a bistro-style eatery. The lease on the boutique runs out soon. They're behind on their rent, and I doubt they'll try to catch up.

"Hey, Surf Dude, I'm gonna make like a banana and split." Both Mark and I look across the way and see Joel sauntering toward the bridge to Manteo.

Mark plants a kiss on my hair, then whispers, "I'd better give him *the talk* again. He heads off to school in the morning."

Mark jogs away, and I watch him go because . . . he looks good jogging . . . and going.

I'm just hovering there, mooning after him, when I realize someone's standing nearby. I turn, and she's perhaps ten feet from our tent, in the shade of a tree. She's looking at the festival program, then at me, then at the festival program again, then at me. She's tall and thin, willowy and beautiful, a thick black braid lying over her shoulder. The light bleeds through her white sundress, outlining her slender form. She looks like an actress or a model. Maybe she was with one of the musical acts that performed today. Maybe she's lost.

"Can I help you?" I move a few steps closer.

She checks the program again, then me. Her eyes narrow, then widen. "I was afraid we were too late." Her voice is soft and musical, her words laced with the melody of a slow Southern drawl. Maybe she's a singer. There were some gorgeous voices on stage today.

A set of keys dangles from her fingers, and I notice that she looks fresh and neat, not windblown and sweaty like the rest of us. I hope she hasn't just arrived here. "The festival is over. It just ended." I hate to be the one to break the news, but it's kind of obvious, anyway.

She approaches tentatively, until we're standing face to face. Something about her seems vaguely familiar, but I can't place what. Maybe I've talked to her before. Maybe she was supposed to be involved in the goings-on today, but she's late getting here?

I would remember her if I'd ever met her, though. She's striking.

"We got stuck in traffic for*ever*," she complains. "I didn't think we'd make it here in time."

What *is* it that I recognize about her? She reminds me of somebody I know. Who? "Well . . ." *Sorry, but you're not in time.* "They just closed down the stage. We've got a few food samples left in our booth. Some other people might too. You could probably still eat." Poor kid. She can't be more than about twenty or so.

"I brought my granny." She thumbs over her shoulder toward the boardwalk that leads to the water. "We came to find *you*. Granny saw you in a magazine story."

Ohhhh . . . maybe that explains something. Between the cookbook, the press releases for the festival, and the coverage of the planned story keeper exhibit at Benoit House Museum, it's definitely a possibility.

Lily. The name trips through my mind. *Maybe this girl reminds me of Lily, the intern at Benoit House. . . . Maybe they resemble one another a little?* I take the opportunity to scrutinize her as she glances over her shoulder again.

"Can you just come talk to her for a little bit? We drove in from Tennessee."

"Tennessee? And you came here to see me? Why?" Now I'm afraid that they've traveled all this way with an expectation—that they're hoping for something I can't deliver. I have absolutely no idea what it could be.

"She won't tell me." The girl's silver-blue eyes plead for me to come with her. "She wanted to see the water, so I left her down there on the bench. It's not far. Please?"

"Okay." Now I'm curious. "Sure. Okay."

We cross the park together, and on the way we make innocuous chatter about the traffic and her grandma. The girl's name is Angela. She's a college student from Knoxville. I have a fleeting thought that I should try to introduce her to Joel, since he and Kayla didn't work out. Angela's grandmother is ninety-four. Angela is one of thirty-seven grandchildren. The number staggers me.

"Her and Grandpa Tom had twelve kids, so thirty-seven grandkids isn't that many." Her laugh is quick and melodious. "Granny Abby always liked to tease that they didn't stop until they got an even dozen."

I barely hear the joke. My mind is running ahead. Tennessee . . . Grandpa *Tom*, Granny *Abby*.

When we finally reach the bay and I see an old woman sitting there, time has stopped moving around me. She seems almost like a statue, staring out at the water, a lace shawl wrapped over her old-fashioned floral dress. A chill travels over my body, even though the day is warm. I circle around her, catch my reflection in cloudy eyes that were once a bright blue-gray, like Angela's.

I know who I'm looking at.

"Able?" The word is little more than a whiff of breeze. It seems to come off the sea.

The woman takes a moment to turn away from the view.

"She's never been to the ocean, not in her whole life, until today," Angela interjects sweetly.

I sit down on the bench, because I'm afraid if I don't, I'll fall. I'm conscious of Angela's curious regard flying back and forth between us, but even if I wanted to, I couldn't explain this to her right now. I can only stare at Able, only feel the trembling warmth of her hand as it slowly circles mine.

"You come by my necklace," she says, her gaze searching me, seeming to reach inside me, groping for something. "You was the one. I seen your picture."

"Yes. Yes, I found the necklace in my grandmother Ziltha's building. It was hidden away in an old desk." The sea keeper necklace I unearthed . . . was it *Able's* necklace? Perhaps she'd given it to Alice, or maybe to Grandmother Ziltha, in gratitude? *I thank you for what you have done for Able*—that's what Thomas's letter had said.

Tears frame her eyes now, wash into the folds and estuaries of her skin. Her hand squeezes tight, and I'm conscious of nothing around us. Not people moving, not waves lapping at the shore, not boats motoring along in the distance. All hangs suspended. Even time.

I don't know how long it is before she speaks.

Her other hand rises, touches my face, cups my cheek, trembling against me. Her skin is sun-warmed. "I put that necklace on my boy. Wrapped it in the swaddlin' blanket 'fore I's to hand him over to her at that hospital. Was all I had to give 'im, and him just a tiny little thang, borned too soon, while my body was all broke up. She give me a promise that she'd git 'im cared for and find 'im a good home. Her bein' in a fam'ly way her own self, I figured she knowed how to look after 'im 'til she got him to a safe place. She told me it were best thang I could do for 'im, to let 'im go and not ask after 'im no more, so that's what I done. Guess I's always thinkin' that, some yander day, that bitty boy would git all growed up and hist on home ag'in, but he never come. Thought somehow's he'd know he was mine, even if nobody'd ever told't him."

I'm caught off guard. I can't breathe. I'm trying to make sense of it all. Beside the bench, Angela sinks to her knees in the grass, and we stare at one another, and I realize why she seems familiar. She looks like my *father*. Like the pictures of him. Like the small shreds of memory I still carry.

"My *dad*?" I babble.

"When I seen you, I knowed." Able's thumb strokes my cheek, rough and bent and calloused. The hand of a woman who's worked hard and raised twelve children and lived ninety-four years. "Welcome home, child."

She beckons me close and begins to weep, and we wrap our arms around one another and hang on. As I hold her, my mind fills with questions. *How can this be? How could Ziltha take another woman's child and tell everyone he was hers? What happened to the baby she was carrying? Did it die? Was it stillborn? Is it possible that she was never pregnant at all—that after losing several pregnancies, she invented one as a way of clinging to Benjamin?*

Did the Benoits figure it out?

Maybe Ziltha and her son weren't disinherited because of a family feud, but because the truth became obvious eventually. Babies may look alike when they're small, but as children mature, their heritage shows. Perhaps Girard Benoit knew that the son Ziltha was raising couldn't be Benjamin's?

Despite the lack of answers, I know I've found the truth of who I am and where I come from. The path isn't straight. It winds and bends in magnificent ways, its course shepherded by strong women who've left their footprints behind.

I think of my mother, who raised me and loved me.

I think of Nurse Merry Walker, who brought a frightened girl down the mountain.

I think of Alice, who journeyed into the wilderness to discover the stories of others, but instead found the echoes of her own voice. I think of the baby she was determined to protect, the baby she saved from those who would have seen it perish.

I think of Able Kerth. My grandmother. I feel the flesh and bone and marrow of this woman, this daughter of those who long ago crossed the sea.

I am not just one person. I am the sum of those who have come before me.

My blood rises up, embracing an inexplicable knowing that has been there as long as I can remember. It is the legacy passed from mother to daughter for generation upon generation, and now from my grandmother to me.

The sea whispers, and so does its Keeper. For all the generations, in the old world and the new, we have been his daughters, and he has guided us on our journeys.

We have come full circle, and now the sea has called us home.

Note to Readers

Dear Reader,

It's my hope that, at this point, *The Sea Keeper's Daughters* has taken you on a journey and that now, at the journey's end, you are returning with moments of adventure, romance, and discovery that are yours to keep. The best stories are the ones that become part of our own personal histories.

Speaking of history, I hope Alice's letters have stirred an interest in the true tales of the Federal Writers and the stories they gathered. Never before in American history had such a thing been attempted. Yet through the work of thousands of field interviewers, who were out-of-work writers, secretaries, housewives, professors, and so forth, a struggling America was preserved for all to revisit.

Those involved in "Federal One" were far ahead of their time. They were the beginning of the Civil Rights movement before there was a Civil Rights movement. They pushed toward equality for women before anyone was openly discussing equal opportunity. Their mandate was to be all-inclusive, to break down hard and fast societal boundaries, much like Kathryn

Stockett's main character does in *The Help*, when she interviews black maids in the South. The Federal Writers not only documented the natural wonders of the country, but the hidden lives of minorities, working women, immigrant laborers, sharecroppers, and others typically ignored by the history books. Their writings helped to inspire Steinbeck's *The Grapes of Wrath*, among other classics. Sadly, much of the Federal Writers' work was stored away as the Red Scare heated up, congressional committees held hearings to search for communist infiltrators on American soil, and World War II gripped the nation.

Now, many of the field interviewers' original works are available via Internet. Lives long gone and places long past can be yours at the touch of a button. I hope you'll spend a bit of time with them. (See below for some links to get you started.) You may even find names you recognize and places you know. Most certainly, you'll realize that so many of the things we struggle with as human beings are not unique to our generation. There are lessons to be learned from those who've wandered these paths before us.

I doubt that writers like Alice could have ever imagined their stories would fly through the air, spanning the globe in an instant. I can't help believing that, eighty years after they traveled the hills and dales and back roads, the Federal Writers would be happy to know that many long-silenced voices can now be heard.

May your journey be filled with great stories,

Lisa

Links:

Library of Congress Federal Writers' Project information:
http://www.loc.gov/rr/program/bib/newdeal/fwp.html

Manuscripts from the Federal Writers' Project:
http://www.loc.gov/collection/federal-writers-project

WPA Depression-era photographs:
http://www.loc.gov/pictures/collection/fsa/

Slave narratives transcriptions and recordings:
http://memory.loc.gov/ammem/snhtml/snhome.html

WPA posters and advertisements:
http://www.loc.gov/pictures/search/?st=grid&co=wpapos

CHAPTER 1

WHEN TROUBLE BLOWS IN, my mind always reaches for a single, perfect day in Rodanthe. The memory falls over me like a blanket, a worn quilt of sand and sky, the fibers washed soft with time. I wrap it around myself, picture the house along the shore, its bones bare to the wind and the sun, the wooden shingles clinging loosely, sliding to the ground now and then, like scales from some mythical sea creature washed ashore. Overhead, a hurricane shutter dangles by one nail, rocking back and forth in the breeze, protecting an intact window on the third story. Gulls swoop in and out, landing on the salt-sprayed rafters—scavengers come to pick at the carcass left behind by the storm.

Years later, after the place was repaired, a production company filmed a movie there. A love story.

But to me, the story of that house, of Rodanthe, will always be the story of a day with my grandfather. A safe day.

When I squint long into the sun off the water, I can see him yet. He is a shadow, stooped and crooked in his overalls and the old plaid shirt with the pearl snaps. The heels of his worn work boots hang in the air as he balances on the third-floor joists, assessing the damage. Calculating everything it will take to fix the house for its owners.

He's searching for something on his belt. In a minute, he'll call down to me and ask for whatever he can't find. *Tandi, bring me that blue tape measure*, or *Tandi Jo, I need the green level, out in the truck. . . .* I'll fish objects from the toolbox and scamper upstairs, a little brown-haired girl anxious to please, hoping that while I'm up there, he'll tell me some bit of a story. Here in this place where he was raised, he is filled with them. He wants me to know these islands of the Outer Banks, and I yearn to know them. Every inch. Every story. Every piece of the family my mother has both depended on and waged war with.

Despite the wreckage left behind by the storm, this place is heaven. Here, my father talks, my mother sings, and everything is, for once, calm. Day after day, for weeks. Here, we are all together in a decaying sixties-vintage trailer court while my father works construction jobs that my grandfather has sent his way. No one is slamming doors or walking out them. This place is magic—I know it.

We walked in Rodanthe after assessing the house on the shore that day, Pap-pap's hand rough-hewn against mine, his knobby driftwood fingers promising that everything broken can be fixed. We passed homes under repair, piles of soggy furniture and debris, the old Chicamacomico Life-Saving Station, where the Salvation Army was handing out hot lunches in the parking lot.

Outside a boarded-up shop in the village, a shirtless guitar player with long blond dreadlocks winked and smiled at me.

At twelve years old, I fluttered my gaze away and blushed, then braved another glance, a peculiar new electricity shivering through my body. Strumming his guitar, he tapped one ragged tennis shoe against a surfboard, reciting words more than singing them.

Ring the bells bold and strong
Let all the broken add their song
Inside the perfect shells is dim
It's through the cracks, the light comes in. . . .

I'd forgotten those lines from the guitar player, until now.

The memory of them, of my grandfather's strong hand holding mine, circled me as I stood on Iola Anne Poole's porch. It was my first indication of a knowing, an undeniable sense that something inside the house had gone very wrong.

I pushed the door inward cautiously, admitting a slice of early sun and a whiff of breeze off Pamlico Sound. The entryway was old, tall, the walls white with heavy gold-leafed trim around rectangular panels. A fresh breeze skirted the shadows on mouse feet, too slight to displace the stale, musty smell of the house. The scent of a forgotten place. Instinct told me what I would find inside. You don't forget the feeling of stepping through a door and understanding in some unexplainable way that death has walked in before you.

I hesitated on the threshold, options running through my mind and then giving way to a racing kind of craziness. *Close the door. Call the police or . . . somebody. Let someone else take care of it.*

You shouldn't have touched the doorknob—now your fingerprints will be on it. What if the police think you did something to her? Innocent people are accused all the time, especially strangers in town. Strangers like you, who show up out of the blue and try to blend in . . .

What if people thought I was after the old woman's money, trying to steal her valuables or find a hidden stash of cash? What if someone really *had* broken in to rob the place? It happened, even in idyllic locations like Hatteras Island. Massive vacation homes sat empty, and local boys with bad habits were looking for easy income. What if a thief had broken into the house thinking it was unoccupied, then realized too late that it wasn't? Right now I could be contaminating the evidence.

Tandi Jo, sometimes I swear you haven't got half a brain. The voice in my head sounded like my aunt Marney's—harsh, irritated, thick with the Texas accent of my father's family, impatient with flights of fancy, especially mine.

"Mrs. Poole?" I leaned close to the opening, trying to get a better view without touching anything else. "Iola Anne Poole? Are you in there? This is Tandi Reese. From the little rental cottage out front. . . . Can you hear me?"

Again, silence.

A whirlwind spun along the porch, sweeping up last year's pine straw and dried live oak leaves. Loose strands of hair swirled over my eyes, and my thoughts tangled with it, my reflection melting against the waves of leaded glass—flyaway brown hair, nervous blue eyes, lips hanging slightly parted, uncertain.

What now? How in the world would I explain to people that it'd taken me days to notice there were no lights turning on and off in Iola Poole's big Victorian house, no window heat-and-air units running at night when the spring chill gathered? I was living less than forty yards away. How could I not have noticed?

Maybe she was sleeping—having a midday nap—and by going inside, I'd scare her half to death. From what I could tell, my new landlady kept to herself. Other than groceries being delivered and the UPS and FedEx trucks coming with packages, the only signs of

Iola Poole were the lights and the window units going off and on as she moved through the rooms at different times of day. I'd only caught sight of her a time or two since the kids and I had rolled into town with no more gas and no place else to go. We'd reached the last strip of land before you'd drive off into the Atlantic Ocean, which was just about as far as we could get from Dallas, Texas, and Trammel Clarke. I hadn't even realized, until we'd crossed the North Carolina border, where I was headed or why. I was looking for a hiding place.

By our fourth day on Hatteras, I knew we wouldn't get by with sleeping in the SUV at a campground much longer. People on an island notice things. When a real estate lady offered an off-season rental, cheap, I figured it was meant to be. We needed a good place more than anything.

Considering that we were into April now, and six weeks had passed since we'd moved into the cottage, and the rent was two weeks overdue, the last person I wanted to contact about Iola was the real estate agent who'd brought us here, Alice Faye Tucker.

Touching the door, I called into the entry hall again. "Iola Poole? Mrs. Poole? Are you in there?" Another gust of wind danced across the porch, scratching crape myrtle branches against gingerbread trim that seemed to be clinging by Confederate jasmine vines and dried paint rather than nails. The opening in the doorway widened on its own. Fear shimmied over my shoulders, tickling like the trace of a fingernail.

"I'm coming in, okay?" Maybe the feeling of death was nothing more than my imagination. Maybe the poor woman had fallen and trapped herself in some tight spot she couldn't get out of. I could help her up and bring her some water or food or whatever, and there wouldn't be any need to call 911. First responders would take a while, anyway. There was no police presence here.

Fairhope wasn't much more than a fish market, a small marina, a village store, a few dozen houses, and a church. Tucked in the live oaks along Mosey Creek, it was the sort of place that seemed to make no apologies for itself, a scabby little burg where fishermen docked storm-weary boats and raised families in salt-weathered houses. First responders would have to come from someplace larger, maybe Buxton or Hatteras Village.

The best thing I could do for Iola Anne Poole, and for myself, was to go into the house, find out what had happened, and see if there was any way I could keep it quiet.

The door was ajar just enough for me to slip through. I slid past, not touching anything, and left it open behind me. If I had to run out of the place in a hurry, I didn't want any obstacles between me and the front porch.

Something shifted in the corner of my eye as I moved deeper into the entry hall. I jumped, then realized I was passing by an arrangement of fading photographs, my reflection melting ghost-like over the cloudy glass. In sepia tones, the images stared back at me—a soldier in uniform with the inscription *Avery 1917* engraved on a brass plate. A little girl with pipe curls on a white pony. A group of people posed under an oak tree, the women wearing big sun hats like the one Kate Winslet donned in *Titanic*. A wedding photo from the thirties or forties, the happy couple in the center, surrounded by several dozen adults and two rows of cross-legged children. Was Iola the bride in the picture? Had a big family lived in this house at one time? What had happened to them? As far as I could tell, Iola Poole didn't have any family now, at least none who visited.

"Hello . . . hello? Anyone up there?" I peered toward the graceful curve of the long stairway. Shadows melted rich and thick over the dark wood, giving the stairs a foreboding look that made me turn to the right instead and cross through a wide archway into a large, open room. It would have been sunny but for the heavy brocade curtains. The grand piano and a grouping of antique chairs and settees looked like they'd been plucked from a tourist brochure or a history book. Above the fireplace, an oil portrait of a young woman in a peach-colored satin gown hung in an ornate oval frame. She was sitting at the piano, posed in a position that appeared uncomfortable. Perhaps this was the girl on the pony from the hallway photo, but I wasn't sure.

The shadows seemed to follow me as I hurried out of the room. The deeper I traveled into the house, the less the place resembled the open area by the stairway. The inner sections were cluttered with what seemed to be several lifetimes of belongings, most looking as if they'd been piled in the same place for years, as if someone had started spring-cleaning multiple times, then abruptly stopped. In the kitchen, dishes had been washed and stacked neatly in a draining rack, but the edges of the room were heaped with stored food, much of it contained in big plastic bins. I stood in awe, taking in a multicolored waterfall of canned vegetables that tumbled haphazardly from an open pantry door.

Bristle tips of apprehension tickled my arms as I checked the rest of the lower floor. Maybe Iola wasn't here, after all. The downstairs bedroom with the window air unit was empty, the single bed fully made. Maybe she'd gone away somewhere days ago or been checked into a nursing home, and right now I was actually breaking into a vacant house. Alice Faye Tucker had mentioned that Iola was ninety-one years old. She probably couldn't even climb the stairs to the second story.

I didn't want to go up there, but I moved toward the second floor one reluctant step at a time, stopping on the landing to call her name once, twice, again. The old balusters and treads creaked and groaned, making enough noise to wake the dead, but no one stirred.

Upstairs, the hallway smelled of drying wallpaper, mold, old fabric, water damage, and the kind of stillness that said the rooms hadn't been lived in for years. The tables and lamps in the wood-paneled hallway were gray with dust, as was the furniture in five bedrooms, two bathrooms, a sewing room with a quilt frame in the middle, and a nursery with white furniture and an iron cradle. Odd-shaped water stains dotted the ceilings, the damage recent enough that the plaster had bowed and cracked but only begun to fall through. An assortment of buckets sat here and there on the nursery floor, the remnants of dirty water and plaster slowly drying to a paste inside. No doubt shingles had been ripped from the roof during last fall's hurricane. It was a shame to let a beautiful old house go to rot like this. My grandfather would have hated it. When he inspected historic houses for the insurance company, he was always bent on saving them.

A thin watermark traced a line down the hallway ceiling to a small sitting area surrounded by bookshelves. The door on the opposite side, the last one at the end of the hall, was closed, a small stream of light reflecting off the wooden floor beneath it. Someone had passed through recently, clearing a trail in the silty layer of dust on the floor.

"Mrs. Poole? Iola? I didn't mean to scare—"

A rustle in the faded velvet curtains by the bookshelves made me jump, breath hitching in my chest as I drew closer.

A black streak bolted from behind the curtain and raced away. A cat. Mrs. Poole had a cat. Probably the wild, one-eared tom that J.T. had been trying to lure to our porch with bowls of milk. I'd told him to quit—we couldn't afford the milk—but a nine-year-old boy can't resist a stray. Ross had offered to bring over a live trap and catch the cat. Good thing I'd told him not to worry about it. Letting your new boyfriend haul off your landlady's pet is a good way to get kicked out of your happy little home, especially when the rent's overdue.

The glass doorknob felt cool against my fingers when I touched it, the facets surprisingly sharp. "I'm coming in . . . okay?" Every muscle in my body tightened, preparing for fight or flight. "It's just Tandi Reese . . . from the cottage. I hope I'm not scaring you, but I was wor—" The rest of *worried* never passed my lips. I turned the handle. The lock assembly clicked, and the heavy wooden door fell open with such force that it felt like someone had pulled it from the other side. The doorknob struck the wall, vibrating the floor beneath my feet. Behind me, the cat hissed, then scrambled off down the stairs.

Picture frames inside the room shivered on the pale-blue walls, reflecting orbs of light over the furniture. Beyond the jog created by the hallway nook, the footboard of an ornate bed pulled at me as the shuddering frames settled into place and the light stopped dancing. By the bedpost, a neatly cornered blue quilt grazed the floor, and a pair of shoes—the sensible, rubber-soled kind that Zoey, with her fourteen-year-old fashion sense, referred to as *grandma shoes*—were tucked along the edge of a faded Persian rug, the heels and toes exactly even.

The feet that belonged in the shoes had not traveled far away. Covered in thin black stockings, they rested atop the bed near the footboard, the folded, crooked toes pointing outward slightly, in a position that seemed natural enough for someone taking a midday nap.

But the feet didn't move, despite the explosion of the door hitting the wall. I tasted the bile of my last meal. No one could sleep through that.

The bedroom lay in perfect silence as I stepped inside, my footfalls seeming loud, out of place. I didn't speak again or call out or say her name to warn her that I was coming. Without even seeing her face, I knew there was no need.

Gruesome scenes from Zoey's favorite horror movies flashed through my mind, but when I crept past the corner, forced myself to turn her way, Iola Anne Poole looked peaceful, like she'd just stopped for a quick nap and forgotten to get up again. She was flat on her back atop the bed, a pressed cotton dress—white with tiny blue flower baskets—falling over her long, thin legs and seeming to disappear into a wedding ring quilt sewn in all the colors of sky and sea. Her leathery, wrinkled arms lay folded neatly across her stomach, the gnarled fingers intertwined in a posture that looked both contented and confident. Prepared. The chalky-gray hue of her skin told me it would be cold if I touched it.

I didn't. I turned away instead, pressed a hand over my mouth and nose. As much as the body looked like someone had carefully laid it out to give a peaceful appearance, there were no signs that anyone else had been in the room. The only trails on the dusty floor led from the door to the bed, from the bed to what appeared to be a closet tucked behind the hallway nook, and past the foot of the bed to a small writing desk by the window. Whatever she was doing up here, she didn't come often. What was the lure of this turret room at the end of the upstairs hall, with its gold-trimmed walls painted in faded shades of cream and milky blue? Did she know she was approaching her last hours? Was this where she wanted to die? Where she wanted to be found?

Could I have helped if I'd checked on her sooner?

The questions drove me from the room, sent me into the hall, gasping for air. I didn't want to think about how long she'd been there or whether she'd known death was coming for her, whether she'd been afraid when it happened or completely at peace.

Truthfully, I didn't want anything more to do with the situation.

But an hour later, I was back in the house, watching two sheriff's deputies walk into the blue room. The deputy in back was more interested in getting a look inside the house than in the fact that a woman had died. For some reason, it seemed wrong to leave them alone with her body. I felt responsible for making sure they gave what was left of her some respect.

I waited in the doorway of the blue room, letting the wall hide all but the view of her stocking-clad feet as the men stood over the bed. They'd already asked me at least a dozen questions I couldn't answer: How long did I think she'd been dead? When was the last time I'd talked to her? Had she been ill that I knew of?

All I could tell them was that I was staying in her cottage out front. I'd used the term *renting* to make it sound good. The lead deputy was a thin, matter-of-fact man with an accordion of permanent frown lines around his mouth. He didn't seem to care much one way or the other. He checked his watch several times like he had somewhere to go.

"Well," he said finally, the floor creaking under his weight in a way that told me he was leaning over the bed near her face, "looks like natural causes to me."

The younger man answered with a snarky laugh. "Shoot, Jim, she had to be somewhere up around a hundred. I remember when my granddad retired, Mama wanted to buy the altar flowers for church, to get his name in the bulletin, but she couldn't. The pastor had already ordered the altar flowers that week, on account of Iola Poole's birthday. She was turning eighty then, and that was back when I was in middle school. Mama was mighty hot about it all, I'll tell ya. Granddaddy'd been a deacon at Fairhope Fellowship for forty years, and Mama wasn't about to be having him share altar flowers with the likes of Iola Anne Poole. Our family helped move that old chapel here to start the church. Iola was just there to play the organ, and they paid her for that, anyway. It's not like she was a member, even. Mama figured, if Iola wanted altar flowers for her birthday, she could put some at a church down in New Orleans, where her people come from."

Deputy Jim clicked his tongue against his teeth. "Women."

His partner laughed again. "You haven't been down here long enough to know how things are. Stuff like that might not matter much up in Boston, but it sure enough matters in Fairhope. Believe me, if they could've found anybody—and I mean *anybody* else who knew how to play that old pipe organ over to the church, they would've. That's half the reason my mama pushed for that new band director at the high school in Buxton a few years ago; he said he could play a pipe organ. I never saw the church ladies so happy as the week the band director took over at Sunday services and they sent Iola Poole packing."

"Okay, Selmer, we might as well get the right people out here to wrap this up." Deputy Jim ended the discussion. "Looks pretty cut-and-dried. She have any family we should call?"

"None that I'd know how to find. And that's a can of worms you don't wanna open either, by the way, Jim."

"No next of kin. . . ." The older man drew the words out, probably writing them down at the same time.

Sadness slid over me like a heavy wool blanket, making the air too stale and thick. I stood gazing through the blue room to the tall bay windows of the turret. Outside, a rock dove flitted along the veranda railing. What had Iola Poole done, I wondered, to have ended up this way, alone in this big house, laid out in her flowered dress, dead for who knew how long, and nobody cared?

Did she realize this was how things would turn out? Was this what she'd pictured when she placed herself there on the bed, closed her eyes, and let the life seep out of her?

The dove fluttered to the windowsill, then hopped back and forth, its shadow sliding over the gray marble top of the writing desk. A yellowed Thom McAn shoe box sat on the edge, the lid ajar, a piece of gold rickrack trailing from the corner. On the windowsill, half a dozen scraps of ribbon lay strewn about. As the dove's shadow passed again, I noticed something else. Little specks of gold shimmered in the dust on the sill. I wanted to walk into the room and look closer, but there wasn't time. The deputies were headed to the door.

Hugging my arms tightly, I followed the men downstairs and onto the front porch. It wasn't until we'd reached the driveway that I looked at the cottage and my stomach began churning for a different reason. With Iola gone, it would only be a matter of time before Alice Faye Tucker came to evict us. I had less than fifty dollars left, and that was from the last thing I could find to pawn—a sterling watch that Trammel had given me. The watch was only in my suitcase by accident—left behind after a trip to a horse event somewhere, undoubtedly in better times. If Trammel knew I still had it, he would have taken it away, along with everything else of value. He made sure I never had access to enough money to get out.

What were the kids and I going to do now?

The question gained weight and muscle as the afternoon passed. The coroner's van had just left when Zoey and J.T. came in from school. I didn't even tell them our new landlady had died. They'd find out soon enough. At nine years old, J.T. might not make the connections, but at fourteen-going-on-thirty, Zoey would know that the loss of the cottage spelled disaster for us. The minute we reemerged on the grid—credit card payment at a motel, job application with actual references provided, visit to a bank for cash—Trammel Clarke would find us.

I slipped into bed at twelve thirty, boneless and weary, guilt ridden for not being honest with the kids, even though it was nothing new. Outside, the water teased the shores of the sedges, and a slow-rising Hatteras moon climbed the roof of Iola's house, hanging above the turret like a scoop of vanilla ice cream on an upside-down cone.

How could someone who owned an estate like this one end up alone in her room, gone from this world without a soul to cry at her bedside?

The image of Iola as a young woman taunted my thoughts. I imagined her walking the veranda in a milky-white dress. The moon shadows shifted and danced among the live oaks and the loblolly pines, and I felt the old house calling to me, whispering the secrets of the long and mysterious life of Iola Anne Poole.

Discussion Questions

1. As the story opens, Whitney finds herself facing the death of her dream. Have you ever experienced the loss of something you desperately wanted? How did the experience change you? Do you believe the disappointments in our lives happen for a reason? What can we learn from adverse circumstances or unfair treatment?
2. Whitney has spent her adult life traveling around, never forming close associations with people. Why do you think she has chosen this? Are you one to get involved or to keep your distance?
3. On Roanoke Island, Whitney is confronted with memories she isn't prepared for. Have you ever returned to a childhood place and experienced memories you didn't realize you had? Is there a place that harbors the ancestral history of your family?
4. Whitney is surprised to learn more about her mother's relationship with Clyde. Why do you think her mother never told her the truth? Have you ever uncovered a secret that rewrote family history? Were you better off knowing or not knowing?

5. In Alice's letters, Whitney discovers the broken sister-bond between Ziltha and Alice. Why do you think Ziltha destroyed the letters? Was this a justified response? How do you think the young Ziltha was different from the woman Whitney knew?

6. Alice seems to view her new position with the Federal Writers' Project as an opportunity to break the cycle of grief that has held her prisoner. Have you ever found yourself trapped in one place in life, seeming to go nowhere? How did you break out?

7. In her journey, Alice visits people she would never have spent time with, had her life not taken an unexpected turn. Has a change of circumstances ever thrown you into unexpected company? How did you react? Do you think Alice reacts well to the people she meets? Is she naive, or hopeful, or both?

8. Why does Whitney have such a difficult time trusting Mark and forming close friendships? How do our pasts dictate our futures? Do we always judge new people in light of past wounds? Do you think we're doomed to act based on past wounds, or can we be made new? How?

9. Alice is confronted with cruelty and prejudice in the mountains. Have you experienced these things? Are we called to act, even if the injustice doesn't directly affect us? In what ways?

10. Have you ever spent time with someone who lived through the Great Depression? Did their morals, values, and habits differ from your own? What can we learn from those who have suffered through sparse times?

11. Whitney sets out with one goal in mind—to get what she thinks she needs—yet in the end, she discovers that happiness lies in a completely different direction. Has life ever surprised you in a similar way?

12. Do you know your family stories? What's one of your favorites, or the one that most defines you? How did you learn it? What's your favorite way to share stories with the next generation?

About the Author

Selected among *Booklist*'s Top 10 for two consecutive years, Lisa Wingate skillfully weaves lyrical writing and unforgettable settings with elements of traditional Southern storytelling, history, and mystery to create novels that *Publishers Weekly* calls "masterful" and *Library Journal* refers to as "a good option for fans of Nicholas Sparks and Mary Alice Monroe."

Lisa is a journalist, an inspirational speaker, and the author of twenty-five novels. She is a seven-time ACFW Carol Award nominee, a multiple Christy Award nominee, a two-time Carol Award winner, and a 2015 *RT Book Reviews* Reviewers' Choice award winner for mystery/suspense. Recently, the group Americans for More Civility, a kindness watchdog organization, selected Lisa along with Bill Ford, Camille Cosby, and six others as recipients of the National Civies Award, which celebrates public figures who work to promote greater kindness and civility in American life. *Booklist* summed up her work by saying, "Lisa Wingate is, quite simply, a master storyteller."

Lisa was inspired to become a writer by a first-grade teacher who said she expected to see Lisa's name in a magazine one day.

Lisa also entertained childhood dreams of being an Olympic gymnast and winning the National Finals Rodeo but was stalled by a mental block against backflips on the balance beam and by parents who stubbornly refused to finance a rodeo career. She was lucky enough to marry into a big family of Southern tall tale tellers who would inspire any lover of story. Of all the things she treasures about being a writer, she enjoys connecting with people, both real and imaginary, the most. More information about her novels can be found at www.lisawingate.com.